The Angry Island

The Angry Island

Peter Haden

GUILD PUBLISHING LONDON

This edition published 1987 by
Book Club Associates
by arrangement with
Piatkus Books

Printed in Great Britain

Chapter 1

The last mile. His breathing changed. In – one step, two step; out – three, four. He sucked cold air into his lungs, and when they felt full vacuumed in a tiny extra volume – more oxygen for a starving bloodstream. A bead of sweat rolled into his right eye. He blinked against the salted sting. An irritated swipe across his forehead with an absorbent tracksuit sleeve, then he was round the last bend. Along the roadway he could see the entrance to the marina.

A voice infiltrated his mind. 'Relax, slow down. You don't have to do this any more. Just jog it out to keep the muscles in trim. That all you need.'

His conscience retaliated. 'You're thirty-seven, unemployed, and you had too much beer last night. Now sweat it out.'

A third voice, rasping, deliberately unkind. The regimental physical training instructor, scourging some lagging soldier. '*Push*, you idle bastard. Open those legs. Nothing will fall off, lad. Now *move* it.'

The last two hundred yards. Happy to be pre-metric. Never comfortable with metres. His pace lengthened; faster, too, breathing matching the increased tempo. One hundred yards. Fifty. Elbows going like wheel rods on some ancient locomotive. Gasping now, but he held the sprint, running shoes thumping the pavement slabs as if to make them pay for his agony. Relentless. All the way to the gatepost. A rising ball of nausea told he had reached a limit but he was there, pressing the stopwatch button on his wristwatch, savouring sweet pleasure as the torture ceased.

1

He sat on a low wall by the entrance, head bowed, droplets of sweat falling from the end of his nose, oblivious to stares from early morning passers-by. Five miles, not a bad time, but it had been hard. Too hard. It wouldn't have hurt so much if he had been fitter – or perhaps it was the beer. A few more seconds rest then, hands on knees, he levered his body upright.

Sweat was cooling on his skin. It was important to take a shower before muscles chilled and stiffened. He made his way through the entrance and along a row of wooden pontoon fingers. *Soprano* lay at the end, alive and ready for the sea, contrasting sharply with the closed-down, unwanted, Monday morning appearance of most of the other yachts. He packed clean clothes into a bag. Five minutes under a steaming clubhouse shower would be a last luxury before he sailed.

There was no farewell party, no group of well-wishers to wave him away. At half-past ten, as the tide turned in the Solent, Simon Anthony Miles Verle started the Perkins marine diesel engine and left it to warm up. Soon *Soprano* was secured only by a single line at her bow and stern. He looked again, judging the strength and direction of wind and current.

Sam walked for'ard, pausing for ten seconds to gaze back over his shoulder at a town bustling under the early June sunshine. It would be his last close view of England for months, possibly years. He unwound one end of the bow warp from its cleat, and from the other, still-secured and pulled his line through a ring and back on to the yacht. Even as he checked to make sure that the line, now flaked loosely on deck, wouldn't slip over the side and foul the propeller, *Soprano*'s bow was being carried slowly away from the pontoon.

He walked aft to the sternline. When he had finished she lay about three feet off, swinging through and just beyond a course for the marina exit. A final check over the side for floating warps and he bent to throttle back and put the engine in gear.

He ran downriver under engine, lining up each leg on the autopilot whilst he stowed warps and fenders. Once out in the Solent he set course into wind and hoisted sail, letting the big main flap and slat whilst he settled himself back into the cockpit. Sam pulled another line, and a portion of fores'l

2

unwound itself from a roller reefing forestay. With the auto-pilot switched off he backed the jib, holding it against the wind to turn *Soprano*'s bow towards the Hurst Narrows, the westerly exit between the Isle of Wight and the mainland. As he sheeted home the sails, *Soprano* heeled gently. Switching off the diesel unveiled a familiar chuckle as the sea tumbled in curls and eddies along her waterline.

Sam connected the windvane, a fin-shaped weathercock at the yacht's stern. A series of lines translated the shifting of this mechanical sensor into movements of the rudder. Finally he checked the radar. Its antenna, set at the mast's lower crosstrees, relayed to a display unit by the chart table. Along-side the display unit was an audio alarm. Any solid object which came within a certain distance, be it land mass, a buoy or another vessel, would trigger a high-pitched bleep. The yacht carried a good bank of batteries, more than enough to light her at night, and fuel for her diesel to recharge them for many weeks at sea. If the wind powered his steering gear, Sam would use the spare battery capacity whilst he slept: for a few hours each day, radar would be his eyes and ears.

Soprano lifted and curtsied her way from the English Channel, standing out into the Atlantic before bearing away south, well clear of the north-west tip of France, the Bay of Biscay, and the coast of first Spain and then Portugal.

Sam entered the details of his latest fix in the passage log. He was seven days out, on a voyage of three and a half thousand miles. *Soprano*'s position, taken a few minutes earlier when twilight offered evening stars but still a firm horizon for his sextant, was about eighty miles off the Spanish point of Cape Finisterre. He would stop off at Gibraltar to top up tanks and provisions, then on to Cyprus, calling just short of his destination to visit an old Army friend now running a yacht charter venture in southern Turkey.

He poured himself a gin and tonic, switched off the light above the chart table and went up into the cockpit. It was appreciably warmer now, the climate definitely Mediterra-nean. His eyes adjusted, Sam used the last traces of light to make a final inspection of the deck. There was only a gentle movement as *Soprano*'s bow rose and fell to low Atlantic

3

rollers. Even so, without a safety harness he was careful to move from one handhold to another, always retaining a firm grip. If he fell overboard, *Soprano* would steer on without him. There would be no second chance.

From the foot of the mast he looked up along the powerful curve of her mainsail. At the masthead his burgee, its inner part illuminated by a tricolour light, streamed away into darkness. He was standing, Sam reflected, on almost everything he owned.

Soprano, at thirty-seven feet from stem to stern, was near the upper limit of what he cared to handle alone, day in, day out. Her welded steel construction was designed to be robust and seakindly, rather than to give the last ounce of speed. He had bought her second-hand for forty thousand pounds, spending another five on modifications and equipment.

Back in the cockpit Sam checked the course, retrieved his glass and sat, not for the first time, thinking about the events of the past year.

His trip to Cyprus was a pilgrimage, something he felt moved to do before setting off to explore the rest of the world. There were no graves, no memorial to the wife with whom he had shared over ten years, or their young son who had known only five summers.

Sam was a career soldier, promoted to the rank of Lieutenant Colonel at an early age and privileged to be given command of his Battalion. He was said to have a good future, every chance of becoming a Brigadier and probably a General. His motivation was the family. He had done well enough, joining the Army after taking a modern languages degree at a provincial university, but his background, if not poor, was certainly on the uncomfortable side of modest. Sam intended to spare his children the embarrassing frugality which had marred his own earlier years.

He thought of that day, twelve months ago. Jenny and young Sam were off to England for her sister's wedding. He drove them to Larnaca airport. They were twenty minutes outbound from Cyprus when the aircraft apparently exploded and dropped from the radar screen. The pilot's mayday was half finished, then nothing – the only wreckage a few bits of flotsam mid-way between Cyprus and Crete. No

4

one knew whether it was a bomb planted by some terrorist group, a hijack which went disastrously wrong, or just massive, unprecedented mechanical failure. Either way, on that sunny morning, Sam Verle's world sank to the depths of the Mediterranean.

The Army were considerate. He was given an almost immediate posting. It would have been difficult to have stayed on in the Commanding Officer's house, living and working within the Battalion's close-knit community. They transferred him to a busy staff officer's appointment in the Ministry of Defence, presumably in the hope that a high-pressure career job would help take his mind from the loss.

At first it worked, although there was a difficult period after the tenants left when he moved back into the house in Hertfordshire which he and Jenny had bought together, but at least her clothes, her intimate possessions, had been taken care of in Cyprus.

He left the house at a quarter-past seven each morning, caught the train to Euston, the tube to Embankment, and arrived at the office by nine. In the evenings he was rarely home before half-past eight. Weekends were divided between brief but essential periods of relaxation and frantic efforts to keep up with the administration of himself and the house.

It wasn't a sudden decision. The seeds were planted as the novelty of his employment wore off. They germinated and prospered during the summer months, cultivated by the deadly monotony of his existence. It seemed he was running his heart out in order only to stand still. And for what? He was almost forty with no wish to start again, even if he led the sort of life which brought him into contact with eligible women, which he didn't. Financially, he owed a few thousand on a house worth over eighty. If he retired there would be a good gratuity, more than enough to pay off the mortgage, and a modest but under certain circumstances perfectly adequate pension.

Over the months his priorities changed. At the end of a three week period of late summer leave he wrote out his formal notification. 'Sir, I have the honour to submit this my request to resign my Commission . . .'

5

He sold the house on a rising market. The furniture had been bought with uncaring tenants in mind and held neither intrinsic nor sentimental value. He kept only a few precious belongings. These, together with a box containing papers and family photograph albums, he left with his bank. After ruthless pruning, he was able to pack almost all his other possessions into a few metal, seagoing trunks.

Sam found *Soprano* during that irritating gap between agreeing the sale price of a house and exchanging contracts. She was exactly what he wanted: long-keeled, cutter-rigged, and built to stay at sea in any weather. He bought her at the close of the season, and with the house sale completed was forced to move onboard at the onset of winter. His first purchase was an efficient diesel-fed heating system.

During the months spent preparing *Soprano* for her future nomadic existence, Sam made tentative plans for the first few years. He would sail to the far end of the Mediterranean, working back slowly in a leisurely exploration of Turkey, the Greek Islands, Yugoslavia, Italy and the Balearics, then he would take the trade route, south to the Azores and across the Atlantic. But first, he would go to the low cliffs near their former home on the south coast of Cyprus. Once, and only once, he would stand where he and Jenny had so often stood to watch the purple-gold of a Mediterranean sunset. After that pilgrimage he would leave the island and never return.

Summer north-westerlies pushed *Soprano* eastward for almost a thousand miles, then further south along the coast of Sicily and through the Malta Channel into the Ionian Sea. Broad-reaching under reefed main and a generous unfurling of genoa, *Soprano* carved her way smoothly through sparkling waters but throughout the passage Sam was conscious, from past experience, that the Mediterranean had moods other than the sunshine and breezes beloved by millions of holiday-makers.

Even in summer, her winds could reach gale force. In the Balearics, or in Aegean or southern Turkish waters, they did so on average at least once between early June and late August. Then the Mediterranean, blown by the wind rather than moved by tidal forces, could pile into short, steep peaks and valleys infinitely more dangerous than long, ocean rollers. In extremis a small yacht could be pitch-poled, flipped stern over bow to an inversion from which she would be lucky to recover. If allowed to broach sideways before steep seas, she might literally fall off a wave, dropping perhaps twenty feet from the crest to be stove in on a valley floor which could split a fibreglass hull as effectively as concrete. Sam took comfort from *Soprano*'s steel construction and seaworthy lines, but even so kept a careful watch on the weather.

The days were gently but pleasurably busy. Every other morning he baked, using an uncomplicated soda bread recipe which required neither yeast nor rising time. The small gas oven, swaying in its gimbals to the motion of the waves, emitted an aroma which usually led to an orgy of mid-day indulgence.

Another routine chore was keeping clean. Freshwater showers were a rare luxury, and he had yet to discover a soap which lathered properly in seawater so used cheap hair shampoo instead. Ideally the method was to dive overboard then climb back and achieve an all-over lather with just a little shampoo. Another dive over the side, a quick swim, and the skin would dry without the rime of irritating salt crystals left after normal bathing. At sea Sam would never risk leaving *Soprano*, but by rigging the portable emergency bilge pump he could lift a gush of clean seawater over her side and into the cockpit. The soapy water was channelled away through drainage pipes, leaving a trail of bubbles to mark their progress.

Sometimes he listened to music, the recent marvels of miniaturisation providing a standard of high fidelity hitherto undreamt of on a small yacht. He had a selection of paperbacks which would be exchanged with other yachtsmen in various ports of call. Twice, nature provided the entertainment when schools of porpoises kept pace with *Soprano*, their sleek, black bodies leaping and curving through the water, so close yet somehow not touching.

At night he never failed to be impressed by the spectacle of the stars, seen offshore with a clarity unknown in cloudier temperate latitudes. The Milky Way appeared as a ceiling of countless, crystal specks, each an individual within a broad

7

carpet of light. Soon, the company of other people would be appreciated, a welcome change after almost a month of solitude, but now he was finding a release from stress, emotional as well as physical. Self-sufficiency, and the pleasure of being his own master, brought a measure of contentment.

Off the south-easterly tip of Crete, a light on the offshore island of Kupho Nisi fell abeam and astern. Sam brought *Soprano* on to a more northerly course to curve around the coasts of Scarpanto and southern Rhodes. With Cape Prasonisi and the rocky outcrops of Khina cleared safely, he set her on zero four five degrees true. By now it was almost pilotage, the yacht rarely out of sight of land. During the day he fixed his position by compass bearings on low peaks along the rocky spine of Rhodes. That night, with less than fifty miles to run, he reduced sail. There could be no sleep; a constant stream of shipping crossed his bows, steaming to or from the Rhodes Channel, the busy route for coasters transitting the narrow gap between the island of Rhodes and the mainland. At dawn he could see Asia Minor, her interior guarded by a massive mountain range rising steeply from the narrow coastal plain of southern Turkey.

Sam knew Anatolia, the southern province of Turkey, to be one of the most beautiful but least explored littorals of the Mediterranean. Its heritage was Lycian, Greek and Roman, its coastline wild and barren and indented with deep fjords, many of them uninhabited. Apart from a few, isolated areas of urbanisation, notably at Marmaris – opposite Rhodes – and Fethiye, his destination, the area was primitive even by Turkish standards. Only in the past few years had Europeans become aware of this unexploited treasure. As yet eastern Anatolia, from Sam's own cruising knowledge, remained relatively untouched. In the west, however, both Marmaris and Fethiye were bases for yacht flotillas, pandering to Europe's insatiable appetite for new holiday grounds. Eventually, he supposed, the coasts of Turkey and Syria would become as blighted as those of Spain or France.

Having retired from the Regiment after an injury in Northern Ireland which left him less than totally fit, and therefore unlikely ever to be promoted, it was in Fethiye, pronounced

8

Fet-tea-yea, that Sam's friend Angus Monro had chosen to establish his business. He had a small pension on which he and his wife Jean subsisted whilst using his gratuity, the injury compensation and the proceeds from the sale of their house to set up their yacht charter business, now in its fourth season. Sam had received a letter from Jean and Angus the previous summer, after the accident. They were thoughtful enough to insist that he did not reply at the time, but before leaving England he had sent a note warning them of his arrival.

For eight miles from the Gulf of Fethiye he followed a broad channel to its hammer-shaped head, the right-hand pein a particularly well protected lagoon two miles from north to south and a mile wide. On its southern shore lay the town of Fethiye.

A small group of people stood on the end of the jetty. Through binoculars Sam recognised Jean and Angus who must have spotted *Soprano* as she passed up-channel. They were waving frantically. As he drew nearer they gestured to where he should come alongside. Local boys competed for his lines and made them fast. To avoid giving offence he would check them later, after the boys had gone, but these young- sters grew up with the sea and Sam had little doubt that *Soprano* would be secure.

He killed the diesel and stepped ashore, only to stagger until Angus and Jean grabbed his arms. After so long at sea the land seemed to have acquired the swelling motion of the waves. He was glad of Jean's and Angus's support and in a moment all three were talking and embracing simultaneously.

With Angus in tow, and clutching his passport and *Soprano*'s papers, Sam walked to a quayside office. Jean sat quietly on the jetty, content to watch small boys fishing and to keep an eye on the yacht. Despite the increase in the number of tourists, Sam found the officials no less courteous than on previous visits, although Angus's presence – and, to Sam, fluent-sounding Turkish – obviously helped.

Back at the jetty he invited Angus and Jean on board for a drink – beer or wine, chilled whilst he motored up-channel. Angus advised him to put *Soprano* on one of the vacant orange buoys in the harbour.

"Take the big one next to the charter yacht." He pointed as

9

he spoke. "She's one of my fleet. The buoy will hold you all right. I laid it myself and it's galvanised chain all the way down. Then you won't have to worry about small boys pinching your gear or pestering you for cigarettes."

"We'll leave you to sort things out and have a nap," offered Jean as they finished their drinks. "But we'll expect you for a meal tonight, eightish. That's our house, with the green-tiled roof." She gestured towards a villa set on the shore opposite the moorings. "The people from the charter yacht are coming too, so we'll have a barbecue."

She spoke a few words in Turkish to a small boy standing on the jetty. He promptly leapt on to *Soprano*'s foredeck and stood there, basking in the envy of his friends.

"He'll pick up the mooring for you," said Angus, "save you running up and down the deck. No need to give him anything, he does odd jobs for us. His name's Necdet."

As Sam restarted the engine Necdet scampered about, releasing warps and fending off. Sam realised there was no way he could give orders. It was extremely unlikely that the boy spoke English, and he himself knew less than twenty words of Turkish.

He needn't have worried. Necdet untied a boathook, picked up the buoy, fed the chain over *Soprano*'s bow roller and took a few turns around the samson post, a vertical pillar set through the yacht's foredeck. Sam was about to go below and find the jar of sweets when the boy waved, said something, and dived over the side into sixteen feet of gin-clear water.

Suddenly Sam felt very tired. He opened the last can of chilled beer and relaxed in the cockpit. He would have to rig the cotton awning, to protect what would become a living area from the midday sun, but for now he was content to enjoy the cold beer and look back on his voyage. It was not remarkable by present day standards, but still a considerable achievement. Only the thoughtlessly loud transistor played by the party onboard Angus's charter yacht disturbed his tranquillity.

10

Chapter 2

His homing radar ranged around, searching for its target . . .
A second later Sam's subconscious locked on, memory in
control. He wasn't at sea. There was no need to scramble
on deck. *Soprano* was at rest in the placid waters of the
lagoon.

It was six o'clock. He must have slept for four hours. The
cabin had retained the heat of the afternoon – a sheen of
sweat coated his chest and arms. Sam pulled on a pair of
shorts and went on deck. It took a quarter of an hour to unlash
the seven-foot wooden tender from the coachroof and heave
it over the side. Next, not having filled the freshwater tanks,
he settled for a shampoo and swim with just a quick final rinse
under the shower.

Last time he had eaten with Angus and Jean, Sam reflected,
Jenny had been with them. Black tie for dinner, in those days
. . . That he could pass on to thinking about what to wear for
this evening, rather than lapsing into melancholy, he put
down to the effect of his new lifestyle. He selected his most
formal clothes. Angus and Jean were to be honoured by a
clean pair of lightweight slacks, a seawater-washed,
freshwater-rinsed non-iron shirt, and his ancient but still
serviceable blue blazer.

Old habits die slowly. At a correct five minutes-past eight
he pulled the last few strokes to a low wall bordering Angus's
patio. The dinghy was floating in about two feet of water as
Angus took its painter and made it fast to a metal ring set into
the stonework. Sam shipped the oars and handed himself
alongside.

"Welcome," Angus boomed, his six feet five inches and sixteen stone all but lifting Sam over the wall. "Come and have a beer."

A hospitable arm encircled his shoulders. Sam was slim but well-muscled and a fraction over six feet yet he felt dwarfed by the Scotsman's bulk. A lager can almost disappeared inside his friend's huge fist.

"Can't guarantee the quality," he called over his shoulder, taking another can from a drinks fridge in the corner of the patio. "The Turks nationalised the factory so the Danes upped and pissed off home. They didn't wait to give the locals a quick course, not that it stopped them brewing anyway, so the result's a bit variable."

Sam took a cautious swig. It hadn't quite the taste of a European lager but it was cold and acceptable.

"Good can?"

Sam nodded.

"Listen," Angus went on, "we have about half an hour before the others arrive. Jean told them half-past eight to give us time for a chat before the business entertaining starts. So – " he looked Sam up and down – "you seem to be in good shape. Physically, I mean. You're . . . er . . . over the worst of it?"

Sam nodded. Angus clearly felt it was necessary to say something, they were old friends, but that was enough. He changed the subject. "How's business?"

Angus pursed his lips and stared intently at the can in his hand.

"We're surviving," he said at last, "but I won't pretend it's easy. Chartering is a competitive market, and Fethiye isn't everyone's cup of tea. My brochure can't offer bright lights on the doorstep so we don't get too many young people making up a holiday party. And the recession hasn't exactly helped. I suspect that a good few who might have come here are more worried about finding themselves a job."

"But for all that," Sam persisted, "you are winning? I mean, you're not going broke or anything, are you?"

It was a measure of their friendship that he was able to put the question. The response was one of Angus's infectious bursts of laughter.

12

"Hell, man, if you'd asked me six months ago I would have said yes. Talk about cash flow! What with the insurance on the yachts, and the maintenance. Some of these charterers have no fucking idea. They think that two hundred quid a head entitles them to bounce off every rock in the Mediterranean."

Sam was used to Angus's language.

"But now," he pressed, "this has been a better season?"

"Oh, aye, it's been better. We've worked our arses off for four years and with any luck we'll fill a few more vacancies each season. This year there'll be a small profit but it's touch and go, Sam, even now. I have to get some return on the capital so that we can begin to refurbish."

He waved his hand. "Once you let an outfit start to go downhill, it's the end of the road. But at least there's light at the end of the tunnel, even if it's just a speck."

A splashing of oars and the sound of women's voices carried through the darkness. Angus put down his can, glanced around the patio as if anxious to be sure that all was in order, and stood up.

"It's the charter party – early. Do me a favour, Sam. You might feel like throwing them in the 'oggin, but turn on the charm, if only for old times' sake."

Angus's move to the patio wall coincided with Jean's arrival through a sliding glass door. She stepped quickly towards Sam, kissing him with an expression on her face he couldn't read.

"Sorry I wasn't here when you came." Jean glanced over at three people, two women and a man, who were stepping down from the wall. "They're early." The emphasis was on the first word. Sam detected more than a hint of disapproval. "We'll talk later." She patted his forearm and turned to greet her other guests.

Angus, whose natural manner was rarely less than ebullient, could become positively overwhelming when he chose to make an effort. Arms encompassing the two women, he swept them to the rear of the patio.

"I want you to meet a very old friend – you probably saw him arrive today. He's sailed *Soprano* single-handed from the UK." Angus turned first to one girl then the other.

13

"Fiona Marchant . . . Sally Forbes – " a wave of his right arm – "Sam Verle."

They shook hands and Angus indicated the third member of the group.

"And Julian Cranleigh. Now," he turned back to the women, "what can I offer you to drink?"

Whilst they were discovering what was – and what was not – available in southern Turkey, Sam took the opportunity to make a first appraisal.

If there were a centrepiece to the trio it had to be Fiona Marchant who was undeniably attractive. She was tall, perhaps five feet nine. In close-cut slacks and sleeveless tee-shirt she seemed almost skinny but Sam had to make a conscious effort to level his gaze on her face. Miss Marchant had a far from boyish figure.

Her voice was well modulated, hinting at an expensive education. She had a straight rather severe mouth counter-balanced by attractively slanted high cheekbones. Her demeanour had the confidence of one who expected – and generally received – attention.

Sally Forbes seemed an unlikely companion. She was not unattractive but her regular features and long blonde hair were in distinct contrast to the striking brunette. Sam detected a trace of north-country vowel sound, the 'a' shorter and more open. Of the trio she was definitely the odd one out.

Julian Cranleigh seemed pleasant enough, something of a male version of Fiona. Sam had seen hundreds of similar young men during his brief sojourn in the City: flocks of conservatively-suited fledgelings of the financial, legal or Government establishment.

Anxious though he was to assist Angus, Sam was acutely aware that small talk, even with those he knew well, wasn't his forte. Fortunately the guests' curiosity about his passage from England prompted a stream of questions from which developed almost a narrative account of the voyage. Although he wasn't too keen on social chatter, Sam could be a fluent raconteur. Interrupted only by the occasional query, his resumé lasted a good five minutes.

Shortly afterwards, Jean excused herself to carry out a few

last-minute tasks in the kitchen. Angus levelled the barbecue coals, now almost white, and freshened his visitors' drinks.

Despite his regular contact with charter parties, it was not often that Angus had the opportunity to spend a few hours in the company of a group of English people. He tried to keep up with the news by listening to short-wave radio broadcasts but after four years abroad he had no shortage of questions with which to fill any gaps in the conversation.

Sam's thoughts drifted. He, too, was curious, but about the three visitors. Angus and Jean seemed almost apprehensive of them, the traces of hostility which they had let slip entirely out of character. After several minutes of making no contribution whatsoever to a round up of London's more recent theatrical triumphs, Sam volunteered to go and talk to Jean: "Keep her company. See if there's anything I can do, or bring through."

He threaded his way through a large, open-plan living area to a kitchen built on to the side of the villa. He found Jean busily slicing peppers, brushing the pieces off a chopping board into a large wooden bowl.

They fell naturally into an exchange of news, of what had happened to friends and acquaintances and within the broader family of the Regiment. Jean meanwhile deftly assembled a platter of steaks and kebabs. Her preparations seemed to be almost complete.

"Are you going to tell me about those three outside?" Sam asked, trying to sound casual. "I mean," he gestured with his hands, indicating a willingness to drop the subject if necessary, "it might be none of my business – I shan't mind, if that's what you want to tell me – but I would have thought that they'd have been out sailing, not sitting in the harbour putting the pair of you on edge."

Jean studied him for several seconds. She didn't seem annoyed but as if she was struggling to reach a decision. Her abrupt movement towards a dark green glass carafe seemed to indicate that she had made up her mind. She poured two beakers of red wine.

"Cheers."

She swallowed a quarter of her drink at one go. Sam raised his own glass politely.

15

"Local stuff," she went on, seeking refuge in trivia. "Not brilliant, but quite passable once you get used to it."

She began to peel a clove of garlic. "Do you mind if I do this whilst we talk? Somehow it's easier, having something to do with your hands."

There was no need to reply.

"Angus said I wasn't to tell you . . . we argued about it for most of the afternoon."

She was cutting the garlic into gauze-thin slivers. Sam waited patiently.

"I know it gets to him, sometimes – all the work he puts in, and the worry of having invested everything . . . You're right about those three out there." She put down the knife, picked up her beaker again and turned to face him. "Believe it or not, they're important to us. Things have been pretty tight with the business but we're just on the point of a breakthrough."

"That's exactly what Angus said," encouraged Sam. "But I take his point about having to refurbish and so on."

"Fiona Marchant works for one of the glossy yachting magazines at home. Apparently her father is a director of the publishing group." Committed to explaining now, Jean relaxed and spoke more easily. "Angus wrote to them earlier in the year, enclosing our brochure and inviting a few journalists to come out. We offered a free boat for a week or so, but it's worth it in terms of bookings after they've featured the company in the magazine – if you get a good write-up, that is. Anyway," she grinned at him, "we weren't fully booked, so it wasn't as though we were losing income by making the offer."

"So what happened?" asked Sam. "They're here."

"The trouble is, we were so pressed to keep the business going that we were offering either skippered or bare-boat charter. That way, we could sweep up less experienced customers."

"Who would have been anxious about taking a boat on their own from one of the bigger charter firms," Sam prompted.

Jean nodded. "Angus took a few parties himself, and persuaded qualified friends to take the rest. A small levy on the charter party helped towards the air fare – we paid the balance – and the skipper had almost a free holiday. It cut into our profit, but we were able to keep going."

16

Sam guessed the problem.

"Those three outside," he asked, "would they by any chance be minus a skipper?"

"Yes, they are, and it's their own bloody fault."

Jean tried to quell her anger by setting down the beaker and reaching mechanically for a bowl of huge black olives. She cut a slit into the side of each olive and inserted a sliver of garlic.

"Try one," she offered, "they're good. When they booked," she went on more calmly, "they didn't ask for a skipper. Originally there were four of them. The two women are flatmates, Cranleigh is Fiona Marchant's boyfriend, the other man was a friend of Sally's, the only one with enough experience to take the yacht.

"Anyway, it seems that he had to cry off at the last minute – something to do with his work. The trouble is, instead of letting us know, they just turned up anyway. Obviously Marchant's using our offer to the firm as a ticket for free hols for herself and friends. It's no skin off our nose, provided we get our write-up, but it explains why she didn't want to come clean – in case we suggested some other time, when we could have arranged for a skipper."

"And Angus couldn't take them," observed Sam, "or they'd be out there now."

"That's right. We do try and stagger the changeover days, but most of our customers want to arrive and leave at the weekend. Tomorrow is Friday when most of the yachts will be back. Right now they're all bare-boat charters with no additional skippers. Angus and I will be flat out cleaning, re-provisioning, doing any repairs – you know what's involved. Then it's off to the airport, and a new lot to be settled in. We give them a barbecue and briefing party on Saturday evening, and they sail on Sunday. After that, Angus could take the Marchant party."

She helped herself to some more wine.

"Unfortunately, they only have ten days. And as they arrived last night, half of that time will have been spent swinging on a buoy in Fethiye harbour."

"And that," Sam hypothesised, "is the requiem for your good report?"

17

"I'm afraid so." She ran a hand through her hair. "They won't see much if they wait till Sunday. Besides, that Marchant girl was a bit hoity-toity when she found out there wasn't a skipper waiting, just on the off-chance. You can imagine Angus's reaction! And the trouble is, she could so easily damn us with faint praise."

She topped up his glass, then gave an embarrassed smile.

"I'm not trying to get you drunk, but you can see why Angus and I have been arguing. I said you would be annoyed if you had been in a position to help us but didn't know because Angus was too stubborn to ask. He said it wasn't fair – you had your own plans, and besides, because of the Ireland incident, you might feel you couldn't refuse . . ."

The Battalion had been in South Armagh. The lead vehicle was thrown into the air by a remotely controlled mine. All four occupants were killed outright. A well-placed sniper had calculated precisely where the second Rover would be. His first shot wounded Sam's driver. The Land-Rover rammed a stone parapet and caught fire. Sam was badly concussed so it was Angus, then a junior captain, who galvanised the occupants of the third vehicle into action, setting them to watch for the sniper's position whilst he ran forward to help those in the Company Commander's Rover.

Ignoring the risk from the sniper he got both of them out from the front, collecting painful burns in the process, and the radio operator managed to extract himself from the rear. The incident, at the time not altogether unusual during a Battalion's tour in that troubled province, nevertheless earned Captain Monro the award of the Queen's Gallantry Medal. On a more personal level Sam knew that had it not been for Angus's courage, he would probably have been just another cross on some terrorist's scoresheet.

He suppressed a burst of incredulous laughter.

"Thank heaven you told me! What does he think I'm on my way to? Some high-level business conference?"

He picked up the platter of meat.

"Believe me, Jean, if I can solve a problem by spending a few days sailing around with these people, I'm only too glad to do it. Whether I arrive in Cyprus next month, or in time for Christmas, doesn't make a scrap of difference." He paused, then winked at her. "If he says anything later, tell him it was all my idea."

When they carried through the ingredients, the barbecue was ready. It was a long, rectangular tin trough, the sort used by locals, every bit as efficient as the more expensive versions marketed in England for the suburban patio.

As well as traditional kebabs, Jean produced highly-spiced Turkish sausages. The steaks, she confessed, were an imported barter. After a rudder-bending crunch with a local fishing boat, the crew of an American charter yacht had sought the use of their slipway.

"It was a huge thing." She laughed at the memory. "Complete with a twelve cubic foot freezer." That she should choose to dispense her only stock of frozen T-bone steaks, thought Sam, indicated the degree of importance she attributed to the evening.

After supper they sat round the long refectory table, drinking wine and helping themselves from dishes of figs, olives and local cheeses. Angus, Sam noticed, hardly touched his own wine although he was at pains never to leave his guests with an empty glass.

Conversation flowed easily till eventually Sam saw his opportunity. Julian Cranleigh, learning that Sam had explored Turkey during his time in Cyprus, asked his opinion of the local cruising grounds.

"It depends," he replied carefully, "on what you want. If it's coves and beaches by day, but a few evenings in the tavernas as well, I would go west. Marmaris is a lively enough place, and I can point you towards some attractive empty fjords on the way. Alternatively, if it's the tourist scene you want, try Rhodes. The main town gets crowded but Lindos is worth a visit. I can show you a good anchorage on the chart."

He sipped his wine. "That's going west. Personally, I'd go the other way."

"Why?" The question came from Sally Forbes who had been quiet up till now.

"That's the advantage of Fethiye," he told them, conscious that his words might finish up in print. "You can go for the tourist spots," he emphasised the 'can', "but right here you're on what I would call the edge of the flotilla fringe. In a week

19

you could explore parts of original unspoiled Asia Minor, places that most Europeans can't even imagine. It's a fascinating part of the world, a bit primitive, perhaps, but exciting for all that. It seems a pity not to take the opportunity before the area becomes popular and loses its character forever.

"There are some superb bays to explore." Sam turned to their host. "Angus knows them as well as I do. If he'll fetch us a chart, I can show you where I would recommend. He can tell us if my knowledge is out of date. It's a year or so since I was last there, but it can't have changed all that much."

Deliberately, he lit the touchpaper.

"It takes about a week, by yacht. You ought to have a marvellous time."

As he expected, there was an instant hiatus.

"Unfortunately," it was Fiona Marchant who spoke, "we don't have a week. We were obliged to arrive without our skipper. Mr Monro – er, Angus – has agreed to sail with us, but not until Sunday. That gives us only a few days."

Her tone was even rather than icy. At least, thought Sam, the use of Angus's Christian name indicated a partial thaw.

As deliberately as he had lit the conversational touchpaper, he allowed a brief silence to fall. Angus would be as suspicious as hell but it must look as though Sam's just might have been an unprompted offer. Angus could tackle Jean about it later, but by then the die would be cast.

"It's a pity to come so far and then miss out on the best cruising area. If you only have a few days Rhodes might be possible, unless . . ."

"Unless what?" asked Julian.

"Well – " Sam turned his hands palms uppermost in a self-deprecating gesture – "I suppose *I* could take you. It would be up to Angus, of course," he went on hastily, "as well as yourselves but I'm spending a couple of years in this part of the world so there's no urgent rush to move on."

He grinned disarmingly. "I haven't discussed this with Angus yet but I was going to ask him if, at some stage, I could come back here to slip and re-antifoul *Soprano*. Perhaps if I escorted a charter party for him, I might get a discount on the use of his slipway."

He stood up to stretch his legs and looked across at Angus.

20

"It ought to be fun. I could enjoy showing people around Kekova and Kastellorizon."

"I think," said Fiona Marchant, taking charge automatically, "that we have to pass the decision to Angus." She turned towards him. "It's a very kind offer, which for my part I would accept gratefully. I really don't see us enjoying much more of swinging on a buoy in Fethiye harbour, despite the scenery and Jean's excellent hospitality."

Out-manoeuvred, there was no way Angus could refuse. Sam's ability as a skipper was beyond question. The three visitors seemed to have taken to him, and he could trust his friend to make sure that they had a good time. He glanced at Jean. Her expression warned him not be churlish; that after all their work, if he wanted her future support this was an offer she wouldn't allow him to throw away.

There was a tense five seconds and then Angus laughed. His fist closed around the neck of the carafe and he poured himself a generous beaker of wine.

"All right." He raised the glass. "Here's to your holiday."

He turned to his friend. "Seriously, Sam, I'm grateful. It's a fair trade. Bring *Soprano* back whenever you wish, and I'll have her hauled out for you."

Sam responded to the toast. "I'm not complaining. If I slipped in Tel Aviv they'd screw me for several hundred dollars. As you say, a fair exchange."

He raised his own glass. "Ladies, Julian, it will be my pleasure to take you east in the morning."

He was up with the sun. After an early morning swim, which included an inspection of the mooring on which he would leave *Soprano* for the next seven days, he was packed, breakfasted and ready before the first signs of life on *Windsong*.

Julian rowed across to collect him. Whilst the three charterers were doing last-minute shopping, Sam checked the yacht thoroughly. By mid-morning they were ready to slip and he gathered his crew around him in the cockpit, a chart unfolded on the seat.

"This is where I suggest we go. Remember, I'm here for your benefit, so if you want to stay longer somewhere, or move on, you only have to say. For now, I propose that we

21

start by sailing to Kekova. It's about seventy-five miles, but if we do it in one leg we can port-hop back again gradually."

"What's at Kekova?" asked Fiona bluntly.

"It's the most fascinating place I know in southern Turkey," said Sam gently, implying an element of privilege in the shared knowledge. "There's a series of bays for about four miles, protected by an offshore island. We can get into the lagoon from either end and, once inside, the island provides almost perfect shelter. I won't spoil it for you by going into too much detail, but remember, it's very primitive and I doubt if you will see another yacht. There's a superb ruined castle, complete with its own amphitheatre, two tiny villages, and in one place, where the water level has risen, you can snorkel down to look at ruined buildings."

There were murmurs of interest and enthusiasm.

"After that, we'll call back via Kastellorizon." His finger moved across the chart. "It's a Greek island, but only a mile or so off the Turkish mainland. I'll tell you its history later, but I always think of it as an unspoiled paradise."

He sensed that the itinerary had caught their imagination.

"Right then, first we have to get there so it's 'cards on the table' time. Julian, we'll start with you. How much sailing have you done?"

"A fair amount," he answered after a moment. "Crewing, mostly; cross channel races, that sort of thing."

He sounded experienced enough, Sam decided. "Fiona, Sally, what about you two?" he asked the girls.

"Father has a motor yacht," Fiona offered rather unhelpfully. "It has a crew."

Sally appeared to be embarrassed by this response. "My father taught me to sail a dinghy," she said quickly, "but I've never been on a big boat before."

They spent the morning in the lagoon, Sam showing them how to set and reef sails. Finally he gave them practice at the helm.

"Supposing," he explained, "I fell overboard. One of you has to be able to take command of the yacht, put her about, come back for me and then stop her alongside." He talked through the technique, then made them go back, under sail, to collect a rubber fender.

22

They decided that Fiona would best be employed with the sheets and boathook, but after a few attempts Sally and Julian more or less had the hang of it.

At least, Sam thought to himself, if he did fall over the side his instruction might give him an evens chance. But he resolved to take great care not to have to put it to the test.

They sailed after lunch. If the wind held, *Windsong* would probably average five knots. She was a modern, thirty-two foot fibreglass sloop, smaller than *Soprano* but with her cruiser-racer lines likely to be about as fast. Passage time would be around fifteen hours, which would set them off Kekova shortly before dawn. Sam would not risk the entrance at night; if necessary they could shorten sail, or even heave-to for a while. Once inside, there would be time for a few hours' sleep then they would be reasonably fresh to go exploring. He sensed that even Fiona was developing a mild enthusiasm for the trip.

His first problem, however, was that unlike *Soprano* the charter yacht lacked any form of self-steering. One of them must always be at the tiller, steering by compass. In one sense this proved useful; observing watches and taking turns on the helm served to fill their time but Fiona, and surprisingly Julian as well, had some difficulty in maintaining an accurate course.

With Fiona it was understandable, but in Julian's case it was disappointing, although it occurred to Sam that as a junior crew member he would not have been invited to steer a racing yacht. Fortunately, Sally Forbes compensated for Julian's lack of experience. Dinghy sailing had at least taught her to handle a boat. As soon as she learned not to over-correct for every small shift of course, but to relax and take advantage of the greater stability of a keel boat, Sam found she could reliably be left alone at the helm.

By early evening they were off Kotu Burnu, or Kotu Point, sixteen miles south of Fethiye. Fiona volunteered to produce an evening meal, which he suggested they ate before the added complication of nightfall. It was, he had explained to them, a straightforward passage, simply a question of standing out for a few miles then following the Turkish coast as it curved along the base of an elongated U-shape then gently up

23

again. There were a number of lighthouses along the way which he would use to keep track of their position.

Despite her good intentions, Fiona discovered that preparing a meal in a small yacht at sea could be a testing process. The wind was behind them and just offset to their port quarter. It was an uncomfortable point of sail, the waves superimposing a twisting, corkscrew motion on her natural pitch and roll. Sam had been watching the sea for some time. A fair sized swell was developing, greater than he would have expected from the still modest press of wind.

Grey-faced, Fiona scrambled up the steps and into the cockpit. "I'm sorry," she said after a few seconds, "but if I'd stayed down there, I would have been sick." There was a telling pause. "In fact . . ." She turned, leaned over the side and retched.

"Julian, keep an eye on Fiona. Sally, take the helm." Sam went below.

First he made safe a few tins and plates which threatened to cascade all over the sole. Unlike *Soprano*, *Windsong* had a short keel. Reducing the wetted surface made a yacht faster through the water, but without that long blade running almost from stem to stern she was twisting uncomfortably in what, without doubt, was a rising sea.

He looked at the barometer. Down two millibars in less than an hour. Sam studied the chart. There was no convenient bolt-hole. With an inexperienced crew he did not fancy pounding the yacht against wind and waves in an attempt to beat back into Fethiye. He tapped his dividers on the chart table, steadying himself as *Windsong* gave another lurch. If they were in for a blow, they were going to have to ride it out at sea.

He rejoined the others. Even in the few minutes spent below, the wind had freshened. It was probably at the top end of force four. A good stiff sailing breeze, but in gathering darkness it would appear far more threatening to the inexperienced. The corkscrew was more pronounced now as each passing wave attempted to push the stern sideways before Sally could correct with the tiller.

"Anticipate it, Sally. When you feel her start to lift, put the helm on early, before the stern swings. That way, you'll keep a

24

straighter track." Concentrating on steering, she could only nod her acknowledgement.

Fiona was wedged in a corner of the cockpit. She seemed to be recovering but for practical purposes was unlikely to be of much use. She would have to go below, despite her protests about wanting to be in the fresh air, and lie down in a sleeping bag. Sam reached inside the cabin, towards the bulkhead locker into which he had slipped his safety harness.

"Right," he shouted, his voice carried away into the blackness on a rising wind, "it looks as if we're in for a bumpy night. There's no need to worry. If I've seen one storm like this I've seen a thousand."

The patent exaggeration obviously amused Sally. A smile broke briefly through the mask of concentration on her face. Julian looked as though he would rather be a million miles away. Sam wriggled into his harness and clipped the other end of his lifeline on to a wire jackstay which ran the length of the deck.

"Listen to me, all of you. I'm going to take the helm, then bring her round on to the wind. When we do that, it'll be bumpy. She'll pitch quite a lot. Julian – as we come round, you winch in the jib so that she stays driving up to windward. Sally, when she's on the wind I'll give you the helm. I'm going to free the mainsheet, so there will be a fair bit of noise and flapping, then go up on deck and drop the main. After that, we'll turn and run under just a fores'l, but she'll be quieter without so much canvas."

He went through it once more to be sure that they understood what would happen and what each had to do. Even so, as the yacht came on to the wind he had to nudge Julian into activity. Before long, he told himself, half the crew would be suffering from seasickness.

Sam crawled along the deck to the mast, up on to the coachroof, and raised himself with one arm braced round the aluminium trunk. He observed the age-old saying 'One hand for me, and one for the ship' while he unfastened the halliard, but inevitably some of the sail slides jammed in the groove. The main had to be clawed down, yard by yard. Finally, he won but the sail was streaming out in an almost horizontal loop from the boom. Sam fished the sail ties from his pocket.

He should have thought about oilskins. With each slam into the waves a solid wall of spray was coming back over the bows. He worked his way aft, towards the cockpit, tying the flogging sail into a series of sausages.

Back in the cockpit, he let fly the jib. The wind took *Windsong*'s bow back towards her original course. Before the sail came under pressure again, Sam winched it into the roller-luff until only a pocket-handkerchief triangle remained. Without the main, and under a reduced jib, the motion was easier but even during that last manoeuvre the wind had freshened. Despite almost total reefing, *Windsong* was still doing a good six knots. For the first time Sam's habitual caution was tinged with real concern.

There was no way he could have foreseen the situation. In that part of the world there were none of the weather forecasts or gale warnings upon which the European sailor is so dependent. It looked as if they had put to sea only to meet a summer *Meltemi*, the gale which sweeps down from the Turkish hinterland. According to the Mediterranean volume of his *Admiralty Pilot* it happened, on average, only once each summer. Sam, at sea with an inexperienced crew, had a sneaking suspicion that *Windsong* lay in the path of a spiteful depression.

Not without difficulty he persuaded Julian and Fiona to go below and lie down in their sleeping bags, knowing that if they were allowed to remain on deck they would become cold, miserable and lethargic. Sam had brought his own foul weather gear from *Soprano*, but he was pleased to see that the protective clothing provided for the charter party was in pretty good condition. Not, as he pointed out to Sally as she struggled to pull a safety harness over her oilskins, that it would normally receive much use.

They chatted as Sam helmed the twisting, heaving yacht, Sally giving him the occasional break whilst he snatched a bearing on a coastal light or went below to mark their position on the chart. Shortly after ten they caught sight of the light on Catal Adasi, or Catal Island, away on the port beam. It marked the base of the U-shape where the coast began to run due east.

The wind, Sam told her, had set them further south, away

from land, so they were in no danger. He did not tell her that the barometer was still falling. The last of the fores'l had been furled in an hour ago, but even under bare poles *Windsong* was beginning to worry him. As each wave, higher now, collected under her stern, the yacht lifted as if cupped by some giant palm then surfed in a headlong, crazy rush with the foaming, frothy crest alongside her. She stopped, dropping into the trough with an arresting lurch, her bows driving deep before buoyancy brought them to the surface again, shedding aside solid green water only just in time for the sequence to begin again.

It was the classic problem of a small yacht in short, steep seas. If a wave caught her before the bows recovered she could be pitch-poled, end over end. He had to slow her, so that with less downhill momentum she ought not to bury so deep. After a bruising five minutes going through the lockers, he had assembled every fathom of warp which *Windsong* possessed. It was barely long enough to have effect, even streamed in a U-shaped bight from her stern. He needed something else as a sea anchor and it had to be soft. Any solid object picked up by a wave and driven forward could overtake the yacht and possibly damage the hull.

A sail! *Windsong* carried a spare jib, in case the roller-furling fores'l failed. The replacement was an old-fashioned, hoisted variety, a large triangle of heavyweight terylene. He made his way below and for'ard to the sail locker in the forepeak. Down here the noise was deafening, the crash as her bows went down sounding as though she were dropping on to something solid and unyielding.

Using one hand to prevent himself from being thrown around the cabin, Sam dragged the sail bag aft, finding it easier to crawl along the sole rather than stand upright. Fiona and Julian were looking anxious, faces pale against dark quilting, but otherwise they were all right. Lee cloths fastened to form a wall along the open side of their bunks saved them from being thrown around. He had to shout to make himself heard.

"Bad blow. Probably go on all night. We'll have to ride it out. Best stay here for now. Julian, you'll have to relieve Sally at some stage. Get what rest you can now."

27

Julian's head moved in acknowledgement and Sam crawled on aft. It took him ten minutes, sitting on the floor of the cockpit, to make up the lines.

At each corner of the sail a brass ring was sewn stoutly into the cloth. Through two of these cringles he led the eye of a bowline, so that the sail, its full height streaming aft, would be held at each end of its base, or foot, by a line leading forward to the yacht's stern. Another five minutes and he had the makeshift sea anchor rolled up on the after deck.

It would be hopeless to try lowering the sail gradually; the wind would pick it out of the water and throw it back on to the yacht. He waited till she was about to rise, and therefore accelerate, then threw the carefully bundled sail and rope down into the sea. As *Windsong* lifted away, the lines paid out. Twice he had to unscramble a snag, pulling in several yards when a large bight threatened to tangle itself into a knot.

Inside the oilskins he was sweating. Lying on deck, his arms working from under the guardrail, it was exhausting to handle the heavy, wet warps. He could brace himself only by spreading his feet. With every lurch, fittings and coamings on the deck under him raised another bruise. He would be black and blue by morning. Eventually, after what probably took five minutes but seemed like twenty, the sea anchor was streamed properly. *Windsong* had slowed perceptibly, the long, down-hill rush less wild, her bows burrowing less deeply and recovering more quickly.

Eleven o'clock. Between them, he and Sally had been sailing the yacht for over five hours. Sam was used to the sea but Sally was still reacting to every movement of the hull. She hadn't said anything but her arms and shoulders must be aching from the unaccustomed exercise of helming. She was his most valuable crew member. It was important that she did not become exhausted.

If anything the wind was stronger, certainly at the top end of a force eight gale. Near to the yacht, he could see wave crests being lifted and blown away in solid streaks of spume. A short while ago, somewhere forward of the port beam, Sam thought he had glimpsed Strongili Light on the tiny island just past the southern shore of Kastellorizon, but now spray was affecting visibility. Sam wasn't too concerned. He knew where they were, and there were no obstacles in their path until Cyprus, one hundred and fifty miles away.

Sam didn't expect the *Meltemi* to last for many hours. He was conscious of the sudden, unpredictable drop of the barometer. 'Long foretold, long last – short notice, soon past.'

In the meantime the wind seemed to be holding a peak. Even for Sam, accustomed as he was to bad weather, it was an impressive performance. They were cut off, isolated in their own small world by spray and blackness. In the rigging was a cacophony of sound, devil musicians playing like demented harpists. He had to shout in Sally's ear.

"Go below. Get some rest. Send up Julian. Tell him to wear his harness, and to pass me the hook so that I can clip him on before he climbs out through the hatch."

She nodded, and shuffled forward towards the cabin. Sam concentrated on the weather, trying to decide what the wind was doing. It was still screaming, but at least it wasn't any louder. After a while he relaxed, helming automatically as each successive wave tried to have its way with *Windsong*. He missed the directional stability of *Soprano*'s full-length keel, but this yacht seemed to be taking the storm well enough.

Perhaps it was some mariner's instinct, or else he was alerted by a deeper tumble and roar. He looked over his shoulder and saw a giant rogue wave – a solid, high wall of water advancing on *Windsong*'s transom. The coachroof hatch slid open and Julian appeared, unsuspecting. The next moment he saw the wave and his jaw dropped.

Sam screamed: "Get back. Shut that hatch!"

Pushed ahead, the advance swell was on them, lifting and twisting. Sam braced his feet on the far side of the cockpit and threw all his strength into holding the tiller amidships. He managed to hook an elbow underneath it and lock himself rigid, teeth clenched, neck sinews straining as he fought to stop the yacht from being set sideways.

He watched four feet of warp snake back to hang slack over the rail. One of the lines securing the sea anchor had parted. The yacht slewed, all the weight now on the wrong corner. She was starting to broach, presenting her side to a solid curlover of water.

The rogue wave took them, stern first, pushing it round to complete the broach. At the same time tons of seawater dropped against *Windsong*'s cockpit and lower superstructure. She was going over.

Vignettes burned onto his memory. Sam registered her masthead dipping majestically to the sea as the yacht was laid on her beam ends before a violent lurch threw him out of a vertical cockpit.

'This is it', he thought, as he fell into the maelstrom beneath.

There was a bone-breaking snatch as he came to the limit of his lifeline. It made him catch his breath but then he was submerged, gagging on a throatful of solid water even as something sharp caught him in the stomach and lifted him clear of the foam. It was *Windsong*'s guardrail, the wire fence around her deck.

He had to breathe. Frantically, he coughed and retched, trying to control muscle spasms so that he could suck air into his starving lungs.

Even that attention was divided. Harness and lifeline had saved him. When the yacht went over he had been thrown out, but now five thousand pounds of ballast in her keel was re-asserting control. Eventually, if the hull held, she had to come upright. It was her only stable position.

He was like a cat stranded half-way over a wall. Another lurch could throw him back again but the harness mightn't hold a second time, and once *Windsong* was upright, he would be unable to board her from down in the water. Frantically, even as he retched and sawed for breath, Sam scrabbled at the wire.

He was over, collapsing into the well of the cockpit, when he looked up. As the yacht described her return arc, the mast swung to the sky. But it was a hollow, aluminium stem, its top section now partly filled with water. It whipped vertical, but the roll-over proved too much for supporting shrouds; first one parted, then another. Sam watched, as almost in slow motion she was dismasted from the lower crosstrees. A forest of mast and rigging crashed towards him.

Chapter 3

Of six steel multistrand wires bracing the masthead, only the backstay, running from aloft to *Windsong*'s stern, withstood the overload. Tension snatched mast and rigging down to the cockpit. Seated normally, the helmsman would certainly have been injured – probably killed – by the crashing mast and flailing wires. Sam's undignified collapse into the cockpit protected him as though he were in a slit trench. He closed his eyes in reflex self-protection as aluminium and stainless steel slammed against coamings.

The cockpit was draining fast, seawater escaping through one and a half inch pipes set in each corner. He was wet, bruised and cold. There was an overwhelming temptation to rest, just for a while . . . His conscience assumed the rasping tones of the regimental physical training instructor.

'Move, you idle bastard! Those people depend on you. The hatch was open, there'll be water below. If it gets for'ard into the bows, she'll go down!'

Forcing himself into action, he crawled towards the companionway, found a gap and struggled to kneel up through a tangle of wire. All the lights had gone. Below, someone was moving. Scudding clouds gave a glimpse of the moon, her pale light reflected on an oily surface as water swirled with the sluggish movement of a crippled yacht. It was level with the bunks. So far the stern anchor had stopped her being lifted by a passing wave, but one more big roller and she would tip, bows down. If that water ran into her forecabin, beyond reach of the bilge pumps, she would be condemned to float, stern cocked high, gradually taking the sea till she was pulled into an inevitable slide to the bottom.

Sam opened a cockpit locker, felt for a long steel handle and yanked it free. Crawling back beneath the wire he raised a sprung flap near the cockpit sole and set the tubular steel into its socket. Two up and down strokes to prime. He had no idea how many gallons of water were below. The pump was rated at fifty a minute.

He set up a steady rhythm, shouldering aside fallen rigging so that back muscles could take some of the strain off his arms. After a while he lost all track of time. Despite his soaked clothing he was sweating profusely. His arms and shoulders ached then the stabs of pain began, like a red-hot wire being inserted into his joints with each stroke. Sam closed his eyes, clenched his teeth and pumped on, using body weight for each down stroke, pulling back for the return.

A singing monotone rang in his ears. Blood thumped past his temples, marking each heartbeat with a booming throb. Coloured lights danced under his eyelids. When the first dry stroke sucked air and the handle plunged freely, Sam collapsed on top of it. He had shifted over a ton of seawater.

He lay in the cockpit. Given back her buoyancy, *Windsong* responded more to the waves. She was lifting now, up and clear of the water. Without most of her rigging she offered little resistance to the wind. The sea anchor, having caused her troubles by starting that fateful swing, now held her steady and almost in line with the wave pattern. *Windsong* had survived the nightmare of all yachtsmen: a knock-down. A figure clambered through the hatchway. It was Julian.

Sam eased himself on to an elbow. "What's it like below? Are the girls all right?"

Julian didn't reply immediately but stared at the kinked mast with its festoon of wires.

"Christ, what a mess."

"The girls," Sam repeated, levering himself into a sitting position, "are they all right?"

"I think so. Fiona was pitched across the cabin. Sally was on the downhill side. I managed to hold on. Didn't you hear the screams?"

Sam shook his head. "I was thrown out. Lucky to get back. Harness held."

He thought of his marathon at the bilge pump. "What on earth have you been doing?" he demanded.

"Looking after Fiona; she took a nasty bang on the head and we fished her out from under the water. I think she's going to be all right, though. It took a minute or two to climb out – the upper crosstrees were jammed across the companionway. I could see you pumping like mad but you were finished before I could get clear."

Sam nodded. It must have been terrifying down below in pitch blackness, the yacht on her side and water pouring in through the hatchway. They had done well enough not to panic.

"Are we all right?" asked Julian, gesturing towards the fallen rigging.

"For the moment," Sam answered. He was aware of the two girls, one helping the other, emerging from the cabin. He looked up at the remains of the mast.

"There's nothing much we can do in the dark. The wind seems to be easing, and the hull will look after itself. See if you can find the spare torch, Julian. I'll lash this lot down on deck so it can't cause any more damage, then we'll see if there's any chance of a hot drink and some dry clothes."

The gale was subsiding as quickly as it arrived, but there would have to be daylight and less wind and sea before he could work on deck. There was little Sam could do to influence the course of the yacht. Without electric power they couldn't start the diesel, which in any case would have to be stripped and cleaned after being underwater. For the moment she was safe enough, drifting to her stern anchor – and it would be light in a couple of hours. Working mostly from the cockpit, he tied down fallen fittings; the tiller he lashed amidships. A stab of light from the companionway told him that Julian had found the torch. After a last glance around the horizon, Sam went below.

She was a depressing sight. He played the beam over what had once been a snug, orderly cabin. The upper port side was dry and the cooker apparently in one piece, but most of the lockers had burst open. The cabin sole was ankle deep in waterlogged food, books and personal belongings. Water dripped from the roof lining. Mattresses and bedding were sodden. The three charterers perched on the edge of a bunk, their faces a canvas of misery and discomfort.

Sam bullied them into activity. They searched through holdalls for dry clothing. Wet mattresses were stuffed for'ard and from the forecabin, which had escaped serious flooding, dry ones brought aft. Sam checked the gas connections then lit the cooker to boil some water. After half an hour they rested in a semi-destroyed cabin, but they had dry clothes, somewhere to sit, warmth from the cooker and a hot drink laced liberally from a salvaged bottle of rum.

Sam's waterproof Seiko told him that it was half-past two. Soon it would be dawn. He used the torch to make a cursory inspection of the engine and battery compartment. It would take a day to strip, clean and reassemble the diesel but *Windsong* carried neither enough tools nor replacement engine oil. One of the batteries had been torn from its mount and had severed a cable which explained the total loss of power, but he would leave that job until he could sort out the damaged wiring in the mast.

"The first priority," he told them, settling himself back on to a bunk, "is to build a jury rig. Fortunately, with part of the mast still standing, we ought to be able to set enough canvas to give some control over our direction."

"Then what do we do?" asked Sally.

"Come daylight, I'll see where we are. The chart's no use – its a papier mâché lump. Don't worry, though, I know the coastline well enough. It's my guess we'll drift somewhere south of Kekova. With any luck we can sail north and find a fishing village. Once I can get to a telephone and be in touch with Angus, we should be able to organise something fairly quickly." He paused. "So far, I'm afraid, it's been a pretty ghastly sort of holiday for you."

"I shall dine out on the experience for weeks," said Fiona enigmatically.

After a few more desultory remarks, conversation lapsed. Each was left to private thoughts in a swaying corner of darkness.

Sam dozed for nearly three hours, waking to the sound of someone working in the galley. He saw that Julian and Fiona were still asleep and as he moved to ease the stiffness from his limbs, Sally handed him a fried egg sandwich.

"A carton of eggs and a loaf survived in the bread locker. Here, you must be starving."

He accepted the plate gratefully, and the steaming mug of coffee Sally set on the saloon table. He squeezed past her to stand on the companionway steps and poke his head above the hatch. It was broad daylight. The wind had backed more southerly, setting them in towards the coast, but it was down to a modest sailing breeze. Only a residual swell and the shambles of the wrecked mast on *Windsong*'s deck bore witness to the ferocity of last night's gale.

"That," said Sam as he licked his fingers and reached for the coffee mug, "was fantastic. Well done you."

Julian and Fiona were stirring.

"I'm going to get started. Someone can give me a hand when they're ready."

He retrieved a toolbox from under the chart table and went on deck. They were about five miles off the coast. He recognised the islands of Kastellorizon and Strongili, past which they had drifted whilst he slept. If he moved quickly, it ought to be possible to lay a course for Kekova inlet. From memory, it was about nine miles to the north-east. He tried to picture the chart. Beyond Kekova, the coast was barren and inhospitable for quite some distance.

It took three-quarters of an hour to build a jury rig. The mast had snapped just above the crosstrees but lower shrouds on either side were still in place. Using lengths of wire salvaged from the original rigging, Sam lassoed the stump with temporary back and forestays. The mast secured in all four directions, he passed a line over the crosstrees and hauled up a block through which he had already reeved the mainsail halliard. With the block at a new masthead, and the other end of the halliard attached to the sail, he was able to lift part of the mainsail up a remaining eighteen feet of mast. The spare sail area he lashed down, threading sail ties through deep reefing cringles and knotting them underneath the boom. When he had finished, *Windsong* was setting about a third of her original mainsail and no jib.

He moved back to the cockpit and experimented. The yacht wouldn't make much to windward, but she would lay a course of about seventy degrees off or more. She was about as efficient as an old square-rigger and those, he reminded them, had circumnavigated the world long before engines were invented.

The sun came up, a huge, dull-orange disc lifting rapidly off the eastern horizon. An impressionist blur of coastline developed detail – trees and vegetation and barren rock.

"Where are the buildings?" asked Sally.

"There aren't any," Sam responded, "not facing the open sea."

He pointed. "You can't make it out yet but over there, about thirty degrees off to starboard, is the entrance to our lagoon. From here it all looks to be one piece of land but that low hump, apparently on the foreshore, is Kekova Island. The channel is where that left-hand edge dips to the sea.

"Why don't we steer straight for it?" asked Fiona. "We seem to be heading a long way left."

"Out here," he told her, "the wind is blowing more or less towards the entrance, but near land it'll be deflected by the coastline. With this rig we can't claw back upwind, so to be safe I'm aiming well to one side. As we pass the gap I can turn across the wind and reach into the lagoon. If we headed straight towards it now, we probably wouldn't make it."

It grew hotter as the sun shed its orange hue to become a yellow ball of fire. Sweaters were discarded. Sam's only worry was that the breeze might die away altogether, leaving them to drift helplessly in a current which would sweep them past the entrance. *Windsong* was moving slowly, at barely more than two knots. The entrance to the lagoon was less than two hundred yards wide. He detailed Fiona to stand in the bows and watch out for submerged rocks.

The yacht slipped through successfully. Once in the lee of the island there was even less wind. Sam pointed out two small villages three-quarters of a mile away on the shore, but they could steer only towards an empty bay almost two miles beyond.

The scenery was breathtaking. Forested foothills reached away to the interior. Set on the highest hill, a ruined castle dominated the four-mile length of the lagoon. At the far end another narrow entrance led back to the Mediterranean.

Sam laid out anchor and chain. When they were a hundred

36

yards off, he left Sally at the helm and joined Fiona in the bow. They were hardly moving. He waited till he could see a patch of sand about fifteen feet down then lowered the anchor.

"Drop the sail," he called to Julian. They had just made it. A dying breath of wind swung the yacht to her anchor. Flukes bedded into sand and disappeared. *Windsong* lay in the centre of a semi-circular bay, about forty yards from a narrow strip of beach. Everything around them was beautiful, barren, and absolutely deserted.

Sam waited in the bow until *Windsong* had settled to her anchor then walked aft. It was only when he sat down in the cockpit that he realised how exhausted he felt after the night's events.

"I would be grateful," he began, "if some kind person would fetch up a few cans of beer. Those in the forecabin should be fairly cool."

"What's the programme?" asked Julian, passing a pack up through the hatchway.

"I suggest that we have a drink, and relax for what's left of the morning – I feel absolutely knackered. After lunch, perhaps you three will restore the maincabin to some semblance of order, then you might like to take the dinghy and either explore or loaf on the beach. I shall walk to the villages. Unfortunately, I don't think they have a telephone. There wasn't one last time I was here. They weren't even connected by road. There's just a track leading along the coast to Kas."

"How far's that," asked Fiona. "On to Kas, I mean?"

"Just under ten miles, from memory. It's the small fishing village opposite Kastellorizon, but they have customs officials so there will almost certainly be a telephone."

He thought out loud. "It's hilly country with no public transport. At a brisk pace, say, two hours. Leaving after lunch, I should be back by nightfall."

In Sam's exhausted state two cans of beer were as effective as a bottle of sleeping pills. He woke after two and a half hours feeling considerably refreshed. Fortunately he had packed a pair of suede desert boots for trips ashore which would be ideal for hill walking. Despite the heat he put on a pair of slacks, and into his sailing jacket pocket he placed passport, ship's papers and money.

Julian rowed him ashore. He watched Sam set off up the hillside at a pace which, he suspected, the older man could sustain for hour after hour.

It took some time to sort out the yacht. Seawater had spoiled most of their fresh food but they had an adequate supply of tins. Bunk mattresses and clothes were laid on the deck where they dried quickly in the afternoon sun. After an hour or so there were few signs below of their ordeal.

"We've spent the first night of our sailing holiday in fear for our lives, and the next day engaged in housework," Fiona observed. "I expect that we're going to be here for at least twenty-four hours, so I suggest we leave the exploring until tomorrow and be content with a trip to the beach and a swim."

The girls swam to the shore whilst Julian rowed the inflatable. A narrow strip of coarse gravel-sand separated sea from scrub, marking a no-man's-land between two encroaching forces. As Julian pulled up the dinghy, Fiona removed a holdall. With a large bath towel spread to the sun she looked around then up at the foothills. Murmuring insects set up a background hum beneath the solo cries of birds. Air shimmered off rocks too hot to touch. They were enveloped by a heady scent of vegetation. There was neither sight nor sound of anything attributable to man.

"He was right." Fiona broke their silence. "This really is quite a place. It's absolutely deserted."

Julian lay back on his towel. Squinting against the sun, he watched Fiona untie her bikini top. Her breasts bobbed gently as she dropped it into the holdall. A hand moved to the knot on her right hip.

"Do you think that's wise?" he asked.

She shrugged her shoulders.

"Why not? There's only us three here. I'm going skinny-dipping, then I shall oil myself up for an all-over tan."

"It's a nice thought," offered Sally, "but this place isn't exactly the South of France. For all we know they might have strict laws."

"And who," demanded Fiona, "is going to report us?"

Rejecting Sally's caution, she untied the knot. Previous sunbathing had left a pale triangle of skin not much larger than the area of tight, brown curls. She turned and walked into the sea.

"She can be bloody headstrong," Sally commented as Fiona swam in a strong crawl towards the yacht, "but just this once, she might be right. It's a tempting thought."

"All right then," laughed Julian. "Let's all go skinny-dipping."

He stood up and pushed down his trunks. Unused to being naked in the open air, he made straight for the concealing shelter of the water. Floating just beyond his depth, he turned in time to see Sally walk into the sea. He was used to the sight of Fiona's body, although he never tired of looking at it, but when he called at the flat if Sally were not dressed she always wore a housecoat.

He found her nudity exciting. Her breasts were smaller than Fiona's but well-shaped, ending in a delightful upturn. She was a natural blonde, he noticed, and turned on to his stomach again. A few seconds later he was startled by a hand which brushed playfully over his genitals. Fiona surfaced, laughing, a few feet away.

They swam for some time before returning, no longer self-conscious, to the beach. Still recovering from the loss of a night's sleep, all three of them dozed under a hot sun. Fiona was the first to hear a quiet splash then the creaking of rowlocks under shipped oars.

She lifted her head then sat up sharply, eyes blinking against the glare from the sea. It was a wooden fishing boat, twelve or fifteen feet long. Nets and marker buoys were piled in the bow, and cases of beer . . . they had been on to *Windsong*. As its prow touched the shore, three men jumped into the shallows to lift and drag their craft up on to the beach.

The two groups looked at each other. The fishermen were dressed alike in frayed canvas plimsolls, shapeless baggy trousers rolled to the knees and a dirty, unbuttoned shirt. One of them said something. It was a guttural, unintelligible sound.

"Do you speak English?" asked Julian hesitantly. A

39

forlorn hope. He was acutely aware of their vulnerability as the three men burst into a rattle of words.

Sally picked up her bikini. Fiona's was in the holdall. She reached out for it but drew back when the oldest man moved towards her. His eyes scanned her body. He looked around the bay, said something else equally unintelligible, and began to untie the string holding up his trousers.

"Wait a minute! Please . . ." Fiona stopped speaking, panic rising.

The trousers fell away. He wore no underclothing, and she saw his erection growing, a brown penis pointing from between curtains of grubby shirt.

Julian moved to intercept but one of the others clamped a powerful grip on his arm and swung him sideways. He turned to aim a blow but before it landed an unseen fist slammed on to the back of his neck. The fisherman let go of his arm and drove his fist savagely into the pit of Julian's stomach. He dropped into the sand, hopelessly winded.

The third man advanced on Sally. Julian's attacker seized Fiona's arms, pulling them over her head and kneeling on her wrists. She tried to lash out with her feet but the oldest man caught them and then sat on her legs. Fiona screamed. The sound rolled up to the empty hills. He laughed, exposing yellow and brown teeth, then slapped her face with a force which made her head sing.

His knees were between her thighs. A rough palm cupped briefly against her genitals before he dropped on to her and pushed. She was dry and whimpered with pain as he began to move inside her, his rank, fishy-smelling body and foul breath suffocating her last resistance.

Sally cried out. Her captor twisted her arm savagely behind her up to her neck, tugging at her hair to restrain her. For now he was content to fondle roughly at her breasts while he watched the main entertainment.

Fiona felt the first man's orgasm. He pulled away, kneeling, his penis still hard and glistening. The one holding her arms shouted impatiently.

Oh God, she was going to be raped again. Perhaps by all three . . .

"No!" Recovering his breath, Julian shouted hoarsely and

40

launched himself at the two men. The one behind Fiona released his grip and rose to meet him. He pulled something from his pocket. There was a sharp click as a blade flicked out.

Julian went for the knife arm. It was a brave enough attempt but in his way of life, power and authority stemmed only from wealth or position. He was ill-equipped to match the Turk who accepted the duel as a matter of course. He was as wild as his background. Even so, had he not been reasonable? The women were fair game but the man was weak and soft so he had not been harmed. But since he chose to fight again . . .

Expertly, the fisherman side-stepped Julian's rush and with no more thought than would have been given to a fish, slipped the blade into his stomach.

Julian staggered. Something felt wrong . . . he was on his knees . . . for the first few seconds anaesthetised by shock. Hands clutched at his belly. But as redness spread between his fingers waves of pain radiated from the wound. Screams from both women receded down a hall of consciousness.

Ignoring Julian's body, his assailant returned to Fiona and changed places with the older man. He was erect and ready.

"Please, no. No more," she pleaded, even though he wouldn't understand.

Like the first man, his knees landed between her thighs. He was grinning at her and pointing to his penis, showing her what she was about to experience.

She threw her head to one side. He laughed at the gesture and said something, whether to her or to the other man she had no idea. He moved . . . but away, and she dared to hope before calloused hands seized her ankles, crossing them and giving a harsh twist which the other man matched with her arms. Helpless, she was flipped efficiently on to her stomach.

The knee was back between her legs, and hands were parting her buttocks. In sick disbelief, she realised what was about to happen to her, and for the first time in her life Fiona experienced the raw fear of total panic. Wildly, she heaved and thrashed but her arms and legs were pinned. The side of her face was pressed into the beach. There was sand in her mouth. His thumbs hooked deeper into her flesh . . .

41

She wailed. It was a frenzied, animal sound, curving up from the shore and all but dying on the hillside before being met with a sharp, reverberating crack.

The fisherman was lifted and thrown back. The other two looked up at the hillside then scrambled for their boat. There was an irregular, crackling sound and they fell into the shallows, red tendrils sprouting and curling about them in the rippling water.

Fiona lay on her side, arms tight about her knees, sobbing uncontrollably. Sally crawled over to her then moved on to Julian who was stirring.

A group of twelve men in khaki-green uniforms advanced down the hillside. Their leader stopped his party at the edge of the beach and came on alone. Sally raised her head to look at him. He was tall for a Turk, his dark skin and hooked nose denoting mixed ancestry.

"Sie sind Deutsch? Französisch?"

She shook her head.

"Nein. Englisch. Sprechen Sie Englisch?"

He looked closely at her, then spoke slowly. *"Ein bisschen* . . . a little. You have some troubles, I think."

She told him, in a few words, about the yacht being dismasted and how the captain had gone for help.

"Then these men came. It was horrible . . ."

"Ja. We see something of what happen."

He looked at the bodies, then shrugged carelessly.

"Afterwards, they would have . . ." His meaning was unmistakable as he drew an index finger across his throat. They were interrupted by a gasp of pain from Julian.

"He needs a doctor," said Sally, looking up again. "Can you help us, Mr . . . er . . ."

"Samandag." He bowed slightly. "Major Ragip Samandag. There is no hospital for many miles. Fethiye, yes, but not here."

He thought for a moment. "We make manoeuvres. There is exercise camp." He pointed to the hills. "You come with us. We carry him. I have medical orderly."

Sally looked at Julian. He was pale and sweating but his skin felt cold. His breathing was shallow. He had all the classic symptoms of shock, and his stomach was still bleeding. He

42

had to have medical attention. It was no use staying with the boat. She made up her mind.

"Fiona, you can't stay here on your own. We'll both have to go. I'll row out to the yacht, get some clothes and leave a note for Sam. Can you wash yourself, in the sea?"

Fiona nodded dumbly. Sally hoped she, too, wasn't going into shock. For the moment it seemed she must think for all three of them, and care for Julian.

As Sally led Fiona to the shallows, Samandag shouted an order. Two of his men produced machetes from their packs and set off towards the undergrowth while a third put a temporary field dressing on Julian's wound. Twenty minutes later, with the girls dressed in jeans and sweatshirts and Julian wrapped in blankets and placed on a makeshift stretcher of wooden poles and a groundsheet, they set off towards the foothills.

At first the swaying and jolting caused him considerable pain but mercifully, after a while, he lapsed back into unconsciousness. Neither of the girls had a watch but they seemed to walk for half an hour at a time and then rest for a few minutes. In the third session they came to the edge of a pine forest where a track led in through the trees. Samandag halted the procession.

"Not far. Few minutes, maybe. I go back – bring your friend. My men speak not English but they look after you. Yes?"

Sally answered for all of them.

"Yes, Major. You have been most kind. Thank you. We will go with your men."

They arrived at sunset. It was a tented camp, set out in as near a rectangle as the trees would allow, but on the far side were three wooden huts. Judging by the equipment which overflowed on to the verandah, the centre one was some sort of storeroom. The one on the left supported a roof aerial, so it was probably their headquarters. The hut on the right bore a sign whose red crescent on a white background identified it as the camp medical centre.

The medical orderly, a fleshy individual whose plump appearance contrasted sharply with the lean fitness of

Samandag's soldiers, seemed to know what he was doing. Whilst he examined Julian, Sally established that his training had been in Germany, as a *gastarbeiter* in a general hospital. She guessed that his knowledge was probably no more than that of a state enrolled nurse.

In good German he told her that Julian was suffering from shock and had lost a lot of fluid. He had facilities neither for surgery nor for matching blood, but he would keep the patient warm and administer an intravenous drip of plasma, saline and dextrose. The young man should recover unless there was internal bleeding. If so . . . He shrugged. Then such was the will of Allah.

Sally tried to find out what contact they had with the outside world – how, if necessary, Julian might be transferred to a civilian hospital. The orderly would answer only medical questions, insisting to all others that she ask '*Der Kommandeur*', who would be along later.

There were two beds and a washstand in the main room of the hut. A short passageway led past a small office and then a storeroom to an end cubicle housing a chemical toilet. With Julian resting comfortably, though in some pain when conscious, the orderly produced two camp beds, and shortly afterwards a platter of bread, cold meats and cheeses. Sally was ravenous but had to encourage Fiona to nibble at some cheese. Later in the evening the orderly returned to look at Julian, bringing with him a second hurricane lamp.

When he left, Sally settled Fiona into the spare bed and lay on one of the camp beds to wait for Sam. Despite the horror of the afternoon, after a night at sea and the long trek into the hills she drifted off into an exhausted sleep.

44

Chapter 4

Villagers accustomed to seeing the occasional charter yacht were no longer astonished at what, by their standards, was the amazing wealth of foreigners. If they resented the disparity, thought Sam, they managed not to show it. Two cafés in Kekova now offered primitive restaurant facilities, the owners rowing out to greet and compete for a new arrival, conscious that they could charge the occupants of a visiting yacht more for grilled fish, bread and salad than they would otherwise make in a month.

Striding through the shoreline outskirts, Sam studied people at a transition stage – members of an isolated, subsistence level rural community becoming aware of the world outside. Most *gastarbeiters* left the slums of Istanbul and the north to earn vast sums in German cities, but news of this twentieth-century gold rush had spread even to Kekova. From each hamlet one or two young men departed. Some never returned. Others, preferring a traditional way of life to the stresses of modern, industrial Europe, drew out their savings and came home. Here they were rich men, able to marry well, their trappings of affluence bringing the first incongruous modernisation to their community.

Sam looked around. There was no point in returning with the worshipped Mercedes, as many did, for the roads had yet to reach Kekova. Here the equivalent was an outboard motor on a fibreglass speedboat. They had no mains electricity, but what status accrued from a Honda generator driving the electric light, a refrigerator or even a television set. They could not receive Turkish television programmes, which came from the other side of the mountains, but Israeli broadcasts, sometimes in English, reached across from Tel Aviv. Sam thought back to previous evenings spent in the village café. No matter that children glued to the screen couldn't understand the words, it was enough for them to squat on a brushed earth floor and absorb scenes of western civilisation.

Sam quickly established that neither hamlet offered a telephone, which came as no surprise. Following a well trodden track, he set off across the grain of the country towards Kas.

Near the village he met two women walking back towards the settlement. They wore the traditional upturned slippers, baggy trousers and sari-like swathe of tunic and headscarves. Each carried a shoulder yoke supporting two lidded wooden buckets which he assumed to contain goats' milk. Sam was about to offer a greeting but at the sight of him the women crossed to the other side of the track, shielded their faces by pulling forward a headscarf and hurried on by.

Despite the urgency of his mission he could not resist pausing as he crested the next ridge. A patchwork carpet of greens and bright yellows, surrealist in sunlight, led along the floor of the valley. Sam looked down at a view which couldn't have changed since the Middle Ages. There were no houses, just a small group of single-storey huts in the distance. There were no roads, only tracks. There were no pylons, telegraph poles, vehicles, nor any other evidence of twentieth-century 'progress'. A large bird, hawk or buzzard, circled in thermal currents rising from the valley floor, soaring over territory once familiar to generations of its ancestors.

Sam pressed on to Kas, a small, harbourside community. Thanks to a mixture of words, sign language and money he was able eventually to speak with Angus from a telephone in the local post office. He was obviously relieved to learn of their safety but Sam told him apologetically about the knock down and dismasting, adding hurriedly that *Windsong* was otherwise all right.

"My dear laddie," boomed the Scots voice over the crackling line, "the mere fact that you saved the yacht is good news. Half the local fishing fleet isn't back yet, and that storm caught dozens of charter boats. A lot of them were wrecked, or

46

abandoned prematurely by inexperienced skippers. I went out and picked up at least a dozen people from liferafts this morning."

"What about the rest of your fleet?" enquired Sam.

"We were lucky. They were either in port or near enough to run for shelter. So all I have to do is step a new mast in *Windsong*, and it's business as usual. What's more, some of the competition are going to need my boats to honour their bookings so it's an ill wind, as they say."

"Do you have a new mast to put in?" asked Sam anxiously.

"Aye, that's why we run identical yachts. A few spares fit them all. But it's a yard job – I need the crane to lift her mast down through the coachroof. We'll pick our weather and I'll tow you back with the launch. Now, where exactly are you anchored?"

Sam told him. Angus hoped that by morning the swell would have disappeared completely. If at first light conditions looked favourable for towing, he would set off.

Daylight was fading fast when Sam crossed the last hill before the bay. *Windsong*'s dinghy was pulled up on a deserted beach. As he dropped to the water's edge her cockpit came into view from behind the coachroof. There was a man sitting there, smoking a cigarette, but it wasn't Julian. There was no sign of the girls. The stranger waved, pointed at the dinghy and beckoned Sam towards the yacht.

Sam was surprised and suspicious, but if he wanted to find out who the stranger was it looked as if he would have to row out. He peered at the yacht, trying to see if the other three – or anyone else – were below. It was impossible to tell in the twilight.

He called. "Sally . . . Fiona . . . Juliaaan." His voice echoed against the hillside, rolling around the bay and out across the water. The man stood up.

"Please," he shouted across, "I mean you no harm. Your friends are not here. I try to help. I ask you again, come aboard." He pointed once more at the dinghy.

Sam slipped off his desert boots and socks, launched the inflatable and rowed out, turning the dinghy for the last few yards to approach stern first and facing the stranger. The man made no move as Sam tied his painter to a shroud and climbed on board halfway along the yacht.

"My name is Major Ragip Samandag of the Turkish Army. Please," he indicated the cockpit, "won't you sit down? I will tell you what has happened to your crew, and on the chart table you will find a note from the girl called Sally."

Sam interrupted only once to ask what had happened to the fishermen's boat and their bodies.

"We do not know which village they came from," replied Samandag. "I will ask tomorrow. Do you know this part of Turkey at all, Mr . . ."

"Verle. Sam Verle." He nodded. "I've been here before. That was over a year ago."

"Then you will probably be aware," went on Samandag, "that there is very little here of what you would call 'law and order'. We have our own ways of settling these matters. I could not leave the corpses. By tomorrow they would have been rotting and bloated in the heat. I borrowed your dinghy, weighted the fishing boat and bodies with stones, tied the dinghy behind and rowed to the centre of the inlet."

He shrugged. "Then I smashed a hole in her planking." He nodded towards the water. "It is very deep.

"After that I rowed back to your yacht, left my clothes on board, took the dinghy to the beach ready for your return and swam back out here to wait for you."

Sam studied the man as he talked. After so many years with soldiers he prided himself on being a reasonable judge of character and, after all, the Turk had rescued and befriended his crew. But summary execution and an arbitrary disposal of bodies indicated a degree of power unknown to western armed forces, whilst his cavalier solution served as a blunt reminder that hereabouts the veneer of civilisation was thin in the extreme. Nevertheless, Sam locked up the yacht, content for now to follow the officer to his camp in the foothills.

There was little conversation as they marched, the Turk setting a brisk pace up the rough incline. There were no pauses for rest. Samandag knew that the Englishman had covered nearly thirty kilometres already. He had spoken of a walk to Kas, and of his conversation there with a man called

Angus. Samandag had offered to place one of his men on the shore tomorrow, to wait for the other boat.

But was it not unusual for a man from one of the richer countries to march so well? Samandag did not ask, but played with the thought, putting it finally to one side but not discarding it completely.

Sam pushed his tiring limbs to keep pace with a man not much younger than himself but obviously fit and much fresher. He chose not to reveal his own background but from time to time posed carefully casual questions – the sort which on many occasions civilians had asked about his military unit or career.

He learned that Samandag was an infantryman, now commanding a company which trained national service recruits. The Turk confirmed that the camp hadn't existed last time Sam was in the area. It was, he said, a recent project. At the culmination of their training, soldiers were taken to be exercised where there were none of the restrictions imposed by proximity to more populous areas. Being near the coast, detachments could be brought and collected by sea; otherwise, they were self-sufficient for two weeks at a time. This group was halfway through – it would be another six days before the supply boat returned. Until then, even if they carried the injured young man to Kas, there was no hospital. And the doctor there was not trained in the ways of modern medicine. The best treatment, Samandag reassured him, would be from his own orderly in their well-equipped medical centre. If the patient's condition deteriorated he would be too ill to be carried on a stretcher, in which case Samandag would send one of his men to Kas with orders to telephone for a helicopter, either to bring in a military doctor or, if necessary, to fly out the casualty.

Sam was used to the Middle East where for prestige purposes high-sounding names were given to basic facilities, and where promises were often not translated into action, but if there was one organisation likely to be able to produce a helicopter in this part of Turkey, it was their armed forces.

It was a relief to see the clean, fairly sterile-looking interior of the medical centre. By the soft, yellow light of the hurricane lamps he saw that Julian was resting quietly, a tube set

49

into his arm. A heavy sheen of sweat, not caused entirely by the heat of the night, was the only other sign that all was not normal. He could make out Fiona's head on the pillow of the second bed. Sally lay on a camp bed.

Samandag stood waiting by the door. It was late. Sam was too tired to worry about food. He whispered his thanks to their host, closed the door, removed his boots and stretched out gratefully on the remaining camp bed.

They were woken shortly after daybreak by sounds strange to the others but familiar and nostalgic to Sam – the roar of a petrol-driven field burner throwing its jets of flame into a low metal tunnel to heat huge dixies set on top; men queuing for breakfast clanking mess tins, cutlery and tin mugs; and every now and then a brisk shout as non-commissioned officers competed for the attention of their squad. Sam sat on his camp bed, running his fingers through tousled hair. There was a knock on the door.

"Come in."

No sooner had he called out when it occurred to him that their visitor probably spoke no English. There was another knock. Sam padded across the hut to let in the orderly who was bearing a bowl of steaming water.

They stood aside to give him room as he washed and made comfortable the patient. Julian was fully conscious but the wound made it too painful for him to sit up. Sam moved forward to inspect it when the orderly changed the dressing. The damaged flesh looked clean enough, although there was a trace more blood seepage than he would have liked. The orderly noticed it, too, and looked at Sam, holding his palm down and rocking it slowly. It was a gesture which said that it might be all right, but there again it might not.

They passed a quiet morning. The girls occupied themselves by talking to Julian and taking over routine nursing duties. From time to time they sponged his face and chest to keep him cool, or lifted his head for a sip of water. At least, thought Sally, the occupation had a therapeutic effect on Fiona, who was still quiet but considerably less morose than yesterday. There was nothing, however, for Sam to do – there was nothing he could do for Julian until either his condition

50

improved or it became necessary to ask Samandag for a helicopter.

He hadn't spoken with the Turk that morning. Samandag had left with his men after breakfast, and according to the orderly did not usually return until late afternoon. By mid-morning, despite anxieties over Julian, Sam was thoroughly bored. He walked slowly round the camp, now occupied only by cooks, fatigue men, the medical orderly, a soldier with one ankle bandaged heavily, and a supervising non-commissioned officer. The man with the damaged ankle had a medium calibre machine gun disassembled on a blanket in front of his tent. He ignored Sam. Each was killing time; one cleaning a weapon, the other content to watch.

Having wiped each part with an oily rag, the Turk reassembled his machine gun. Sam had watched many a recruit and inexperienced soldier. They did it carefully, sliding one part on to the next, checking back time after time. The Turk's fingers moved with careless competence born only of long use and total familiarity. His hands were a blur of activity as he clamped on the magazine, cocked his weapon, pulled the trigger, repeated the sequence as a final check and reset the safety catch. Finally he laid it down with the ejection port uppermost as a precaution against grit and dust. The soldier looked up, a grin on his face. That had shown the foreigner his skill.

Sam returned the smile, offering a nod of congratulation. The man had to be an instructor with that standard of weapon handling but his uniform was that of a private soldier. Sam glanced back casually to confirm that the man's sleeve, collar and epaulettes were devoid of badges of rank. Perhaps he was one of life's natural soldiers – invaluable in war, but incapable of avoiding brushes with peacetime authority – men who tended to oscillate between the ranks of private and lance corporal throughout their service.

He strolled on round the rectangle, looking over the camp. The non-commissioned officer, he noticed, was never more than fifty yards away. Samandag might have instructed him to look after the foreigner, but the man's unsubtle observation was more in tune with not letting him out of his sight.

Having exhausted the possibilities of the camp, Sam went

51

back to the medical centre. At mid-day the orderly brought cheese, bread and a bottle of wine. Sam was relieved to see Fiona eating again.

He thought about Angus. If he left at, say, five o'clock, and the launch made eight knots, it was about seventy-five miles to Kekova – so, nine hours to cover the distance which meant that he could arrive by two o'clock. He wondered if Samandag had remembered his promise to station a man near *Windsong*.

Sam finished his beaker of wine.

"I'm going back to the yacht," he told the others abruptly. "There's nothing I can do here, not until tonight, anyway, so I might as well go and meet Angus. I could occupy myself with sorting out some of the rigging or having a look at that engine."

"All right," answered Sally after a moment's pause, "but I think you should know that I'm concerned about Julian, even though the orderly hasn't said anything. So far, there doesn't seem to be any improvement."

"Mmm." Sam scratched his stubbled chin. "I wonder if it mightn't take a day or two to get over that journey? We probably won't be able to establish a definite trend until tomorrow, although if he gets any worse I could always ask Samandag tonight about a helicopter. There's no sign of any deterioration so far, is there?"

She shook her head.

He hesitated, wondering how to frame his next remark without making the girls anxious.

"Look, the NCO in charge of this place has been following me round all morning like a pet dog. Samandag has probably told him to keep an eye on us. I can't speak Turkish, and I doubt whether the NCO knows a word of English, but if I start to wander off he might get agitated. He could even make it pretty plain that he wants me to stay here. Rather than put either of us in a difficult position, I'm just going to drift away when he's not looking. If he notices that I'm missing he'll probably ask the orderly to find out where I am, in which case you merely say that I got bored and went for a stroll. All right?"

They were distracted by a murmur from Julian. Sam went out and sat on the verandah – midway between the door and

52

the end of the hut, leaning back against the wall with his arms folded. At first the NCO, playing cards with the soldier who had been weapon cleaning, looked at him every few minutes but after a quarter of an hour he was once more engrossed in his game.

"Sally," Sam called quietly, "don't come out here. Can you hear me all right?"

"Yes." Her voice was muffled from inside the hut.

"Give me thirty seconds," he went on, "then open the door a foot or so, will you, and leave it like that?"

Sam unfolded his arms and shuffled sideways, keeping one eye on the NCO. A last glance, and then a two-foot drop into deep shadow alongside the verandah. Looking underneath the corner between the hut's foundation stilts and weeds he could just see the two men fifty yards away. He heard a door open. The sudden movement caught the NCO's eye. He looked up, seeing the empty verandah and the door now ajar. The Englishman had obviously gone inside. The NCO turned back to his card game.

Keeping the hut between himself and the two men, Sam crossed ten yards of cleared ground and slipped into the forest. Undergrowth was dense in patches but he was able to work back for fifty yards before moving parallel with the camp perimeter. When he came to the track leading from the coast he retreated again, walking deep enough in the trees to be sure of seeing before being seen.

After a quarter of a mile he stopped, smelling something not belonging to the forest. There was a rising column of blue-grey cigarette smoke just off the pathway in the undergrowth. It must be a Turkish soldier. Sam couldn't see the man, only the top of his hat and the muzzle of a rifle sticking up above foliage. But why, he wondered, put a sentry in such a position? The man wouldn't be able to alert the camp of an approach, unless he did something drastic such as firing his weapon. An unpleasant suspicion formed in Sam's mind. It looked very much as if the soldier had been sited to intercept anyone coming from, rather than going to, the camp.

He circled around towards the coast five miles away. It was nearly all downhill, the going easier as the forest thinned out. From the edge of the tree line, Sam looked over a series of

53

valleys which led to the sea. They ran not at right angles but at forty-five degrees, so that each one had to be crossed diagonally. The path lay somewhere over to his right. He moved off, aiming for an intersection just before the final rise.

Each small, uncultivated valley was bare-sided but for tiny plants and clumps of long, spine-leafed cactus. Only the floors offered shade from an occasional wild olive or carob tree. The heat bouncing off the rocks was intense but fortunately this was a desert climate not the humid, debilitating steam of tropical rain forest. Even so, Sam was sweating freely by the time he crossed a last dune before the bay.

It was empty. The sea danced and sparkled, a thousand blue-white crystals reflecting the afternoon sun, but *Windsong* had gone. There was no sign of Angus. Sam sat down, staring at the empty lagoon whilst he thought things over.

Angus wouldn't have taken the yacht, not without her crew. And last evening he and Samandag hadn't left till dusk. It was highly unlikely that another yacht would enter the lagoon by night, moor in the bay rather than off one of the village tavernas, and then break into and tow away a vessel which had obviously been left there deliberately. Fishermen from the village might have moved her, but he doubted it. If so, without sails and engine they couldn't have taken her far; probably only to Kekova jetty for safety. Otherwise, *Windsong*'s disappearance had to be connected in some way with Samandag . . . It was as if, despite having rescued the girls, he intended that the yacht and her crew should neither be found nor return to Fethiye.

Sam weighed a pebble in one hand, trying to decide what to do next. Angus would arrive sooner or later, but it might not be for several hours, or even today. He would have made a decision based on the weather at Fethiye. Sam thought about staying put and waiting for the launch. Otherwise, if Angus found the bay empty, what would he do? Ask at the village, probably. Not that the locals would be able to tell him very much, unless *Windsong* had been towed there in which case Angus would wait for her crew to turn up.

He threw the pebble aside. If *Windsong* was at the village, Samandag was in the clear; if not, then he had to be responsible.

54

If the Turk were innocent, he couldn't object to Sam returning to the yacht. But if Samandag were responsible for the yacht's disappearance, Sam knew that he wouldn't be left at large to meet up with Angus – which might explain the interest in keeping an eye on him back at camp. They would let Angus ask around fruitlessly, or possibly tell him that *Windsong* had been able to start her engine and had motored off towards Fethiye. Either way, this part of the Mediterranean was devoid of coastguard or search and rescue services so Angus would probably start motoring back, checking at ports and anchorages along the way.

Sam rose to his feet, mind made up. He would walk to the village. If *Windsong* wasn't there, then it would be better if Samandag were not aware of his outing. No doubt the Turk would tell them that Angus had failed to turn up. So be it. The first priority was Julian's recovery. If Sam declared his hand, he wondered how long the courtesy and medical treatment might last. Much as he would have liked to sit and wait for Angus, if the yacht wasn't at one of the village jetties he would go back to camp before his absence was noticed.

By climbing a ridge and walking as far as the ruined castle, Sam was able to look down over the two hamlets. There were local fishing boats but no visiting cruising yachts, no launch, and certainly no sign of *Windsong*.

His sixth sense operated as a sort of internal tension, a gut sensation that all was not well. Sam had known the feeling on more than one occasion; in Aden, when he split up his platoon seconds before the first terrorist mortar round landed, in Borneo, on a jungle track just a shade too quiet, and in South Armagh when the warning came too late and Angus had stepped in to the rescue. Sam opened into a steady jog back down the valley. He had that feeling now.

He made it in one and a half hours which was not bad for nearly seven miles, mostly uphill and across rough country. Once back in the pine forest he retraced his outward route, giving the sentry an even wider berth. He slowed down near to camp. By the time he found the back of the medical hut, his breathing was normal and he had stopped sweating. The NCO was nowhere in sight.

Sam leant over the verandah rail, as if he had just come out for a breath of fresh air. Not long afterwards the NCO emerged from the cookhouse tent. A turn of his head showed that Sam had been noticed but there was no other reaction. With the NCO still watching him, he walked along the verandah and into the hut.

Sally was lying on a camp bed, hands behind her head, staring at the ceiling. There was no sign of Fiona. Julian appeared to be asleep.

"You're back early," she said softly. "Did you meet up with Angus?"

He shook his head. "How's the patient?"

She thought for a moment, obviously choosing her words carefully.

"I'm not sure." She swept back from her forehead hair damp with sweat, looked at the moisture on her palm and wiped it unceremoniously on her slacks. "God, it's hot in here. Fiona's gone for a stroll round the camp to cool off.

"Julian's wound looks all right," she went on, "but it's still seeping blood. He was sick not long after you left. Not much, just some sort of nasty-smelling green bile, but he seemed more comfortable afterwards."

Sam mulled over the news. He had little experience of knife injuries, but a better than average understanding of bullet wounds. He had given first aid to a number of soldiers over the years, once for nearly thirty-six hours until a helicopter could lift the casualty out of the jungle through a hole in the monsoon. The vomiting worried him. If there was internal bleeding from a damaged blood vessel it could build up pressure in the peritoneal cavity, hence the nausea. On the other hand, it might be just the tail end of shock, part of Julian's general condition which had not been helped by being carried over rough country and having to lie in a stifling hut without air conditioning. Either way, they ought to know by tomorrow.

He stood up. "I'm going out on to the verandah. You wouldn't like to come with me, please? I've something to tell you."

They leant over the fence, side by side, forearms resting on the rail.

56

"First of all, though, how's Fiona? I've hardly spoken to her since . . ."

"Since she was raped." Sally spoke the word firmly, deliberately matter-of-fact. "Better than she was yesterday. Right now she's hurt, bitter and angry, all rolled into one, but she'll get over it."

She shook her head. "What's worrying her most is that she wasn't on the pill. It didn't suit her, or something. She bosses her boyfriends into using a French letter, apparently. The trouble is, she won't know for a week or two whether she's pregnant. I think that particular prospect hanging over her is causing most of the depression."

Sally met his eye and smiled reassuringly. "Don't worry. It's not very pleasant for her, but I know Fiona. She'll survive."

Her voice took on a lighter note. "Now, tell me about *Windsong*. You say that Angus hasn't arrived?"

He told her about the events of the afternoon and his suspicions but suggested that for the moment it might be better if they spared Fiona any further anxiety.

Sally agreed. "But what are we going to do?" she queried. "Samandag should be back soon. Why not ask him straight out about the yacht?"

Sam shook his head.

"No. At the moment, he's being very helpful and for all we know, there might be some perfectly simple explanation, although for the life of me I can't think of one. Even so, I have a feeling that now is not the time to tell Samandag that I spent the afternoon wandering around that lagoon."

For the first time Sam found himself in Sally's company with an opportunity for idle conversation. He asked how it was that with apparently different backgrounds, Fiona and she came to be sharing a flat.

She laughed. "It's simple, really. We met at university, living in the same hall of residence. You could only spend two years in hall. For you final year you had to move out into a flat or lodgings. To be able to afford a flat I had to share, and Fiona didn't want to live on her own. When we graduated, and both of us found jobs in London, it seemed convenient to keep the arrangement going."

"And you get on all right?" Sam asked pointedly.

"Most of the time." She kept her voice even. "I'm not going to play the 'poor-little-rich-girl' tune for her but she hasn't found it easy, moving from an over-protective education into the everyday world. For what it's worth, she doesn't rely on her father's money at all. Fiona's establishing her own reputation in the magazine business."

She looked at him directly. "I know her better than most people. Fiona can be very kind when she's absolutely sure that she's not going to be ripped off. Unfortunately that has a habit of happening in her emotional life as well as financially."

They continued to look out over the camp and the conversation turned to Sally's career in marketing. In response to her questions, his own background was summed up succinctly.

"I was in the Army for nearly twenty years – an ambitious young Lieutenant Colonel. Then my wife and son were killed in an air crash about a year ago. I took an early pension, and now I sail my boat."

She was silent, not wanting to offer some banal comment. She had taken him for a well-off bachelor, able to afford time off from some enterprise or other to go yachting. There had been no hint of personal tragedy, and he certainly didn't fit her image of an ex-Army Officer or a modern sailing hobo.

Uncertain how to react to Sam's disclosure, Sally was spared a response by Fiona's return. She managed a smile, but rather than join them walked into the hut.

A figure in fatigue denims festooned with belt, webbing and pouches ran into the camp and collapsed. His dark green shirt was soaked with sweat. After a few seconds he wriggled out of his equipment. Another dark stain had run down his spine to spread in an inverted triangle across the small of his back. The soldier checked his weapon, flicking the handle back and forth to eject any last round from the chamber. Finally he squeezed the trigger, reset the safety catch and laid the weapon chamber-side up on his pouches. Taking out his water bottle he drank sparingly, wiped sweat from his eyes and looked towards the entrance.

More figures appeared to repeat the performance.

58

Amongst the first half dozen in what had obviously been a gruelling race home came Samandag, his shirt open to the waist, massive chest heaving, beads of sweat hanging on a forest of hairs turning grey with the onset of middle age. He waited for the last few stragglers before walking across to them.

"The boy," he enquired, "how is he?"

"I'm not sure, Ragip. I think tomorrow will tell. There might be some bleeding inside, in which case he will need surgery."

The Turk weighed Sam's words carefully.

"So. I will see you later. We will have a meal, drink some wine together. Now you will excuse me, please."

Shouldering his sub-machine gun, he walked off towards the headquarters hut.

"What do you make of that?" Sally asked him.

"Nothing. It's what I would have expected – non-committal. But I do make something of that."

Sam inclined his head towards the groups of soldiers dispersing to their tents.

"It adds to what I said earlier. Armies do things in different ways, but I've seen a few armies in my time and there are certain basic facets common to all."

She was curious.

"One, you don't leave recruits alone like that after the end of a training session. They would just lie around in a mindless huddle. Recruits have to be rounded up into squads, told what to do and then given the command to get on with it."

Sam ticked off his observations on his fingers.

"Two, recruits are generally youngsters, particularly when you have national service as they do in Turkey. The average age of those soldiers must be about twenty-four.

"Three, recruits tend to be wayward, needing encouragement all the time. So you need more staff to drive them on and supervise. This camp doesn't have the entourage of bullying instructors which I've never failed to see around a bunch of trainees. Yet those so-called recruits have just completed a crippling forced march, in unholy conditions, and all of them finished within a few minutes of each other.

"Fourth, those men are used to soldiering in a hot climate.

59

Look how they drank, slow and sparingly, so they wouldn't get stomach cramp. That comes from experience. Civilians don't sweat like those men have to – not many of them, at any rate. Even with fairly advanced recruits, some of them would have up-ended their water bottle, either through forgetfulness or because they gave in to temptation, but not those men – I was watching. Every one took just enough. You don't get that sort of self-discipline with a recruit platoon."

He paused, but Sally was content to listen, fascinated.

"Finally," he concluded, "every one of them is an expert weapon handler. It wasn't an instructor I was watching today. That was the norm. If you want proof, look at the way every man jack of them took care of his weapon, making sure it was unloaded and putting it down properly, even before taking a drink of water. A recruit can be told countless times that one day his survival might depend on being able to fire his rifle, but you're lucky if half of them remember."

"So what you're saying . . ." she began slowly.

"I'm not just saying," he told her, "I know for sure. Those men are no more recruits than I'm Clare Francis. They have the unmistakable hallmark of fit, hand-picked professionals. The question is: why does Samandag want us to believe they're recruits on manoeuvres?"

They watched a group of officers and senior NCOs gather outside the headquarters. Each carried a notepad or folder, indicating some sort of briefing. At six o'clock Samandag opened the door and beckoned them inside. Sam would dearly have loved to listen but besides his lack of Turkish, with the camp bustling with solders there was no chance of eavesdropping without being detected.

After the meeting Samandag called round to the hospital hut. He invited the three mobile members of the party to join him at a long trestle table being set out near the field kitchen for officers and senior NCOs. The soldiers, Sam noticed, were expected to eat by their tents.

"In honour of the occasion," announced Samandag as bottles of Kavaklidere and Buzbag were set in front of them.

He played the perfect host, introducing each man at the table even though he was the only one who spoke English. Both Kavaklidere, a sort of white burgundy, and Buzbag, which turned out to be not unlike Chianti, proved surprisingly good. A ragout of lamb was served with aubergine and tomato side salad and yoghurt, and followed by fruit and cheese. The local villages, commented Samandag, were able to grow enough only for themselves. They had no surplus to sell. Therefore, he concluded, food was good at the beginning of a camp, quite reasonable – he hoped – in the middle, but poor at the end.

The others were keen to ask questions, particularly about the girls' way of life: where they lived, what they did for a living, and how their leisure time was spent. Patiently Samandag translated each query and answer.

In response to another question, Sam described himself dismissively as a retired civil servant, but even as he spoke detected raised eyebrows from their host.

Samandag apologised for not being able to offer *sekerli*, or coffee, but small glasses of tea without milk were produced, and finally *raki*. The Turk added water to the girls' measures of spirit and swirled the liquid till their drinks turned white.

"I should have thought of it earlier," Sam said turning towards Samandag, "but on our yacht there is more coffee than we could possibly need. Perhaps tomorrow it might be a good idea if I made an expedition and presented some to you."

Sam noticed Sally's eyes scanning the Turk as she monitored his reaction. An initial flicker of concern reverted almost immediately to an urbane, even disinterested expression. A clap of the hands, an order in Turkish and a young NCO poured more *raki*. Sam, a survivor of many invitations to the Sergeants' mess, had barely touched his drink. He made a show of accepting a top-up gratefully, even though there was room only for half a tot.

As darkness fell hurricane lamps were set on the table. In the relaxed atmosphere conversation flowed, despite the language difficulty. It was impossible not to enjoy the occasion – more than once Sam had to remind himself of the reality of their situation.

As more wine and *raki* were consumed, men disappeared from time to time into the trees. Several were equipped with torches which they used to light their way over a mass of tent

61

ropes. Sam noticed that when they came back to the table, they didn't always sit at the same place. A young Turk was delighted to find a gap between Sam and Fiona. Before stepping over the bench he placed his torch on the table. After a few minutes Sam picked it up and walked off into the darkness. He returned to sit opposite, the torch safely in his pocket.

By nine o'clock the party was losing impetus. Tired after an arduous day, and conscious of the need for an early start next morning, Samandag's men were courteous but content to let conversation lapse. Sam thanked their host for his hospitality and concluded the evening successfully by inviting the girls to join him in a toast to the Turkish Army. They drained their glasses.

The time dragged by atrociously. After two hours, the temptation to leave had to be slapped down at five-minute intervals. By a quarter to midnight, the other occupants of the hut fast asleep, his vigil was over. Two and a half hours – long enough for the effects of food and wine to have helped the Turks into solid slumber.

Sam opened the door, slipped along the verandah to the position he had occupied that afternoon, and rolled right under the boards. Visibility was excellent – better than he had dared hope. An almost full moon threw pools of strong light against patches of deep shadow. The camp was a three-dimensional photograph in black, sepia and silver, a photograph that was coming to life . . . Across the square a soldier emerged from between two tents, stepping carefully over guy ropes which he could scarcely see. Sam felt he was watching a ciné film in the unnatural hues of an old time movie.

He waited. Footsteps were inaudible on the soft earth and he couldn't afford to be surprised by another soldier working parallel with the man opposite.

Shielding its dial, Sam pressed a button to illuminate the display on his Seiko. Five-past twelve. He had been there for twenty minutes. It was tempting to press on, but more reconnaissance came to grief through impatience than for any other reason.

By half-past twelve he had established that circuits around

the camp, weaving in and out of tents and buildings, took about twenty minutes. He looked up. The sentry had disappeared. Seconds later a tent flap moved on the far side of the square and two figures ducked out. The second man yawned, stretched, and bent to lace up his boots. He was next on stag. His predecessor backtracked for a few tents before disappearing into his own.

It was a rudimentary system, relying on a solo guard to alert his relief. The duty was being performed conscientiously – and from what Sam knew of discipline in the Turkish Army, it was unlikely that anyone would risk an illegal rest under the trees – but even so, one man was little more than a fire picket. He could be overwhelmed without the rest of the camp being alerted. It wasn't a system which Sam would have countenanced, even in peacetime, but in such a remote area Samandag obviously felt totally secure.

He waited whilst the new sentry completed a couple of circuits, so that he would be more relaxed. For a third time the guard gave the medical centre a wide berth, presumably to avoid disturbing the patient. On each occasion he walked along the headquarters verandah but made no attempt to open the door or look inside. Sam lay safely concealed in his hole beneath the boards.

When the guard disappeared fifty yards on between tents, Sam walked quietly past the stores hut to the headquarters. Its door was the same as their own, a flimsy, framed-lattice affair held shut only by a spring. He winced at the mild squeak from its hinges but although unbearably loud to his heightened senses, the sound wouldn't carry as far as the sentry. Sam closed the door gently and looked around.

Like their own hut, its windows were covered only by a loose-hanging mosquito curtain. The verandah windows were in shadow but two shafts of moonlight slanted through those at the rear. He could make out the shape of objects – a desk, a chair and a low table – but little else. The hut appeared to have an identical layout to the medical centre. He moved along the corridor. The smaller room was another office containing a flat-topped folding table and a small filing cabinet. Obviously Samandag used the main office and this one was for his clerk. Sam checked his watch. Five minutes.

Another ten before he stopped to wait for the sentry to pass.

He stepped back from the table and into something which made a sharp scraping sound as wooden legs skittered across the floor.

A coatstand?

He spun round, expecting a splintering crash at any second. Something flat but not heavy fell against him. Automatically his arms went up to stop whatever it was from dropping to the floor. He was supporting what appeared to be a large rectangle of wood resting on its bottom edge. Another scrape from the floor warned him that something within this delicate equilibrium was becoming unbalanced.

Clues of shape, size and sound tripped in microseconds across his memory. Sam moved a hand slippery with sweat to the blackboard's lower edge, taking weight and backward pressure off the easel. Carefully he teased its legs apart, reset the board, eased away his hands . . . and exhaled with relief.

With fingers over the glass he switched on his torch. In a dim, diffused beam of light he saw that the board had been wiped clean. Sam was about to start on the filing cabinet when a sudden thought prompted him to lean round and shine his light on the reverse side.

It took five seconds to lift the board down, turn it round and rest it against the table. It wasn't clear immediately because the dimmed light illuminated only a small patch at a time. His beam slowly traced the outline of a well-sketched map: a pear-shaped island, tilted slightly to one side, and with a familiar harbour in the top right-hand corner. For several minutes Sam studied superimposed symbols and arrows. It seemed impossible yet there was only one logical interpretation: he was looking at a diagrammatic plan for an amphibious assault.

Chapter 5

It had to be an academic exercise, some sort of military study for the instruction of junior officers. It was inconceivable that the Turks intended to capture Greek territory, even an island as small as Kastellorizon. Athens would never accept occupation – it would mean war in the Aegean. And yet Samandag had lied about his men, and he was probably responsible for the removal of *Windsong* . . . Once more Sam experienced a feeling of unease, that familiar sensation that something was wrong.

He needed a camera or some means of making notes. In one of those drawers there might be paperwork amplifying the diagram. Sam checked his watch. There was time to look over the rest of the office before Samandag's guard came round again. He knelt in front of the cabinet. It was a simple file depository with two deep drawers and no lock. But security shouldn't have been necessary. Samandag had no reason to expect a visit from locals, the nearest of whom were probably in Kekova, seven miles away.

Sam pulled open the top drawer and shone his torch inside, discovering a few folded papers which looked to be maps. He lifted the largest one out, and with the torchlight still shielded by his fingers unfolded a zig-zag concertina on to the table. It wasn't a map but a chart, showing the coastline from Levant Syria round to the Bosphorous. His beam tracked upwards, over the Sea of Marmara towards Istanbul and the edge of the Black Sea. It picked up the chart's title and various notes for mariners printed along the upper margin. Letters danced at him from the paper – not the Roman alphabet. He couldn't

65

understand the words, but Sam recognised occasional, familiar shapes of Cyrillic script.

For several seconds he stared whilst his brain sprinted along any number of avenues in a vain attempt to rationalise the discovery. As a member of NATO, Turkey turned to her western allies if she needed assistance. Besides, she had charts of her own. Relations between Turkey and her Russian neighbour, with whom she shared a common border in the north-east, were cordial but reserved. Certainly there was no military contact. It was highly improbable that a unit of the Turkish armed forces would rely on a survey and chart quite clearly produced by the Union of Soviet Socialist Republics.

Sam shone his torch back into the cabinet. More charts. A land map of Kastellorizon, but not annotated. He flicked open each one, confirmed their common origin then tossed the papers back into the drawer. He pushed it shut and opened the one below.

The diffused beam settled on to a rectangular object about one and a half times the size of a house brick. Meters and switches . . . It was a portable field radio, similar to models used by western armies. Sam picked it up. It had no tuning dial, only a knob which turned through a number of set channels. Although size and shape gave only a crude indication, a set like this might have a range of thirty miles, perhaps more from high up or over the sea. The Russian border was the best part of a thousand miles away. This looked to be a compact, very high frequency set, probably fitted with secure speech scramble, but strictly for local communication.

It was heavy for its size. Stamped on to one side was the crest of the Russian Army's Corps of Signals. Sam put the radio on the table. Perhaps there was a book or some message log giving schedule times and channels. As he turned to take another look into the bottom drawer, his peripheral vision caught the tip of a beam of light reaching across the verandah.

Sam's heartbeat accelerated. Could he have misjudged the time, or was the sentry early? There were no footsteps – he couldn't be on the verandah yet. Sam scooped up and put back the radio. Mercifully the drawer pushed shut quietly. He squatted alongside the window, back against the wall.

One slow thud after another. The light grew brighter. After

66

almost total darkness, even the fringe of the sentry's beam was enough to throw the inside of the hut into sharp relief.

Christ, the blackboard! It was still on the floor. If that light were played through the transparent gauze . . .

No sooner had panic seared his stomach when the beam passed harmlessly by the window. Sam exhaled slowly.

The door squeaked. Bloody hell! The sentry was coming into the hut. The footsteps stopped. Sam was holding his breath again. Flashes of light came through the door from the corridor as a torch played over the main office. If he checked the rest of the hut . . .

Sam stood up. That beam would be his first clue. If it steadied on the corridor and there were any more footsteps he had five, maybe seven seconds. He could take out the sentry, but that offered only temporary respite – visitors would be prime suspects. Sam realised he'd have to take a chance on not moving the blackboard. He would climb out on to the verandah.

A steady beam of white light, the distinct double-tap of heel and toe on wooden boards . . . Sam had one foot through the window, thigh on the sill, weight transferred to hands, head bowed for a silent shift through the gap. Two more double taps. Body through, left foot in contact with boards outside. One hand was on the upright, the other helping to lift his foot and ankle clear of the ledge.

Thank God, a silent exit. He slid down, back against the wall. The night above brightened as a wedge of light turned into the small office and settled on the curtain. When it swung away he would move round to the side of the hut. The sentry oughtn't to be alerted by the blackboard. Sam would wait until the Turk was well round the circuit then go back inside and put it away. But after that, he still had to work out what the hell to do as a result of his discovery.

The beam failed to lift. It stayed there, illuminating the window and spilling light on to the verandah. Sam felt a surge of adrenalin, and with it the heat of fear in the pit of his stomach. What the hell was that sentry playing at? He resisted an animal urge to run, but his muscles tightened involuntarily.

A single, shouted command and three lances of brilliant white light split the darkness to converge on his crouching

67

form. For half a second he contemplated a frantic break-out but from behind the lights a familiar rattle warned of cocking handles being pulled back and allowed to spring forward, each one shifting a mechanism which collected a live round from a magazine and fed it into the breach. By now they were holding the aim. A gentle tightening of just one finger would be enough to set a lump of metal tumbling and tearing through his body.

Sam forced his muscles to relax. Slowly, very slowly, he held up a hand to shield his eyes from the blinding beams. A black shape advanced on to the perimeter of light.

"Mr Verle." The voice was Samandag's. "How very wise. You do not move, or my soldiers have orders to fire. I shall speak to my men. Afterwards, on my word of command, you will stand up and walk slowly back inside the headquarters. It is time, I think, for you and me to have another talk."

Sam was directed to a chair in front of the desk. A soldier set two lamps in front of him and rejoined his companions by the door. The light was on Sam's face but only Samandag's torso as he stood facing his prisoner from behind the desk. The Turk blew down a cloud of cigar smoke which swirled and eddied in blue-grey curls as man-made momentum surrendered to thermal vortices from the hurricane lamps.

"So, Mr Verle, if that really is your name, it is time for you and me to be more honest with each other."

Coming from beyond the circle of light, his voice was vacuous and unnerving.

"You assumed, Mr Verle, that only one sentry had been posted. No doubt such a slovenly system was all your prejudice expected from a Turk."

Samandag warmed to his discourse. "The patrol sentry was no more than a blind. My real security came from four two-man observation trenches, sited to look both inwards and out from just beyond the camp perimeter. You would not have seen them. There is no system of relief. In each position one man sleeps, the other watches. They take it in turns throughout the night."

Outwardly, Sam was impassive. Inwardly, he groaned. He'd been so bloody confident, lying out there watching the sentry. They must have spotted him leaving the medical centre, seen every move. No doubt when he went into the headquarters hut one of them had alerted Samandag. The reaction group must have been standing by, ready to surround him silently in a matter of minutes. Samandag had played him brilliantly all evening. Now, like a prize fish, he was landed. Sam waited for the interrogation to begin.

"I know," went on the Turk, "that you had time to explore these two offices. Also, you did not put away the blackboard. So, perhaps you would be kind enough to tell me of your conclusions."

Sam said nothing. His mind was searching frantically for a plausible line, some statement of partial truth which might satisfy Samandag. It was still racing when the Turk began again.

"Come on, Mr Verle, I will help you. Let me tell you what I have observed, then hopefully we shall avoid childish insults to our respective intellects. First, your passport. It appears to be genuine – it even gives your occupation as 'Government Service'. Now, what sort of service is that, I must ask myself?"

Sam raised his eyebrows.

"Don't be surprised," soothed Samandag, one hand lifted almost in benediction, "my orderly collected the passport from your jacket pocket whilst we were having supper. It also tells me that you are well travelled – Europe, Turkey and Cyprus as well as most of the Middle East.

"Next, you are conveniently shipwrecked in the nearest bay to my camp." He raised a hand to prevent Sam speaking. "Yes, I agree, the damage appears to be genuine" – stress on the 'appears' – "and you did not find us, we found you. That rape was most unpleasant. But if it had not taken place, and had we not intervened, could it have been that you might have come looking for us?"

He lifted his shoulders, hands turning outwards in a typically Middle Eastern gesture. "I don't know, Mr Verle. But you have to agree that whereas your three companions may have the hallmark of innocent civilians, you cannot claim to share their image."

As if to press his point, Samandag walked round to the

front of the desk and leaned against it. His face was still in shadow.

"You trekked to Kas and back, yet after a journey of which many Europeans would be incapable you were still able to march to our camp. Finally, you decide to explore my head-quarters in the middle of the night. As you have discovered, I have no means of locking things away. It ought not to be necessary. But if you have explored this building, then you must be assumed to possess what can only be described as extremely sensitive, even dangerous, information."

The Turk's voice grew harder, his delivery more staccato. "You have seen the charts, some of our radio equipment, and the blackboard. Why did you go exploring? That is not what a normal person would have done. But a normal person would not be interested in what you have seen, whereas you, Mr Verle, are a 'Government Servant'."

Samandag paused. "I have been anxious to offer humanitarian assistance," he went on more quietly, "and I would not wish that policy to change. But right now, the future of your companions lies more within your province than mine."

He tapped one forefinger against his thigh. "You owe me an explanation, Mr Verle. Perhaps you should give it before my forebearance is exhausted."

Sam was only too aware that failure to provide a reasonable answer would jeopardise the girls' safety and Julian's recovery. As long as the three of them were presumed innocent, they were probably safe. He had led them into enough trouble already. The only sensible course was a degree of honesty. Samandag had to be convinced that their arrival was coincidental, that they represented no threat.

He told the truth about his background, and about the events which led to their arrival in Kekova. Samandag nodded slowly when Sam assured him that until a few days ago he had never set eyes on Julian or the two girls.

"It was a series of accidents," he went on, "that storm, a disabled yacht, those fishermen, and finally your intervention. I'm very grateful for what you have done, but if you hadn't helped us we would never even have suspected your presence here."

70

"And yet," responded Samandag after a moment's silence, "you were moved to explore my camp, to go on a spying expedition in the middle of the night."

The suggestion of spying brought a shivering sensation to Sam's skin, despite the heat of the night.

"It was more a case of trying to find out what sort of set-up we had accidentally blundered into," he responded carefully. "Particularly as you were not being entirely honest."

The outline of Samandag's head lifted in response to the allegation.

"You should be aware," Sam pressed on, "that I took a walk this afternoon. Largely through boredom, although I timed it to coincide with the possible arrival of the chap I phoned yesterday. As you well know, *Windsong* is no longer there. Neither, incidentally, was the soldier you agreed to station by my boat in order to link us up with our rescue party." He looked blindly towards a face outside the pool of light. "I wouldn't mind betting that *Windsong* isn't far away, probably underneath a couple of hundred feet of water. As for Angus, what was he told? Or have you left him to make a one-man search of the seventy-odd miles of coastline from here back to Fethiye?"

As if to acknowledge the new note of honesty in their exchange, Samandag pulled a canvas chair from one side of the room and sat down near Sam, in front of the desk. His expression neither confirmed nor denied the accusation.

"Nevertheless," he responded suspiciously, "you did not ask if I knew anything about *Windsong*. Instead, you chose to creep around at dead of night."

"That," Sam replied, "was simply because I assumed our expectations of help, particularly medical, would be better if you thought we accepted entirely what you had chosen to tell us."

"But you had not." It was both question and statement.

"No. Don't forget, I was a professional soldier for nearly twenty years." Sam recounted his observations of the afternoon. "So it was clear," he concluded, "that your men were the absolute opposite of recruits. I chose not to tell the others," he lied smoothly, "because they had enough to worry about already. What I had in mind was to take a look at your

71

headquarters, then make a decision. I'm not sure what else I might have done – in the end, probably nothing. Anyway," he shrugged his shoulders, "that particular dilemma seems to have been overtaken by events."

Samandag walked back behind his desk, took a bottle of *raki* and two glasses from a drawer, poured a brace of generous measures and handed one to Sam.

"And so," he replied eventually, settling back into his chair, "you have made your reconnaissance." He sipped at his drink. "I think I am even prepared to believe that you are being honest. But what, my friend, did you learn from your examination of our headquarters?"

There was no way out. Whatever he said would be unlikely to influence Samandag's plans for his own future, but a degree of truth might bolster the Turk's belief that the others were innocent.

"It's quite clear," said Sam, keeping his voice as even as possible, "that you have assembled a small unit of highly trained men – probably the equivalent of our Special Forces. I find a detailed plan for an amphibious assault on a Greek island for which this deserted area would make an ideal mounting base."

He stopped, wondering if he might be allowed to get away with that much and no more. But Samandag pressed immediately for the final piece of the jigsaw.

"The charts? Those maps? The radio equipment? Do they tell you nothing, Mr Verle, after your twenty-odd years as a soldier?"

"Russian," said Sam flatly. "All of them. So presumably you are working for the Soviets." He paused to sip at the *raki*, wondering for how long this artificially civilised session of question and answer would continue. A pity. In different circumstances he and Samandag might have got along quite well. Sam decided to play his final card whilst the game was still open.

"That's really about all I can tell you. I've been absolutely honest. You would have suspected a degree of knowledge even if I hadn't confirmed it, so no amount of denial on my part could have affected the outcome for me, but by being honest I hope to have convinced you that the other three

72

aren't involved. All I ask is that you continue to look after them until such time as the young man can be moved to hospital." His pitch finished, Sam knocked back the rest of the *raki*.

They sat in a silence as oppressive as the humid, kerosene-odoured air. Sam felt a trickle of sweat work its way down his chest. Eventually Samandag spoke a few words of Turkish. Two of the soldiers came forward to take station on either side of Sam's chair.

"You will go with them," he said. "Your co-operation is the guarantee of your friends' safety. I will decide by morning what is to happen."

A few more unintelligible words and Sam was led firmly but not unkindly through the door. A third soldier requisitioned one of the hurricane lamps from Samandag's desk and showed them to a tent in the furthest corner of the camp. Once inside, Sam's wrists and ankles were tied expertly. They motioned him to lie on a canvas camp bed. With arms fastened behind his back, he wriggled into a more or less comfortable position. The light stayed on, a soldier sitting in shadow, watching him. After about three-quarters of an hour, despite discomfort from his stiffening limbs, Sam dozed.

It was too close. He screwed up his eyes to focus them and made out a toecap on the edge of the bed, shaking its frame to wake him. Sam turned his head towards the light. It was Samandag, wearing full combat kit. He tried to lever himself upright but there was no power in his left arm. Pinned under his body, it had gone to sleep completely. Samandag helped him to stand and twisted him round. A soldier cut the ties at his wrists and ankles.

"You will accompany us." The words were blunt and business-like. "If you try to run, my men will open fire. You will walk beside me." Samandag handed Sam his sailing jacket. "Come."

Sam followed, rubbing his arm to restore circulation. Outside, in the moonlight, almost all of Samandag's soldiers were assembled in double file. In addition to his weapon each man carried a bandolier or belt festooned with extra rounds, grenades or mortar bombs.

He marched behind Samandag to the head of the procession and they led off at a brisk pace towards the southern exit. As they passed opposite the medical centre, Sam took a long look across the square but there was no sign of anyone there being awake. It was half-past two.

Behind them soft-soled boots settled into a quiet rhythm. These men were not new to night operations. Other than the muted fall of footsteps, theirs was a soundless procession. Not one item of equipment had been left unchecked to flap or rattle. As they approached the edge of the tree line a sentry stood up and waved them on. Without a word of command half a dozen men detached themselves from the main body and ran ahead, scouting in a protective, fan formation. By the time the party arrived at the bay where once *Windsong* had been anchored, their scouts were in position on the crest, lying face outwards to provide an all-round defensive cordon through which the procession passed on its way to the beach below. Drawn up on to the sand, outboard motors angled forward to protect propellers, were six large, high-speed inflatables.

Samandag looked at his watch and raised a hand, fingers extended, towards his company sergeant major. Five minutes' rest. The men sat down, an unclipped belt the only concession to comfort. After a final glance at his sentries, Samandag sank into the cluster comprising Sam and the headquarters group. It was Sam's first opportunity to talk since their rather one-sided conversation in the headquarters hut.

"Where are we going?" he asked bluntly. The time for finesse was past. Samandag could either answer the question or tell him to shut up.

The Turk looked at him, teeth showing unnaturally white in the moonlight. He gave a short laugh and lifted his shoulders, implying that it was of little consequence whether Sam knew or not.

"To Kastellorizon." The words exuded anticipation, as in the Middle Ages a crusader might have spoken of the Holy Land.

"Then tonight . . ."

"Yes," interrupted Samandag, "tonight, or more accurately this morning, is the date for the operation."

74

"And you intend that I should accompany you?"

Samandag lit a cigarette. "Only, my friend, because I believe what you told me – about your colleagues, that is. They will remain with my rear party, who are under orders to do what they can for them but you might as well know that my medical orderly fears the young man has internal injuries which require surgery. That is beyond the orderly's competence." He paused. "We are both soldiers . . . You will understand if I tell you that although I am able to contact our support ships, there is no question of risking the entire operation in an attempt to save your friend."

Samandag's voice was soft but his speech quicker than normal. Sam recognised the symptoms: acute, pre-operation nerves . . . Samandag's body was high on adrenalin. He needed to talk and tension was making him garrulous. Sam kept silent.

"I could not let you speak to your friends, not after you had investigated my headquarters. Rather than leave you to be guarded by a small rear party, it was easier to bring you along for the ride. Afterwards, we shall be recovered by submarine. Besides," a direct glance suggested that Sam was receiving the truth, "you will have to be interrogated eventually by people with better facilities than mine." Sam thought he detected a hint of empathy. "I hope the investigation will not be too uncomfortable. I am not an expert in such matters, but my understanding is that providing one is telling the truth there is not too much mental disturbance."

Sam thought of twitching bodies injected intravenously with heavy overdoses of valium; shivering, half-alive humanity stammering out information during the crucial gap between self-control and oblivion.

"And where will that interrogation take place?" he asked evenly.

Samandag laughed. "In Russia, of course." He stood up, brushing sand from his trousers.

Sam clambered to his feet, suspicion firming in his mind. "It's not just a case of working for them, is it?" he demanded. "You really are . . ."

"Yes," interjected Samandag, "Russian soldiers. All of us."

"Even though you speak Turkish. So, it appears, do all of your men. And physically you could pass for Turks."

"You western Europeans are all the same," complained Samandag, "assuming that every Russian is caucasian and comes from the suburbs of Moscow. We are many races. A large part of our population does not have Russian as its mother tongue. We have Asians, Moslems, Mongols . . . My mother was a Kurd, from the eastern province where nomadic peoples have crossed the border for centuries."

He shrugged. "My father was a Georgian. I am a citizen of the Union of Soviet Socialist Republics. I am also bilingual, of course, as are my men, all of us indistinguishable from Turks. That is why we were selected and trained for this mission."

"And you are going to attack Kastellorizon," said Sam. It was a conclusion, not a question.

"We shall take it," retorted Samandag, "and, in the old-fashioned sense, we shall sack it."

His voice hardened. "We do not wish to cause unnecessary casualties, but there are bound to be a few. I'm afraid that some of the young women will have to make a particularly personal contribution to the success of our mission." He looked at Sam. "There is no hypocrisy to what I say. I was glad to be able to help your friends, but when we abandon this island, Greek outrage must be all-consuming and absolute. The political and military benefits to my country will be enormous."

Samandag looked at his watch. The time for talking was over. A wave of his hand and men filed to waiting inflatables, four to each side. Boats were lowered into the water with no exchange of words. It was a practised drill. Samandag indicated that Sam should take station in the centre of his headquarters group inflatable. Disregarding the outboards, men picked up wooden paddles.

As the small but heavily armed flotilla began its passage to the exit, Sam estimated that it would take forty minutes before they were out into the Mediterranean. Hard against the dark silhouette of Kekova Island, it was extremely unlikely that the low black inflatables would be discernible from the mainland.

Eight paddles moved in easy rhythm, blades dipping vertically into the water with a soft, almost unison plop. Ripples sucked and burst at the edges as back, shoulder and arm muscles tightened and pulled. The only undisciplined noise came from trickles and droplets as paddles were lifted clear for the next stroke.

There was time to think during this gentle, somehow unreal beginning to the operation. The origins of the present-day animosity between Greeks and Turks lay in centuries of conflict and barbarity. The Turks were no more than wary of the Greeks, treating them with aloof disdain, but the Greek had an insane, almost pathological fear of the Turk, rooted more in history than in modern reality.

Kastellorizon was the most easterly of Greece's inhabited islands. With a weekly steamer from Rhodes and one under-water telephone cable providing the only links with the outside world, it was ideal for the Russians' purpose. Presumably Samandag didn't intend to stay around until the cavalry arrived. Nevertheless, if his men did their job, the reaction of all Greeks, mainland and islanders, would be so passionate that no amount of Turkish denial would be believed.

It had to spill over into the Aegean. The Turks had never accepted sea and air limits claimed by Greece round her numerous Aegean islands, some of which, like Kastellorizon, were almost on the coast of mainland Turkey. The Greeks were bound to make a show of force, establishing a sea and air presence which would close the Aegean to Turkish shipping. A confrontation would be inevitable. And even if war were somehow averted, Graeco-Turkish relations, hardly cordial even now, would be totally soured. In the nineteen-seventies, when Turkey invaded Cyprus, Greece had left NATO. Another dispute like that and she could do so again, perhaps forever. Russia would not weep to see a coach and horses driven through Alliance solidarity in the eastern Mediterranean.

They were almost at the exit. Sam could see an occasional light from the villages. Whilst the remainder slowed, one crew increased their tempo. The first inflatable slipped through the gap, presumably to check against the untimely arrival of some local fishing boat. Sam caught the whirr of a starter. Once outside the channel they paused to unite the formation. At tick-over the engines, muffled by an intervening spit of land, would be inaudible from the inlet.

They set off slowly, Samandag's inflatable leading. Five minutes later his helmsman shouted a warning and opened the throttle. From its size Sam judged the outboard to be somewhere around seventy-five horsepower, more than enough to lift the rigid vee-hull on to a plane. At something like twenty knots they crashed over the surface, bouncing and thumping as though the sea were made of concrete, low waves lashing back needles of spray. The occupants clutched safety ropes attached to the walls of the inflatable and huddled for shelter.

Only when they reached a cluster of small, uninhabited islands guarding the entrance to Kastellorizon harbour did Samandag give the order to ease back. Sam watched an inflatable peel off and run up against an island no more than one hundred feet in diameter. Figures lifted waist high cylinders to its central hummock.

"Mortars," shouted Samandag, seeing Sam's interest. It was a soldierly precaution. If the assault group ran into unexpected opposition, they would be able to call down high explosive rapid fire. Sam recognised a pair of American-made eighty-one millimetre tubes. A single round through the roof would probably destroy any of the houses on Kastellorizon. Samandag took a final glance at his fire support base and they were through the entrance, running across a quarter-mile of flat water to the jetty at the head of the harbour.

All the houses on Kastellorizon were built around the quay. Beyond the village, rocky ground rose sharply to a summit which marked the northern end of the island's spinal ridge. Heading south, land dropped away steeply on either side into the Mediterranean. Only on the northern coast, the bulbous part of the island's inverted pear shape, were contours gentle enough for a fishing village on the thin strip of land surrounding an almost enclosed harbour.

Guarding the eastern shore of the narrow entrance was a small, ancient castle, whose red-hued stone had earned it the nickname of 'Castel Rosso' from Genoese traders. On the opposite side a ridge of rock ran on from the main spine in a protective arm. Once through the entrance the harbour

78

opened out to its full width of almost three hundred yards. There were buildings on either side. They passed a small, modern hotel on the western shore.

Sam had called at Kastellorizon several times during his Cyprus days. With no more than a weekly steamer from Rhodes and no contact with the Turkish mainland, there were only three types of visitor – the occasional more intrepid tourist, long-distance cruising yachtsmen, and expatriates with relatives or property on the island.

From visits to the museum Sam knew that Kastellorizon had once been a prosperous trading station, its natural harbour offering shelter first to Venetian ships, plying to Syria and the Nile Delta, and in the twentieth century to flying boats reaching from England and France to Cairo and beyond. But prosperity died with the flying boat era. Facing starvation, thousands of the population emigrated to Australia. Today Sydney still had a thriving Kastellorizon Society whose members made occasional voyages to view empty family property, their voices bringing incongruous tones of Strine to a small café behind the jetty.

A modest trickle of visitors made little impact on the one hundred and fifty or so inhabitants, who lived out each year at the pace of the Middle Ages. A per capita pension, paid by the government to prevent total exodus and loss of the island to Turkey, was supplemented by local fishing in the fifteen-foot boats which dotted the harbour wall. Sam had always been attracted to the island – to him it was an unspoiled paradise where life had drawn back from the twentieth century and returned to the sanity of a less frenzied age. It seemed that this day its innocence was to be sacrificed.

The harbour front was almost deserted. A few fishermen, mostly older men, were taking advantage of the cool early morning to mend nets or refuel small, single cylinder diesel engines in their boats. Soon they would tonk out to coastal waters around the island, returning before the full heat of mid-day.

The inflatables fanned out across a sector of waterfront. Fishermen stared in surprise. The high-pitched roar of outboards reverberated from stone houses and up to the hillside. Sam heard firing from behind and right. He ducked

79

instinctively. One of the boats had run ashore opposite a small stone building housing the post office and telephone exchange – one end of a seventy-mile submarine cable to Rhodes. They were inside, the door sagging on its hinges, the lock smashed by a burst from a machine gun. Figures reappeared and threw themselves on to the ground. An explosion blasted the building. Ancient stone walls contained the force but directed it upwards. The roof lifted, almost in one piece, then collapsed inwards on to wrecked equipment in a shower of tiles, wooden beams and dust. Until the next steamer on Friday, four days away, Kastellorizon was cut off from the outside world.

They were at the jetty. By the time the invaders were close enough for Turkish Army insignia to be distinguishable on their combat uniforms, the visible destruction of their telephone exchange had confirmed the worst fears of the incredulous fishermen. One young Greek, his handsome, bronzed face furrowed by query and indignation, ran towards the nearest group of soldiers. A raised machine gun signified clearly that he should stop. Perhaps, thought Sam, the young man couldn't conceive that he was in real danger. He came on, shouting and gesticulating. Without hesitation the soldier lowered his muzzle a fraction and stitched a short burst across the man's thighs. The body shook two or three times, hovered for half a second and was swept to the ground like a rag doll. At first the man lay still, dulled by shock, then he screamed over and over again, legs twitching, hands padding his wounds to contain the blood and the pain. Other men backed off, turned and fled into narrow alleys leading away from the harbour.

Besides Samandag and himself there were eight men in the headquarters group. Two ran to the centre of the jetty where a Greek naval patrol boat lay secured alongside. It was a small vessel, perhaps forty-five feet long, and carried no visible armament. The boat, kept permanently at Kastellorizon, was used by the Greeks for occasional bouts of showing the flag – maintaining a military presence to remind Turkey of the sovereignty of the island and its coastal waters. From her closed down appearance the Greek crew eschewed sleeping on board, no doubt preferring the comfort of a shore billet. One Russian stayed on deck. His companion kicked open the wheelhouse door and disappeared below. A minute later he emerged, a wave of the arm signifying to Samandag that the boat was empty. They ran back to rejoin the headquarters group, now setting up base at the head of the jetty.

Samandag gave another command. Six of the group detached themselves, three to either side, and began a systematic destruction of the open wooden fishing boats. Into the floor of each boat a soldier fired about ten rounds. Bullets went straight through the planking. Low fountains welled and bubbled as boats began to fill. Soon they would sink into ten feet of water. It would take days of repair, replacing splintered planks and stripping engines, before they would be usable again. Seeing Sam's disapproval, Samandag tapped him on the shoulder.

"It's necessary." He had to shout above the noise of firing. "I don't have enough men to collect the boats together and mount a guard over them."

He was distracted by men's shouts and women's screams from houses around the small square at the head of the jetty.

"We have to search," he explained, "in case those Greeks have weapons. Besides," he lifted his shoulders, as if to emphasise that he was not personally responsible, "we have our orders."

All along the waterfront, doors were being blasted or kicked open. Frightened faces appeared at upstairs windows; shutters were thrown back as families, alarmed by the noise, peered anxiously into the street.

House by house, occupants were herded out on to the quay. Once empty, homes were searched with deliberate disregard for the few pieces of furniture or meagre family possessions. Through open balcony doors, Sam saw mattresses overturned and drawers tipped out. Downstairs, whole shelves of crockery were swept clear with a stroke of the arm or the sweep of a gun butt. Outside, small groups of islanders, many of them still in nightclothes, were guarded by three or four men. Most of the women were in tears. A few gave way to despair and began to wail abuse at the soldiers but were restrained by their husbands. Recognising that resistance was hopeless the men stared, sullen and helpless, the hatred of centuries rekindled in their dark eyes.

As soon as a house had been searched the family was made

to go back inside, an occasional shot on to stone walls identifying the penalty for returning to the streets. So far, thought Sam, the invaders hadn't behaved with undue inhumanity. Considering their orders, which were doubtless designed to alienate the population as much as possible, the Russians were behaving with reasonable restraint. Property had been smashed and homes violated, but apart from the shooting of one young fisherman, perhaps as a necessary declaration of intent, the people of Kastellorizon had suffered little physical maltreatment.

The search of the harbourfront terraces was almost complete. Some of the Russians had already moved into the warren of back streets. Now that people knew what to expect there was less commotion. It was no longer necessary to shoot through a lock. Occupants opened their door and came out, albeit with their faces reflecting a mixture of loathing and dumb resignation.

But even as Sam realised that such bland measures wouldn't be enough for the Russians' purpose a young Greek wife, overcome by sounds of destruction coming from within their home, slipped past her husband to scream abuse and pound her fists into the face of the nearest soldier.

He could fend her off with only one hand, the other committed to keeping a tight grip on his weapon. After a glance at his colleague, he dodged another blow and lifted the butt of his sub-machine gun to deliver a stunning parry to the side of the woman's head.

She staggered back, her heels drumming staccato steps, an intense hotness around her left ear and temple. Before she could recover her balance another soldier hooked his elbow through her upper arms, pinning them tightly behind her back. His other hand twisted into her long, black hair and pulled viciously. She cried out in pain. A mist of tears obscured the morning sky.

Her husband leapt at the soldiers. A Russian sidestepped the rush, lifted his knee to the Greek's stomach and followed through with a butt-swing strong enough to fracture his skull. The man was courageous but ineffectual; he collapsed like a young heifer Sam had once seen slaughtered with a bolt to the brain.

The couple lived at the right-hand edge of the harbour, before it curved round to the hotel. There had been time for them to dress hastily before the soldiers reached their door. Her white cotton blouse was a simple, sleeveless garment gathered at the top in an elasticated ruche. Without warning her former victim snatched at the front of the blouse and hauled it to her waist. Full, olive breasts heaved as she strained against his unyielding grip.

Sadly, it was all too obvious to Sam that the woman was to be the victim of condoned rape. He wondered if Samandag's young soldiers shared the conscience which had moved their leader to intervene in Turkey.

But to Private Mikhail Romanov she was only a Greek. Besides, they had been given permission, even encouraged. The woman could be enjoyed without fear of reprisal.

They had her on the ground, blouse and skirt around her waist, legs held apart, whisps of thick, black curls vibrating in the morning breeze. The soldier kneeling in front of her said something to his comrades and began to unbutton his trousers. She screamed again as he lay on top of her.

Sam looked away, unwilling to witness what was clearly regarded as part of the morning's entertainment.

At the back of the square black smoke and tongues of flame billowed from a ground floor window. There was a smell of burning paraffin – they must have kicked over a lamp. His eyes followed the pall of smoke to the hillside above. It was pure chance that he caught the spasmodic flickers of light. They were in deep shadow, underneath a large overhang of rock, otherwise he wouldn't have seen what, to a soldier, were the unmistakable muzzle flashes of a group of riflemen.

In a moment of pure, subconscious survival reaction, Sam dived for his only immediate cover, the lee of a mound of ropes and fishing nets piled on the edge of the jetty. As he rolled on the planking, wooden chips flew into the air. Behind him, white marks showed the fall of shot as rounds from the hillside splintered away the brown creosoted surface. Sam had taken the only shelter on the jetty. Samandag and his headquarters group ran forward, closing up to buildings on the edge of the square for protection.

They were pinned down. A few of the Greeks must have

escaped through the back of the village, taking with them weapons which had probably been oiled, wrapped and stored since the Second World War. A nineteen-forties rifle, Sam thought, could kill just as effectively as a modern equivalent.

Samandag was shouting to his radio operator. This had to be the support weapons commander's trade test, a chance for the mortar crew – prudently dropped off on the outer island – to justify their pay.

They were good. Very good. In seconds the familiar 'plop-plop-plop' sound of rounds from tubes belied the devastating effect of high explosive shells about to detonate in quick succession against hard rock. The commander had aimed to suppress the Greeks' fire. It was a tricky shot, judging both range and elevation to the hillside. The first salvo was fifty yards short but it would keep the Greeks' heads down. Unless they had sense enough to shift quickly, the next rounds would be corrected on to their position.

Sam looked around. For the first time since they had landed he was unguarded. Samandag's headquarters group, up against the walls of the square, was otherwise occupied – probably content that their prisoner, having taken cover on the jetty, had nowhere else to go. To his right the rape party had disappeared, possibly to worse excess inside a building. The rest of the Russians were in narrow side streets. On his left, smoke from the burning building drifted out to the centre of the harbour.

Behind him, also unguarded, lay what ought to be a fast, seaworthy patrol boat. Ahead of him, all attention was focused on the hillside. Sam rolled over, clamped his fingers on to the edge of the jetty and eased first one leg, then the other, and finally his torso down into clear water.

He swam under the jetty till he was level with the patrol boat's stern. There was more noise and shouting from the shore. There wasn't much time – as soon as the commotion died down they would start looking for him.

Heavy, manilla warps were secured through metal rings set into the side of the jetty. Fortunately he could reach the rings from the water. Had there been bollards set higher up it might not have been possible. Because a narrow harbour mouth protected the inner bay from any swell, the crew had used only a single warp at each end. With the breeze pushing the boat forwards, towards the entrance, her stern line was under tension. He hung from it, pulling the boat nearer to the jetty to induce some slack. He would have given his pension for a knife! Twice he repeated the nerve-wracking procedure before a round turn and two half hitches could be untied and slipped through the ring.

Slowly the breeze prised the boat's stern away from the jetty. There was no time to swim round the outside. Taking a chance on a wind shift, which could catch him between a steel hull and wooden piles, Sam handed himself along the jetty to the bow warp. He clawed to release its knot before the wind took the boat out too far and tightened the line.

Freed from her berth the patrol boat settled with her stern some sixty degrees off the wind, drifting slowly sideways out into the harbour. Sam used the bow warp to haul himself on to the foredeck. Another salvo exploded against the hillside. Mentally wishing the Greeks luck, he ran aft down the port side, keeping wheelhouse and superstructure between himself and the shore. Kneeling to reduce his profile, Sam pulled the stern warp on deck – it couldn't be left to foul the propellers. He ran back to the wheelhouse. The patrol boat was five yards clear of the end of the jetty.

His eyes darted over an unfamiliar control panel. Twin throttle levers . . . He tested them and found they moved freely. Where the hell were the starters? Two red buttons, above the levers. Setting each engine for a quarter throttle, he pressed the starboard button. Nothing happened.

Sam forced himself to fight down a rising panic. This had to be thought through logically. There was no power which meant there must be battery isolators.

On the port sidewall of the wheelhouse were two boxes, pipe-conduit wiring leading out from underneath. Isolator switches, similar to those on *Soprano*, protruded from one side. He threw them down to be rewarded with a red glow from raised warning lights alongside each starter button.

He pressed again for starboard engine. It turned over, sluggish at first, then fired. Compression ignition gave more and more help to the batteries – and took over completely. Sam laughed aloud as the engine clattered into life.

85

He throttled back and engaged gear on the starboard shaft. Christ, the revs were dropping! Frantically he shoved the lever forwards to catch the engine before it stalled, breathing again as it picked up to a healthy roar.

There was no time to worry about cold bearings. As his right hand switched to spin the wheel hard a'port, his left repeated the start sequence on port engine. With both diesels running, her stern swung out in a skidding turn. Glancing over his shoulder, he saw figures sprinting along the jetty towards him. The boat was accelerating to the plane but he was twenty yards short of the entrance when a finger of tracer curled past, ten feet from his starboard beam.

Heading through the gap, Sam spun the wheel irregularly to put the gunner off his aim. If she hit one of those rocky outcrops at this speed . . . There was a hammering sound astern. He prayed that tracer wouldn't find the fuel tanks.

On the bulkhead behind him a glass porthole shattered as the boat slewed across a line of fire. They were nearly at the northern tip of the island. Sam twitched the wheel to starboard. Tracer moved with them, just too far. That gunner knew his job – instead of fine correction he was waiting for the boat to cross into his aim.

Sam ran in almost to caress an orange wall of light. Just a few more seconds. Now, hard over! She banked to port and before the gunner could switch left his target had disappeared. At thirty knots the patrol boat curved behind a headland to streak south along the western shore of the island and out into the Mediterranean.

Chapter 6

He ran the boat south under autopilot, for the first five miles with diesels hard against the governors and giving an indicated thirty-five knots. Once out of mortar range, and sure that there was no attempt to follow him, Sam eased back the throttles. Below decks a screaming, rattling clatter of engines subsided to a steady, vibrating rumble. As the bow came down whiskers of white water relaxed into the Mediterranean.

Sam stepped through the wheelhouse door and stood on the side deck, facing aft. It would be some time before the hump of Kastellorizon disappeared over the horizon. At ten knots the patrol boat was steady enough for him to go exploring without having to cling from one hand-hold to another. After a final three hundred and sixty degree search, Sam descended into his acquisition.

Rising decibels hammered his ears as he opened the heavy steel door to the engine room. Fortunately he wouldn't have to spend time down here. The wheelhouse gauges showed two fuel tanks, both full. Presumably they were somewhere underfoot. He could only guess, but at cruising speed a craft such as this ought to have a range of about a thousand miles.

Moving for'ard he found the accommodation area, a none-too-clean galley and rest room with berths for the crew, one single cabin to port, presumably for the skipper, and beyond it a shower and heads compartment. There were very few personal belongings lying around and the lockers were almost empty of clothing. Clearly her crew spent only the minimum time aboard.

87

Through a final watertight bulkhead lay the bow section. Part of the space was taken up by lockers which contained the usual bosun's stores: paint, cordage, oil, and a mass of ships' bits and pieces, but about a third of the area was partitioned off into a separate cupboard by full-length, steel walls and a locked metal door.

Sam went back to the captain's cabin. Inside the wardrobe he found a small safe-box welded to the floor. It would almost certainly contain the ship's code books, and hopefully the required key.

He had no chance of defeating the dial and tumbler lock, however unsophisticated it might be to a professional safe-breaker, but forcing open that box could take time. He ran up to the wheelhouse and scanned the horizon. Returning to the forepeak, Sam rummaged through the bosun's stores. Five minutes later he was relieved to see the stout, metal hinges of the captain's safe-box surrender to the soldierly logic of a five-pound hammer driving a one-inch cold chisel.

As he expected, the forepeak store contained the ship's arms and ammunition. Her largest weapon was a medium calibre deck pom-pom gun in two sections; a seat and shield attached to a base plinth, presumably intended to be fitted to a ring of stud-bolts somewhere on the foredeck, and a breach and barrel assembly wrapped in preservative and oily paper. Above the pom-pom, slung from a row of hooks, were five sub-machine guns. They were of Greek manufacture but appeared to be modelled on the British Army Stirling. Exploring the metal boxes stacked in a corner of the cupboard, Sam found a Very pistol, complete with a selection of coloured cartridges, a generous supply of both small-arms and pom-pom ammunition, and finally a box of white polystyrene trays coddling layers of grey, segmented, fragmentation hand grenades.

Sam could not reasonably have hoped for more. It was very much the standard armament for a patrol boat; sufficient to enable the crew to stop and search a suspect vessel or, in extremis, achieve a measure of self-defence.

He returned to the wheelhouse. The sea was clear of shipping, Kastellorizon now only a smudge under the northern sky. Another five minutes and the patrol boat would be invisible from the island. He became aware of mild, abdominal pain, overshadowed till now by more urgent matters. After a night of intense activity, an early-morning sea passage, a swim in the harbour and the adrenalin-consuming theft of a foreign naval vessel he was experiencing the stomach contraction and light-headedness caused by lack of food. Sam took a half-step towards the galley, then stopped. Blood sugar level couldn't be ignored but there was one higher priority. He wouldn't feel secure until he had assembled the means to protect his prize.

For the next hour he sweated and heaved to pull the disassembled pom-pom on deck, bolt the plinth to its ring mount and fit the heavy barrel and breach assembly. Each part had to be stripped of a layer of preservative and wiped with an oily rag. Shirtless, his arms and chest were soon lined by channels marking the progress of rivulets of sweat through accumulated grease and grim.

There was no instruction manual, but after half a lifetime of weapon-handling Sam was able to deduce the assembly sequence and work out the intricacies of the pom-pom's load and firing mechanism. His only indulgence was a glass of cold water, taken on the way below for the final item, a box of belted, high explosive shells so heavy that he had to drag it along the cabin sole, up the companionway and over the deck to the gun position.

Sam gave the barrel a final wipe, stepped back to admire his handiwork then slipped into the firing seat. With the sights set for five hundred yards he selected a wave crest.

His foot found the pedal. Without ear defenders the familiar crash of explosions left a singing monotone inside his skull. A row of white flecks on the Mediterranean gave no indication of the destructive power of each explosive round against a soft-skinned target, but Sam was content with the results of his labour.

Rather less enjoyable were the next ten minutes, given to scrubbing tacky preservative from his arms and chest with a mound of cotton waste dipped in detergent. He took care to swill all the slippery, grease-laden scum from the deck, then dressed and set off to explore the galley.

It wouldn't have survived the divisional rounds of the

89

Royal Navy. A gimballed stove was coated with spattered remains from past cooking. Sam shrugged. He had put up with worse squalor in the field. And the store of tinned food ought to be safe enough. Pictures on labels identified the contents despite the unintelligible lettering. Ten minutes later he carried aloft to the wheelhouse a steaming plate of fish pieces in tomato sauce topped with a pyramid of baked beans.

The island had disappeared. Disconnecting the autopilot, he forked in another mouthful of breakfast and spun the wheel to bring the patrol boat round to zero four three degrees compass – as near as mattered due east. With the autopilot re-set, Sam raided the chart locker. Brushing aside a fallen baked bean, which avenged itself by obscuring two miles of Levant Syria, he studied the Turkish coastline.

The 'hump' of Kastellorizon was about nine hundred feet above sea level, which meant that given perfect visibility, a lookout would be able to see for over thirty miles. There was a slight haze, but Kastellorizon had sunk to the horizon before it disappeared so he had to be about that distance south of the island. He set one point of the dividers on Kastellorizon, the other on Kekova: only thirteen miles, but at Kekova the coastline was curving north again. If he circled round to approach from the east, the boat would be shielded from Kastellorizon by a more southerly spit of land.

He thought about using the ship's radio on Channel Sixteen, the international call and distress frequency, but decided against it. There were no coastguard stations in the area and the set had only a limited range. The chances of any positive help, even if some local freighter were maintaining a listening watch, were not encouraging. Besides, Samandag would almost certainly have been in radio contact both with Kekova and the submarine . . .

The realisation brought an instant shudder. Why the hell hadn't he thought of it before? Tiredness. Anxiously Sam scanned the water, half expecting to see a tell-tale white feather of spray and stalking periscope.

He thought back to his service days; in the Ministry of Defence he had been involved with joint operations. They wouldn't use a nuclear submarine, not in these waters, so how fast could a diesel sub go, running submerged? Depended on type, but probably not more than fifteen knots. Maybe twenty on the surface.

He pushed the throttles forward till the gauge settled on twenty-five. If the submarine were in the immediate area she would have picked him up on sonar, but unless she lay ahead he ought to be running clear. That ruled out the radio. If he transmitted they would snatch a fix in seconds, and long-range detection might give them a better chance of making an intercept.

Starboard twenty . . . might as well fade from any contact on a false heading. Sam wedged his empty plate in a corner of the chart table and settled to keeping a proper lookout. He wasn't too proud of the fact that for the past couple of hours he had allowed himself to be a sitting target.

It was eleven o'clock. Having steamed towards Israel for sixty miles before turning north towards the Turkish coast, by dead reckoning he was now about twenty-five miles south-east of Kekova. The precaution had taken him beyond all visual or sonar range and he stood a fair chance of arriving back at the inlet unannounced – but he couldn't risk going inside.

Immediately beyond Kekova Island the mainland was indented deeply by a bay over a mile wide. Around this bay the coastline was irregular, and at its western lip two small islands opposite the tip of Kekova Island marked the shoreline side of the lagoon's eastern entrance. Barely a mile from this channel lay the cove into which a disabled *Windsong* had drifted only forty-eight hours earlier. If he made landfall five miles this side of the eastern entrance, and followed the coast round to the lee of those two small islands, he ought to be able to run in unseen.

Sam motored slowly round the bay, bracing the wheel with his knee, alternately scanning the flat water ahead for un-charted rocks and lifting binoculars to search the hillside above. Eventually he was fairly confident that the sparsely vegetated, rocky foothills immediately surrounding the bay were unoccupied. For the last cable all his attention was given to the process of anchoring. His eyes were never away from the echo sounder for more than two or three seconds. A red spot moved gradually round the circumference of a graduated

91

dial. Ten fathoms . . . Sixty feet of water and a half-cable off, but one hundred yards was too far out. The closer in he could anchor, the more she would be concealed from inland under the lee of the foothills.

Sixty yards. Hills fronting up nicely, but depth down to eight fathoms. Back to nine again. The boat's draught was probably about five feet, so he needed room to swing in something like three fathoms. But a gentle shoreline indicated that the seabed would probably shelve slowly. Seven fathoms . . . five . . . shit! His hand moved to the gear levers, but before he could put her astern the red blob nudged back to seven fathoms. They had crossed an underwater ridge.

Sam spotted what he was looking for, a gulley where during the rainy season silt would be carried into the sea. Cautiously he nosed in. Off its mouth, the bottom lifted gradually to meet her keel. The anchor would bed securely into soft mud. Three and a half fathoms. A safe twenty-one feet and less than twenty-five yards from the shore. He jiggled the gears to take the way off her and ran for'ard to release the anchor pin.

He was tired, having had only ten hours' sleep in the last three nights. He recognised the familiar sensations of gritty eyes, of unconscious activity until the brain jumped to catch up with what his body was doing. He picked up two more magazines. They slotted into the side of the sub-machine gun. If he taped one magazine on top of another, feed apertures protruding and at opposite ends, when one magazine was exhausted he had only to release the catch, swing both magazines through one hundred and eighty degrees and ram home a replacement. Thirty rounds, a two-second reload and another thirty rounds of automatic fire. He would carry two weapons, one on his back as a spare, with additional loaded magazines and a box of loose rounds in a haversack.

Sub-machine guns organised, he turned to the grenades, unscrewing each base plug and inserting a detonator. He should have tested one out at sea, to measure the delay. Now it was too late – he couldn't risk the noise. Sam taped a pair of grenades to his belt, ready for use. The rest he stowed in the haversack.

During his initial tour of the ship, he hadn't noticed a dinghy, or even an inflatable. Another search confirmed that

92

the harbour-minded Greeks had dispensed with what could be a vital piece of equipment. He lowered a boarding ladder into the water, undressed, and parcelled shoes, clothing and weaponry into a crewman's oilskin jacket. Half into the water he lifted his bundle, knots uppermost, down from the deck. Guiding it with his head, he breast-stroked for the shore.

Systematically, he checked the weapons, loaded them, and distributed the modest arsenal about his body then set off eastwards along the beach to a headland, crawling the last few yards to its skyline. Over an intervening valley and another, lower ridge he could see the bay where *Windsong* had been anchored. Close inshore a large caique, about seventy feet long, snubbed gently at her chain. With her raised after-deck she resembled a cross between a Syrian schooner and an Arab dhow. The mast remained, but for most of the time the captains of these coastal traders relied on a modern diesel engine. They were a common enough sight, thrashing along the eastern Mediterranean or through the Aegean islands, occasionally easing fuel consumption with a carelessly hoisted sail.

It made sense to use an inconspicuous trader for the last stage of the journey. A submarine, drawing about twenty feet, would have to come in on the surface. There was always a chance of being seen, even at night. Worse still, she might foul some fisherman's nets. Judging by the pile of equipment already on the beach, it looked as if the Russians were vacating their base camp and taking the evidence with them.

Two figures moved along the shore: guards. Each carried a rifle slung over his shoulder. Fortunately the light prevailing westerly would have carried away the sound of the patrol boat's engines.

It took some time to reach the tree line. Sam couldn't risk being caught on the floor of a valley, so he retreated to half a mile beyond the patrol boat before turning inland. The track to the caique was now around a corner and over a mile and a half away. He reached the edge of the forest without incident and turned towards the track.

Sam approached cautiously, but a thorough search of the surrounding area confirmed that there was no sentry. Finally he squatted alongside the track itself. It was well scuffed, with more recent footprints superimposed on those made by Samandag's booted squad during their early morning march to the inflatables. The Russians were still using the same route to the beach.

Sam moved back into the forest. Slowly, like an ornithologist anxious not to disturb his subjects, he traced a path between trees and clumps of vegetation. Halfway to the camp he stopped. He could smell burning wood; not the rich, pine-heavy scent of a forest fire, more the creosote and woodash smell of preservative-treated timber. He resumed his slow, patient advance, crawling the last two hundred yards to an observation position in deep shade under a clump of bushes, still ten yards inside the forest. It was unlikely that he would be seen from the brightly sunlit clearing.

He was at the eastern end of the rectangle. In the centre, where they had dined the previous evening, men were raking over the remains of what had been a sizeable bonfire. Wooden huts and tentage had all been burned. Nearby, the last few non-combustible stores were stacked for a final departure. He searched for Julian and the girls. Could they be on board the caique? Sam was beginning to wonder if his trek had been a waste of time when the wind shifted, swirling a low drift of smoke in the opposite direction. Through an eddy of half-clear air he caught a glimpse of Sally, seated on the ground where once had stood the medical centre. There was no sign of the others. Smoke surged back, as if reluctant to assist him further.

It was enough. When the rear party left for the beach, Julian and the girls would be with them. Still facing the clearing Sam wriggled back slowly, deeper into the forest.

Safely away from the camp, he stood up in the shade of a young conifer. Dirt and debris were engrained into his skin and clothing but Sam made no effort to brush himself down as he set off parallel with the track. Already he was reverting to animal hygiene.

Sam turned his mind to more immediate matters. There were half a dozen men in the rear party, and it looked as though about eighteen had come ashore from the caique. It would be one against a couple of dozen, so choice of ground, and surprise, would be all important.

Eventually he settled for the final clearing where trees funnelled out on to fifty yards of open ground before the crest of the first valley. He dug his position with a broken branch, but only after lying down underneath a cluster of deciduous saplings to confirm his fields of fire. There were limits to what could be achieved quickly with a stump of wood and bare hands, but after fifteen minutes Sam had scraped out and camouflaged a shallow trench which would protect his body. If he had made a mistake, they could use it for his grave.

He mulled over the likely pattern of the ambush. If those from the caique were as well trained as the rest of Samandag's men they would run from the killing zone and go to ground, using every rock and tree trunk. He might hold them off for a while, but if they were expert at fire and manoeuvre, one group pinning him down whilst the other made a flanking advance, they would get to him eventually. That said, with any luck most of them wouldn't be trained infantrymen. Sam was gambling on a different reaction from naval ratings.

From his haversack he took a ball of cordage, lifted from the patrol boat's locker, and half a dozen grenades. Glancing frequently along the track he set to work, first near his own position and then on the edge of the tree line. The haversack, with its spare grenades and ammunition, he placed inside his fire trench. Both sub-machine guns had a taped, double magazine, and a spare set for each was loaded and ready. Two hundred and forty rounds and a few grenades against twenty-four men. It was a bit tight. And afterwards, they still had to escape from the survivors. He lay in the trench and pulled cut branches over his head.

Two and a half hours. Despite the tightness in his stomach, Sam had to make a conscious effort to stay awake. When finally they came he heard noise and clatter long before the first men entered his restricted field of vision. The advance was in reassuring contrast to the silent, professional march of earlier that morning but the few soldiers had not forgotten their training.

There was a vanguard, about ten yards ahead of the main party of sailors. They walked past twenty feet away, rifles held casually by trigger and stock, pointing down and ahead but

95

ready to be lifted immediately into the aim. The sailors' weapons were shouldered, their hands full of equipment not consigned to the bonfire. The girls were at the tail end of the main body, with two more soldiers a few feet behind them, but there was no sign of Julian. Sam made a snap decision to press on. First, he would have to take out the afterguard.

The girls were drawing level. Sam sighted on the nearest of the two soldiers behind them and with the change lever on automatic put a double tap into his target. He switched, and in that first second of reaction time, when the group were disorientated, dropped two more rounds on to the next man.

They had barely registered that it was an ambush, far less had time to trace his position. At a throat-tearing volume he articulated three well-spaced words.

"Girls . . . lie . . . down."

It was the crucial moment. Unless they reacted to the English language, which only they would understand, his plan was in ruins.

They were going down! Thank God. He selected a group of milling sailors in front of the girls and set to work.

For the next ten seconds it was distasteful, organised slaughter. Kneeling, only his head and shoulders visible above the earth, Sam fired in short bursts, adjusting his aim but letting recoil elevate the barrel. He began at a man's groin, lifted to his neighbour's stomach, swung to an adjacent chest and dipped on to the next target.

It was more difficult now, they were splitting up. Someone had shouted a command. Sam registered the click of an empty chamber and switched magazines. This time he risked a longer burst of his precious ammunition. It worked, completing the panic. Two or three men fled into the trees on the far side of the track. The lead group and a remaining half dozen or so sailors were sprinting for the shelter of the valley.

He changed weapons, scrambled from his position and ran towards the track. The girls looked up, the shock and fatigue on their faces giving way to disbelief as they saw him slithering alongside the nearest tree. Sam jerked his head over a shoulder.

"That way. Run fifty yards, then wait for me."

He peered along the track towards the valley. There were also a few men somewhere away to his right. The exposed

96

flank worried him but it was vital that he reduced the size of any force which might pursue them. Most of the Russians were on open ground, fanning out and almost at the crest. He pulled the weapon to his cheek and began a series of carefully aimed shots. Four men pitched forward and lay still. A fifth dropped over the crest, but whether propelled by a hit or by panic he couldn't be sure.

They were all over. The earlier ones would be crawling back up the slope to identify his position. It was time to move. Sam rolled sideways, back into the trees.

Rifle fire from the other side of the track was echoed by a wet slapping sound of bullets hitting bark and leaves. He looked up. The gashes were all at chest height which implied that the Russians, lying in a safe fire position, weren't too anxious to come forward for a better view. He scrambled behind a tree and up into a crouch. Poised like a sprinter on starting blocks Sam took several deep breaths, searched the ground for any debris which might break his run, and launched forwards. He ran low and fast for his shell-scrape, jinking like a frightened hare. A bullet cracked past, not too far from his ear. Then he was diving, almost in slow motion, willing his body to relax before it hit baked earth.

He raised his eyes above the shallow parapet. Clear in front. He looked back. Where the hell were the girls? Less than twenty-five yards away, crouching behind a cluster of saplings which gave some concealment but absolutely no protection. He shouted, and waved urgently.

"Go on! Further back. Another hundred yards and wait for me again."

Dont let them freeze up now. Sally emerged, a hand clamped on Fiona's wrist, half-pulling her. Then they were away.

He turned and loosed off a few random shots across the track. It was prophylactic fire, intended only to keep heads down whilst the girls cleared the immediate area. From time to time Sam glanced over his shoulder. He was lucky enough to see where the girls went to ground.

Neither bird nor cicada would risk a sound. In a silent forest, Sam settled deeper into his trench. Looking left, through the trees, he could see patches of open ground leading to the crest. To his front, over the parapet, he studied the far side of the track.

It took four minutes before curiosity overcame fear. Perhaps they suspected that he had pulled back to break from contact, or even been hit by one of their rounds. Across the track figures emerged through foliage. Sam pulled the string.

It lifted and stretched tight, but despite his care to ensure a direct lead the line snagged on a piece of bark. Sam felt a bead of sweat ooze on to his forehead. He pulled again, harder. Mercifully the chip of bark lifted free. The other end of his line divided to steel rings set ten feet apart. Each ring passed through a metal pin, which Sam had withdrawn as far as he dared after lashing the grenade body to the base of a tree.

They were advancing slowly, weapons ready, eyes darting over the forest. Perhaps it was their all-consuming caution which made them forget one golden rule. They were bunched. Two of them would be separated by the left-hand grenade. The third was advancing directly towards the one on the right.

They heard two soft 'pings' and a leafy descent as springs launched handles from fragmentation cases into the undergrowth. All three of them flinched nervously and dropped to a crouch, weapon at the shoulder, eyes searching frantically for the source of noise. The two on the left were about eight feet from their tree. The one on the right was further forward.

Sam counted silently. 'And two and three and . . .'

They looked about. Perhaps it was a forest animal or a bird fluttering the branches. Frightened minds accepted what they wanted desperately to believe.

'. . . five and six and . . .'

Reassured by the silence, they were standing. The nearest man raised a hand, signalling to the others – who were half-way upright – to stay where they were. He took four quick paces towards the cover of a large tree.

'. . . seven and . . .'

A double crash. The forest seemed to lift and scatter, splinters of wood and metal radiating in a two-thirds arc. Sam was protected by tree trunks. He started into the cloud of dust, searching for signs of movement.

Satisfied, he ran forward, dropping behind a tree on the

edge of the explosion area. Two of the bodies had been hit by several fragments. They lay motionless, blown over backwards, the front of their uniforms bloody and shredded. Their companion had caught the full blast effect from only a few inches. It brought back memories which Sam had hoped never to relive. He swallowed hard to control his throat and stomach muscles. Subjected to so much blast and over-pressure the corpse was almost nude, its stomach split like an over-ripe tomato. In death the sailor had discoloured, disfigured and fertilised one-fiftieth of a Turkish acre.

From his position at the edge of the track, Sam could see clearly across the gap to the crest. Heads were appearing on the skyline. They would be anxious to know what was happening. He sighted carefully. About seventy-five yards. It would be a lucky hit at that range, with an un-zeroed weapon. As the foresight came up to cover a human blob Sam fired a single round. He saw the fall of shot a foot below his point of aim but flying rock splinters would concentrate the imagination. Heads disappeared. After a final glance around the area, Sam ran back to his trench. He paused only to collect his weaponry and pull a second piece of string. As soon as it jerked into slackness he let it fall, and at a steady run retreated to the girls' position.

He was barely halfway when a multiple explosion, more distant this time, boomed into the forest. Sam had no idea what was happening at the crest. His single shot wouldn't hold them for long. If the officer or NCO in charge knew his trade he would soon be probing forward on a flank, ready to use covering fire as soon as the enemy position could be identified. But those grenades would make them cautious. With luck it would be a while before they could organise a fire and manoeuvre assault and find his old position. By the time the Russians discovered that he had pulled out, Sam hoped to have the girls well clear.

They stood up as he approached. He had only one question. "Julian?"

Fiona was silent. Sally shook her head slowly. It was enough for the moment.

"Listen." His voice was urgent and uncompromising. "There's a boat a couple of miles east of here. We stay in the trees to the far corner of this forest, then cross two valleys and meet the coast where it curves inland."

He jerked his head towards the track behind them. "They might not be far behind. Let's go."

Sam led off at a fast jog. They were safe, but not for long. He had achieved one of the more difficult military manoeuvres – a clean break from contact – but Samandag would have warned his rear party about the patrol boat, and they would guess that it couldn't be far away. Once the Russians had checked the ambush area it would be obvious which way they had fled.

"Mind how you go," he called to them, "and for God's sake don't turn an ankle."

They were making good progress. The girls were breathing hard and sweating, but they were young and could keep going. His mind went back to the Russians. If there was anyone senior enough still alive, he would be bound to make the attempt. Given the Soviets' problem, Sam knew what he would do – run along the edge of the tree line, where the going was fastest, until the forest turned inland parallel with the coast. Where the party had to break cover to cross the valleys – that would be the place to find them.

Trees were thinning out, the ground beginning to slope downhill. Both girls were winded. Soon they would have to leave the forest. Now was as good a time as any. Sam eased the pace and turned to face them. Fiona and Sally collapsed with relief.

His tone was demanding.

"Okay, get your breath back but listen to me – and for Christ's sake *concentrate*." He laid heavy stress on the last word, catching their attention.

"The boat's over there. Dead ahead." Through a dozen or so trees and beyond a crest, way out to sea, were the blue waters of the Mediterranean.

"If they catch us in a valley we're sitting ducks, but with any luck we have just enough time. So, I shall hold this position until you two are on the next ridge. When you are over the skyline, pick a solid chunk of rock and lie behind it. Watch my run. If anyone, and I mean *anyone*, approaches this lip, you fire at them."

He set down his own weapon, unslung the spare from his back and removed the magazine. They recoiled a fraction as he moved towards them, the sub-machine gun in his palms.

"Don't be so damn stupid. If those Russians catch us, they'll kill us. We're wasting time."

His finger pointed at the side of the weapon.

"This is called the change lever. Back here, it's on 'safe'." He moved the lever forward, cocked the sub-machine gun, re-applied the safety catch and held the weapon upright, his finger curved around its trigger.

"See? It won't fire. Now, if I move the lever one position down, like so . . ." He squeezed the trigger again. Working parts snapped forward with a heavy click.

"Remember that position. It sets the weapon to fire single rounds. Under no circumstances push the change lever right forwards, to there," he demonstrated, "Because that's the setting for bursts, and besides the risk of losing control, you don't have that much ammunition."

He untaped and inserted a full magazine. The half-empty one could be refilled whilst he waited. In any case, the girls were already under enough strain and it was unlikely that they would remember the reload procedure. Finally, he showed them how to sight along the weapon.

"But don't get fussed about the aim. All you have to do is keep their heads down." Sam re-cocked the weapon and set the change lever to 'safe'.

"Here." He passed the sub-machine gun to Sally who took it gingerly. "It's all set up. Just move the lever, aim, and squeeze gently."

He repeated the sequence to lock it in her mind. "Lever, aim and squeeze. Up to thirty rounds. Try to count your shots and save enough to see me over the ridge. Then I'll reload for you."

She held the weapon awkwardly. Sam read doubt and fear in her expression. He seized her forearm and squeezed it hard.

"Listen, if they catch me halfway up that valley and you freeze solid . . ."

His face was rigid. Sally realised that for the moment she and Fiona were no more than parts of a machine. He was

101

forcing the weaker components to accept their share of the load. She nodded slowly.

His grip relaxed. He gave her arm a small shake of encouragement. "Don't worry. I'm covering you. Go on, fast as you can."

The girls set off into the valley. Sam moved along the ridge towards the right-angled corner of the tree line. That was the most likely approach, along the edge. If not, and they came through the forest, he would take them from the side.

He could see along the tree line for about a mile. Sam settled into a patch of shade and began to thumb replacement rounds into a magazine. Two minutes gone. He glanced over his shoulder. The girls were out of sight. After four a half minutes they emerged, going reasonably well on the far side of the valley floor. He turned back to the tree line. Birdsong told him that no one was blundering through the forest in their footsteps.

The girls were climbing now, progress reduced to agonising slowness. Each time he looked they seemed to have advanced only a few more yards. Finally they were on the summit slope, slipping and scrambling on some loose scree.

They were there, damning his hopes just when he dared to wonder if there would be no pursuit. Four of them. Presumably their leader had sent most of the party on to the caique and set out after the fugitives with a small group of picked men. They were a mile away and moving quickly. There might be more of them in the trees – not the best place for an ambush so not here. He had eight, maybe nine minutes.

Sam crawled back round the corner, ran along the top of the ridge for thirty yards, turned hard right and launched himself down the slope. The Soviets wouldn't overlook the valley till they reached that corner. By then he intended to be over the next crest but it would be a close-run thing.

Having marked the point where the girls crossed the sky-line, Sam turned all his attention to the slope. He bounded down in a series of runs and jumps, from time to time landing sideways, feet and knees together as he para-dropped on to a level patch to control his descent. Nearer the bottom the slope was less steep. Now it was level. The honeymoon was over.

Sam picked a spot well aside from the girls, in case they had to open fire, and set off up the escarpment.

The descent had taken two and a half minutes. He had five and a half, or not much more, to reach the top. It was impossible to run. Climbing the thin turf and rocky outcrops was like stepping up a steep and irregular stairway. Thigh muscles were the first to complain, growing more leaden with each movement. He was breathing hard. There had to be an equilibrium, some acceptable level of discomfort which would underwrite enough continuous physical exertion.

Sam used hands and shoulders to bear down on his knees, counting paces to distract his mind. Beads of sweat ran along his eyebrows. He tried ineffectively to brush them away with wrists already wet and slippery. A hot ball expanded inside his stomach. He hadn't eaten since breakfast so when the nausea came it was mostly bile. Sam retched and spat, head to one side, but kept moving. This was no athletics meeting where sporting effort would earn polite applause. He was being hunted.

Once through the pain barrier, nausea subsided and he was able to hold the pace. On to the final stage: the summit slope. It was gentler, even concave for a few precious yards, but for centuries a scoop of soft rock had collected pebbles from above. It was a nightmare run, two slithering steps forward and a slide back. His calf muscles were on fire but this was the critical time. In his mind's eye he saw a Russian taking careful aim at the back of a human fly on the far wall. His feet smashed into the shingle until he broke free, on to a smooth, sloping fault which marked the apex of the ridge.

He was over, and on his back, blood steam-hammering through his ears and temple. Blue sky and white puff-balls were misty through salt-stung eyes. Sam forced himself to breathe deeply, to control the spasms. Leaning up on one elbow he saw the girls running towards him. He crawled back to the crest and studied the tree line.

"They're coming." Even now he could manage only two or three words at a time.

"Four of them." Another deep breath. "About a mile behind." He spat, and wiped the remaining mucous from his

103

mouth with the back of a hand. "That's why I had to move so fast."

He rolled on to his back. There must be no mistake. But on the way out he had anticipated a hasty return and had studied the terrain. He pointed to a distinctive patch of darker, scrub-covered rock.

"Just to the left of it there's a dent in the ridge. Our bay is immediately behind that shallow pass."

He forced enthusiasm into his voice. "Right, same again, one more time. All clear?"

"What about you?" asked Sally. "Can you get back? If they turn up, I mean."

He nodded. "This valley is the same width as the one we have just crossed, but the far slope is only half as high."

His head dipped urgently. "Fast as you can. We're losing time."

The girls were moving quickly, pursuit pushing them on harder. Sam refilled his last empty magazine. Every few seconds he looked up. He missed their arrival. Suddenly all four of them were standing at the corner of the tree line, staring out across the valley.

Sam waited. Every extra second was to his advantage. The Russians were obviously making a decision. They might turn back, but he wasn't counting on it. In their place he would cross to the last ridge, so that he could look into the bay. Only then, if he found nothing, would he assume that the fugitives had escaped.

They were slinging weapons across their backs to leave hands free for a steep descent. His thumb found the change lever. It was time to impose a delay.

It was extreme range for a small calibre sub-machine gun, certainly too far for accurate shooting. He would try a short burst on automatic, aiming low and letting recoil lift his fire through the target. He might be rewarded with a lucky shot.

Sam stitched off a six or seven-round burst. Dust lifted from the hillside. Shit, lower than he'd expected. Even so, splinters of rock at their feet sent the Russians diving for cover.

He glanced back. Spurred on by the sound of firing, the girls were racing for the far slope. To his front three men were

104

moving. Sam bowed his head in wry tribute to their patrol commander. The Russian had recognised the light chatter of a small calibre weapon, and knew that Sam was firing at extreme range so was spreading his force. Galloping down from the crest they would be difficult and scattered targets, and as they dropped into the valley it was unlikely that Sam would come forward to keep them in view. There was every chance that some, if not all of them, would reach the safety of 'dead ground' below him.

Sam loosed off a few more rounds at a running figure, but flinched as the patrol leader's heavier calibre weapon sprayed his immediate area with disturbing accuracy.

He was off again. Like a startled bloody rabbit, he thought, as he bounded into the valley but unless one of them turned out to be an olympic athlete, Sam was fairly confident that he could be over the next crest before the Russians appeared. There had been time for muscles to recover, and the far slope was easier. He was still going well when he reached the ridge.

"Run," he shouted at the girls. "They're into the first valley." It was four hundred yards to the shore – fairly steep but with only the occasional low bush. A final sixty feet of sand slowed their headlong, striding rush. At the water's edge he looked back. The ridge was clear.

"Come on." As the girls drew level he ran into the surf, stepping high till water pressed against his thighs. They waded, then in shoes and clothing it was a short, anxious swim to the boarding ladder suspended from the far side. All three of them were coughing and gasping as Sam helped the girls on deck. He had to shout for their attention.

"Fiona, into the wheelhouse." He lifted the spare weapon over Sally's head. It should still fire, despite a short immersion. He pointed. "See that liferaft? Take cover behind it. If they come, let them have a good long burst."

He ran to join Fiona. She was leaning against a wall and looked drained, physically and emotionally. Both engines started immediately. Sam took a wrist and pulled her gently but firmly to the control panel.

"You must have steered your father's yacht at least once?" he demanded urgently.

She gave a nervous, barely perceptible nod.

105

"These are the clutch and throttle levers. If I shout for engines, engage gear" – he demonstrated – "push both throttles about halfway forward, and steer out into the bay. Got that?"

Fiona wiped a strand of hair from her forehead and managed a subdued 'yes'. There wasn't time to go over it again. Sam ran along the deck. The anchor windlass was operated by a lever connected to a paul and ratchet. He sawed fore and aft. Link after link clanked over her bow roller and crawled across the deck, till chain led vertically into the water.

Sally's prolonged burst of firing warned him that they had run out of time. For several seconds nothing else happened. Presumably the Russians had gone to ground.

Sam worked frantically. A distant, crackling sound came down from the hillside. The lever locked tight as anchor flukes bedded on to her bow plates. Seawater was spitting into the air. Steel raindrops bounced off the deck. Framed in the wheelhouse window, Fiona's face was pale and anxious.

He screamed: "Engines!" reinforcing the order with a mime, the palm of his right hand pushing forward imaginary throttles. He heard the diesels pick up. The patrol boat gathered way through the water.

On the hillside above, the Russians were on their starboard beam. As Fiona turned the boat almost through one hundred and eighty degrees, they came on to the port quarter. Sally was firing again, but the range was too great. More rounds were smashing into hull and deck plates. It would be two minutes before they were clear of the bay. With her stern and port side exposed to the Russians, it was a matter of time before they hit something vital.

Sam moved back to the pom-pom. Something sliced at his calf. He stumbled and clutched at the mounting, pulling himself into the seat. He straightened the leg. It functioned, swinging the weapon round. The Russians were all together, up on the ridge.

His foot stamped on the pedal. The noise was deafening. It was difficult to hold an aim, the weapon seemed to dance on the deck. Across the bay high explosive shells detonated on the Russians' position. A body lifted into the air, arms spread in a ghastly parody of crucifixion. Sam stopped firing. They

106

were far enough out into the bay to be clear of any rocks or shoals. He shouted towards the wheelhouse: "Fiona, faster! Push the levers right forward."

A nearby ricochet produced a metallic, whanging sound. On the port side of the wheelhouse a last pane of glass shattered. He swung the muzzle back to the hilltop and fired a creeping barrage. They wouldn't be safe until they were beyond effective range of the Russians' small arms.

What the hell was Fiona doing? The engines weren't picking up and he couldn't see her. Sam slipped from his seat and ran along the starboard deck to the wheelhouse. He found her slumped over the wheel and console. Lifting her to one side, he slapped both handles forward and attempted to steer the boat whilst lowering her gently to the deck. Sally appeared at the wheelhouse door, still holding her sub-machine gun, and rushed to help him.

Five minutes later he was able to throttle back and disengage engines. Safely beyond a headland, the patrol boat settled into the water and wallowed in a low swell.

Supported by Sally, Fiona was sitting in a corner of the wheelhouse. Sam eased her forward and lifted the neck of her shirt. The entry hole was small and puckered. Gently, he rolled the blood-soaked cloth above her chest. The exit was a mess. One of the last rounds had caught her under the left scapula and crossed to tear out through her right breast. Sam placed his middle finger lightly on her neck, above the carotid artery. Nothing.

Sally clenched both fists and pressed them to her mouth, shaking. Sam replaced the tee shirt and lowered Fiona on to planking littered with shattered glass. In death her looks defied the red-stained clothing and matted hair, but now served only to emphasise the senseless waste of a young woman's life.

Sam lifted Sally away. With one arm round the sobbing girl's shoulders he opened the throttles and turned the patrol boat towards open sea.

Chapter 7

Fine tuning could be done later. Clear of the mainland, Sam set the boat on an approximate course for the western tip of Cyprus then managed to persuade Sally to rest below for a while. He followed her down for a quick preliminary inspection of engines and bilges.

She would probably be back on deck inside twenty minutes, too keyed up to sleep, but in the past seventy-two hours the girl had drawn heavily against her mental reserves and he was anxious to spare her from what had to be done next.

He intended to follow Middle Eastern tradition, performing final rites before the catalyst of heat accelerated bacterial decay. Sam weighted the body's ankles with a length of spare chain. He wasn't religious but stood, head bowed, and recited the Lord's Prayer – from a surfeit of experience he knew that confirmation of a Christian burial would comfort her next of kin. Finally, he raised the inboard end of a gangplank. What had once been Fiona Marchant slipped into the froth of the patrol boat's wake.

Next he looked to his leg. Fortunately the bullet had furrowed only a surface gash on the side of his calf. It was no more than a deep graze. Provided he guarded against infection it oughtn't to cause problems. The patrol boat was equipped with a reasonable first aid box, probably because the crew had no access to a doctor during their weeks at Kastellorizon. Sam used Savlon solution to swab away tiny fragments of cloth, then rather than a dressing applied aerosol Nobecutane which solidified into plastic skin. He paid in advance, however, for future convenience. Cold, antiseptic spray on raw flesh brought tears to his eyes.

With Sally still below, he took the opportunity to sweep up the broken glass and wash the blood-stained boards. All the port side windows were smashed but the for'ard screens were intact. The wheelhouse would be a bit draughty, but perfectly serviceable.

Below decks it could have been much worse. Fortunately, with the Russians firing from above, the chine angle – where just under the water line her plating angled towards the keel – had protected the submerged part of the hull. A number of rounds had penetrated her sides, but thankfully without damaging anything crucial. He plugged the holes with conical wooden stoppers from the bosun's emergency repair kit. She was seaworthy again, although Sam was only too aware that given an extra thirty seconds at anchor under the Russians' fire, there might have been a different outcome.

Sally, unrested and totally alert, joined him as he finished the inspection and followed him back to an almost restored wheelhouse. When he explained that Fiona had been buried at sea she lowered her head in dry-eyed acknowledgement. There might be tears later, but self-indulgent over-reaction was the product of a more cossetted lifestyle. She responded quickly enough when he disconnected the autopilot and invited her to take the wheel.

"What happened to Julian?" Sam asked quietly. He was anxious to put all the unpleasant news behind them, at least for a while.

She thought for a few seconds before replying.

"I made a conscious effort to remember the details – in case there might be some sort of inquest – and to translate the orderly's German carefully. We had to call him. It was about half an hour after you all left, or so he said.

"Julian woke up in a lot of pain. His stomach was very tight, and distended. By dawn his pulse was much weaker and he wasn't breathing properly, it was more a sort of shallow panting. He kept crying out . . ."

She hesitated then went on in a steadier voice: "There was only morphine. The orderly said he couldn't stop the bleeding. All he could do was ease the pain, even though the drug

109

might cause more vomiting. I remember him saying '*zwanzig milligram*' – twenty milligrams – every four hours.

"It was soon after mid-day. I don't think Julian even knew what was happening. There wasn't enough blood left for the heart to pump. That caused ventricular failure, which led to cardiac arrest."

"I'm sorry." It sounded facile but it was all he could think of.

"It's funny. The wound seemed so small. It didn't look serious, did it? But he must have needed surgery . . ." She took two or three deep breaths. "I think the orderly did everything he could. They took the body away in a long, black plastic sack."

'Brought expressly for the purpose,' thought Sam. 'What the Army used to call "bags – human remains".'

"Steer one two zero," he said gently, to bring her mind back to the present. After a few minutes he left her occupied with the therapy of helming and went outside to check for any other damage. It was all cosmetic, nothing serious, and afterwards he took the chance to stand relaxed at the guardrail in the last of the afternoon sun, if only for a few moments.

He looked at his watch. Five o'clock. In two and a half hours it would be dark. He was reluctant to leave Sally on watch at night, steaming at speed and having to recognise the size and course of other ships from their lights. Neither would he have wished to leave her alone so soon, but after the last three nights he needed sleep urgently if he were to come on deck at dusk.

Sam went back inside the wheelhouse and leaned over the chart table. For a few seconds he bounced the end of a pencil against surrounding woodwork, then marked a point some thirty miles to the west of Cyprus. Behind an almost uninhabited coastline the hills rose quickly to two thousand feet. Devoid of buoys or a lighthouse, it wasn't a stretch of land to approach at night. By day it would theoretically be visible at a range of over fifty miles, but that would be reduced by haze. If they were about thirty miles off at dawn, he could close the coast at first light. Sam spanned the dividers between their present position and his dawn arrival point, measuring the gap against a scale along the vertical edge of the chart. A

110

hundred and twenty-five miles, it would take just over six hours.

He thought about the submarine. It couldn't catch them, and they were probably clear of the Russian skipper's patrol area by now. If he kept the boat at twenty knots whilst he slept it would be safe enough to throttle back after dark. He confirmed that Sally felt happy about steering and keeping watch for a while.

"Where are we headed?" came the inevitable question.

"Cyprus." Sam outlined the passage plan. "But we'll talk later about what happens when we get there," he offered, fending off her curiosity. "Right now, I'm tired enough to be a menace in charge of a boat."

He explained the gauges and asked her to call him if there were any significant changes in reading.

"Or if anything else bothers you," he added, "like what to do about a patch of shipping. Just throttle right back, and come below."

Finally he mentioned the submarine.

"But if you do see anything," he concluded, "push the throttles wide open. The noise and motion will wake me fast enough."

He would have to trust Sally's judgement. Unless he seized the opportunity to rest, he would be committing the unpardonable sin of exhausting himself to the point of being unable to react quickly enough to an emergency. He took off his shoes and lay down on the captain's bunk. Ninety seconds later he was asleep.

At some stage he was vaguely aware of a reduction in engine speed and an easing of the boat's motion, but the recharging of his batteries had barely begun. There was insufficient energy left in him to spark an alert. He fell back into oblivion.

There was blackness all around him but he was awake. Memory scavenged his senses. Engine noise, movement . . . In an engulfing flood of recollection, Sam knew that he had overslept. He stretched upwards and swatted the bulkhead, fingers reeling for a switch. One push, and the cabin was suffused in a dull red glow which wouldn't destroy his night vision. Twenty-past eleven. Christ! He had been asleep for over six hours.

Sam pulled on his desert boots and swayed towards the companionway. He found her in the wheelhouse, leaning over a chart table illuminated only by a small, red bulb at the end of a flexible, coiled-metal stalk.

"Are you all right? I thought you were going to wake me before it got dark?" He could see only her face and shoulders clearly.

"It was obvious you were pretty well all in." She turned towards him and stood upright.

"Besides, after you went below I grew bored with just steering, so I experimented." The voice came from a silhouette. "It didn't take long to work out how to switch in the autopilot. I kept an eye on the gauges, and there have only been half a dozen other ships, none of them close enough to worry about. So," she concluded, "it seemed a pity to wake you."

Her hand moved towards dots of beta light on the panel. "Trial and error, but we're showing a red and green light to port and starboard, a white light on the aerial mast and another white one astern. Those three switches were grouped together, and I think that's what you pointed out the other night as the lighting for a small power vessel. Anyway, I thought it would be near enough, especially as I altered course to stay well clear of other ships."

It was all common sense, but must have taken a degree of determination. Sam moved to the panel and peered out through the screen. An almost full moon showed the low undulations of a calm sea. Way out on the starboard bow was a blaze of white lights; a cruise liner, lit up like a Christmas tree. He picked out the small blob of green on her starboard superstructure. She had crossed well in front of them and was steaming clear.

"Do you think I've passed my watchkeeper's exam?"

The voice was at his side. He put an arm round her shoulders and gave her a grateful squeeze.

"I think you've done marvellously well. And I feel a hell of a lot better for a few hours' sleep."

He crossed to the chart table and spoke over his shoulder.

"What time did you throttle back?"

112

"Eight o'clock. Half an hour after it got dark. Three hours at twenty knots put us nearly halfway to Cyprus. We're doing ten now, so we should be at your thirty-miles-off point by two o'clock."

Sam took a reading from the distance-run log, measured off the miles and marked their position on his rhumb line. Next, he switched on the radar unit and experimented with the controls. It was an ancient American-built set with a series of range bands out to a maximum of fourteen miles. After some adjustment he achieved a sharp blip marking the cruise liner, otherwise the screen was blank. He switched it off, finally turning out the red light over the chart table. When Sally volunteered to make something to eat, Sam realised that his last meal had been that mid-morning breakfast.

"I was starving earlier on," she confided, "so I had a good look over the galley. There are the ingredients for a stew, and there's plenty of fruit. All tinned, I'm afraid, but the peaches are good – I had some a couple of hours ago. And in the cupboard under the sink I found a case of canned beer. It's Greek stuff, but I'll bring you a couple, if you like."

They ate in the wheelhouse.

"Why are we going to Cyprus?" she asked, talking and eating simultaneously. "I mean," there was a pause as she swallowed, "couldn't we have gone back to Fethiye to link up with Angus and the authorities?"

"Maybe, although I wouldn't fancy steaming into a Turkish harbour with a Greek gunboat. But that's not really the point."

Sam took a drink of the lukewarm beer and set down the can with a grunt of disgust.

"Look, tomorrow's Tuesday, the second day of occupation for Kastellorizon. With the telephone exchange destroyed, the island is cut off from Rhodes completely. I doubt if it's the first time the phone has gone on the blink, so I can't imagine the Greeks being too excited. They'll probably send out an engineer on the next steamer, as a matter of routine. And that's on Friday – only three days away."

"But in the meantime, what do the Russians expect to achieve?" she asked.

113

"A hell of a lot. In this part of the world, memories are kept alive from generation to generation. Even in the nineteen-eighties Greek leaders have been claiming that the main threat is from Turkey, not the Warsaw Pact – albeit to distract attention from internal problems. And that's why the Russians have come up with a very clever idea."

He spent a few minutes explaining the centuries of conflict and barbarity between Greek and Turk.

"It's one of man's traditional hostilities," he concluded, "like that between Jew and Arab, or Christian and Moslem. This Aegean dispute, which is basically a disagreement over sea and airspace limits but also involves seabed oil and mineral rights, is just the modern aspect of an ancient struggle. More recently, the issue has been complicated by events in Cyprus. Graeco-Turkish relations weren't improved in 'seventy-four, when the Turks invaded to protect the Turkish minority from Greek Cypriots, nor in 'eighty-three when the Turkish half in the north declared independence. But Cyprus is a long way from Greece and only forty miles from southern Turkey, so a Greek military expedition would have been hopeless. All they could do was whine to the European Community and the United Nations, and in 'seventy-four pull out of the military structure of NATO for a few years."

"But Kastellorizon . . ." she began.

"Exactly. Kastellorizon's different. It's Greek national territory. If it appears that the Turks have sacked a Greek island, every Greek peasant and coffee-shop politician will be screaming for revenge. This time, if it wanted to survive, a Greek government would have to take some sort of action."

"So what could they do?" asked Sally. "Presumably Samandag and his men won't wait around to be caught, so Greece won't have to recapture the island."

"Correct," agreed Sam, "but nevertheless there will have to be a response – for my money somewhere within a spectrum which starts at withdrawal from NATO and finishes with an attempt to close the Aegean to Turkish shipping."

"Go on," she invited.

He shrugged his shoulders. "It only needs thinking through. It's not difficult to see the scenario. As always, the Greeks will try to extract maximum political capital. There

114

will be demands for NATO action, as well as EEC economic sanctions. NATO won't do anything – the Alliance has always refused to get involved with bilateral squabbles between its members. Neither will the EEC. Turkey is a valuable export market, not least for arms sales. Even if one country suspended trade relations, another would be delighted to step forward. But it wouldn't happen. Sales, and jobs at home, are far more important to European politicians than a fit of Greek pique."

He pulled a wry face. "Anyway, Greece wouldn't pull out of the EEC – she makes a fat profit from her membership. So that leaves NATO. She knows the West is keen for her to stay within the Alliance, and given no response to her demands for action against Turkey, the only face-saver and retaliation would be to pull out. I think it's a certainty, and this time it would probably be for good."

"But where, at the end of the day, would that leave Greece?" argued Sally. "Wouldn't she be isolated?"

"Not really," responded Sam. "If she needed military assistance – arms, for example – the Soviet Union would be delighted to oblige. Particularly if, as a quid pro quo, Greece allowed them further use of her shipyards. The Russians have been desperate for a decent Mediterranean naval base ever since the Egyptians kicked them out of Alexandria. In the end, they could achieve the fragmentation of NATO, earn hard currency by selling arms to the Greeks – paid for at least in part by European Community subsidies – and have the Soviet Mediterranean Squadron operating from an Aegean harbour. Not a bad return," he reflected, "for a few days' work on an isolated Greek outpost."

The patrol boat droned on, intermittent rattles and vibrations in concert with shafts and engines.

"You say that's one end of the spectrum," Sally observed after a couple of minutes' silence. "Wouldn't withdrawal from NATO be enough?"

"It depends on how the Greek government chose to manipulate domestic opninion," he replied, crossing to the chart table and switching on the light. He lifted the lid and pulled an Admiralty Chart from the drawer beneath. "Take a look at this." Sally moved closer and followed his finger along the chart headed 'Mediterranean Sea – Eastern Sheet'.

"These are all Greek islands." The finger traced an east-west belt across the bottom of the Aegean, beginning with islands just off the Greek mainland and finishing at Kos, hard against the Turkish coast.

"So are these." A hand circled the Aegean archepelagoes and settled finally against Limnos, lying in the northern Aegean off the entrance to the Dardanelles.

"Greece would love to claim a twelve-mile limit for each island. It would give her total control of the Aegean, and that would include valuable oil and mineral resources on the sea-bed. So far she hasn't risked Turkish reaction, not to mention international condemnation."

"But in response to Kastellorizon – " broke in Sally.

"Precisely."

He turned to face her, half-sitting on the edge of the chart table. "Put it in context. Excuse the barrack room language, but generations of Greeks have been brought up to be scared fartless of the Turkish threat. Then there was the invasion of Cyprus and Turkish U.D.I. Finally, Kastellorizon.

"The population will be working themselves into a steady frenzy, demanding whatever they can think of with their usual mega-machismo. The Greek government will have a field day, scoring points like crazy off the Turks. But despite Greek demands, NATO and the EEC will do nothing. And above all else, the over-riding priority of that Greek government will be to stay in office.

"Out of NATO? Definitely, and it wouldn't surprise me if they decided to kill two birds with one stone because the Greeks won't be slow to realise that with international opinion on their side, and Turkey isolated, there's never going to be a better time to go all-out in the Aegean. It's the one place where they could satisfy popular demand by tweaking the Turkish tail, and achieve a historic ambition into the bargain. You claim territorial waters for each of those islands, and the Turks on the Aegean coast, and through the Dardanelles and Bosphorous into the Black Sea, are cut off from the Mediterranean. It would cripple them both militarily and economically."

"So the Turks would fight," she concluded flatly.

"Possibly," he countered, "although a lot would depend

116

upon how the rest of the international community lined up. The Turks might start with a token challenge, perhaps by sailing through a few merchantmen escorted by a warship. But if the Greeks interfered, then yes, at the end of the day, they're risking an Aegean war. Not only would NATO's southern flank be a dead duck, but the whole of the Eastern Mediterranean would be up for grabs."

They stared through the screens at an empty sea. Occasionally a larger wave lifted the patrol boat's bow till it dropped with an easy splash into the trough beyond.

"Surely," Sally began again after a few minutes, "it depends upon what the Greeks believe? When we reach Cyprus, couldn't you warn the authorities, or even the news agencies? Turkey could issue a denial and don't forget, we would be independent witnesses. That has to count for something."

"Maybe, but I wouldn't gamble on it," Sam responded. "First, we have to reach Cyprus. For all I know there's an Ilyushin reconnaissance aircraft searching for us right now. But in any case, leave us out of the equation, just for a moment. Samandag won't stay on at Kastellorizon to be caught by the Greeks. He'll bug out, either just before the ferry arrives or soon afterwards. Thinking about it, in his position I'd sink the ferry as she entered the harbour and use the inflatables to rendezvous with the submarine. Then the news would be out, and no amount of Turkish denial is going to be believed."

"Except by us," she persisted. "Let's assume we reach Cyprus. There has to be something we can do."

He was quiet for a few seconds.

"Our first choice," he began eventually, "would be to make the whole thing public. But that means international news agencies, which the Russians also monitor. They would radio a message via the submarine and Samandag would pull out. By the time anyone arrived there would only be a ravaged island and the overwhelming testimony of its inhabitants. And you can be sure that in the meantime there will have been a few more, high media value atrocities."

He paused, choosing his words carefully. "If we turn up with a gunboat pinched from the very island which has been

117

attacked, with some story about the group of men from Turkey who were responsible actually being Russians, Athens and Moscow are probably going to accuse us of being implicated in a Turkish cover-up."

"All right," she countered, "in that case, why don't we contact the British authorities? They could pass a private warning to the Greek government."

"So then what happens?" he queried. "If the Greeks send a gunboat or a helicopter, Samandag will destroy it and pull out. And you can bet your life there's a Bulgarian registered trawler or merchantman sitting astride the sea approaches from Greece. Any major amphibious or warship deployment towards Kastellorizon, and Samandag will be into that submarine before the Greeks are through the Rhodes channel. All they will find is a bunch of distraught islanders. Back to square one."

"So there's no way we are going to be believed?" The note of frustration in her voice was unmistakable.

"I know this will sound cynical," he replied softly, "and I dare say we shall raise a few doubts in some minds, but at the end of the day the Greek government will believe what it wants to believe. And that's why the scheme is so very, very clever."

Sally walked over to the windscreen, mulling over what he had said.

"So why are we steaming towards Cyprus," she asked, "if there's nothing we can do? Are we just running for safety to the nearest British military base?"

Sam turned off the chart table light and joined her.

"I didn't say," he replied in a deliberately even voice, "that there was nothing we could do. Only that in the final analysis, the Greeks will choose what they want to believe. There is a counter to the Soviet gambit – " he emphasised the 'is' – "but I believe that the solution lies in retaking Kastellorizon whilst Samandag and his men are still on it. And it's essential that at least some of them are captured alive."

"What? You're not expecting to lead a British attempt, surely?"

There was enough light from the control panel for her to see him shaking his head. "The Greeks would never allow it,

118

even if the Foreign Office could make a fast enough decision, which I doubt."

"So?"

"I shan't go anywhere near the British bases." His relaxed delivery implied that he had made up his mind some time ago.

"I shall do what the Greeks, for a variety of reasons, are incapable of doing. My approach will be from the one direction in which I suspect the Soviets will neither risk – nor assess that they need – a trawler or submarine. I intend to follow in Samandag's wake, and land from the narrow band of water between Kastellorizon and the Turkish mainland.

"What's more," he went on before she could interrupt, "if we are to succeed, it won't be with some obvious, unwieldy Armada, which there isn't time to assemble anyway. This has to be a job for a small team of experienced specialists."

She watched him check gauges and the horizon.

"Fortunately," he concluded almost casually, "I think I know exactly where to find them."

During the night the wind died, and with it the low swell. Even stationary, without the portside windows, it was cool in the wheelhouse. Fingers around a mug of steaming black coffee, Sam turned for the fiftieth time towards the eastern horizon. The first temporary paleness of false dawn had passed, but due east the sky was definitely a lighter shade of grey and purple. Looking towards the break of day he could distinguish the surface of a slate-coloured sea. He set down the mug and went out on to the side deck. Even in those few seconds the band of visibility had widened. Only tiny ripples from an occasional uncertain zephyr distorted the boat's reflection. Soon it would be an easy target for aerial reconnaissance. It was time to move.

Sam tapped his palm on the flat surface of the guardrail and turned back to the wheelhouse. Both diesels rattled affably to life and settled to a steady rumble, sharpening to a rasping bark as he pushed open the throttles and brought the bow round towards the coast of Cyprus.

It was a good landfall, within a mile of prediction. Hills sweeping away to Cape Arnauti on his port bow were an inky silhouette against a brightening sky. Sam closed to within a

119

quarter mile of the coast, so that from seaward the patrol boat would be inconspicuous against a backdrop of land shadow, then turned to follow the southern shore of possibly the most beautiful of all Mediterranean islands.

He recalled reading somewhere that civilisation on Cyprus dated back to six thousand years before Christ. Over the centuries Aphrodite's Island had been occupied by a number of emerging powers: Persians, Romans, the English Knights Templar, Venetians, and for over three hundred years, until eighteen seventy, by the Turks. In that year began a British occupation which was to last until independence, achieved under the Treaty of Establishment in 1960, which also ceded to Great Britain two military base areas as sovereign territory.

Once there were two communities living side by side throughout the island but for many years the Greek Cypriot, four-fifths majority harassed and provoked the Turkish Cypriot minority. Following the 1974 Athens-inspired military coup in Nicosia, which deposed Archbishop Makarios, Turkish Cypriots fled north to the protection of invading Turkish armed forces, who without serious difficulty occupied some thirty-six per cent of the island, securing a partition which endured beyond the 1985 initiatives of United Nations Secretary General Perez De Cuellar.

Steering just east of south, Sam knew that the coastline was uninhabited until the village of Peyia, twelve miles away. A further nine miles beyond this first settlement lay Paphos, once a small fishing village but now a major tourist area, a southern coast replacement for Kyrenia lost to the North.

Sam had wide experience of the *babu* mentality of Greek Cypriot bureaucracy, and knew that were he to enter even a fishing harbour, their arrival would set in train a web of investigation from which neither he nor the patrol boat would escape for weeks. Fortunately the local predilection for pen-waving stopped short of writing a cheque to pay for a coastguard service.

Sam's destination was Lara Bay, an isolated and sheltered anchorage six miles short of Peyia. By land the only approach was along a rough track, at times impassable even to four-wheel-drive vehicles. Provided the anchorage was deserted,

Sam knew their arrival would be unobserved and that they could lie there, perhaps for weeks, before news of the patrol boat reached the authorities.

It was over a year since Sam had visited Lara, last time in a small sailing yacht. Even without a detailed chart he established the bay's entrance easily enough, then once inside nosed gently towards the shore, finally dropping anchor through fifteen feet of clear water on to a sandy bottom. With a generous scope of chain paid out, he ran the diesels astern to bite in the flukes. Her anchor held. He killed the engines and she settled to chain within about sixty yards of a narrow sandy beach.

Even as thinning, grey-white curls of exhaust smoke died on the water, a golden rim edged above the foothills. Within minutes morning freshness would warm to a pleasant heat, but inside two hours it would no longer be comfortable.

Whilst Sally was sleeping Sam intended to bathe, but he was reluctant to dress again in dirty, sweat-stained clothing. He recalled seeing some washing up liquid and a bucket in the galley. Minutes later he stripped in the morning sun and gave his entire wardrobe a rudimentary pummelling in seawater and detergent, allowing himself fresh water only for the final rinse. His clean laundry he draped over the guardrail. In half an hour the lighter garments, if not dry, would be comfortable enough to put back on.

With a piece of cordage attached to the handle, Sam hauled up another gallon of seawater and poured it slowly over his head. Like a swimmer greasing up for a channel crossing he anointed himself with green detergent, then plunged overboard to tread water whilst he rubbed away the tacky coating. His makeshift toilet completed, Sam dived to inspect the anchor before treating himself to a leisurely swim around the boat. His arrival at the top of the boarding ladder coincided precisely with Sally's emergence from the wheelhouse.

She blinked in surprise, smiled, and greeted him almost simultaneously. Her gazed traversed to a circle of soapy water alongside the patrol boat, past the bucket and wet foredeck, and across to a festooned guardrail on the starboard bow. Finally she looked down at her own stained tee shirt and slacks.

"I stink" she announced with disgust, sniffing cautiously at first one armpit and then the other. "How did you set about doing your laundry?"

He told her, as well as how to bathe in seawater. She walked to the foredeck and collected a bucketful from over the side. Standing with her back towards him, she lifted off her tee shirt and stepped clear of her slacks.

Sam felt he oughtn't to be standing there, like a schoolboy receiving his first, accidental revelation of the adult female form, but despite his best intentions he stared as first her bra and then a pair of matching, natural-coloured briefs were dropped into the bucket.

She was the first naked woman he had seen for over a year. At first it had seemed disloyal not to avoid sexual thoughts; later, celibacy had become a way of life. Confronted by this nudity – intensified by a pale, bikini-cast triangle – Sam was embarrassed by his voyeurism. He turned and dived back into the Mediterranean. When next he twisted in the water, Sally had all but disappeared from view as she knelt to her laundry.

On his third circuit around the hull he saw her standing poised at the top of the boarding ladder, covered in streaks of soapy green. She surfaced from a long, shallow dive, laughing at the struggle to tread water and at the same time wipe away the glutinous liquid. Sam made his way amidships to rest with one arm hooked through a rung of the ladder. Sally swam back towards him in a slow, even breast stroke. She, too, held on, facing him.

He couldn't stop himself from looking down at her compact but perfectly proportioned body and experienced a long-forgotten emotion of uncertainty and excitement. Sally looked at him directly, her face calm and candid. She slipped one arm under his and her hand arched to encompass his shoulder. The other passed around his waist, pulling their bodies together.

Swaying in the water, his right thigh drifted between hers, which tightened gently. He felt the firmness of her nipples, the softness of her breasts as they brushed his chest. They clung together, lips salty from seawater. His erection pushed against her then she was away, underwater, swimming fast. Sam let go of the boarding ladder and followed slowly on the

122

surface, controlling his breathing. After a few minutes they were together again, treading water. Her fingertips brushed his cheek.

"I'm going to dress. Will you give me a few minutes?"

When he climbed aboard, Sally had gone below. Only her slacks remained on the guardrail. He dressed, following her example. It would be at least an hour before the heavier garments were dry.

He found her in the galley, opening tins of fruit. The combination of briefs and tee shirt was almost as erotic as her naked body, but it was a dispassionate observation. The mood had passed, by unspoken agreement set aside for some more apposite, less dangerous time.

'Twice within twenty-four hours', thought Sam, wrapping shoes and clothing in an oilskin for a swim to the shore. From Lara to Paphos was thirteen and a half miles, and he would have to walk, at first cross-country and then because he had no wish to advertise his presence by trying to hitch a ride. Once he reached Paphos he would be inconspicuous within the tourist hordes.

His final destination was Limassol, a further thirty-five miles beyond Paphos and, since the partition of Nicosia, the economic capital of the South. Unfortunately, he had no Cypriot money. To exchange sterling, a bank official would ask to see his passport and he couldn't risk some observant official noticing that he lacked a re-entry stamp since his last exit over a year ago.

But once in Paphos, Sam was counting on being able to exploit a particular facet of life on the island. In Cypriot eyes, to cheat the government or any large organisation was fair game, but theft from a fellow villager was unworthy, bringing only dishonour to the thief and his family. Sam knew that were he to park a military Land-Rover in a quiet lay-by for the night, next morning he could expect to find it minus wheels and engine. A private car, complete with expensive radio, would be left untouched. This unwritten law survived even in the cities where few of the island's inhabitants bothered to lock their vehicles.

It was a long, hot and dusty walk. His clean but unkempt

123

appearance, now with four days' growth of beard, attracted little attention as he passed through villages. He had been in the Mediterranean long enough to acquire the bleached hair and deep tan of a local, easily distinguishable from hasty, red-brown tourist hues.

As he walked towards the harbour through the narrow, cobbled streets of old Paphos, Sam was aware of incipient dehydration. He sat beneath a long canvas awning which shaded a line of tables belonging to a café across the street.

A waiter set down small dishes of nuts and olives. Sam ordered two colas, and for the next ten minutes exercised the self-discipline of drinking them slowly.

Choosing a moment when the waiter was engrossed in taking an order from a large party of tourists, Sam extracted an English five-pound note from his wallet. Catching the waiter's eye he waved the note, slipped it under the empty olive saucer, and held out an open palm in the international gesture of declining change. Before the note could be collected, Sam had disappeared into a crowd along the sea wall.

The waiter would recognise the note and know that its value greatly exceeded the price of two drinks. He might grumble at having to exchange it himself, but he had received a generous tip. There could be no question of theft, and certainly no reason to go after Sam.

There were two distinct categories in the line of parked cars. Many were at least ten years old, bodywork well preserved in the dry heat despite the proximity of salt water. Some were considerably older: Morris Minors with split front windscreens, Standard Tens and Vanguards, Vauxhall Crestas and Wyverns, all of them collectors' items in the United Kingdom. The minority of new vehicles belong either to wealthy local businessmen or, for the most part, to foreigners from either the military communities of the two British bases or the United Nations in Nicosia.

Sam strolled up and down alongside the low sea wall. It was forty minutes before he saw what he wanted. A family parked a fairly new, small Volvo and walked off towards the old town market.

The man's tee shirt proclaimed membership of the Royal

Air Force Station at Akrotiri. He had fallen in to the way of the islanders. The car's windows were down so that the interior wouldn't be unbearably hot when they returned, and it had seemed unnecessary to fill the pocket of his shorts with a bunch of keys. They had been tossed on to the parcel shelf.

After waiting a few minutes, to give other onlookers time to move on and to be sure that no member of the family dashed back for some forgotten item, Sam drove the car unobtrusively out of Paphos.

There was always the possibility of a random police check, more prevalent in Cyprus than in the United Kingdom and particularly likely where the road passed through British Sovereign Base territory at Episkopi, on the edge of the Western Sovereign Base Area. These checks were not because of stolen cars, which were almost unknown on the island, but because licence evasion, not least in rural areas, was something of a national pastime. But being foreign-owned, the Volvo was properly registered and displayed a current tax disc. Sam was reasonably confident that he could bluff his way through a checkpoint.

Having driven out from Akrotiri, the owners of the car would probably spend some time strolling around the market and then almost certainly settle somewhere for a cool drink. He should be safe for at least an hour, and even then police communications on the island were basic by European standards. It was unlikely that there would be a general alert before he reached Limassol.

It was an attractive drive, sometimes along the coastal plain, occasionally through foothills. After twelve miles he looked down over a superb view of Aphrodite's Rocks, a cluster of small stones in the surf marking the legendary birthplace of the goddess Venus Aphrodite, born of the sea.

Traffic was light in the sprawling Cypriot city no larger than an English town. Because of the summer heat, shops and offices closed at midday and re-opened for a few hours in the early evening. Sam knew that Phivo would be resting at the flat which he used as a *pied-à-terre* during the week. At weekends he usually disappeared to join his family at their house in his native hillside village. As a final precaution Sam parked the Volvo and walked for the last mile.

At first there was no response to the doorbell. But just as Sam was beginning to wonder if he had chosen a singularly unfortunate time, he caught the grudging shuffle of flip-flops on the marble floor of the entrance lobby.

It was not a time when any Cypriot would call. The door opened, slowly at first, then was flung wide.

"Sam! It really *is* you. Come in, come in. Why didn't you tell me? How long have you been in Cyprus?"

Phivo's surprise and pleasure at Sam's unannounced arrival gave way almost immediately to comment on his dishevelled appearance.

"Give me a large, cold beer," Sam begged his friend, "then sit down, and don't interrupt. What I have to tell you, even by your standards, is quite a story."

His host returned from the kitchen with two frosted cans in one hand. At five foot ten, Phivo Karakoulas was an inch or two taller than the average Cypriot. What gripped the attention, however, was not height but build. He was almost obscenely stocky, from his unbelievably short, thick neck, which barely separated a balding head from massive, bull-like shoulders, to calf muscles which displaced almost horizontally the hem of a white towelling robe. On his wrist a large gold Rolex sank into a mass of thick black hair. Around him drifted the odour of some expensive European fragrance. Phivo exuded money – and power.

Sam had first met him at one of the periodic receptions intended to enable more senior members of the British community on the island, for so Sam found himself as commander of the largest Army unit, to become acquainted with some of the local business and political *prominenti*.

A common interest in boats led to an invitation to a barbecue party on board the *Maria*, Phivo's forty-two foot Riva Caribe sports fisherman. Although the *Maria*'s twin three hundred and twenty horsepower Cummins diesels gave her a maximum speed of thirty-three knots, and a range of over a thousand miles, like so many Cypriots Phivo was a coastal mariner, rarely beyond sight of land for very long. Sam taught him the rudiments of offshore navigation, which they tested on excursions to Tel Aviv and Port Said, and advised on the installation of more advanced equipment.

One evening Sam mentioned that he was thinking of buying a sailing yacht, which though British-owned and registered had been berthed for many years in the northern port of Kyrenia. Her owners had lived in the North, before and after the Turkish invasion, until advancing years and a need for specialist medical treatment forced them to return to the United Kingdom. Now they were attempting to dispose of their assets. Unfortunately, in those days, Sam wasn't permitted to cross the border.

"Where's the problem?" Phivo had asked. "Do you want to be taken into the North, or shall I have the boat brought to another port so that you can collect her – somewhere on the Turkish coast, perhaps, or maybe Syria?"

Sam knew that a Greek Cypriot couldn't have access legally to the Turkish Federated State of Cyprus. They talked around the subject but he avoided making a firm commitment. A few days later he mentioned the conversation to someone whose duty it was to be aware of the unadvertised activities of the island's personalities and political factions.

"My dear chap, I can't say you astonish me," came the bland reply. "How much do you know about Phivo Karakoulas?"

"Not an enormous amount," confessed Sam guardedly, "although we meet fairly frequently."

"Some people," began his informant, knocking a pipe bowl against the trunk of a carob tree, "will tell you that our Phivo is now a respectable businessman. I can give you my own opinion, for what it's worth, because there's no hard evidence. If there was, Karakoulas would be behind bars. But I don't think there are many pies in which he doesn't have the proverbial finger.

"Some say that he's one of the main procurement agents for the Palestinians: anything from aspirins to an Armalite rifle. Others reckon he's just a crook, organising the delivery of proscribed cargoes into any country you care to name."

He paused, looking out over the clifftop at a pair of rock eagles soaring on the uplift.

"If you want a cargo of illicit liquor in Saudi, see Phivo. If you need a middle man to launder hi-tech defence equipment to Libya, or to arrange for arms to be re-directed from the country quoted on your export licence, they say he can do it."

Sam was hardly surprised. The Middle East spawned an abundance of such characters.

"No wonder a trip to the North didn't seem too difficult," he observed.

They walked on slowly. "There's still a lot of smuggling between the two communities," commented his informant, "luxury goods and hard currency one way, gold and antiquities the other."

"What's Phivo's history?" asked Sam. "Was he always a sort of local mafioso?"

The intelligence officer was in the process of relighting his pipe. "No." A shake of his head spread the noxious smoke in a wide arc. "He used to be one of Grivas' bright young lieutenants, back in EOKA days. I dare say if the British could have laid hands on him before Independence, they would have stretched that fat neck. There are any number of important Greeks around who once fought the British. Some of them are now in politics; others, like Phivo, went into business. But unlike him, most of them have stuck more or less to the straight and narrow."

Despite this information, the friendship developed. Sam was something of a specialist in counter terrorist operations, although he was too young to have been in the Army during the EOKA campaign. He spent many evenings on the balcony of Phivo's flat, talking of past times and looking out from the foothills over the lights of Limassol to the bay beyond.

In response to Sam's interest Phivo occasionally invited others, older men with deeply wrinkled faces, their long, flowing moustaches still thick and luxuriant but now silver or white. They accepted him as a friend of Phivo, a student of recent military history in which they had been intimately involved. Over numerous cups of coffee or glasses of wine, their natural caution gradually relaxed. Out of deference to their visitor they spoke in English, although some of them found difficulty with the language. Sam listened, fascinated, to reminiscences of fishing boats delivering arms and explosives to small harbours, of pack mules moving supplies by

128

night along mountain tracks to remote villages, of ambushes against British patrols, and of top-level meetings in safe houses which included the monasteries of the Greek Orthodox Church.

Only through the occasional accidental meeting, or inadvertently overheard snatch of conversation, did Sam ever receive a hint of Phivo's current activities. Accepting that it would be unfair to strain Sam's loyalty as a member of the island's British administration, itself a part of the overall government establishment, Phivo separated strictly his social and business affairs. Within this framework, and despite a disparity of background and profession, by the time he came to leave the island Sam counted Phivo as one of his closest friends.

Sam talked continuously for ten minutes. The Cypriot hung on his every word.

"So that's it, Phivo," Sam concluded. "There isn't time to do anything else. I'm not bound by any of my former constraints, and besides, you're the one person I know who can probably produce what I need. So, how about it?"

The Cypriot lit an American cigarette and studied the spiral of rising smoke.

"You say at least eight men?" he confirmed eventually.

"Plus you and me, yes. And we need the weapons."

Another long silence.

"Money?"

Sam shook his head. "If it comes off, there should be a pretty handsome response from a few grateful governments. The media rights alone ought to be worth a small fortune. The survivors should finish up as fairly wealthy men." He grimaced. "But there is nothing 'up front', as you say, and nothing is guaranteed.

"That said," he was playing his last card, and the only ace, "I wouldn't fancy being a Greek Cypriot if there were an all-out war between Greece and Turkey. It didn't take the Turks long to capture over a third of the island in 'seventy-four. If it came to a set-to over the Greek islands, I can't see Turkey leaving an isolated Greek outpost only forty miles from her southern shore. This time she might decide to lay the

Cyprus ghost for ever and grab the lot – a quid pro quo for whatever the Greeks get up to in the Aegean."

He paused for effect. "What I need won't cost very much – perhaps it would be worth your while underwriting the operation, if only as a small insurance premium on your investments in this part of the world."

It was a telling remark. For the first time Phivo's bland expression disappeared. His legitimate hotel business alone was worth about ten million sterling, most of it financed initially from laundered profits. If there were a war he could move on, perhaps to Sicily or Malta, but he still stood to lose an uncomfortable slice of accumulated wealth. Fleeing from a war zone, even as a blue-chip refugee, held no appeal.

Phivo opened a full-length, louvred door and stood looking out across the balcony. Sam could sense the thought process. He timed the silence. It lasted for half a minute and felt like an hour.

"What weapons did you say you wanted?"

He exhaled silently with relief. How much Phivo's decision owed to their friendship, or to an argument which must have struck home, was impossible to gauge.

"Right, let's talk business. We must have some sort of pill-box buster. An anti-tank weapon will do – they used them to good effect like that in the Falklands. Something akin to the Milan system, if you can get it. We shall need mortars, ideally around eighty millimetre calibre and with high explosive rounds. Each man will need a respirator, preferably the British Army pattern because it's the least uncomfortable, and I shall want a good supply of CS gas canisters. The rest shouldn't be too difficult: heavy and light machine guns, grenades, some plastic and a few detonators – don't forget wire and a remote control initiator – and four man-pack radios."

Sam had been thinking aloud while staring intently at the carpet. Now he glanced up at Phivo.

"And by not later than lunchtime tomorrow."

Chapter 8

He was not an accredited diplomat but ostensibly a member of the Soviet Trade Mission to the Republic of Cyprus. In midsummer Nicosia's one hundred and five degrees, Anatoly Makarov lay naked on his bed, mentally cursing the vagaries of the Cyprus Electricity Authority which for the second time in a month had deprived him of fans and air conditioning.

Unlike the stone houses and shaded courtyards of the old quarter, his modern concrete apartment block offered little protection from the heat. Windows were open wide to the noise of traffic below but the hot, dusty air barely stirred. Rivulets of sweat from his chest and armpits soaked into a cotton sheet. He longed for the cool of the evening.

Makarov scratched his groin. Five weeks in this stifling heat, and still he wasn't acclimatised. He got up to walk to the shower, even though relief from the tepid water would be short-lived, but was diverted by the jangling of his telephone.

A curt summons to the office induced a brisk reply which belied his true feelings. It would not be prudent to show ill grace, especially so soon on his first foreign assignment. He could have wished for an easier climate, but even Nicosia in high summer compared favourably with the lifestyle of his family in Moscow, who would not be permitted to join him until at least one of the children was old enough to be left behind.

An hour and a half later, driving an inconspicuous Fiat rather than his usual Soviet-made Lada, Makarov turned into the car park at Larnaca Airport. After several enquiries and a telephone call to his destination by a security guard, he was allowed on to the airfield. A few hundred yards from the cluster of inadequate buildings supporting a presumptuous 'Larnaca International' sign, he found a line of Portakabins, in one of them the offices of Cyprus Air Services Limited.

As Makarov entered a middle-aged man wearing well-pressed cotton slacks and a short-sleeved bush jacket rose to greet him.

"Ted Mottram." He extended a hand. "You'll be Mister Fischer?"

Makarov nodded.

"Your secretary tells me you want to fly the southern coastline? A German company, she said, looking for another tourist base to develop?"

"It's a possibility. I wish to examine the whole coast, particularly harbours and anchorages." He looked at his watch. "When can we start?"

If Mottram was put out by his client's unforthcoming attitude, it didn't show.

"Flight plan's filed. As soon as you're ready, Mister Fischer. There's just the . . . er . . ."

"Of course." Makarov produced an envelope and placed it on the desk.

"Two hundred. In Cyprus pounds. That will be for today. If I need more time tomorrow, you will be paid again in the morning."

The single-engined Cessna bounced through thermal turbulence rising from the land. Makarov disliked flying, but once out over the sea at two thousand feet he welcomed the drop in temperature. For most of the time they followed the coast, circling over the marina at Larnaca, the port and bay at Limassol, and the harbour at Paphos.

"There isn't much, further on. Just a small anchorage at Coral Bay, and I think I remember seeing the odd sheltered beach between here and Cape Arnauti. Otherwise, that's about it."

"You will go there, please."

"Sure." Mottram banked to avoid the area of the airport at Paphos, rejoining the coast as it turned north towards the western tip of the island.

They rounded Cape Drepanum with its tiny, offlying island

132

of Ayios Yeorgiou. Three miles ahead lay a peninsula which pushed out from the foothills to form the southern arm of Lara Bay. And there, on the other side of that low curve of land, nestled what was unmistakably a battleship-grey naval patrol vessel. They closed to within a mile. Makarov raised his binoculars. The boat looked deserted, but that was it, all right. He had found it! His hand reached for the microphone switch.

"Okay. We go back, please. There is no point in going further. No roads."

Mottram nodded. It made sense. A successful charter, even if it was the first for days. Humming contentedly, he turned to port away from the low sun and set course for Larnaca International.

The door to the companionway was closed and bolted. It was hot in the cabin, but tolerable with the small porthole open to a soft, onshore breeze. Even at its nearest point, in the prevailing westerly the Cessna was safely downwind, its engine almost inaudible, no louder than the murmur of a distant dragonfly. A light film of sweat oiled Sally's naked skin but after the strain of the last few days she slept on soundly.

Phivo was away all afternoon. By invitation, Sam raided the kitchen for a late lunch, buttering wedges of crusty cottage loaf to go with slices of salty, slightly squeaky *haloumi* cheese. A bottle of Olympus claret complemented his nostalgic feast – an inexpensive, local wine not often seen outside Cyprus but a rival for any European *vin de table*. After a surfeit of fresh air, exercise and lunch he slept on the sofa until disturbed by a door being slammed and a torrent of Greek from the entrance lobby.

Sam glanced at his watch. Five o'clock. As he levered himself upright Phivo entered the drawing-room, followed by a man whose face was vaguely familiar.

"This is Stavros." Phivo gestured towards the sofa. "Sam Verle."

He stood up and they shook hands. Stavros was much younger than Phivo, perhaps in his late twenties or early thirties, slim-built and wiry. Sinews and tight balls of muscle were clearly visible under his olive skin. It was not the build of

133

a sedentary man. Stavros's large, almost thyrotoxic, brown eyes could have been considered effeminate, but from that gaunt face Sam recognised the stare of one of nature's predators.

"Colonel." Just the one word. Confident, not ingratiating, and he knew of Sam's background.

"Stavros is my procurement executive."

It was a description consistent with the local habit of embellishment. Sam took it to mean that Stavros was in charge of gun running. They sat down.

"What you ask," began Stavros in heavily accented English, "is difficult to get quick in Cyprus."

He pronounced it 'sigheye . . . prus', the middle syllable stretched disproportionately, so he was a native islander. His shoulders lifted, hands turned over, like an Arab bazaar trader.

"The guns is not problem. Radios, okay. Plastic, maybe. Mortars, anti tank rockets, gas canisters, I have to find." He held up his fingers. "Two, maybe three days. By ship, or you can collect. Syria or Lebanon. I can arrange, if you can wait."

"The days are long gone," said Phivo, "when I used to have that sort of thing available immediately. Stavros knows his job. If he says it will take two or three days to get the stuff on to the island, that's gospel. We can telegraph now but even if you collect from a foreign port, by the time it's loaded, taken to the docks . . ."

"All right," broke in Sam, "I'm convinced."

It was his turn to stand and stare out to sea. If they got ashore successfully, Samandag's men would take cover in the old, stone buildings. There had to be some means of neutralising the Russians before they could recover their balance. Once the assault lost momentum, and the small attacking force were pinned down, they would soon run low on ammunition and be vulnerable to a counter attack. Tear gas and anti-tank missiles gave them belt and braces, with the mortars for counter-battery fire. Without all three it wasn't impossible but he would need more men and it would be a bloody exercise.

Shit! His fingers clenched in frustration; so near, and yet a million miles away.

"Sam." It was Phivo, at his shoulder. "It is possible to get what you need sooner. It's on Cyprus, but not within my gift."

A nasty suspicion began to form in his mind. "Not from my own . . . ?"

"My friend." Phivo smiled, "Forgive me, but that was a predictable reaction. No, if I wanted to steal arms your British bases are the last places I would consider."

His voice grew more serious, even persuasive. "There are many other foreign troops on our small island, not all of them as security-minded as you British . . ." He broke off, leaving the idea hanging.

"Go on," Sam said abruptly.

Phivo turned towards Stavros.

"Three places," began the younger man. "United Nations – not good. Many British troops, so too dangerous. Next, units from Greek National Guard. Maybe, but we are not happy to attack Greeks. Besides, they will complain to our government. Big investigation, and we still have to live here after you are gone. But the Turks, they have what you need. Is possible." The corners of his mouth edged into a thin smile. "And against Turks, we do not mind helping you."

"You mean I have to lead a bunch of cut throats in a raid across a federal border," Sam interjected, making no effort to hide his exasperation.

Phivo saw Stavros's neck redden with anger. Tempers were about to flare.

"Enough," he snapped, more to his employee than to Sam. "We can cross into the North," he explained more quietly. "That's not the problem."

With the situation smoothed over, he shrugged his shoulders fatalistically.

"Believe me, my friend, if I had what you want, you would receive it. But this is the only answer. The Turks are Moslem. If you need those weapons quickly then, to adapt your English saying, this time the mountain will have to go to Mahomet."

The four-wheel-drive Datsun Patrol swayed, lurched and bounced along a rutted track. Seated beside Phivo, Sam glanced in the mirror at the two in the back. Stavros and his cousin sat impassively, apparently unconcerned by a sheer drop of several hundred feet only inches from the offside wheels.

From Limassol progress had been quick at first, but as they left the coastal plain the road grew narrower, the hills steeper. At times they ground along in second gear, bonnet pointing to the sky, air cooling progressively as the big diesel pulled them from a temperature of around a hundred degrees at sea level to a noticeable chill and freshness at four thousand feet.

They left the winding, metalled road for a forest track where the scent of earth and pine reminded Sam of Bavaria. All the time they were heading north, navigating across country on centuries-old paths now widened for the occasional forestry commission vehicle.

Several times Phivo stopped to confer with Stavros, or to consult a map on to which uncharted tracks had been superimposed. Throughout their journey the other young Greek, almost a carbon copy of Stavros – to whom he undoubtedly owed his position – remained silent. Taking advantage of his cousin's success, he would accept patronage under the nepotism which riddled Cypriot business and public institutions. Even Phivo, Sam recalled, had been known to take advantage of the wider family circle which binds all Cypriots, asking some distant relative in a useful government position to free an inconvenient, bureaucratic log-jam, or to oil financial wheels.

Phivo stopped the Datsun, jumped down and walked along the track. Forest shade enhanced the gloom of approaching nightfall. He halted, looked carefully to one side, then ran back to the vehicle.

They turned off into what appeared to be inpenetrable foliage. It parted, to reveal an even narrower pathway flanked by vegetation which made it look impassable even to a small car, but Sam noticed that the branches divided easily enough, and just as smoothly swung back again. Linking numerous deep pot-holes were two distinct ruts separated by a low hump. The vehicle path had been carefully planted on either side with frond-like bushes, giving it the appearance of a goat track or at best a disused and now thoroughly overgrown forestry commission by-way.

It was almost dark. They were climbing again, without lights. Phivo appeared to know the route but, as he pointed out, it was hardly necessary to steer. The wheels were almost trapped by parallel grooves. Suddenly it grew lighter. They were in a small clearing.

Phivo invited the passengers to step down, then reversed off the track and deep into undergrowth. He had to fight his way out but from a few feet away, or from the air, the Datsun would be invisible. Sam could smell woodsmoke, and hear the bells of sheep or goats. Trees would deaden sound, so the source couldn't be too far away.

From the other side of the clearing they climbed a gently sloping path which had definitely not been used by vehicles. For the last fifty feet it narrowed to a single-file passage through an otherwise solid barrier of thorn cactus and brambles growing chest high between trees. Finally they emerged on to the edge of a tiny village.

There were no more than forty dwellings built around a central rectangle of open ground. On one side was a café, paraffin lamps suspended from a verandah, the door open, groups of men seated around tables inside.

Phivo beckoned Sam to follow. They crossed the dirt square and passed between two houses. Eighty yards on, the ground dropped away at a cliff edge. A narrow stairway zig-zagged down to what appeared to be a rubble-based road two hundred feet below.

Sam walked along the clifftop. The place was a natural fortress. To left and right the rock faulted vertically, leaving a great plateau of land standing proud from the face of an escarpment. The only approaches were up the stairway or, on a broader front, through the forest where a man-made barrier had grown as wild and impassable as primary jungle. In modern times the village would almost certainly have been an EOKA base, a refuge impossible for British patrols to have approached unseen.

They turned from the cliff face and walked back to the village. Behind each stone dwelling was an outer layer of construction, mostly large lean-to affairs attached to the rear of the main house. They were animal sheds, part-timber and part-stone. This was a sheep and goat farming community

137

where the way of life could scarcely have changed for hundreds of years. A smell of animals and their dung blended with the scent of pine logs, burning even at the height of summer to ward off the cold of the mountain.

They made their way to the café and found Stavros and his cousin seated at a table just inside the door. Phivo was received with much courtesy by an elderly proprietor who moved tables and chairs deftly to create a discreet space around the four men. Sam noticed that there were no women. This was the traditional coffee and wine shop, the exclusive preserve of the men. Most of them were elderly, many wearing traditional black, baggy trousers with a dhoti-like loop of cloth gathered up at the rear, their trouser legs tucked into black, highly-polished, knee-high leather boots.

Olives, taramasalata and fresh, crusty soda bread were set before them. Phivo asked for wine. Their arrival, albeit an event in such an isolated community, aroused only passing interest. Conversation gradually resumed its former level. In the corner a huge, open fire threw out sporadic bursts of sparks on to a stone floor, and on to any of the cats foolish enough to be lying too close.

They drank their wine, content for the moment in the drowsy, smoke-filled fug of the tavern. Finally, however, Phivo leant forward, his elbows on the table. The others drew in their chair.

"Costas."

The one word was an acknowledgement and an order to speak. The young man sipped hastily at his wine, glanced at Stavros and swallowed nervously. It was important to justify – and retain – his patronage. Never before had he, Costas Araouzos, been instructed personally by Mister Karakoulas to make such important arrangements, and at such short notice.

Costas hesitated. He had left their only map in the car. The proprietor was hovering discreetly out of earshot. Costas's shout brought him scurrying across the room to their table.

He might be diffident with us, thought Sam, but that doesn't stop him basking in a spot of reflected glory and lording it over the locals.

There was a torrent of rough dialect Greek. Several times

138

the landlord repeated a sound resembling the first syllable of 'never'. Sam recognised the Greek word for 'yes', sounding confusingly like a negative. He caught Phivo's eye and each registered the other's distaste for Costas's demeanour. The young man had yet to come to terms gracefully with his transition from peasant poverty to relative power.

The proprietor returned with a grubby rectangle of folded paper. Phivo made a point of thanking him whilst Costas opened it out. It wasn't exactly the product of an Ordnance Survey, or even a petrol company road map, but an approximate sketch plan torn from some tourist guide book.

"We are here." A nicotine-stained finger covered an area of about five square miles.

"It is twenty minutes' drive to the border. We shall leave at three o'clock."

After the briefing they were served a supper of barbecued pork chops with salad and chips. The pork was unlike anything available in England. Sam's chop hung generously over the side of his plate. The pig had been fed on the left-overs of wine pressing, a diet which produced not only an enormous animal but meat intensely succulent – virtually marinated on the trotter. The salad was the traditional affair of shredded cabbage with tomato, grated fetta cheese and black olives. But for the chipped potatoes, which added an incongruously modern touch, it was a meal which might have been served to the villagers' ancestors.

Conversation was desultory, and rarely strayed from their plans for the morning. They finished two more bottles of Arsinoë, a rather mediocre dry white wine much inferior to hock, and which Sam found palatable only after the first few glasses. It was barely ten o'clock, but men who would be up before sunrise were already drifting from the café. Phivo pushed back his chair.

"It is time for us to retire. My friend," he turned towards Sam, "Costas will show you to your accommodation. I trust you will have a restful night." Sam detected the flicker of a grin on his guide's face. "I have instructed Costas to make sure that you are called in the morning."

Outside the café, Phivo and Stavros set off across the square.

139

Costas made a sign for Sam to follow him then walked along one side to the end building, a single-storey stone structure with a tiled roof sloping up towards the rear wall. Costas knocked with his fist against a planked door. Neither waiting for a reply nor wishing Sam good night, he set off back towards the café.

Framed in a crack of light was the outline of a woman, her features in shadow from the dull, yellow light of a hurricane lamp hanging from a crossbeam inside the house.

"Please, come in."

Sam was assaulted by a gush of heat and odour. In a fireplace on the far side of what appeared to be the only room, burning logs surmounted a hill of white ash. Straight in front of him, right of the chimney breast, was a divided door. Through the upper half residual light illuminated part of what appeared to be a small barn, built as a lean-to against the rear of the tiny dwelling. From a depth of darkness emanated the sounds, and the smell, of animals.

"My name is Andoula. Please . . ." She pointed to one of two wickerwork armchairs. After nearly two hours in the café Sam would have preferred to stand, but didn't want to appear discourteous. As he sat down, he looked around. There was a small sideboard, a table not more than a yard square and two dining chairs, all made from wood long since scrubbed white. The only other item of furniture on a bare flagstoned floor was a three-quarter-sized bed, in the corner diagonally opposite the door to the barn.

"You would like something to drink?"

A statement more than a question. From the sideboard she produced a bottle of Commanderia, its name a legacy from the Grand Commanderie of the Order of Knight Hospitallers, fifteenth-century inhabitants of Kolossi Castle, near modern Limassol, where vineyards still produced the sweet red dessert wine.

She poured two glasses, handed one to Sam and settled into the other chair on the opposite side of the fireplace. Her arm swung up, and back, to close the top half of the barn door.

In many Cypriot familes women wore black traditional dress almost continuously, because within the greater family community no sooner had one period of mourning elapsed

140

but another began. Andoula, however, was dressed in a one-piece dark green flying suit. It was difficult to be sure, but Sam would have placed her in her mid- to late-twenties. Her pale-olive skin, slightly hooked nose and closely curled black hair hinted at a mixture of Greek and Moorish ancestry. Like Phivo she, too, was tall by Cypriot standards, perhaps five feet seven, and unlike most of her countrywomen Andoula appeared to be keeping her figure. Twisting to locate the door, her right breast was contoured through the thin cotton fabric. Catching his appraisal, she smiled to reveal small, even teeth and shook her head slightly so that her large gold hoop earrings caught the light.

"You live here?" Sam asked, not entirely by way of polite conversation. He was curious. People who worked in the cities but returned to their village by night had to cope with a clash of cultures, but this girl didn't give the impression of being part of a migrating rural generation. Besides, had she been from the village, it was inconceivable that they would have been left alone together.

Another shake of the head, this time more vigorous.

"Limassol. I work for Phivo. My mother was his sister."

"Was?" invited Sam.

"They were killed in the invasion of 'seventy-four – my parents, I mean. We lived in the North. I managed to reach the South. Phivo paid for my education, first at the English School in Limassol, then in the United Kingdom so that I could take a business studies degree. Now I work for him." She laughed. "He knows he can trust me."

The story explained her somewhat cosmopolitan appearance. "And this place?" asked Sam,.

She twisted the glass by its stem, holding it up to study a refracted glow from the hurricane lamp through the red-tinged bowl.

"It's mine. A sort of occasional retreat. It used to belong to my mother's family – part of her bride price. I come here only at weekends, or when Phivo wants to use the village. He owns most of it."

She tucked her legs up on to the chair. "One of the local men looks after my animals."

It was an unusual situation for a young Cypriot woman.

141

"And the family haven't tried to marry you off?" Sam conjectured.

"Who to?" Andoula asked bluntly. "Phivo bought me my freedom," she went on, "and now he's getting value for money. And in any case, what else is there for me on the island? Marriage to a rich old man, or some young peasant who could never accept my way of life? Or perhaps one of your so-called eligible young British officers who believes that any modern Cypriot girl is bound to be an easy lay?"

She raised her eyes to look at him directly. "You know perfectly well they hardly ever marry a local girl, and even then her family have to be rich enough to make up for the disadvantage of a Cypriot wife in the officers' mess."

She spoke factually rather than with discernible bitterness.

"Well, I'm rich enough but from what I've seen, most of your young officers are bankrupt: either in money, or in intelligence, or both."

Sam was taken aback for a moment, unsure quite how to respond. Andoula took his silence for disagreement.

"Come on," she chided, "you know the scene. Regimental cocktail party, silver on display, uniformed waiters holding trays of brandy sours whilst the band beats a retreat outside."

Her forefinger extended accusingly from the glass. "Apart from the Mediterranean background, it's a setting from the last days of the Raj, right down to the just-too-loud remark in some slurred, minor public school accent. 'Touch of the tar brush there, old man,' " she mimicked, " 'but her uncle is Phivo Karakoulas. He's loaded, so get in there. Look at her! She'll go like a diesel-driven doughnut.' "

It was a cutting imitation. Sam winced.

"I'm sorry," she said, "it's hardly your fault." She stood up and lifted the bottle of Commanderia by its neck, then hesitated.

"The trouble is, whether I'm with your people or mine, returning to Cyprus after living in London is like stepping back fifty years."

She walked over to his chair and topped up their glasses.

"What really gets to me is being denied a normal, uncomplicated social life. Sometimes I feel more in tune with you British, but in all honesty your young officers are a pretty

142

mediocre bunch. Yet if I let myself get involved with a local, even a modern version, there would inevitably be some forfeit of liberty. They're incapable of thinking in any other way."

She sat down again and stared, brooding, into her glass. 'She's trapped,' thought Sam, 'and will remain so for as long as she stays on the island.'

"We have an early start," he reminded her gently. "Where would you like me to sleep?"

"You can have that one." She lowered her head towards the bed in the corner. "I'll sleep out there. It's warm enough, by the back of the chimney breast."

It wasn't what he had expected. "Let me sleep in the barn," he protested. "I can't deprive you . . ."

"It's all right," she broke in, "there's a camp bed. Besides, I'm used to the animals, and Phivo said it was important for you to rest."

Sam looked at his watch. Eleven o'clock. They would be up again in four hours.

She lit another hurricane lamp. "Take this, there's a sink out in the barn, and a jerrican full of water. I wouldn't recommend the loo – if I were you, I'd find a tree."

Sam had to be content with a cold-water wash and a begged squeeze of toothpaste applied with his finger. At least he felt fresher. She stood by the camp bed, waiting for him to leave.

In deference to the luxury of clean bed linen – presumably brought from Limassol – Sam undressed. Having lifted the glass he turned down the wick until a blue flame popped from side to side, blew gently to extinguish it then set the hot lamp down on the stone floor.

It was only half-dark, the glowing remains of the fire a neon moon set low in the far wall. Despite the food and wine, Sam was wide awake. He recognised the symptoms. What they intended to do wasn't particularly dangerous – though all things were relative – but adrenalin was already fuelling his imagination. He knew from experience that it would take two hours of twisting and turning before he dropped eventually into a shallow, troubled sleep. In the morning he would feel bloody awful. The cycle could go on for days, until the body surrendered to exhaustion.

143

The room was noticeably colder. After half an hour he got up. If he had to lie awake, he might as well make up the fire from the basket of logs near the hearth. He was settling back beneath the bedclothes when the barn door latch clicked.

"You couldn't sleep either." Andoula emerged, wrapped in a fluffy ankle-length dressing gown which looked to have been woven locally from pure wool. Flames flickering around new logs brightened the gloom.

"Shall we have some more wine?"

He ought to have said no, but if it bought an extra half-hour of sleep it was worth the price of a mild hangover. Besides, in the cold morning air any slight headache would disappear before they reached the border.

She sat on the edge of his bed.

"I owe you an apology for what I said earlier. It wasn't very polite."

He leant half-upright on one elbow, struggling not to spill Commanderia from his brimful glass.

"Don't worry. I can't say I blame you. It must be difficult." Sam hesitated then continued, "Have you ever thought that perhaps you don't belong here – at least, not for a while?"

There was no response.

"It's none of my business," he began again after a few seconds, "but couldn't you transfer to Europe?"

Andoula sipped at her wine. "Five years," she said abstractedly, "that was the bargain. My degree cost him the best part of thirty thousand, what with air fares, tuition fees and three years' living expenses. He's still very generous, I get a good salary, but he can buy expertise any time. What he needs from me is loyalty."

She looked at Sam. "You're not a fool. You know what kind of business we're in. I might not like it, but a girl has to survive." She shrugged her shoulders. "It's a fair exchange," she said more lightly, "and in any case, it's four years down and only one to go."

"And then what?" asked Sam.

"Phivo knows I want to go back to Europe. By then his eldest son will be ready to take over. With my qualifications and Middle East experience, I should have something to offer a European company."

144

They sat in silence for a few minutes, watching the flames.

"What about you?" she asked eventually.

"This is a temporary aberration," Sam replied. "I retired early. There are no dependants, so I was going sailing. I don't know how much Phivo has told you, but I had to leave my boat in Turkey. I intend to pick up the threads again as soon as this is over."

She turned towards him. The movement opened the neck of her dressing gown. He could see the upper half of a light coffee-coloured breast. She made no move to pull the edges together.

"Phivo told me about your wife and child – I'm sorry. It really was inexcusable of me to complain about the British."

Sam shook his head.

"I don't disbelieve you for one moment, so there's no point in being offended."

"By way of changing the subject, aren't you lonely?" she asked curiously. "Sailing around the Mediterranean on your own?"

He shook his head again and grunted a denial. "The loneliness came in the first few months, after the crash. You get used to it."

He leant over the side of the bed to put his empty glass on the floor. She stood up to make room.

Even afterwards, she wasn't sure to what extent it was a spontaneous decision. Andoula had already decided that he was not unattractive, although his features were regular rather than in any way handsome. She had noticed his slimness and the hardness of his body, unusual in a European of his age. She suspected that he was essentially a kind person and she was sorry about his family, without in any sense being motivated by pity. He was from the other world, the one where she had tasted freedom. Perhaps each had something to offer. As he settled back from depositing the glass she untied the knot at her waist, letting the garment hang loose and open.

"It's better than a sleeping pill," she said softly, moving forward to rest her right hand on his shoulder. Fingertips traced a line down the centre of his chest. After a few seconds'

145

hesitation his right hand reached slowly beneath the robe to her hip.

She moved closer. His hand lifted to her breast. Each pursued a progressive exploration, almost sure but still reluctant to abandon all protection against the humiliation of rejection. Her fingernails reversed lightly over his stomach till the back of her hand brushed the head of his penis.

Confident, now, she discarded the robe and lay alongside him. Afterwards, there was only a series of blurred recollections, vignettes of an anxious, urgent coupling, essentially physical, almost devoid of emotion. His hands moved as if they sought to cover her entire body; at her side, on her back, exploring her buttocks. She was kneeling, catching her breath as she lowered herself on to him. They surrendered to the urgency of two almost unrelated ecstasies; two ritual, rhythmic cadenzas which the gods, in a moment of indulgence, resolved into a synchronous climax.

Chapter 9

Encased in a fibreglass fuselage shell which accentuated the cold of a desert night, Mikhail Artamonov shivered, huddled deeper into his seat and cinched his lap strap a centimetre tighter. A Soviet technician – one of several thousand in Libya – held the wings level by the starboard tip. Apart from a few men around the glider and its tug, the airfield, built and operated exclusively by the Soviet Union, was deserted.

His brain rattled automatically through the mnemonic: C.B., S.I.F.T., C.B..

Controls. Full and free movement. His hands and feet tested column and pedals.

Ballast. Already calculated precisely. They had taken out the dual controls so that behind him Lieutenant Yuri Utkin could accommodate between his knees a kit-bag shaped package containing weapons and equipment.

Straps. His own were tight. He called to Utkin and collected a frozen affirmative grunt through the headphones.

Instruments. Checked in the hangar. Artamonov reset his altimeter.

Flaps. Not fitted.

Trim. Elevator trim pushed well forward for take-off. Once they were airborne he would adjust it to ease forward pressure from the control column.

Canopy. Closed and locked.

Brakes. His left hand pulled back a lever. Rectangular airbrake plates protruded from above and below the wings, retracting as he released with the spring.

Static crackled in his headset. 'Come on, come on,' he

urged mentally. What the hell was the tug pilot waiting for?

"Tower, Bravo Golf ready for take-off."

About bloody time.

"Bravo Golf, clear to take off. Wind light and variable."

"Bravo Golf."

In the tower a fixed red light changed to green. Artamonov waved a white, doeskin-gloved hand at the tip man. Alongside him someone relayed the signal forwards, swinging a light from side to side in an arc describing the base of a circle. A third airman, well in front of the tug, repeated to the pilot Artamonov's instruction for 'up slack'.

The rope tightened until the glider nudged forward on her single, half-protruding belly wheel. Another wave. The man raised his light, still from side to side but above his head, and faster. Even through his headphones Artamonov heard the rising roar of the tug's twin engines.

It was a gradual acceleration. The tip man walked, then trotted. Artamonov's peripheral vision caught the exact moment when he leg go. A bit fucking soon! The fat slob must have knackered himself on the taxi round the peri-track. Shit, the wing was dropping. It wasn't generating enough lift. His left hand settled on to the cable release knob. If that wing touched, he would have to pull off. Heavily loaded, she would ground-loop in a spar-breaking circle.

No use applying aileron to raise a wing already stalled . . . Savagely, he booted on full left rudder. Despite the tug, the glider began a turn to port. Swinging round on the outside of a circle the starboard wing accelerated, increased airflow generating additional lift. Artamonov's eyes oscillated between tug and wing-tip, now inches higher.

They were running out of scope, as far to one side as the rope would allow. He was forced to swing back again, reversing the effect, but in those few precious seconds the tug had also accelerated. Although barely a foot above the ground, the wingtip was holding its own. Slowly, it came up. That prick of a ground crew! Artamonov forced himself to concentrate on settling the glider into position.

Thirty-three knots. Rubber eased from tarmac and the glider was airborne. Artamonov pushed the stick forwards, holding her low and level. If he allowed the glider to climb prematurely she would lift the tail of their tug, which had yet to achieve flying speed. The tug pilot would not be grateful for a forward pitchpole on to his propellors.

She was off. Artamonov brought the glider up a fraction, clear of the towing aircraft's turbulence. Below them converging lines of white lights fell away. As they crossed a right-angled warning line of reds, the airfield plunged into darkness.

"Bravo Golf, climbing straight ahead to clear the circuit."

"Bravo Golf. Call rejoining."

"Bravo Golf."

Reacting to signals from Samandag, and to Nicosia's excellent response to his cipher, the Moscow controller of Operation Red Castle had activated two of the Spetsnaz pre-positioned in Libya as a back-up to Samandag's team.

Both Utkin and Artamonov were members of the Spetsnaz – or Special Forces – of the Soviet Military Intelligence, the GRU. Smaller than the KGB, to which Makarov belonged, but in no way subordinate to it, their rival GRU comprised five departments – reconnaissance, intelligence, information processing, radio interception and the elite Spetsnaz.

Inserted behind enemy lines during a period of tension, Spetsnaz were tasked to assassinate enemy political and military leaders, to seek out enemy nuclear facilities – either to be destroyed by the patrol or designated as targets for air and missile strikes, to identify and neutralise major NATO headquarters, and to attack high-value targets such as airfields, defence radars or naval bases.

In peace they acquired fluency in a western language. In war, as Spetsnaz *reydoviki*, or raiders, Artamonov and Utkin would wear British uniform, gaining access to NATO installations by the capture and impersonation of western personnel. *Reydoviki* knew intimately the country to which they were targeted, generally as a result of covert visits but sometimes even at the invitation of their intended victims, for by virtue of their rigorous selection system many Spetsnaz were also international sportsmen or women. It was impossible for western agencies to monitor them closely, not least because of their peacetime tactic of wearing the same uniform as members of the nearest, ordinary military unit in their area.

149

Spetsnaz ethos combined the professionalism of Special Forces with the dedication of Hitler's SS. Their loyalty was absolute. Like all Spetsnaz, on recruitment Artamonov and Utkin had signed a version of the Official Secrets Act. To break it was to commit espionage, for which the penalty was death. As their leaders intended, intense, incestuous elitism displaced ordinary human values. And to Artamonov and Utkin their orders were succinct and clear.

Artamonov's hands and feet moved automatically, holding the glider on station as they droned above desert towards the coast. His thoughts rarely strayed from Operation Red Castle. It was an appropriate title, drawn from a translation of the island's name.

At half-past nine Tobruk passed beneath their port wing. Now they were just under five hundred miles, or six and a half hours, from the release point.

They followed the Antonov Pchelka – unkindly code-named 'Clod' by NATO, although her name meant 'little bee' – down to two thousand feet. In a way, reflected Artamonov, the pilot and navigator of the Pchelka were taking the greater risk. Even with her interior stripped to accommodate additional fuel tanks, and the two three-hundred horsepower, nine-cylinder Ivchenko radial engines set for an economical seventy-five knots, the An-14 had barely the range to return to Libya. The slightest headwind and she would be forced to ditch, relying on a rescue service of Soviet fast patrol boats. That such a risk should be accepted gave a sobering indication of the importance placed upon their mission by Moscow.

Artamonov squirmed in discomfort. Despite a last-minute, prophylactic visit to the lavatory, the cold was alerting his bladder and he was suffering acutely from a numb backside. He suspected that Utkin was dozing. Artamonov would have given a week's pay to hand over control, loosen his straps and wriggle around in the narrow fuselage.

The tug pilot flicked his transmit switch twice. No messages, except in emergency, but two loud clicks warned Artamonov that it was time for the next descent. They planned to fly progressively lower, underneath Cyprus radar for as long as possible, relying on the accuracy of the tug's radio altimeter to fix their height above the sea. When they were back into straight and level flight, Artamonov re-set his own barometric altimeter to read one thousand feet. Half and hour later he corrected it on to five hundred. They could only hope that air pressure wouldn't change significantly once they were on their own.

Inside the Pchelka's heated cockpit the navigator scanned his electronics. From now on, the battle was his. He would decide upon tactics and pass orders to the pilot. Electronic counter measures, or ECM, were his speciality. Ironically, in the next few hours he faced the very real possibility of death by drowning, which he considered an unfortunate consequence of the recognition which had secured his selection for this mission.

An orange light flickered, went out for a few seconds, then returned, the pulses of darkness increasingly shorter and less frequent. They were being scanned, at extreme range, by Cyprus radar.

The two aircraft ought to be safe for a few seconds. Having barely crossed the radar's horizon, the tiny Pchelka would probably be disguised within a periphery of surface clutter. Even if the radar were switched to Moving Target Indicator – or MTI – mode, in which it would be programmed to record only objects moving at or above a specific velocity, their Pchelka, with its glider in shadow behind, presented only a weak radar profile. Much depended upon the alertness of an anonymous operator at the other end. The navigator smiled, and leant forwards. In ECM warfare the weapons were chaff, decoy flares and wave energy. He was a general, about to deploy his electromagnetic forces.

"Take her right down," he instructed the pilot.

Artamonov's ears received a familiar warning. He eased the stick forward to follow the tug. At fifty feet, flying operationally at well below what a civilian pilot would consider a safe altitude, they were again underneath the radar's horizon, but not for much longer. Eventually they would have to climb whilst the navigator worked to place them, undetected, at the head of a final glidepath.

For planning purposes Artamonov had insisted that all

151

calculations be based on a glide ratio of twenty-five to one, at which the glider achieved through still air a forward distance of the release height multiplied by twenty-five. If he pulled off at a mile high, he could expect to go for twenty-five miles. In practice, despite the additional weight of the weapons pack, he could probably exceed this ratio, perhaps to a glide angle of nearer thirty to one. As an added bonus, they would realease upwind in the prevailing westerly.

But there wouldn't be a mile of height to carry them for twenty-five miles. Artamonov had agreed to a release height of two thousand feet, after which, if they encountered only still air, the glider would be at sea level in just under nine and a half miles.

The orange light blinked again and shone steadily. External antennae in a small radome underneath the Pchelka's nose accepted the signal and relayed it to an on-board computer. As an opening gambit the navigator selected basic noise jamming, the transmission of a signal which, if nothing else, would convert a precise echo to a radial strobe on the operator's display. At best, if noise jamming entered the radar by its antenna side lobes, the entire picture could be obliterated.

"Take her up. We'll look for an inversion layer."

"Roger."

Two clicks warned Artamonov and the Pchelka began to climb.

The initiative lay with the radar operator. If thoroughly alert, he might have noticed deformed activity on the edge of his screen. More probably, however, the effects of subtle jamming at extreme range would disguise the presence of a light aircraft, particularly with the head-on Pchelka offering her smallest radar signature. Provided there were echoes blasting back from a few fast jets or commercial airliners . . .

They were at fifteen hundred feet and climbing when his instruments revealed that the operator had spotted them, or at least had observed an ill-defined signal which he was attempting to identify. The level of radar energy was increasing in an attempt to 'burn through' effects which, at this stage, the Cyprus operator might still be ascribing to natural phenomena.

The navigator sucked in his teeth, considering. He could change the jamming technique, but that would scream 'ECM' at an experienced man.

"Height?"

"Two thousand."

"Any sign of that inversion?"

"Could be any second."

The navigator slowly increased jammer output to match the attempted burnthrough. The operator would be suspicious but hopefully, lacking confirmation, he would bide his time – reluctant to appear foolish by raising a false alarm.

The pilot studied the lights of a small cargo vessel about a mile away. They were definitely murkier.

"Coming in now."

"Thanks."

The navigator grunted with satisfaction. It had been a worthwhile gamble. Having approached below the radar horizon for as long as possible, he had sought to jam their electromagnetic signature whilst looking for a temperature inversion, a lid of cold air holding down rising warmer air from below. Inversions at around two thousand feet were a regular feature of the Mediterranean, particularly in summer. For once their meteorology brief had been right.

He glanced at the altimeter. Two thousand two hundred. Free of the inversion's clouding effect, stars shone with ice-cold clarity.

"Hold two one hundred. That seems to be about the middle."

"Two one hundred." The nose dipped gently.

It was impossible to be sure of the effects of an inversion layer. Sometimes radar waves would literally bounce off; occasionally they could be ducted along the interface, giving greatly extended ranges, but range extension in one direction often resulted in a decrease in range – or even a 'radio hole' – in another. He was gambling on the fact that for a radar operator the consequences of an inversion layer were more often bad rather than good. His instruments told him that the radar beam was still there, but diffused and weakened. Slowly he reduced power on the jammer. With every passing minute their Pchelka was over a mile nearer her destination.

No sooner had the pilot's 'three miles to run' passed through his headphones when the needle oscillated violently. They were approaching the edge of the inversion layer. Any second now and they would step, naked, on to a spotlighted, electromagnetic stage.

Signal reading increasing rapidly ... He needed a few seconds to think, buying them by matching the growing beam strength with increased jammer output. They were almost home and dry. He smiled at the inappropriate expression but they were nearly close enough to give the glider an unmolested run in. If he could sustain a covert approach, Artamonov and Utkin would be spared the attention of any well-meaning but inconvenient search and rescue party.

It was the end of a night, when human reactions were at their lowest ebb. In his air-conditioned radar room the operator missed the first few sweeps but saw it eventually, a fuzzy, enlarged cloud which was impossible to categorise. It might perhaps be an atmospheric condition associated with the inversion layer. Its range was indeterminate but the bearing was the same as that earlier burst of energy which had lifted, intensified, and then mysteriously died away.

George Iocovou reached forward. He would try again to burn through the interference. If that failed, he would change frequency. He was curious rather than suspicious, but if frequency agility failed to produce any additional information, he would have to risk displeasure by interrupting the unofficial rest of his watch supervisor.

In the Pchelka, he was ready. Feline microchips awaited their wave-energy mouse. Instruments signalled its arrival.

Through the radome it passed to be devoured, dissected and analysed by a predatory computer. A digital read out, then a green light. He flicked off the noise screen and simultaneously switched in a repeater jammer. Suddenly the Pchelka was transmitting actively, advertising her presence with a beam from an electromagnetic lighthouse. The navigator concentrated furiously on his computer, directing transmission like a maestro wielding his baton at an airwave

154

orchestra. His targeted Pchelka was receiving the radar signal but delaying it, retransmitting at a slightly later time. Delaying the retransmission would produce a false position, somewhere higher and astern of where they actually were, on the operator's screen.

Iocovou blinked. It was as if a curtain had been pulled aside. There! A signal, clear as crystal, with what appeared to be some sort of echo along the inversion line – where the interference had been.

They were at the release point. A series of rapid clicks confirmed to Artamonov what he had already determined by dead reckoning. The pilot of the Pchelka rocked his wings. It was the signal to pull off.

Artamonov tugged the yellow knob, then once again for safety, catching a glimpse of the metal ring as it snaked forward behind the tug in a gentle, diving turn to the right. He pulled up to port, climbing to convert residual velocity into height. Two thousand two fifty. Not bad. Artamonov set course for the island and concentrated on extracting maximum performance from his glider.

The pilot opened both throttles, sacrificing precious fuel to claw up along a path from the Pchelka's true position to that being given out by the repeater jammer. In the shadow of so much electromagnetic intensity the signature from a slim, head-on, poorly reflecting fibreglass glider was too weak to be of consequence.

On the navigator's display two signals, one behind the other in a direct line from the ground antenna, were converging fast. As they centred he flicked off the jammer, rested back in his seat and exhaled slowly. He had given his electronic recital, and like any artist after a demanding, solo performance, he felt drained. But there was the contentment of knowing that it had been a controlled, virtuoso display.

The Pchelka was at Flight Level Six Zero, or six thousand feet, on Flight Path White Fifteen heading west from Cyprus. Bravo Golf was on course and on her filed flight plan. A night navigation training sortie had taken her to within twenty miles of Cyprus before the first leg home. She was, however, **one hour ahead of schedule, as a precaution against any** curiosity aroused by the flight plan of an aircraft claiming Libyan civil registration.

Iocovou was confused. The aircraft had appeared suddenly. But there had been a lot of interference. She was early, but now that she had turned away there appeared to be little point in waking his supervisor.

The pilot switched on his navigation lights and asked the navigator to pour their thermos of hot soup. As a member of the Soviet Air Army it gave him a peculiar feeling to fly in what was effectively western airspace. Or, more precisely, to fly in an aircraft whose electronic secrets were so precious that if necessary he would ditch without a mayday rather than take the risk that his Pchelka might be recovered by western hands. He studied the fuel gauges. There was a slight crosswind. It would be a close run thing, but with luck they would just about make it.

Artamonov's eyes returned repeatedly to the variometer recording their rate of sink as they followed the glide path. Out over the sea he wasn't expecting to find thermal bubbles of rising warm air in which he could circle to regain height. It would be enough to establish an accurate landfall before they hit the water.

Down to a thousand feet, but the island's profile was firm. In his calculations Artamonov had deliberately ignored the prevailing westerly, but with a benevolent tailwind they would arrive at the coast with height to spare.

A quarter of a mile from the island. Just under five hundred feet. Where the hell was that bay? It was difficult to see anything against the inky backdrop. He abandoned the search for a few seconds to plan the approach. Artamonov was prepared to ditch the glider and sort out their precise position at first light, but the bonus of an extra few hundred feet gave them an alternative.

On the nose a peak, silhouetted against the night sky, rose above them. He could make out another, maybe five hundred feet higher, at twenty degrees to starboard. There was no need to ask Utkin to shine his torch on the map. Ahead lay Vlambouros, to the right, Mount Lara. They would cross the coast two miles north of Lara Bay.

156

In the rear seat Utkin was not privy to his leader's thoughts. Ahead, he was conscious only of two shapes: the back of Artamonov's head and a rising outline of black landmass. So the Captain was going to cross the shoreline and look for lift. It was a risky enterprise, flying low over strange, unlighted territory at night, only too easy to misjudge height or distance and clip the ground or some hillside with a wingtip, but he knew from experience that Artamonov seemed to have almost nocturnal vision. And he was a bloody good pilot. He'd flown Mig fast-jets before joining the Spetsnaz, with his spare time devoted to gliding, a sport at which he still competed internationally.

Utkin forced himself to relax. If they were going to scratch around in the dark at low altitude, then he was probably as well off with Artamonov as with anyone else.

They crossed the beach at four hundred and fifty feet, clearing the cliffs by less than four hundred. Whatever the windspeed, it had been enough to stretch their glide path considerably.

Artamonov was looking for wave lift. A westerly airstream crossing the north-south coastline would be deflected upwards. The limit of this updraft would depend on the strength of the breeze, and how it reacted with cooler air flowing seaward at night. But with luck . . .

The variometer needle twitched, zeroing horizontally at nine o'clock. They were holding their height, upward movement of the airstream cancelling the glider's sink rate. From now on Artamonov would begrudge every second of distraction from that crucial instrument.

The beach was about to disappear behind the cliff. His eyes darted obliquely to white smudges of surf. Just the occasional line of foam, which promised only a low swell. Artamonov peered ahead, into the darkness. If it were going to come . . .

Zero. A half knot of sink, then back to zero again. A hint of turbulence buffeted the glider gently, as if the wind was mocking his anxiety.

A half . . . a knot of lift! He felt the surge under his port wing. If was over there, to the left. Artamonov moved stick and pedals simultaneously, centreing the control column and easing off most of the rudder as she settled into the required

157

angle of bank. He teased back the stick to hold up her nose. Clean, accurate flying was essential. A careless dive or any sloppy sideways-slipping turns would cancel immediately their precious height gain.

After one circuit Artamonov had identified the area of greatest lift. Next time round he adjusted the pattern to best advantage, flying a long oval parallel with the coastline.

It was hardly strong lift – occasionally two knots from a gust, mostly less. He worked hard, feeling the glider through his body and fingers, reacting to every nuance of wind and flicker of the needle. Reward came slowly, but eventually the clifftop was noticeably less distinct. He had scratched and clawed the glider to eight hundred feet. From that height they could glide for something over three and a half miles.

The variometer needle was horizontal and steady. They were soaring on the wave crest. Lift had decayed, and no amount of effort on his part would take them any higher.

He turned south across a valley, and for the first time had a chance to study the land carefully. A couple of miles away a low promontory jutted out to sea. Since crossing the coast he had been incommunicado, senses focussed to pinpoint concentration. Now he could share the triumph with Utkin.

"That's it. There she is – Lara Point."

"Any sign of the boat?"

Artamonov shook his head. "Probably anchored under the lee of the coast."

They flew on. Another cliff reached up from the beach. He followed it, taking advantage of a lift line to restore some height. Even so, as the glider hissed over the northern edge of Lara Bay they were less than four hundred feet above the low hills.

"She's there."

An outline of superstructure sat on the water. The patrol boat lay to her anchor, showing no lights. He banked steeply to avoid flying too close to their target and headed north-west, out to sea.

"I'm going to put her down."

There was no reply. Utkin knew precisely what to expect. Artamonov used the airbrakes to burn off excess height. They would ditch at the chosen position; one mile out on the hundred fathom line, in six hundred feet of water. He turned finals into wind.

They were sinking into a bottomless black cloud. It was impossible to identify the surface with sufficient accuracy for a 'round out', holding the glider a few inches off till she stalled into a perfect touchdown. A late guess and they would fly at speed into the sea, but if he rounded out too soon she would stall with excess height until the nose dropped into a vertical imitation of a high diver.

Yet again Artamonov told himself to resist at all costs any temptation to round out, and to concentrate instead on flying with the lowest possible rate of sink. His attention tracked around horizon, variometer and air speed indicator.

He braced himself for the landing. They must touch now, any second, but still she flew on. He glanced sideways. It was as if they were flying underwater.

A full twenty seconds after Artamonov ignored yet another instinctive urge to pull back on the stick, the glider's belly wheel cut through a wave crest. He checked back – not too much, or the tail would catch and slam the nose down – then they were level, sinking on to the sea at thirty-six knots.

Two more splashes. Each one bounced the glider over the next few crests like a skimming stone. Artamonov concentrated on holding the wings level.

She struck. The underside of her nose caught the face of a wave and she was down, surfing through the water, bumping hard, decelerating violently, pushing them viciously into their straps as she came off the plane and settled into a gentle swell. Neither of the wings had broken away. She was floating, waist deep. They were down.

Artamonov unbuckled himself, pulled back a catch and lifted off the hinged, perspex cockpit canopy. Utkin slipped his knife from a leg sheath and cut the cordage binding the package between his knees. It separated. For the moment he ignored the thinner bundle and concentrated on heaving a bulky, rubberised mass over the cockpit sill. With the painter secured he tugged on it sharply, hearing with relief the welcome hiss of high-pressure, compressed air.

Artamonov rolled over the sill and into the inflatable. Holding it against the glider he received their equipment

159

package and tied it to a thwart. They had been down for less than ninety seconds. Utkin reached to the floor for a six-inch diameter threaded plate. Seizing the raised spine he gave it several half turns before water pressure from below pushed it free. A thick, low fountain welled inside the cockpit.

They paddled a few yards away and watched. Fuselage and wing sections filled with water. Her tail lifted clear, following down vertically with an eerie, whistling noise as air escaped through small apertures in the stern.

She was gone. They were staring at an empty sea. If they had been forced to ditch in shallower water the glider's wavy, sandy-brown and green camouflage pattern would have made her difficult to pick out on the sea bed. At this depth, Artamonov doubted if she would ever be found. He shivered, at the same time noticing a paleness in the eastern sky.

Utkin extended a telescopic, alloy mast and pushed it through a cloth tube sewn into the sail's leading edge. Artamonov slipped a wooden dagger-board through the centre box, clipped a rubber paddle over the transom and sheeted in the sail. Their dinghy and a new dawn converged on the shore.

Chapter 10

Sam's wristwatch alarm sounded at two forty-five. He was alone, and had slept soundly. It was dark and much colder, the fire reduced to a faint glow of embers beneath a mountain of white ash. He lay there for a few seconds, gathering willpower, coiling a mental spring against the moment of abandoning comfort and warmth for the skin-tightening chill of early morning.

His clothes were on a fireside chair. Cold air and stone assaulted his body as he shuffled cautiously, arms outstretched, through the darkness. He located the log basket. Next to it, on the floor, he recalled seeing a few old newspapers. Several ash-scattering puffs teased a small flame from the embers. With a sheet of newspaper burning in the fireplace, he collected the hurricane lamp and applied a twisted taper.

Andoula appeared in the doorway as he finished dressing.

"There isn't time for coffee" she called, turning back towards the barn. "I'll get you some milk."

A metallic clanking noise – presumably the lid of a churn – and she returned with an earthenware mug. Thirsty from too much wine, but fortunately spared any more punitive after-effects, Sam accepted it gratefully. He thanked her for the milk, and for last evening. They were inadequate words, anodyne and urbane, but she smiled and squeezed his wrist gently as he buttoned up his sailing jacket. As Sam closed the heavy, wooden door his final glimpse was of her crouching figure, face half-turned towards him as she paused from re-building the fire.

Costas appeared by his side as he set off for the café. The other two were already there, stamping feet and flapping their arms against the cold. There was enough ambient moonlight to identify substance from shadow. On the ground were two boxes, each about fifteen, by eight, by nine inches deep, with a handle at either end. Ammunition. Around them, barrels resting on the lids to keep working parts clear of the dirt, was a ring of sub-machine guns. Alongside lay a slim, semi-circular basket from which protruded a miscellany of handles.

"We have to shift this lot between us," announced Phivo bluntly, "so let's go."

Sam picked up four weapons by their overhead carrying handle. Phivo hefted a brace of sub-machine guns in one hand and the tool basket in the other, leaving Stavros and Costas to manage the remaining four weapons and ammunition. In single file they set off across the plateau for the stone staircase.

"Mind where you put your feet, there's a lot of loose scrub about," cautioned Phivo as he led them into the descent. "I lost a good man over the edge in 'fifty-seven," he added gratuitously.

Sam concentrated on each step individually, particularly at the corners where the staircase reversed direction from a larger patch of stone twice the normal width but still only a yard wide and crumbling at the edges.

It seemed an interminable descent. When they were almost down to the road a cluster of tiny red dots emerged from beneath an overhang of rock twenty-five yards away. From time to time each dot errupted into a brief and irregular flare. As Phivo stepped on to the road one of them separated from the cluster and advanced towards him, arcing down to disappear as the cigarette butt was discarded and ground underfoot.

Also beneath the overhang were two Land-Rovers, parked nose to tail. Against white bodywork Sam could distinguish the wreath-pattern decals of UNFICYP, the United Nations Force In Cyprus.

"Any trouble?" queried Phivo as they walked past the rear vehicle. The man shook his head. "We lifted them from outside the Amathus Beach Hotel. Probably a couple of

162

officers having a dirty night out in Limassol. I doubt if the trucks will be missed for another three hours."

One of the men dropped the lead vehicle's tailboard and switched on an interior light. All six of them were wearing the lightweight, stone-coloured uniform and blue beret of the United Nations Force. The man pulled out a wicker basket.

"There's a selection of sizes. We earmarked these."

He passed a uniform to Phivo, Stavros and Costas. After inspecting Sam he rummaged back inside the basket.

"This might fit."

"I don't like my brother's wife's cousin," laughed Phivo as he struggled to push his feet through the trousers, "but it comes in handy when the fat little toad has the United Nations laundry contract."

The sleeves of Sam's jacket were a shade long, but otherwise the uniform fitted well enough. They distributed the weapons. Sam was impressed. Phivo had managed to lay hands on the United States consortium of Saco Defense Systems' latest NATO-calibre, nine millimetre sub-machine gun. Looking rather like an overgrown pistol, a butt-grip at the rear of the weapon and its magazine hanging down vertically further forward, a 683 model Saco was the latest in simple, low-cost, light machine guns. For accurate shooting the buttstock extended rearwards on a stalk and the carrying handle incorporated a simple tube-sight. With an unloaded weight of only three and a third kilos, but a fire rate of about six hundred and fifty rounds a minute from thirty-two-round magazines, the robust Saco was ideal for their purpose.

From the raffia tool basket Phivo produced two additional magazines for each weapon.

"We'll take five men in each Rover," he ordered as they thumbed in round after round. "Mr Verle and I will go in the lead vehicle, Stavros and Andreas will be in the front of the second." He spoke in English. All of them seemed to follow him without difficulty.

So the man who had advanced to meet them was called Andreas. He was older than the others, nearer to Phivo's age. His five subordinates, whose names Sam had yet to learn, seemed to be about the same age as Costas. They were a

163

mixed bunch – three Greek, two decidedly Arab-looking, perhaps ex-Palestinian or Lebanese forces. One of the Arabs wore a beard.

It had not been a race, but Sam was reassured when two of them finished loading before he did, which indicated a fair degree of familiarity with small-arms. He wondered what their collective experience might be of operating under fire. In this part of the world it wasn't a tactful question, but the Arabs had probably fired a weapon in anger whilst their European counterparts were still grappling with primary education.

The Greeks, too, were quiet, not chattering like recruits, which was another good sign. Well, Sam mused, he would known soon enough. Today, Phivo would lead. Thereafter, he would assume command but on Kastellorizon the odds would be about four to one. Less favourable, even, than at Port Stanley, and Samandag's professional force was likely to prove a tougher proposition than Argentine conscripts. But even they, he thought abstractly, had caused the transfer of too many names to a marble scroll on the regimental war memorial.

They drove the six and a half miles to the border in silence. Most of the journey was a hair-raising descent without lights through northern escarpments of the Troodos mountains, but for the last two miles they were on the southern edge of the Morphou plain. Fortunately the narrow back-roads were deserted.

When they reached a main, east-west highway Phivo followed it for a few yards before turning north again on to a baked-earth track leading into what appeared to be an orange or lemon plantation. The sky was lightening. Sam judged daybreak to be half an hour away.

A mile into the plantation the track narrowed to a rutted passageway shielded by a canopy of trees. A lighter patch about two hundred yards ahead marked the end of the tunnel. Halfway along, Phivo detailed two of the Greeks to remain with the vehicles and led off on foot. They emerged at the edge of a bare, uncultivated strip of land, perhaps twenty yards across. On the far side Sam could just make out what appeared to be a double row of six-foot high fencing.

164

They sprinted to the wire and knelt, breathing deeply, waiting for any reaction. After about thirty seconds Phivo turned to one of his men.

"Kyriakos!"

The Greek dropped his tool basket and knelt at the foot of a concrete post where two panels of diamond-pattern netting overlapped. The left-hand panel was wired to the post, but the one coming in from the right was secured only by a single strand of thicker, plastic-coated wire, interlaced vertically in line with the post through both layers.

Taking a pair of pliers he gripped the bottom of the single strand and twisted, twice, rolling a length of wire round the tool. With enhanced purchase he was able to overcome the friction pressure of the panels. As the upper end of the wire passed down through the mesh, the outer layer peeled away. The bearded Arab rolled it aside until the gap was wide enough for a Land-Rover.

"There are plenty of crossing places," commented Phivo quietly at Sam's side, "but we prepare the best ones so that they can be re-used. The far side's the same, but from the patrol track you can't see a thing."

They had breached the 'Green Line', a United Nations supervised boundary agreed between Greek and Turk at the end of the fighting in 'seventy-four. Just in front was the patrol track, a single carriageway strip of compacted ground bordered on either side by five yards of defoliated, sandy soil.

In the past Sam had driven along the track, but United Nations vehicle patrols made a point of not straying from the central strip. When the cease-fire had been established, both Greek and Turk had in places mined what might have proved only a temporary front line. United Nations forces had cleared the patrol track, but not necessarily the area on either side where outer limits of old minefields were often designated by fences such as that through which they were about to pass.

Stavros removed two thin metal rods from the tool basket. Each was about two feet long, a short wooden handle at one end, the other sharpened to a point. He offered choice of handles to Sam.

"You help," he invited, "or you want that I ask Greek man

165

to do it?" His features were in shadow, but Stavros's voice carried the challenge very clearly.

"We don't inspect our crossing points regularly," explained Phivo, as if seeking to soften the atmosphere without in any sense letting Sam off the hook.

"A year ago, from time to time, we were using a site in the west. One night, bang! Anti-personnel mine. A man lost his foot." Sam saw the outline of Phivo's shoulders lift and fall. "Might have been from the war – worked its ways to the surface – but if someone from the other side had been watching us, or maybe found where we had prepared the fence . . ." Phivo turned away towards the rolled-up wire.

"So we have to check," concluded Stavros.

It was a very unsubtle examination. 'So be it, and fuck you too, sunshine,' thought Sam. He took a probe.

They knelt, a wheelbase apart, on a line scored by the missing fence. Each man had to clear a path the width of his body, enough to accommodate a Land-Rover tyre with a few inches to spare. Sam lay down, stretching out backwards till only one wrist crossed the start line. Stavros, still kneeling, was about to begin, then thought better of it and adopted Sam's prone position. If either of them made a mistake, blast and fragments would be deflected up and outwards. At least, thought Sam as he made his first row of threading insertions, the Greek was sensible enough not to let his pride cloud his judgement. And equally obviously – he smiled to himself as he inched forward for the next line – nobody had given the Greeks a demonstration of the safest way to breach a minefield.

He wriggled on, row by row, as fast as he dared, reminding himself before every advance to keep his hands and feet inside the cleared lane, resisting any temptation to open the gap between probes.

Sam wasn't worried about vehicle mines – apart from being too big to miss, his weight would be insufficient to set one off. But vehicle mines were often sown in concert with anti-personnel mines, to deter clearance. Some types were designed to be lifted for thirty inches by a primary charge before the main explosion took a man's balls off. Most anti-personnel mines were intended to maim, rather than kill, a living casualty sapping the attacker's morale and resources far more than a corpse. If he missed an A.P. mine . . .

Fortunately the soft, sandy soil offered little resistance – which made it even more of a heart-stopper when the tip of his probe butted something solid.

"Lie down," he called to Stavros, "and cover your head."

Carefully he brushed away the sand, following the downward, diagonal path of his probe. He was expecting, even hoping, to be mocked by a piece of stone but four inches below the surface, eyeballing him as if with a malevolent mind of its own, lay a chunk of dark brown plastic.

Phivo had been wise, reflected Sam as he brushed away more sand to establish an outline, not to rely on just a quick sweep with a metal detector. The prognosis wasn't good. It was a very military-looking piece of dark brown plastic, bearing black letters and numerals. He couldn't make them out. He would have to lift it.

A rectangular shape, about two and a half inches by five. Time and the surrounding world had no meaning for Sam. His mind shut out the noise of insects, ignored the sensation of warm air brushing across the back of his neck. The lightening sky could have belonged to another planet. Sam concentrated exclusively on that small lump of plastic.

As he brushed away at the far end, something sharp sliced into his fingertip. He went back to it, blowing aside the last few grains of sand. Broken glass reflected the dull light, behind it was a short strip of copper – an electrical contact. Confidently Sam pushed his fingers under the plastic and lifted it clear. One last glance, then he raised himself on to an elbow, twisted, and tossed the object back at the others, watching with vindictive pleasure as they scattered.

"Only an old torch," he called with a false note of apology in his voice, returning to his task without waiting for their response. But in a suspected minefield he had identified an unknown object and removed it. The point wouldn't be lost.

Several more times they stopped, but only for large stones. Then they were running across the patrol track to probe again on the far side.

Stavros checked his back pocket for the pliers, climbed over the northern fence and began to pull out its vertical wire.

Phivo's timing was excellent. On either side they could make out nearby trees, but dawn had yet to light up the distance.

Two men walked along cleared paths, guiding the lead Rover. Using strips of soft wire one of the Greeks replaced the first fence and stayed on the far side. Short, wooden pegs were tapped into the ground at each end of the two paths before their tracks were obliterated with a branch. Feverishly, harried by advancing daylight, they repositioned the northern fence and ran into the plantation after the two vehicles.

Ten minutes and two villages later they met their first Turk – or more accurately, Turkish Cypriot – an old man, riding towards them on a donkey grossly overloaded with bulging nets of water melons. Old man and donkey squinted at the United Nations Land Rovers with supreme indifference.

Phivo couldn't resist pointing out to Sam the disparity. Bustling, almost frenetic industrial and tourist development in the South, the apparent indolence of an agrarian lifestyle in the North. Privately, Sam preferred the latter. Rank upon rank of hotels and villas had all but destroyed the character of the southern coastline, even if the development explosion had been an inevitable consequence of losing the North. He contented himself with pointing out to Phivo that at least the deserted roads and more primitive infrastructure worked to their advantage.

Five minutes later Phivo turned cautiously on to the central, cobbled square of a small village. A low, green-stained stone wall circled an algae-coated, stagnant pool. The raised hand of a naked, pedastalled nymph hadn't produced a fount of water for months, possibly years.

Somewhere a rooster stretched his larynx. A few hens clucked and scratched at the dirt. Phivo looked round, taking in the dozen or so houses, most of which backed immediately on to their own smallholding. Outside a closed-up café, tables loaded with last night's cups, glasses and ash trays insulted the new day.

"We should be all right for a while," he offered guardedly. "But we can't stay for long. In half an hour we could be surrounded by children, not to mention a few nosy adults."

Despite the vehicles and uniforms it would be obvious to all but a casual observer that eight of the nine were, to varying

168

degrees, of decidedly Mediterranean or Middle Eastern ancestry. The villagers, seeing a United Nations patrol, would
expect caucasians. It was inconceivable that on close inspection their Greek and Arab force could pass for a group of
British, Canadians or Danes.

"Come with me," Phivo invited. "We'll leave our weapons
behind." He turned to Kyriakos and the two Arabs in the
back. "You three stay here but put your guns on the floor, out
of sight."

Sam and Phivo passed over their own. "Andreas speaks the
best English, and he doesn't look too Cypriot," he announced
to all of them, "so he can pull up alongside and answer any
questions. Remember," he called over his shoulder, "only
English. No Arabic, and no bloody Greek!"

Kyriakos, thought Sam, looked less than delighted at the
prospect of sitting in the middle of a Turkish village. The
Arabs managed an air of contemptuous disinterest.

Whilst Phivo was briefing Andreas, Sam sauntered round
the Rover, studying the layout of the village. They had arrived
from the east, on a road which led into the lower third of a
square and looped around its southern side before departing
westwards, more or less opposite where they had come in.
Several dirt tracks led between houses into fields but there
was only one other metalled exit, a narrower road which
appeared to run due south from two-thirds of the way along
the bottom side, about twenty yards diagonally forwards and
left from the front of the Rover.

Andreas moved up his vehicle with commendable lack of
engine noise. Phivo walked round both Rovers, checking that
rear canopy flaps were fastened down, then reached behind
his seat and extracted a large pair of binoculars.

"Come on." A jerk of his head indicated that Sam should
follow him. They walked at a steady pace towards the southern exit.

It was more of a narrow lane, walled high on either side
with crumbling stone and a riot of overhanging blue bougain-
villaea. Twenty yards on, gardens gave way to barns and
outhouses, all in varying stages of dereliction. Where the
fields began, the lane curved half right. As they approached
the corner Phivo slowed down, stopping when there emerged

from behind a last barn the left-hand side of a strip of tarmac, disappearing in a straight line to the south-west.

"There it is." He spoke softly, even though they had yet to meet a villager. "The large villa, about a mile down the road."

It was a superfluous identification. It was the only villa. Sam took the offered binos, checking automatically that the lenses would be in shade and not throw a flash of reflected light towards their target. Satisfied, he braced himself against the corner of the barn and focussed each eyepiece on to the white edifice.

It wasn't one building but several, perhaps once part of the estate of some wealthy Greek or foreigner. The main residence was a large, two-storey affair, set back about a hundred yards from the road. At the rear it faced south-east, sharing the morning sun with acre after acre of vines. Most of the ground floor was obscured by a long, low outbuilding which appeared to run from the corner of the house to within ten yards of the road. Behind it he could make out another, similar arm, so that between them the house and outbuildings enclosed three sides of a huge, shady rectangle. Surrounding the complex, including a generous lawn at the rear, was a low wall surmounted by a five-foot fence of vertical, black-metal railing.

The entrance, alongside the road, was sealed by two, massive wrought-iron gates. Just inside, through loops and whorls, he could see a lone sentry. Above the main house, on a makeshift pole, fluttered a huge red flag bearing the star and crescent of Turkey.

"As you say," observed Sam quietly, lowering the binoculars, "there it is."

"What do you think?" asked Phivo. Although nominally in charge of the operation his experience was exclusively of guerrilla warfare in which large, well-defended British bases had been subjected to harassment rather than direct assault. He was more than ready to receive the younger man's opinion.

"How good's your intelligence?" Sam queried.

Phivo shrugged. "It's difficult with hardly any Greeks in the North, but it's always been a Battalion Headquarters. Units come here one at a time as a break from the Green Line. They do a bit of training, some of the officers take leave, then they relieve the next company due for a rest, and so on. The point is, in addition to what the company holds, it's here where the Battalion Quartermaster keeps a first line reserve of weapons and ammunition – it's stuff the Turks brought over and have never taken back."

They had no way of knowing whether the Battalion was manned to full establishment. Sam lifted the binoculars for another look at the entrance. One company, and say another twenty or so for Battalion Headquarters.

"Hundred? Hundred and twenty?" he asked. From his left came the sound of saliva being sucked through teeth.

"My contact in these parts takes in the officers' whisky. He mentioned a figure of about eighty. But he's a Turk," Phivo concluded, which Sam took to imply absolutely no guarantee of reliability.

"How do you fancy going in?" Phivo went on after half a minute. Sam continued his silent reconnaissance. Phivo persisted. "Like I mentioned last night, in the café?"

Another long silence. Eventually Sam lowered the binoculars.

"Come back behind the barn."

He broke off a stick and sketched two parallel lines in the dirt.

"It might not work. For a start, the sentry will hear us coming. Land-Rovers have a distinctive sound and there aren't that many around, particularly at this hour of the morning. Besides, he'll be bored rigid. He's bound to take a look."

He marked a curve through ninety degrees.

"Next, it's a tight turn, so we'll have to slow right down. Those gates look pretty substantial, and there seems to be some sort of chain round them. We might not have enough momentum to break through. Worse still, we could knacker the Rover. I'd hate to finish up on the wrong end of a firefight without much cover."

He straightened up and scuffed out the sketch. Fortunately Phivo was old enough, and wise enough, to accept advice.

"Let's roll up the canopy on the lead Rover . . ."

* * *

171

Sam turned into the lane, parting a string of blue flowers with his near side wing mirror. On the straight he accelerated to a sedate thirty miles an hour. Three hundred yards short of the entrance he switched off the ignition.

The engine carried on turning with a subdued, sibilant roar. When, after three of four seconds, he turned the ignition back on, it fired immediately. The Rover lurched forward and obliged with a delicious, raucous backfire. Twice he repeated the performance, each time letting the speed drop off. When he switched on for a third time she picked up with the classic kangaroo-jolts of either a first outing learner or a very sick engine.

Seconds later he passed the gates. Behind them stood the sentry, rifle slung at the shoulder. Sam waved, collecting a half-hearted lift of the right hand in response. Pulling away from the camp he played a couple of encores. Another three-quarters of a mile and the road crested a low rise. Beyond it, Sam reversed off and parked in the shade of a carob tree.

It was important to do things properly. An immediate return and that sentry might be suspicious. He passed the time by checking scrupulously over his weapon and magazines.

Sam looked at his watch. Five minutes. He restarted the Rover, stepped down from the cab and released the catches, heaving up bonnet and spare wheel to pull a connector cap from the sparking plug of number one cylinder. Slow, smooth revolutions degenerated into a lumpy tickover. He dropped the bonnet but didn't refasten it. They might need to fix that engine in a hurry.

Running on only three cylinders, and with Sam manipulating the ignition switch, it was a leukaemic United Nations Land-Rover which died, finally, a vehicle's length short of the gateway.

Grateful for the distraction, the young conscript watched the United Nations officer push up the heavy bonnet and brace its support stays.

Halfway through a two-hour sentry stag. Another hour before he could walk those few yards to the end of the outhouse, stand in front of the table and cough, loudly, until the guard commander opened his eyes.

172

They would pretend that the corporal had not been dozing, merely resting his eyelids for a few seconds. Sleepy and foul-tempered after at least two illegal bottles of wine – which he would not have shared – the corporal would shout into the back room. If there were no response he would rise, grudgingly, to rouse the next hapless conscript from a last few seconds of bliss on his infested palliasse.

The corporal should have been awake, watching the guard. The door should have been locked, all communication through a small, barred window. But it was hot and, besides, nothing of any military significance had happened on the Morphou Plain since 1974. It had to be the most boring shithole of a posting in the entire Turkish Army.

'*Ne mutlu Turkum Diyene.*' Their national saying: 'How happy is he who can say, "I am a Turk." ' It was all right for the officers, or even an NCO. They had privileges and occasional leave, but a national service conscript was sentenced to a term of poverty and harsh discipline with no remission for good conduct.

Now there was a lucky man, working for the United Nations! He must be important to be allocated his own vehicle for he was alone, that much he, Kemel, had observed. The sides were rolled up. The back of the English Land-Rover was empty.

The United Nations man lit a cigarette and stared at the engine, as if trying to decide what to do next. A soft breeze carried tendrils of smoke. American tobacco. Once he had begged – sometimes stolen – such luxuries from Americans in Izmir. On his present pittance he couldn't even afford the rough local cigarettes.

The man turned to face him and walked up to the gate.

"Telephone?"

A mime, one finger dialling on the other palm, blue beret tilted sideways to an imaginary raised receiver. It was unnecessary. Kemel recognised the sound – in Turkish, '*telefon*'. The man would have to be taken to the guardroom.

He hesitated. This was not covered by his orders. But if he woke the guard commander, he would only be told to open the gate and the corporal would be angry at the delay, seeking to show the important, United Nations official that it was

173

entirely the sentry's fault. Kemel knew from experience that he would be cuffed and belittled. Better to open the gate, let him in, and call out loudly to the guardroom.

The man wasn't waiting for a response. He was going back to his Land-Rover. In a moment of mild panic Kemel reached into his trouser pocket for the key to the heavy padlock.

The man was returning for the cigarette packet he had left lying on the front wing, offering one. He could keep it for later, a prize indeed. Kemel unwound three coils of thick chain from adjacent rungs of the gates.

Sam took off his beret and leant against the Rover, for all the world the senior, superior official, disdaining to stand, supplicant, before the entrance. Beside him, on the flat upper surface of the wing, his flip-top cigarette packet was open towards the Turk. For a minute it had looked as though the soldier wasn't going to let him in. Now Sam needed him just a few feet nearer, around the edge of the gateway, out of sight of that guardroom window.

Inward opening gates. The conscript left them a foot ajar and took a couple of steps towards the Rover. Shit, he wasn't going to come any further! At least the gate was open. Should he reach back for the Saco or would the act of slinging it over his shoulder alert the young Turk?

Sam took the packet and stepped, unarmed, towards the guard. Smiling he repeated the offer. The Turk took one delicately between dirt-stained fingers.

"Here."

Sam extracted three more, put the packet back in his trouser pocket and moved the hand containing the cigarettes gently, so as not to alarm him, towards the young soldier's uniform breast pocket. He took a quarter step nearer. They were less than eighteen inches apart. Automatically the Turk's eyes traversed down to the approaching riches.

Sam had to risk a sideways glance, barely moving his head. Nothing in the courtyard, a thin angle, you could hardly see the window.

'Four till six,' Kemel thought. 'The most boring stag of all. But this was his lucky morning. So why had the United Nations man's hand moved to caress the back of his neck? Some NCOs abused younger recruits . . .'

The first traces of fear and alarm clouded his mind. What should he do with his own hands, already raised to re-button the pocket?

Even as he stiffened, the United Nations man's head was flashing forward. Kemel's nose was jerked savagely towards the butting, blond hair. His brain told him to cry out but in that same second, when bone and tissue splayed with a pain which penetrated unbelievable depths of his skull, something was tearing almost in slow motion through the muscle beneath his rib cage.

He was suspended in a double agony, an asphyxiated inanimation. Desperate to breathe in and cry out, he could do neither. Crossed thumbs hooked around his windpipe, using it as a purchase for fingers which jammed together somewhere behind his ears. Kemel had a brief vision of distorted quivering features, the effect of concentrating total energy into double callipers which threatened to penetrate his neck and break down the walls of his throat. Nerve impulses relayed from disparate areas of acute distress competed for attention as they exploded inside his mind, to be subsumed in seconds by merciful blackness.

Even as the Turk passed out, Sam was lowering him to the ground, relaxing his grip immediately to avoid inflicting brain damage. He could still see over the wall. His luck was holding. Nothing stirred in the compound. He used the sentry's belt to strap his arms behind his back, gagging him with a filthy piece of cloth which passed for his handkerchief. As a final precaution Sam tied his boot laces together. It wouldn't hold him forever, but he would be out of the way for long enough. When Sam straightened up to toss the sentry's rifle into his vehicle the others were on their way.

He was anxious to reach the guardroom before any noise from the Rover's tyres or engine reached its inhabitants. Old habits made him feel improperly dressed. It was a reflex action to ram on the United Nations beret before he grabbed his Saco, cocking it as he ran for the wall alongside the guardroom door.

Back flat against the building and pause. Silence. The courtyard was still empty. Crouch in doorway, gun level . . . not a thing. Take two steps. Table – seen, no threat. Bit dark. Back

175

room: tiered bunks, sleeping men – maybe six. Explosive tension drained away.

The wooden trestle table supported an old-fashioned black telephone and the upper torso of a corporal, chair pushed back so that his head could rest sideways on a cushion of podgy forearms.

Sam glanced out of the window. Two of them were opening the gates. Phivo was about to bring his vehicle inside the courtyard. The others were running towards the guardroom.

They came in quietly enough but the corporal stirred. Sam poked him none too gently on the cheek with the Saco's barrel. The guard commander's face indicated precisely the transition from anger, through confusion, to fear. Cradling the Saco in his right arm, Sam raised a forefinger to his pursed lips in the unmistakable gesture for silence.

He flicked his fingers towards the nearest man's weapon and pointed to the guard commander. The bearded Arab covered him immediately.

The back room was hot, smelly and windowless. Somebody moved. There was no point in poking a stick into a bees' nest. Sam closed the door quietly and turned the key of an ancient lock.

"Where's Kyriakos?"

"Here."

A quiet voice from the rear of the group. As a child Kyriakos had played in a northern, predominantly Turkish village. Now, recruited by Phivo from a refugee camp, he earned his living from the language.

"Tell him," ordered Sam, "that if there is any noise from in there," his head jerked sideways towards the back room, "he is to demand silence. If he fails, or if either hand moves from that table, the Arab is instructed to shoot him in the stomach."

Whilst Kyriakos was translating, Sam removed one of eight rifles from a wall rack. Its magazine was empty, the ammunition in a box on the floor. Provided that the Arab kept an eye on the corporal . . .

"You can add," he lied, "that the Arab speaks neither Turkish nor English, but he has never failed to obey an order."

176

The corporal looked in neither physical nor mental condition to threaten anyone. His expression suggested a man already trying to work out what to say at his inevitable court martial.

Sam joined Phivo outside. Apart from the main house, only the guardroom boasted a verandah, probably because it was the only section of the outbuildings in use throughout the day. Its shade gave an element of cover. The two Greeks who had opened the gates were prodding the staggering guard towards them. Sam beckoned for him to hurry.

"He'll do. Untie his arms and take off that gag." The young Turk would already be conveniently softened up.

"Say to him," he instructed Kyriakos, "that if he answers my questions, he will come to no harm. If he chooses not to answer, there will be no discussion: I shall merely ask somebody else. But I will have a length of rope tied around one of his ankles and the other end secured to the back of my Land Rover. When we leave, he will be dragged behind. Tell him that the last time I saw a man flayed in this way, in the Middle East, he screamed for three miles until his face disappeared, but it took him seven to die."

He paused for a few seconds, to give the Turk time to exercise his imagination.

"Now, point for me," he said in a quiet voice made more menacing by its even tone, "where is the armoury and magazine?"

Kemel looked at Sam, then at Phivo and Stavros. He was not without courage, but the Turk's instincts told him that these men would do as they promised. In any case, someone would talk eventually. He would die for nothing. Slowly, he raised his right arm.

Opposite the guardroom. It made sense. Watched permanently, in theory, and on the end so that any fire or explosion would be well away from the headquarters and barrack accommodation.

"Good. Now the soldiers, where do they sleep?"

A finger pointed halfway along from the guardroom and ranged back to the main house.

"And the officers and sergeants?"

The other outbuilding, nearer to the house. And the house itself. That had to be for the officers.

177

"Good," Sam encouraged, "you do not wish to be kissed to death by the roads of Cyprus. So, finally, where is the telephone exchange?"

More readily this time: the main house. The guard said something.

"It's on the ground floor," Kyriakos translated, "in the Battalion office on the left."

Sam had no idea whether the Turks used the civilian telephone system or self-laid military land lines. The only sure cut-off would be to destroy the exchange.

"Andreas, take a man with you. See if you can get into the office, but don't make a noise. So far we haven't stirred up anything. Let's keep it that way. Rip out the phone wires – whatever you can do quietly – but don't smash anything unless it looks as though someone's trying to put through a call."

Andreas nodded and called softly: "John."

A modern name for a young Cypriot. The two men trotted warily towards the main house.

"His nephew," commented Phivo quietly. "Reliable. Like his uncle."

Sam was conscious of having assumed a measure of command, despite their original agreement.

"Will you cover the courtyard," he asked, trying to make it sound like a suggestion, "if Kyriakos and I go for the magazine?"

They hadn't bothered to replace the frame, which suggested that underneath were the original hinges, but some prudent Turk had faced the door with a single piece of sheet metal, leaving only small keyholes to twin locks set high and low. They could break it down quickly enough, especially if they used a Rover, but not without a fair amount of noise. He looked at his watch. They had been in the compound for four and a half minutes. It seemed like half an hour. Reveille wouldn't be before half-past five at the earliest – but if so, they had marginally less than twenty-five minutes left.

Sam tapped Kyriakos on the shoulder and ran back to the guardroom. Outside, from the shadow of the verandah, Phivo and the other three were covering the courtyard and the young sentry, who had intelligently been reposted with an

178

unloaded rifle. Any early morning insomniac taking a casual glance through his window would witness normality.

"We need the sentry."

Stavros fetched him.

"Where does the man sleep," began Sam, pausing to let Kyriakos keep pace, "who holds the key to the armoury and magazine."

A troubled look furrowed the Turk's face. For a second Sam thought that he might refuse to answer. Stavros evidently thought so too, and pulled back his Saco in preparation for a poke of encouragement. Sam placed a restraining hand on the Greek's arm. The boy's panic-stricken rapid eye movements between Sam and Stavros suggested that he was trying desperately to remember. He stammered a few words.

"The duty officer," began Kyriakos quietly, "holds the keys at night." The faster the Turk tried to speak, the more he stuttered.

"The duty officer is a Lieutenant Melleç, but he sleeps in the big house. The boy does not know where. He has never been upstairs."

After a second or two the guard was off again.

"He begs you, sir, to believe," Kyriakos translated faithfully, "that truly, he does not know."

Chapter 11

Blue-black oily water reflected an almost perfect sphere. A blowzy middle-aged moon bathed Lara Bay in monochrome. But, her course barely run, she was harried from the east by the steel-grey overture to a brassy new day.

They landed to the north, on a mean spit of sand below the cliffs. Artamonov and Utkin lowered the mast and carried their dinghy a few yards into a ravine. In winter it was a flash-flood course, squandering precious rainfall even whilst the island's water table threatened to become dangerously saline, but for most of the year the re-entrant provided a steep but navigable path to the summit of a fifty foot cliff.

Lying on a crest, they studied the anchored vessel. Artamonov was first tempted to swim out, then discarded the idea. Samandag's signal implied an older operative – a survivor, a man not to be taken so easily. If they were aboard the patrol boat, there would amost certainly be someone on watch. This man would not waste time by shooting at diving swimmers. When they were within thirty yards of the boat he would step from deep shadow inside the wheelhouse. There would be grenades, arcing towards them to explode a few feet down, stunning their bodies as water transmitted the over-pressure.

Artamonov focussed a sniperscope. Three hundred yards. He pulled back and let fly the cocking handle. Working parts snapped forward, skimming a round from magazine to chamber. At that range he was confident of being able to hit anyone exposed on the foredeck before they could raise the anchor. He wriggled back from the skyline.

"I flew that thing for seven hours, so you can watch the boat. Call me as soon as you see signs of life."

Artamonov scooped a hollow for his hips in the loose scree. Within minutes he was asleep.

Having rested throughout the previous afternoon, Sally was awake soon after daybreak. Pale yellow sunlight shafted through a porthole to track, centimetre by centimetre, down the bulkhead towards her bunk. For a few hours during the night it had been surprisingly cool, but already she was sweating beneath a single, coarse sheet. Sally kicked it away and swung her legs to the floor.

She dressed before pulling aside the partitioning curtain. Through starboard portholes she could see most of the beach. Like yesterday, it was empty.

Sam had left her with strict instructions and a loaded submachine gun for protection but already the events of the past few days were receding into memory, shrouded by the protective mist with which the human mind can obscure the unacceptable. She picked up the weapon, moved its change lever from 'safe' to 'single rounds', and unlocked the bulkhead door. It seemed unreal, over-dramatic, like a poor quality television drama. She tip-toed only half-seriously to a deserted wheelhouse and deck.

Sally's conscience made here search the bay. 'I'll be back tomorrow. There might be a fishing boat, or campers on the beach so keep the gun handy, and don't hesitate to loose off an early warning-shot – we'll be gone before they can complain,' Sam had told her.

But there were neither fishermen nor campers, just a brighter version of the same peaceful anchorage where the night before she had sat on deck with her evening meal to watch the sunset.

The patrol boat's water tanks were fairly full, but the urge to dive over the side into a silky-cool sea was irresistible. Shielded from the beach by superstructure, she raised a two-foot, hinged section of the port guardrail, lowered the boarding ladder and hooked it over the side. Before undressing she walked around the deck for a final check of the shoreline.

She dived vertically, welcoming the chill against her skin as

181

she slipped down through the temperature gradient. Surfacing clear of the hull she circled it with a steady breast-stroke until her muscles began to tire.

Back on board she decided to pass time by keeping up with her laundry – not all at once, in case Sam returned early with his friends. Rinsing slacks and bra in a bucket of fresh water she wondered, idly, when life would return to normal; not least, when she would have a change of clothing.

Already the sun was hot on her legs. She twisted out most of the water. They wouldn't take long, draped incongruously over the pom-pom barrel. Until then she would make do with her briefs and tee shirt. After yesterday's sunbathing she would have to stay in the shade. Sally felt the first whispers of a breeze, and smiled. She would also have to keep an eye on the surface whilst she made breakfast. Too much wind could lead to a morning spent diving for clothes around Lara Bay.

Looking out from the galley, part of the shoreline was obscured by a fierce glare refracting from the water. At first she thought it might be glancing off one of the low, black rocks near the beach. Sally peered more closely. No, sunlight was flashing off wet blades. She could feel her heart thumping. Someone was rowing a dinghy out to the patrol boat.

She ran up to the wheelhouse and watched from the starboard doorway. He rowed steadily, content to glance over his shoulder from time to time. The sub-machine gun, she realised with a stab of guilt, had been left lying on the chart table . . .

He appeared to be wearing some sort of uniform – white shorts and a white shirt, with gold-banded, dark blue slides over the epaulettes.

The dinghy was twenty-five yards away. She edged forward, conscious of being dressed only in briefs and a tee shirt.

"That's near enough."

She tried to imbue her voice with a confidence she didn't feel. One oar stayed in the water, turning the inflatable. The man had on a white, naval-style hat with more gold along the front edge of its blue-black peak.

"What do you want?" she asked abruptly.

He squinted up at her and dropped the other oar into the water, pushing the handles away from him gently, rowing the stern of the dinghy towards the patrol boat as if seeking only to make conversation easier. She was about to shout again when he stopped, now within twenty yards. Fortunately the boarding ladder was on the other side.

"You must be Miss Forbes."

A relaxed voice – sort of BBC nineteen-fifties – but not unfriendly. She was surprised to hear her name, but it was vaguely reassuring, somehow implying that everything would be all right once he explained.

"Richard Saunders, Miss Forbes. Chief British Customs Officer for the island. Is Mr Verle back on board?"

She thought of Sam's remarks less than twenty-four hours ago. 'Have to drop the hook here, walk the rest of the way – can't chance a fishing harbour, probably wouldn't be let out for weeks.'

"Don't worry about me," he called, as if sensing her anxiety. "I'm here to help, not to make life difficult. Just let me have a word with Sam."

All the time the dinghy was edging nearer. If she were going to act, it would have to be soon, but Sally was reluctant to declare her hand.

She shook her head. "He won't be long. Until then, I'm not inviting anyone on board."

His voice modulated a fraction – a shade more official, just a hint of intolerance at being delayed by a young woman. He seemed oblivious of her dress.

"Miss Forbes, I have to tell you that Sam contacted me last night. You must realise, you are in a difficult position: a foreign naval vessel, not flying an ensign, and anchored illegally in Cypriot waters. That's why he telephoned. Sam and I are old friends. If you are discovered, in this uniform I can probably stave off an initial enquiry."

It was a painstaking business, shouting across the water. He seemed authentic, but Sam hadn't been at all concerned about being found by a Cypriot official. Surely it would have occurred to him when he was warning her about campers and fishermen? Yet on the other hand it sounded sensible – and she knew he still had many friends on the island.

Sally hesitated. "Mr Saunders?"

"Commander Saunders, ma'am. Royal Navy. Retired."

"Very well, Commander Saunders." She took a deep breath, "I'm sorry, but being a military man you will understand if I choose to follow Colonel Verle's instructions to the letter." Her decision made, she drew confidence from the use of Sam's rank.

"He shouldn't be long. Perhaps you won't mind waiting on the shore. You could always row out again, if an official vessel does show up."

As her shoulders lifted she opened her hands. "I know you'll think me silly, but I'm afraid that until Sam gets back I really don't feel inclined to let anyone come on board."

There was no reaction. It was as if she hadn't spoken. Sally nerved herself for the next stage of their confrontation and glanced at the weapon a few feet from her left elbow. Saunders had commanded all her attention but now a strange, dark shape trespassed into the acute periphery of her vision.

She spun around and gasped. From deep in her stomach rising heat suffused her face with fear and shock. A watery trail led from the port doorway to a man in a shiny black wetsuit. It was too late to reach for the sub-machine gun. Sally's features twisted with frustration and despair. She was only eighteen inches from the muzzle of a small automatic.

He jerked the weapon, marshalling her aside from the doorway and against the bulkhead. She waited, her initial shock subsiding into nervous apprehension.

Whoever they were, it had been a concerted effort. That plausible voice in the naval uniform . . . Self-reproach fuelled Sally's misery. After Sam's warning, why the hell hadn't she picked up the gun and looked around?

There were footsteps on the boarding ladder. The diver lifted the sub-machine gun, removed its magazine with deft familiarity and flicked the cocking handle. One shiny, brass round ejected on to the wheelhouse floor. The man in white arrived in time to pick it up. In his other hand was a black plastic bag. He passed behind his companion, placed it on the chart table and slipped two rubber bands over his wrist. His hand emerged from the bag holding a pistol identical to his companion's. He nodded to the younger man.

"Search the boat."

Utkin, the diver, disappeared down the companionway.

Sally's guard was fair-haired, like Sam, but this man's head was covered in tight, wiry curls. It struck Sally that for someone with such a pale complexion his forearms were unusually hirsute. He was neither tall nor particularly stocky but heavily muscled, perhaps through regular training with weights. She glimpsed a gold upper canine. It could have been an attractive face but despite the lines which fanned sideways from cornflower blue eyes it was totally devoid of humour, or a glimmer of human kindness.

Sally knew that any protest would be wasted breath. These men had to be connected in some way with Samandag and Kastellorizon. Deep in her abdomen a sick, residual warmth suggested that she would find out soon enough.

Artamonov studied the girl, ignoring her inspection of him. She seemed calm. There had been no screaming, no hysterics. From her description she was one of the two who had escaped with the Englishman. Samandag had done well to provide their names. Without them, he might not have held her attention.

He glanced at the sub-machine gun. It had been loaded and ready, indicating a certain resoluteness, but Samandag suspected only the man of being a professional.

Beneath their feet Utkin slammed a bulkhead door and called out that the ship was clean.

The young man would appreciate the girl. She was good-looking. Legs firm and well-shaped, the stomach flat between narrow briefs and the edge of a tee shirt lifted forward by her breasts. But Artamonov, whose taste was in any case diluted by being entirely bisexual, was interested only in her mind.

Given time, and possibly drugs – which were not, however, his favourite technique – Artamonov believed that he could persuade anyone to talk. But they did not have time.

She looked strong. The good and bad method might work, his own interrogation physically uncompromising – and, more importantly, mentally cruel – with Utkin acting the alternate, gentle interlocutor. But to induce the right state of mind, sufficiently irrational for her ultimately to confide in Utkin, cruelty was best applied progressively, over a period of time.

He considered an intravenous injection of valium, better than more sophisticated, so-called truth drugs. She would talk eventually, in the nirvana halfway to unconsciousness but it might take more than one application to unhinge her, and the intervening recovery could be a slow process.

Utkin was beside him again.

No, there was only one way, an all-or-nothing approach. Not just physical pain – she might stand that until she passed out. Artamonov's challenge was to launch an assault so malevolent that it produced a brainstorm, a burst of uncontrollable panic which would breach her mental fortress from within.

Sally heard a few sentences, Russian-sounding or at least East European. The blond placed his pistol on the chart table and walked towards her. Instinctively Sally tried to back off but she was hard against the bulkhead. He stopped eighteen inches from her.

"You will remove your clothing."

The voice was too calm, too dispassionate. Surely he didn't mean . . . ?

There was no hint of warning. His body barely moved but a hand swung into vision. The open palm slammed Sally's head sideways, cracking her temple against the bulkhead. A loud, electronic-sounding monotone rang in her skull. The side of her face felt as if it was on fire. Something trickled into her mouth. She tasted blood.

Through a curtain of water suspended between her eyelashes the wheelhouse undulated as it began to rotate. She touched her face, knees folding, her other hand clutching the bulkhead in an effort to stay upright.

His voice again, from beyond the tears.

"Your clothes. Take them off."

Her thoughts darted first one way then another. Just an order with no second chance, only brutality, immediate and unrestrained.

Artamonov smiled, savouring the impact, on a mind conditioned to law and order, of the complete loss of all human dignity. Her lower lip was trembling. Even as she realised the full extent of her vulnerability he moved his hand.

"No," Sally cried out, her arm lifting ineffectually against an incipient blow.

"Please. I'll do what you say."

186

Still afraid that he might hit her again, she crossed her arms nervously towards the hem of her shirt.

The second blow came the moment she paused, clutching the tee shirt in front of her. Afterwards he snatched it away.

Sally struggled to catch her breath through jerky, snuffling sobs but she began to push down her briefs.

She stood naked before two strangers, one arm across her chest, the other kept low. The hunched stance and streaming eyes and nose reminded Artamonov of films shot at Dachau and Ravensburg. A successful beginning.

He reached out to the captain's chair and swivelled it round from the control panel.

"Sit here."

She shuffled between them, obedience already conditioned towards survival. The dark-haired man stared at her. She knew he was looking at her buttocks. Keeping her thighs tightly together, she climbed into the pedastalled chair.

"We know your name," came the same detached voice, "and those of your companions. In fact, we know all about you, from your arrival in Kekova, where your friend repaid our kindness with irresponsible probing, to the way in which innocent men were murdered before you fled to Cyprus."

The dark-haired one was moving behind her, out of sight.

"It is my Government's intention," Sally looked to her front, "that you should stand trial. If you are completely innocent, you have nothing to fear."

He sensed her disbelief but no matter. The statement implied that she might live. It was cast deliberately as a straw, a lifebelt for her to clutch when he torpedoed her reason.

"I wish to know where your companions are, Miss Forbes – the man Verle and the other woman, Miss Marchant. Where they have gone, what they are doing, and when they will return. So, let us begin." The voice was so normal it could have belonged to a tutor addressing his pupil. "First, your companions. Where are they?"

The beating had been bad. Her pulses accelerated in the silence. She was a small child again, alone but for a white figure. In hospital, frightened by doctors – and by what they might do to her.

But she wasn't ready to talk. Artamonov spoke softly in

187

Russian. Utkin snatched back her hair. She gasped at the pain. Her throat stretched taut. A head loomed into view in front of the ceiling. His right hand was hurting her breast. She tried to fight off each new source of distress but those wrists were like steel hawsers. In desperation, she clawed for his eyes.

Keeping a grip on her hair he brushed aside the arced fingers, stepped around the chair, and jabbed her viciously in the abdomen. She retched and doubled forward. His left hand propelled her towards a line of rivets which skinned her palms as she reached out to break her fall.

Her body curled in on itself for protection. She fought for breath, mentally begging God not to let her be sick. A knee landed on her spine, pressing her chest on to the steel plates. She could neither resist nor cry out when he pulled at her wrists. The blond man held her tee shirt by the sleeves, twirled it and knotted the bandeau into a tight blindfold.

It was uncomfortable but not too painful when they folded her arms – still behind her back – and lashed them together. Struggling to control her stomach Sally tried to ignore the pain from her pinched skin.

'They haven't really hurt you,' she struggled to reassure herself.

But it did hurt, grazing her elbow and wrenching a shoulder muscle when they turned her over. She lay with her back arched awkwardly. As her breathing stabilised, anxiety crowded in. Like a frightened, hooded animal she turned her head towards every sound.

When a hand gripped her shin she shouted and tried to kick out. Someone sat on her legs, forcing her knees back against the joint. The pressure lifted a fraction. Her ankles were braced wide apart and secured to something which moved with her.

A palm passed across her stomach. Sally was barely conscious of beginning a soft whimper. His hand pushed between her legs, spreading her lips.

She twisted and heaved, wild screams tearing her throat, but they pinned her whilst something small, cold and hard was pushed into her vagina.

They let go, but it was still there. She was weeping freely

when what felt like a strip of adhesive fastened something to her inner thigh. Sally tried to brace herself for an electric shock.

Hands under each armpit hauled her back into the chair. Because of her bound arms she had to sit upright, legs jammed against its sides.

The blindfold was being removed. He used it to wipe her eyes and face. She saw that two wires trailed from inside her, along her thigh and over the oar between her ankles.

It was as if they had suddenly lost interest in her. The fair-haired man was examining a tin can, presumably from the galley. He punched a hole in the lid through which he lowered a small, brass cylinder suspended from two wires. The other man carried the can outside, paying out more wire, and taped it on to the port guardrail.

"Now, my dear, please listen carefully." After all they had done to her, he still spoke in the same flat unemphatic voice.

"I am convinced your friends will come back. It would help if I knew when, and what they were doing."

He shrugged indifferently. "But I can manage without that information if necessary. They will come. Sooner or later, they will come."

The other man was taking something from the plastic bag.

"All I want from you," resumed her interrogator, "is a little co-operation. Before you deny it to me, you must understand the consequences."

At last a change in his tone of voice. It was becoming more coaxing, even reasonable.

He pointed. "It would be a good idea if you watched the can."

Her eyes changed direction automatically. There was a sharp crack. Not a big explosion, although if there had been any left it might have broken the port side windows, but the effect on the can was devastating.

It had bellied up and out, splattering baked beans and tomato sauce from a gaping, jagged zig-zag exit hole. Her legs were splashed and stained.

"A small, electric detonator," the blond man observed academically. "Usually an initiator for a much larger explosion – say a piece of plastic." He lifted a rectangular battery, about seven inches by five. At the top were two threaded, brass stalks, on one of them a knurled, round nut. He loosened it and pulled away the wire.

"You saw what that tiny, explosive charge did to the can." They were back to the flat voice again. "And I have placed another inside your body." He held up a piece of wire. "This is one terminal."

A bared and soldered end hooked under the nut. She caught her breath, but nothing happened. Artamonov tightened down the connection.

Sally began to tremble. She tried to squirm from her seat, but her arms were gripped from behind.

"There can be no second chance," he went on calmly. "It will destroy your lower abdomen. If you do not die, slowly, there will never be a normal life. No husband, no children . . . That is the price. The choice is yours.

"Now," he held another bared wire eighteen inches from the second terminal, "where is Mister Verle?"

His right hand began a slow traverse. He wasn't even looking at her, just concentrating on moving the wire towards the terminal.

That thing, that awful thing, was inside her. Sally started to mewl. When that wire touched . . . She tried to say something – and choked. She was about to lose control of her bladder. Her imagination burst its banks. Sally panicked, completely and utterly, and gave a long, drawn-out scream.

He was still staring, impervious, at the moving wire.

Words boiled and bubbled in her throat. "He'll be back . . . b-back today. Please, I'll tell you! I beg you . . ."

His right hand stopped, two inches away. She was weeping, all impulse to resist drained from her.

He asked her many questions, back to before Fethiye. She stalled only once. He looked at her with a rictus grin and moved the wire.

Afterwards he pulled roughly at the adhesive tape, removing the detonator and wire, and nodded to Utkin.

"Put the girl away for now. We'll keep her till we have the others."

She was curled into a foetal position, crying again. Utkin

190

unlashed her ankles and half-pushed, half-carried her down the companionway.

Artamonov smiled. He had judged well. But there was not much time. As soon as Utkin came back they would have to move.

If he hadn't drunk so much wine he would have slept through instead of waking early, fuzzy-headed and foul-mouthed, with a drum-tight bladder and a raging thirst.

In the downstairs office Andreas and John stood motionless as footsteps creaked across the ceiling, then there was silence. His uncle pointed. John crouched behind a filing cabinet. Andreas stationed himself alongside the door.

The Commanding Officer shook what he could only feel beneath his massive, glistening belly and turned to shuffle back to his bedroom.

Somewhere above them a cistern flushed. They grinned with relief. Eyes followed the sound of footsteps on their return journey. Below, on the floor beside a junction box, lay a tangle of wires. Their work was finished.

Crossing to the washstand basin, the Commanding Officer glanced automatically through an open window. But this morning his habitual cursory inspection stopped abruptly at the end of the courtyard. For a full minute he gazed with mounting apprehension. United Nations uniforms, but why were they at the armoury door? They seemed to be interrogating the sentry, armed men with olive skins and black hair . . .

The Commanding Officer swore softly. He wasn't going out there on his own. He reached for the weapon on his dressing table.

The shot was fired to alert the Guard Commander, to panic the intruders and wake up the camp rather than with any hope of hitting anyone.

Sam recognised the cough of a low velocity round. Eighteen inches from his foot a splinter of earth skipped into the air.

"Cover!"

A small dust cloud drifted downwind, dropping specks of fallout over a six foot lozenge inside an empty courtyard.

191

Sam peered round the door frame, not at the usual height in case someone was aiming at the entrance, but lying on the floor.

The round had been fired from the main house, probably an upstairs window. It would have taken a lucky shot. Eighty yards was almost three times the range for accurate shooting with what sounded like a medium calibre revolver.

It was crowded in the guardroom – the nearest bolt-hole for all of them, including the sentry whom Stavros had dragged in by his hair. The young Turk stood next to his guard commander, both now covered by the bearded Arab. His younger countryman started to say something.

"Aziz," Phivo hissed.

He shut up. A bed creaked warningly in the back room.

They hadn't fled. Whoever they were, the men had disappeared into the guardroom, the one place from which he had been counting on a reaction.

He was sweating but suddenly conscious of a gentle airflow cooling his body. The door! Instinctively the Commanding Officer twisted his upper torso, a stab of hangover following the sideways jerk of his head as he glanced nervously over his right shoulder. It was probably alcohol as much as presence of mind which saved his life. With dulled reactions the Turk was not even tempted to raise his pistol towards the two men in United Nations uniform, each holding a sub-machine gun trained on his ample stomach.

They bundled him outside and along the landing. He tried to hold back, only to collect a painful jab on the spine from the barrel of Andreas' Saco. Another door opened. John fired a short burst inside. It swung ajar, but no one emerged. Somewhere a latch clicked shut.

Once through the front door Andreas shouted in English for the Turk to run, reinforcing his command with a shot between the heels. Alongside, John jogged backwards, his eyes flicking intently from window to window.

On either side of the courtyard doors were opening. Figures emerged, most of them, like their Commanding Officer, wearing only a pair of undershorts. Small groups gathered, hesitant but fascinated.

Encouraged by the appearance of his men, the officer stopped. Andreas reversed the Saco and butted him, very hard, between the shoulders. He gasped with pain and stumbled forward.

They needed help. Sam looked at the two Turks, then turned to the bearded Arab.

"Leave them. Costas can cover the guardroom. When the rest of us move into the courtyard, I need you and Aziz on this verandah. Ignore the crowd, we'll look after them. You two just watch the house. Any sign of a sniper, spray the window." He glanced towards the Greeks. "The rest of you, get ready to follow me."

Sam paused. Had he overlooked anything? There was no time to ask, but the Arabs would probably be the most experienced at street fighting. As if to reassure him the bearded one bowed his head, lips pursed in an expression of confidence.

"Okay Costas, take over."

A nod to the Arabs. They were out, two urban ferrets diving into a fire position. Sam ran for the sunlight where they stood – Phivo, Stavros, Kyriakos and himself – in a thin spaced line.

"Keep him coming," Sam shouted. "We're covering the house," he added for the benefit of John who was still moving backwards.

Both sides of the courtyard were coated with young Turks. Behind the three men, nearer to the house, larger groups were edging towards the middle of the courtyard. Intensely curious, and reassured by their own number, some of them were beginning to follow the procession.

Almost there . . .

Sam turned to Kyriakos.

"Find out who he is, quickly."

They found themselves in an uneasy pause, surrounded by a crowd of onlookers, but in most armies it was routine to lock up weapons and not only for security – a barrack block was no place for firearms after a night in the canteen. Officers sometimes carried them but luckily in this camp only a pistol, or it might have been a different story. Sam was fairly confident that the weapons used by the younger men would be inside the armoury. The Turks had no reason to suspect a threat so a

193

small guard with immediate access to arms should have been more than adequate – if the guard commander had taken his duties seriously.

Kyriakos whispered at his elbow, then, on Sam's instruction, shouted a single word of command in Turkish. The closing phalanx of soldiers halted. The buzz of speculation died as each man strained to hear what the United Nations officer had to say.

"We mean you no harm," began Kyriakos again, translating Sam's words, "but my men intend to borrow from your armoury."

Any reaction was drowned by two bursts of automatic fire from the Arabs. Heads ducked then turned to a residual tinkle of falling glass. Drawn curtains swayed gently at a shattered window.

Sam nudged Kyriakos.

"In ten minutes," he roared to recapture their attention and override nervous chatter, "in ten minutes, we shall be gone." Heads turned to face him again. "Until then, you are to remain in your buildings."

As Kyriakos spoke Sam also scanned the upstairs windows. The Arabs' action would have acted as a strong deterrent to anyone armed only with a pistol.

"If there is any more firing from the house," Kyriakos threw back his head to carry the message, "we shall execute your Commanding Officer." He paused. His throat was beginning to hurt. "In twenty seconds, anyone still on this square, or seen at a window, will be shot."

For a couple of seconds there was no reaction. Sam sighted carefully and placed a short burst in front of the nearest group. Moments later men were jamming doorways as they fought to obey the curfew.

They put the Commanding Officer inside the guardroom, with the corporal and sentry. Sam sent Aziz to cover the courtyard from the other side and ran for his Rover. In under a minute he had replaced the pluglead, clipped down the bonnet and angled the broad, metal bars of the front bumper towards the centre of the armoury door. He stopped two feet away, engaged four-wheel-drive and drove steadily forward.

Metal screeched on metal. The door sagged inwards, hanging only on the last few threads of upper hinge and bolt screws. The Greeks shouldered it down. It hit the floor with an almighty crash but noise no longer mattered, only speed.

It was pleasantly cool inside. A wall-mounted air conditioner attempted to counter the sudden, hot inrush. Sam looked around: rifles chained to racks, heavier weapons on wooden pallets to keep them off the floor, three six-foot metal cabinets, their doors secured by padlocks. He shot them away. In a confined space the noise from the Saco made his ears sing.

Twenty-past five. They were running out of time. Soon, early-morning tradesmen would begin to arrive, and they still had to get back across the border.

They formed a chain, passing weapons to the door. A few larger items had to be manhandled by two people. Sam concentrated desperately to make sure that nothing was forgotten: ancillaries for each weapon; batteries, initiators, plastic and wire; and finally box after box of ammunition, each one checked – they didn't want exercise blanks. Outside, Stavros loaded the Rovers till there was barely room for passengers.

Sam forced himself to make a steady, final inspection, searching every rack, shelf and pallet for any vital item which might have been overlooked. In seven minutes they had selectively stripped the armoury.

Satisfied, he ran outside. The Rovers were waiting, engines running. Apart from himself only the two Arabs, now covering the courtyard from alongside the vehicles, were not aboard. Next to the bearded Arab lay the guardroom ammunition box.

He scrambled into the cab. As Phivo pulled away there was more firing from the house – the ground floor this time – but it was silenced immediately by a long duet from the back of Andreas' Rover. They passed through the gate and stopped, slightly to one side, so that from the back of their vehicle Costas and Kyriakos could cover Andreas' withdrawal. Classic fire and movement. Seconds later two laden Rovers accelerated for the village.

There was more traffic now, mostly farmers' vehicles, ancient pickups laden with produce or livestock. Twice they crawled until Phivo could force past thirty-year-old lorries,

195

dangerously overloaded and throwing out rolling clouds of blue-black hydrocarbon. They were halted just short of the border when Phivo had to commit the unforgivable – they were villagers themselves – and edge his Rover into a flock of sheep, scattering it with his horn. Some of the running ewes would injure themselves. The shepherd hit the second Rover with his stick then they were through, leaving the old man and his dogs to round up the animals.

But they were not pursued. If there had been any vehicles in the camp, and Sam hadn't seen any, by the time the Turks could have opened a garage and armed a patrol the Rovers should have been through the village and safely away.

They stopped in the plantation, fifty yards short of the border. The Arabs stayed with the vehicles. Phivo knelt on the tree line. To left and right the track was deserted, but patrols were irregular.

"Stellios!"

The Greek appeared on the far side. Feverishly they pulled at the wire. Costas and Stavros scuffed carefully between pegs, marking a vehicle lane. Phivo scanned the track anxiously, half expecting to see an armoured car half a mile away or a helicopter on the horizon. If possible they had to cover their traces, not least to avoid accusations from the North sparking a massive police hunt in the South.

Phivo pronounced himself satisfied with the replaced fences and brushed track, but not until the Rovers reached the foothills did any of them breathe freely.

She was waiting for them in the clearing. Wired up to Phivo's Datsun were two electric sprayguns. It was a rough job, but fast and effective. They taped a broad band of masking paper round the bottom of each canopy and over the windscreens. Lights were smeared with jelly. Sacking protected wheels. One man sprayed on a green base, another the black camouflage pattern.

"Emulsion" commented Phivo. "Dries in minutes at this temperature. It's too soft to last long, but it doesn't have to."

With a layer of dust over the fresh colours of the local garrison, they ought to be waved through a Cypriot police check. White vehicles would have been particularly vulnerable to a searching helicopter. Now, even if their crossing place were discovered, the trail would go cold just south of the border.

"We wait a quarter of an hour," ordered Phivo, "to let the paint harden. Meanwhile, let's eat."

Andoula lifted the cloth cover from a basket of cheese, bread and fruit, and opened a flagon of *kokinelli*, or village wine.

"Be careful," she warned softly, handing Sam a paper cup with a smile which it was probably as well Phivo didn't see, "it's almost as strong as Commanderia."

They were away again by seven, lurching down the track, in true Cypriot manner leaving Andoula to load half empty paint tins and the remains of their breakfast into the back of the Patrol.

Chapter 12

The girl wasn't crying any more but her body was tense and unco-operative. She seemed miles away. Utkin had to decide quickly. He forced her into a sitting position on the nearest bunk.

"Stay there."

It was as much a threat as a command, reinforced by an inverted forefinger which quivered briefly under her nostrils. There was no reaction, not that it mattered. He could keep the girl in view whilst he looked for the best place to put her.

Moving for'ard from the companionway his eyes ranged round the cabin. Perhaps she could be tied to a bunk. They were a bit flimsy but might be all right, if there was nothing better.

Utkin opened the bulkhead door and stood sideways inside an oval hole. He glanced left at the girl, then right into the forepeak. The steel door could be locked from outside, but like the main cabin there were portholes. They were too small for an escape, but if she broke loose – as well she might with tools all over the place, never mind what was in that metal cabinet – they could expect some attempt at a signal to the Englishman.

Artamonov's shout chastened him to pull his finger out. Utkin ran back, past the girl and under the companionway steps to the engine room. It was a steel cage with no portholes.

"Couple of minutes," he called up to the wheelhouse to keep Artamonov off his back.

When he tried to push her in she resisted, bracing her left foot against the door frame and locking her body. The sudden, silent act of defiance took him by surprise.

Artamonov was waiting. Utkin over-reacted. He wanted only to stun the girl, but in his haste chopped her a good bit harder than intended. Her left temple caught the edge of the door frame.

Shit! She shouldn't have tried to turn just when he hit her. Artamonov wouldn't accept error, accidental or otherwise. Anxiously, Utkin felt for a pulse and found one with relief. At least now it would easier to tie her ankles.

He checked to make sure her breathing wasn't obstructed, then despite the rush stole a few seconds to look at the girl's body. His hand played with her right breast. Later, if all went well, he knew that Artamonov would give her to him. He left her lying on one side, arms still folded behind her back, spare cordage from her ankles lashed to the heavy duty angle iron which formed a safety barrier around engines and shafts.

Utkin tossed the key on to the chart table.

"Even if she gets free," he argued, "there's nothing she can do. And I doubt she'll start messing about with strange fittings inside a locked engine room."

Artamonov grunted. He, too, was searching for anything which might have been overlooked.

"Let's go," he ordered abruptly. "Back to the equipment. You change, I'll sort out the weapons. Then we'll pick our position."

Sometimes they were on roads, often just tracks. Every few hundred yards they changed direction, but the Rovers were making steady progress through the southern part of Paphos forest – predominantly westward, judging from the direction of the sunlight shafting through the tree tops. Sam tried to follow their route on a two-fifty-thou map. At four miles to the inch most of the tracks weren't marked, although he knew roughly where they were from the contours. At less than fifteen hundred feet above sea level they emerged from the tree line to a dramatic rise in temperature as shady forest gave way to sun-baked vineyards. They were approaching a village.

"Anadbiou," muttered Phivo hoarsely, leaning forward over the wheel to peer apprehensively into an empty sky.

Sam bridged the gap on the map between the village and Lara Bay, bracing his thumb and forefinger. Just under fifteen miles – say, twenty, allowing for the roads – but from now on they were out in the open.

He studied the tiny, stone dwellings beside the road. Living-cum-bedrooms opened directly on to the street. Religious ornaments decorated plain, wooden dressers. Old people sat on kitchen chairs outside their doorway, some raising a hand in uncertain salute. Donkeys outnumbered vehicles.

They were through the village in seconds. In the fields black-garbed women paused, straightening their backs to lean on a hoe and stare – premature crones, faces etched and brown, bodies aged and dessicated from domestic and agricultural labour.

Phiti, Lasa and Simou. Sawn-off one gallon petrol tins bursting with geraniums lent gashes of colour to dusty streets. Earthenware amphorae, direct descendants of the two-handled jars of ancient Greece and Rome, decorated shady squares and courtyards. Like Phivo's village these lowland equivalents were almost self-sufficient, their elders neither wanting nor welcoming infection from the outside world.

For a couple of miles they joined a metalled road from Paphos to Polis then west again, seeking out first a fair-weather surface and finally, for the last five miles, a shifting track from Dhrousha to Lara. Gradually they relaxed. In these parts police patrols, like thunderstorms, were scarcely more than an annual event.

Pain washed through Sally as she floated on a rising tide of consciousness. She felt stabbing pulses from a needle point of light behind her eyes, followed by a burning stiffness in her limbs – except for her left arm which, under the weight of her body, had lost all feeling.

She was confused. Sometimes, first thing in the morning, she couldn't remember which day it was, but that never lasted for more than two or three seconds.

Sally knew who she was, where she came from, what she did for a living. In London she was safe and secure. She had been pursued before by bad dreams which trespassed into the light of day, but they retreated almost immediately. She waited but nothing receded. This was real – she was bound and naked on a metal floor. The answers were there, just inches away. Her mind reached out, but couldn't quite touch them. It frightened her. Frustrated, she tried to move, jarring her legs against a rope around her ankles.

The exertion made her aware of the stifling atmosphere around her, heavy with the fumes of diesel and machine oil. She was going to be sick.

She tried to sit up so that she could lean sideways, but there wasn't time. Unable to stop half of it from running down her cheek and over her shoulder, she managed only a spitting, squirming retreat from each burst of vomit.

At last it was finished. Her head was pounding. Using her other shoulder she brushed clinging shreds of last night's supper from her lips. Sally concentrated on breathing deeply to settle her stomach.

As she conquered the nausea two tiny, silver spheres of memory drifted back.

Sam – she clung desperately to the name – she was with a man called Sam, and they were going to kill him, the two men who had hurt her. Sally's mind stretched for more, but the pain in her head grew worse.

In her distressed, unbalanced state he was a lifeline. She had to tell him about the two strangers! But she was tired and sick and it was easier to give in and close her eyes.

It was a relief to peel off the wetsuit. Whilst Utkin changed, Artamonov extracted three packages from their kit bag. Two were the same shape. He stripped plastic waterproofing from a pair of Israeli Uzzi sub-machine guns then opened the third package: M-D11 grenades, made by Diehl Ordnance of Rothenbach, West Germany. He sorted two piles. Each man would carry an Uzzi, three spare magazines, three grenades and a water bottle.

Israeli and West German. He smiled at the combination. But technically they were a sound choice, although only in the elite Spetsnaz could preference over-ride dogma. Artamonov had always liked the Uzzi – not a lot of range, but compact and reliable. He palmed a grenade. Its heavily ribbed body was easy to grip, important when hands were cold, or slippery with sweat. Embedded in a thick, plastic wall encasing forty-two and a half grams of nitropenta high explosive were three thousand eight hundred steel balls.

Unfortunately there were several approaches to Lara, either on tracks from the east or along what the map dignified as a fair-weather, north-south coast road. With so many approaches, Artamonov's choice was restricted to the area around the bay. For fifteen minutes he jogged out along the tracks to study the ground from each direction, then up and down the surrounding dunes. Finally he lay above a sandy hollow where a track led off to the beach. They had to pass below and a vehicle would at least slow down before leaving the coast road. With luck it might stop, letting someone out to walk for a few yards and check the softer going. They might even decide to unload from the road.

But it was less than ideal, with only two of them. Fine if they could guarantee that the Englishman would be alone, but the girl had mentioned the possibility of Greeks – not that he was troubled by the prospect of taking on a few locals, especially with the advantage of surprise. But more people could mean two vehicles, which might not arrive at the same time. First priority was the man Verle. Afterwards, rather than head for Nicosia or radio for a submarine pick-up close inshore, it might be better to take the patrol boat out and scuttle it. That would remove the evidence. But if at all possible Artamonov did not intend to leave any witnesses.

He positioned Utkin above the hollow and set off along the track. If there were two vehicles he would expect the Englishman to be in the first one, and if they arrived separately, Utkin could take care of the second. Artamonov lay behind a dune and tested his fields of fire. From here he could still see the junction, but also cover the track and part of the beach.

The morning breeze steaded into a gentle westerly, but on land gave little relief from a sun which arced to its zenith. Birds and insects gradually accepted as part of the landscape the two strange figures lying almost motionless on burning sand. A soft, buzzing whine punctuated only by finches and cicadas settled over the hollow.

Sally flinched from a spark inside her head – an electric flash of recollection. She was on a patrol boat! Sam had anchored it

202

somewhere, and one of them had pushed her into the engine room, after they had hurt her.

She was less afraid now that her mind was beginning to function. There was still a lot missing, but the spectre of insanity was receding. Her memory would come back. She had only parts of a jigsaw, but if necessary Sam would provide the missing pieces.

The first priority was to free her ankles. Until then she could do nothing, not even stand. Sally rolled on to her back and heaved herself up into a sitting position. The binding looked like terylene, strong but quite thin. About twelves inches of cordage linked her ankles to the angle iron around which he had taken a dozen or so turns, both above and below the line, before tying a knot.

Using her stomach and leg muscles she jerked upward, twisted her feet sideways, rested them on the line and pushed it down. She repeated the sequence, then shuffled forward for a closer inspection. Snatching the line up and down had opened a tiny gap.

She was panting from exertion in the hot, foul atmosphere, but from now on she could work on her back. Sally kept the line as tight as possible, sawing up and down from the horizontal, trying not to bang her heels on the floor. It took as much effort as doing sit-ups. She adopted a steady rhythm, resting after each group of five, ignoring the rivulets of sweat on her chest and forehead.

She lost count. It might have been the eighth batch of five or the tenth. All her concentration funnelled into fraying a single length of terylene. It parted sooner than she expected.

Sally sat up and smiled, taking simplistic, child-like pleasure from her achievement. Even though her ankles were still tied together, with her legs free she could kneel or stand with her back to the angle iron.

There were a number of separate lashings round her arms. Working backwards she strained to look over her shoulder, but had to feel for the last couple of inches. It was impossible to hold a precise angle. Time after time rough metal rasped red abrasions till they were bleeding sores but although she cried out at some of the deeper cuts Sally worked on, so single-minded in her purpose that nothing else mattered.

The last few strands were easier. Thank God she was at last free to bend down and untie her ankles. She straightened up and massaged her wrists gently, for the first time looking carefully around the engine room. Oblivious of her nakedness, of her arms banded with congealed, red slashes, her matted hair and grease, sweat and vomit-stained skin, Sally turned her attention to the bulkhead door.

It was a watertight partition, designed to give the crew more time to abandon if the boat was holed badly or on fire in the after section. A central wheel operated metal studs which extended sideways into the surrounding frame, bracing the door against water pressure. Sally twisted the wheel as far as it would go. With its studs retracted the door rattled more loosely. It seemed to be held only by the tongue of a single security lock, which she assumed was intended for when the boat was in harbour and unoccupied. Sally gripped the wheel and threw herself backwards, but succeeded only in jarring her wrists.

She began a methodical search for something with which to attack the lock. Drawers in the engineer's bench yielded a mixture of small tools – spanners, screwdrivers and pliers – but no large hammer or cold chisel. Leaving the bench she followed a walkway round to the starboard side of the engine room to search aft. When she turned, her view of the door was obstructed by loops of oval-link chain hanging from a pair of pulleys above the engines. Presumably the chain and pulley systems were used whenever an engine had to be lifted from its bearers.

Her father used to have a bow saw . . . Her mind drifted back into childhood memory. The saw's frame was a broadened H-shape. A blade ran between the bottom of the vertical struts, and the tops were joined by two pieces of string. When he inserted a wooden peg between the strings and twisted it they tightened, tensioning the blade at the other end.

Sally climbed over the angle iron and crouched on the engines. One length would be too short. Fortunately neither chain was an endless run, each loop was joined by a shackle. She clambered down for a pair of pliers to undo the pins.

It wanted a straight pull. Sally converted the two loops into a single length of chain, feeding it round the wheel shank and back through the spokes before joining the ends with a second shackle. She took a tommy bar from a set of socket spanners and passed it between the chains, rotating for a few turns to take up the slack.

There would be five components under stress: the chain and pulleys, which were designed to take the weight of an engine; the door wheel, half inch solid metal on a one inch spindle; and the tongue and bed of the lock. Sally leant on to the tommy bar.

She was hanging from it, all her weight insufficient for one more quarter turn. The door seemed to give, but only by a few millimetres. In desperation she jerked on the end of the bar, a suspended marionette collapsing to the floor as the door screeched and crashed ajar.

Surprisingly the lock fitting was intact but with its studs withdrawn the door had folded slightly along one edge, distorting the frame recess and allowing a now bent tongue to be forced out. Tension had also stiffened the hinges. Sally had to brace one foot on the bulkhead to pull the door wide open.

She explored carefully, keeping behind superstructure or below the wheelhouse windows. Her slacks were lying on deck but her bra had disappeared, presumably blown overboard. Sally found the rest of her clothes on the wheelhouse floor. She went below to her cabin and looked inside the tin box. It was still there – the key to the steel cupboard in the forepeak. They had checked the boat for people, but had not had time to search it.

Sally studied the contents. Sam had oiled and replaced the sub-machine guns, although there was no sign of the one left out for her – they had either taken it with them or tossed it overboard. She wasn't at all confident about loading fresh magazines and putting them on a weapon. She also ignored the grenades, but a strange looking pistol with an unusually wide barrel caught her eye. Next to it was a box of American-made cartridges. Sally picked it up and looked at the lettering. 'One Inch Signal – Red'. It might be the ideal way to warn Sam.

Gingerly Sally lifted up and examined the Very pistol, her bruised face furrowing in concentration. She moved a small lever and the weapon hinged open, exposing a cartridge chamber. Obviously they went in one at a time, like her father's shotgun. She closed the pistol and thumbed back the hammer. It was a similar arrangement to a child's cap gun, when she squeezed the trigger the hammer flew forward with a hollow click.

She bundled the pistol and cartridges and her clothes inside an oilskin, just as Sam had done, and stepped down the boarding ladder. Only when salt water reached her cuts was she prompted to wipe the worst of the filth from her skin.

Sally had no idea where the two men would be but Sam had disappeared inland through a cleft in the foothills, towards the right-hand side of the bay. Pushing her bundle she swam to the bows and examined the shore. It might be safer to go left, towards the point. Then she could make her way round, through the dunes.

Utkin heard the Rovers long before the first vehicle pulled up in the hollow. Looking down on to sagging rectangles of roof canvas, he watched an upper section of aluminium door frame swing open. A mass of fair hair emerged into the gap, only to disappear as the man ducked inside again to talk to the driver. A tailboard crashed down, checked at the horizontal by its chains. Two more men were clambering from the back, each holding a sub-machine gun. He could see the second vehicle now, about two hundred yards away. Artamonov's orders were explicit. He would spring the ambush himself by opening fire. The fair-haired man set off along the track, weapon at waist height but ready. Utkin all but disappeared below the crest to avoid being seen by the second Land-Rover.

Artamonov, too, heard the other vehicle. It looked like the Englishman, walking towards him. Brakes squealed. He followed Utkin's example and slithered back till he could see the Rovers without exposing himself to the advancing figure. More men were getting out.

In the second vehicle Andreas waited patiently, his right foot idly blipping the throttle. Artamonov cursed. Against that engine noise it was impossible to be sure that there were no more vehicles. He peered cautiously up the track. The fair-haired man – it had to be the Englishman – was thirty yards away. Two more were following. Couldn't afford to delay . . . he pulled the pin and lobbed a grenade for the gap between the three men.

Sam's caution was deeply engrained. Not that he particularly expected trouble, but like any survivor from countless patrols, whether in the jungles of Belize, Beirut's Rue Hamra or Belfast's Falls Road, his senses were soaring. Eyes which caught a twitch of curtain at an upstairs window might be the only defence against an Armalite, so they were never at rest: they scanned and searched continuously. Ears strained permanently for any change in background noise level, for the slightest sound which might be out of place. Mentally he was already on starting blocks.

One second. Inside the plastic body a hammer struck and ignited the percussion cap. As the grenade crested the skyline its handle flew off with a distinctive 'ping'.

Two seconds. The delay pellet was burning in its tube. Sam's eyes jerked up to catch a small, dark oval almost at the apex of its parabola. Sound and shape were instantly recognisable.

"Grenade!" Even as he roared a warning, Sam was already running. Get off the track . . . no point in going left. He sprinted towards the thrower, pounding for dead ground at the foot of the dune.

Three seconds. Artamonov's grenade landed with a muted bump into soft sand. The delay pellet was melting a ring of solder, so that a pressure spring could force the detonator down on to a booster charge. Kyriakos and Costas failed to react instantly – they watched it land. Lack of experience cost them a full second before they, too, began to run. Pellet and detonator were now separated only by a single flap valve.

Artamonov had never underestimated the opposition. Even so, the speed of the Englishman's reaction took him slightly by surprise. No time for another grenade. He had to tell Utkin. His Uzzi came up into the aim but the sprinting figure was about to reach cover, shielded by the dune. He managed only a short burst on the running Greeks before they, too, were in dead ground. No matter. Artamonov had sited himself and Utkin so that each could cover the other. He switched to the group around the Land-Rovers. Utkin would have to take care of what the grenade failed to finish.

Four seconds. Another burst, a fraction high – only two rounds on a man's chest before the Uzzi lifted off target. Artamonov swore. The others were diving for cover. Utkin's weapon chattered. Phivo returned Artamonov's fire in long bursts, content at this stage to suppress the ambush whilst his men regrouped. Behind the second Land-Rover the bearded Arab registered a new, overhead fire position. There was no sign of Colonel Verle. Kyriakos and Costas were going to ground. One of them might have taken a hit, the bearded Arab couldn't be sure.

A flash from the pellet struck the flap valve, bending it up to reach detonator and booster charge. The grenade exploded, radiating steel fingers in a glittering pattern up and out from an expanding cloud of smoke and sand. When it cleared the Colonel and the other two, if they were alive, would be at the mercy of the man above. The Arab extracted the pin from his own grenade and let the handle fly off. For a count of two he smiled at the grey-black body, sensing its swelling warmth. Under cover of another burst from Phivo he tossed it over the dune.

Utkin flinched. Rounds were coming through the smoke towards his position too accurately for comfort, even though someone had to be firing almost blind. The explosion still rang in his ears. Below him, at least two more weapons were in action. Having opened fire as ordered, he wriggled back from the skyline. A couple of grenades on the vehicles below, then he would shift sideways to re-engage from a new position. Utkin knelt for the first throw.

An invisible giant whirling a massive, metal railway sleeper slammed it across his back. A laser of noise pierced his eardrums. He was looking through an inky-red gauze spangled with blinding flashes of light. When his face hit the sand, Utkin was unconscious.

More weapons were opening up around the Rovers. Artamonov winced and ducked as a burst of fire raised spits of sand alongside his face. From what should have been a routine ambush the situation was deteriorating rapidly. He lay below the skyline and changed magazines. It was sod's law.

The plan had been sound and it had to be worth trying to get rid of the witnesses. Unfortunately, he suspected, Utkin had fired at the two Greeks, and the Englishman had survived. Now that second grenade, and silence from Utkin . . .

Artamonov accepted the reverse phlegmatically, shifting his position and loosing off another burst to discourage any advance from behind the Rovers. Utkin neither carried nor wore anything which might give a clue to their origin. It was a pity about the Greeks, but they had observed no more than a gun battle. If he could reach the Englishman they would be leaderless, and he might still be able to get back to the boat. Artamonov dropped from the skyline, turned, and sprinted away.

An eerie silence shouted across the valley. Sam squinted at the ridge above the Land-Rovers. There had been nothing since the explosion. A few yards away Kyriakos was kneeling over an inert Costas. Sam suspected that whoever had been behind the hill had broken contact before an assault could be mounted by Phivo's group. The dune was about twenty feet high, its top protected by an overhang. Forty yards on, it sloped to the beach. With the main body largely intact and covering him he ought to be safe from above. Sam rose to his feet, brushed loose sand from the Saco and began a cautious trot to the end of the dune.

Artamonov knew precisely how a soldier's mind would react. The Englishman would reason that if he allowed the attacker to escape, they either had to mount a dangerous search or accept the risk of a later attack – at any moment. He smiled as he ran. In his place Artamonov would reason exactly the same way. All the Englishman's instincts must be telling him to keep the pressure on, not to lose contact.

He reached a second, irregular line of dunes, thirty yards behind the first position, and glanced to his right. Anyone trying to work round from the vehicles faced a long detour or, like the Englishman, an approach across open ground. He dived over the nearest mound and rolled into soft sand.

From the far end Sam could see the reverse slope and ambush position. Lying on his stomach he followed a line of footprints to the row of dunes. Someone had run parallel to the beach, rather than working round towards the interior.

Sam wondered how they had reached Lara. By boat perhaps. He couldn't see all of the bay, but the patrol boat was lying to her anchor, apparently deserted.

For the first time since a grenade had captured his attention, Sam thought of Sally. Unless the Rovers had bounced a hasty ambush, the Russians had probably been on board already. There could be someone out there now, or at any moment the whine of an outboard pushing a small dorey up on to a zig-zag plane for the patrol boat. Apart from the urgent need to track their attacker, he would feel a lot happier when they had secured the beach.

Through tufts of coarse grass Artamonov studied the Englishman – or rather his hair, which was all he could see.

Sam knew what he would do, in the attacker's shoes – make for the interior, probably, and try again later – but he recognised that it might be a come-on. A hundred yards away Phivo's group hadn't moved. It was either go now, or risk losing contact.

Artamonov sighted on where the head had been. A few paces back Sam took several deep breaths. He would come out at speed – just in case – rather than offer a slow, accelerating target, and he would go slightly left towards the beach, crossing the dunes almost at their nearest point and well clear of the Russian's tracks.

Sam launched himself, low and fast, jinking every few yards. Nearer to the beach there was more sand. It was like trying to run through a shifting, granular river.

With a mixture of excitement and relief Artamonov tracked the running figure, his foresight coming up on to the Englishman's body. A swerve. Now the target was almost head on . . . less delection . . .

Not quite half way, but he was slowing. Sam kicked out, desperate to end a nightmare of hands reaching up from the surface to cling by their fingernails from his calf muscles.

Another change of direction. Artamonov traversed smoothly. It was more difficult sideways. On the next shift . . .

His body knew instantly that it had taken a debilitating hit. For a couple of seconds it responded by doubling the effort. But unable to sustain activity, it pitched forward on to the sand.

210

Chapter 13

Paint and equipment she left at the village. The man who looked after her animals could be trusted to make sure that no evidence would be found. Considering the state of the roads, Andoula made good time back to Limassol. Phivo's instructions were typically broad-brush, but she had worked for him long enough to know exactly what he wanted.

The Datsun she parked in its underground garage space. Not for the first time Andoula used her pass key to close down her uncle's flat, packing an assortment of essentials into one large holdall: toilet bag, a few changes of clothing, and from the wall safe one of several passports and his emergency bankroll – two hundred thousand American dollars.

She took a taxi, first to her own modern but less spacious apartment. According to Phivo she ought to be back either later that night or on Thursday morning, but her uncle was a demanding employer and in business there were no concessions to their blood relationship. He expected one hundred per cent service which at times extended to wanting her on an aeroplane at less than an hour's notice. Domestic considerations were scarcely within his vocabulary. With foresight born of experience, Andoula kept her own survival bag packed permanently on top of a wardrobe. Two minutes after unlocking her front door, she was back in the taxi.

Perhaps he was showing off, but her driver made up for the tiredness of his ancient, diesel-engined Mercedes by refusing to lift his foot off the throttle. Andoula conceded that her *sang-froid* had been diluted by European standards – several

211

times she touched an imaginary brake pedal and closed her eyes as he pulled out to overtake blindly.

He asked a ridiculous fare but then she had spoken in English, her normal language for business. From her purse Andoula selected notes to the value of less than half the sum demanded.

"I am not a tourist," she hissed in Greek, "I live here. And I have to tell you that you smell."

Instinctively he gathered up the money tossed on to his lap through the open window. The little bitch had picked up her bags and stalked off into Larnaca Marina. His mother and sisters would not dare to speak in that way. For thirty seconds, until she turned a corner, the driver fingered his worry beads and eyed the alternate twitch of her buttocks encased in tight cotton trousers.

She had driven the Riva before but not on her own, and never in or out of harbour. Fortunately Stavros, whom she cordially detested but who doubled as mate as well as minder, had often tried to impress her by explaining the procedure. If in doubt she could go to the marina engineer, but Phivo wanted her to manage alone if she could. At least she didn't have to worry about fuel or water; there was a standing arrangement with the manager that the *Maria* was topped up after every trip. And liking his home comforts, she knew that her uncle kept the yacht well stocked with food and drink.

The engines started immediately. Andoula left them to warm up. With the ship's electrics switched to battery power she disconnected and coiled up the shore cable. As she singled up on to bow and stern lines no one seemed to be taking the slightest interest in a young woman apparently about to take forty-two feet of power boat to sea. A final check round the wheelhouse . . . She didn't know how to use all the *Maria*'s equipment, but Andoula felt just about confident that she could take the yacht to Lara.

She pulled the bow line on board and ran aft. Pausing only to check that both warps were safely on deck she scurried for the controls, but there was no hurry. In sheltered water the *Maria* had barely moved.

Because she was one of the larger yachts in the marina – or

212

perhaps out of deference to Phivo – the Riva was moored on the end of a pontoon and conveniently near the exit. Throttles back, into astern, revolutions dipping perceptibly as her screws began to bite. Andoula's hands flew back to the throttles but the steady beat gave no hint of a stall. Protected from the pontoon by her fenders, the *Maria* edged back into a narrow channel.

Half a boat length then back to neutral. Her bow was drifting towards the end of the pontoon finger but there wasn't much more room astern. No matter, they ought to be able to clear the boat moored in front. Andoula gave her a burst of for'ard on starboard screw. The yacht checked then gathered way again, inching ahead and out towards the exit. Slow ahead both. She countered the swing and remembered to look for any other craft about to use the entrance.

Unfortunately she wasn't sure how to switch in the auto-pilot, so clear of the marina Andoula throttled back, put both engines in neutral and left the *Maria* to wallow gently whilst she coiled warps and gathered in the big, round fenders. Back inside the wheelhouse she folded a chart of the island to show its southern coastline and wedged it on the console in front of her steering position. Next she raided the fridge for some fruit and a can of Coke. Finally she settled herself into the helmsman's seat and pushed the throttles about one-third open, thrilling to the bubbling roar as two turbocharged Cummins diesels lifted the *Maria* effortlessly to fifteen knots. Mindful of Phivo's caution about her inexperience she resisted the temptation to go faster. Reaching out for an apple, Andoula settled on to a course for the open sea.

Following Phivo's instructions she stood out for about a mile before turning to run more or less parallel with the coast, but cutting across each bay. Fortunately visibility was excellent, because her instructions were at best rudimentary. She had hung on every word, repeating them afterwards until they were safely committed to memory.

'Get out of the bay. You'll see the lighthouse on Cape Kiti, then follow the coast for about twenty-five miles and you should recognise Limassol. Past the city, and the RAF airfield at Akrotiri, till you come to a second lighthouse on Cape Gata. For the next thirty miles there's only the odd village till

213

you get to Paphos, and that's where you have to concentrate. Note the log reading off Paphos Point. From there it's ten miles to Cape Drepanum, and you can't miss it because there's a biggish rock-cum-island a few yards offshore. Now check the log again, because it's only three more miles to Lara. Close the coast to within half a mile, and you're looking for a low spit of land sticking out into the sea. We're in the bay immediately behind it.'

She recalled his final instructions. 'And make sure you get there in daylight – you won't find it at night.'

Twelve o'clock. Ninety-five miles to run. It would be dark at eight, but she ought to be off Lara by about six.

There was sand in his mouth. Why the hell hadn't he been more careful? His body bounced again, slammed a second time.

Immersed in oil, oxidation would have been suspended. But surrounded by blood and tissue, solid slugs of phosphorous began to smoulder.

He knew that the first round had entered his chest. The second was lower down – abdomen or bowel. For a few precious seconds there was hardly any pain but he knew it would come, after the initial shock. Even so he was totally unprepared . . . Two white-hot balls accelerated their expanding burn. Nerve endings no longer muted were transmitting messages of indescribable agony. Fingernails lifted as he tried to prise into his body, but the rounds had entered from behind. It was impossible to touch or contain the fires.

Muscle spasm whipped back his head and spine – he was losing control – but even as he begged for death his last vision was of the girl, a smoking pistol in her hand. In those final seconds he knew . . . Artamonov watched her insert another flare cartridge but by the time she pulled the trigger his heart was entering cardiac arrest.

So it had been a come-on, and if Sally hadn't been there it might well have succeeded. Sam shouted her name and ran diagonally down the dune, first towards the body, which he covered with his Saco till he had kicked away the Russian's sub-machine gun and felt for a pulse, then back to Sally.

She had done it. Sam was back, and safe. A colossal tiredness engulfed her but now she could relax. He was taking the pistol from her fingers – that was all right – now he was touching her arm, and talking. But her mind had been stretched too far. Dislocated and overloaded, it had to rest. She smiled but couldn't respond further. Not yet.

Sam had seen it before, a sort of shell shock. Grown men would turn suddenly mute, tears rolling down their face. There was sometimes acute agrophobia and refusal to leave an imagined sanctuary, but invariably that partial or complete withdrawal. It was one of the classic – and often most distressing – symptoms of mental illness. Sally was obviously blissfully unaware of being at odds with reality. Whatever she did, however withdrawn she became, in her own mind she was entirely sane. Only the outside world could be at fault. With a heavy feeling of guilt Sam studied her closely, but there was no reaction, not even from her eyes. He was looking into a catatonic void.

"There were just the two of them. The other one's dead as well." It was Phivo's voice, at his elbow. Gently Sam put an arm round the girl's shoulders.

"Bring up the Rovers. We'll find another hollow, near the beach, then make sure that the area's secure." He looked at Phivo. The awful question, but it had to be asked.

"Casualties?"

"Stellios is dead. He was about to walk up the track when the first shots were fired. Kyriakos has a piece of shrapnel in one shoulder but he's lucky – I don't think it's serious. Costas was hit by a bullet as well as being caught in the grenade blast. He's unconscious."

It was a measured, factual response but for Costas, Phivo's voice implied, it was only a matter of time. So, effectively, two dead – a loss they could ill afford. They were down to eight men; seven, if Kyriakos were seriously incapacitated.

Sam looked up closely at the Cypriot.

"And the rest?"

Phivo knew what he meant. The Englishman was asking after the morale and courage of his men. For some, it was their first taste of combat.

"It's nothing new for Stavros. All he wants is revenge for

his cousin. The Arabs are fine, but that doesn't surprise me. So is Andreas. Kyriakos and John are a bit shaken, but with the others to stiffen them up they should be all right."

It was an intelligent answer, devoid of the usual Greek bluster. And Sam had to know. With so few of them, he couldn't afford a weak link.

They set themselves up near the beach. Andreas and John were despatched to search the northern quadrant, the two Arabs went south. He sat the girl in the shade, watched over by Kyriakos who appeared to have escaped with a flesh wound. Sam was reasonably confident that he could remove the metal once they were onboard.

With Phivo and Stavros covering him, Sam swam out to the boat. He was mystified by a spatter of baked beans on the side of the wheelhouse – hopefully she would recover to tell him about it eventually – but the message from a windlass of twisted chain and the damaged engine room door was clear enough. He found a bucket and rinsed away the mess, switching on electric pumps to empty the bilges. What the hell had they done, to make her vomit and almost lose her mind?

The area search produced only a dinghy. Inside the kit bag they found a couple of immersion suits, a sniper's rifle, some field rations and a Japanese radio. It confirmed Sam's suspicion that there were only two Russians – the dinghy would have been too low in the water with three men and their equipment. At least the inflatable solved one problem. With lines attached to its bow and stern they could lighter their weapons and ammunition into deeper water.

First priority, however, was Kyriakos's wound. Sam extracted sterile-packed swabs, forceps and scalpel from the first aid chest. They laid Kyriakos face down on a scrubbed cabin table. The fragment had entered from below, presumably because he was diving forward at the time, and pushed up into the fleshy area over his right scapula. There was an angry, purple swelling and a lot of congealed blood but it probably looked worse than it was. Even so, he was not going to enjoy having it removed.

Kyriakos gasped when Sam made a deep cut to widen the entry hole. After that it wasn't too difficult to fish out the metal. It looked like a piece of mechanism. To a permanent

216

accompaniment of the Cypriot sucking in saliva, Sam swabbed away till he was sure that no fragments of metal or cloth remained in the wound.

"Nearly finished," he muttered, to encourage his patient.

He held the Savlon bottle where Kyriakos couldn't see it, measured out a stiff dilution, parted the cut with his fingers and poured antiseptic into the cavity. Kyriakos roared but it was essential to guard against sepsis. Finally Sam closed the wound with strips of tape and bandaged on a dressing.

"Don't start heaving things around," he warned as Kyriakos dabbed tears from his eyes and pulled on his shirt, "or it might start bleeding again. It'll feel stiff, but as far as I could see there's no muscle or bone damage. Make sure you get some rest – it shouldn't be too bad tomorrow."

They were loaded by mid-afternoon, including the bodies of Stellios and Costas and the two Russians, which to avoid complications later would best be buried at sea. Sam was drenched with sweat from helping to hump and stow box after box. Leaving John and Andreas to finish off, he dived over the side to join the shore party. Sally might react badly to coming onboard with strangers. It would be better if he rowed her out himself.

He swam slowly, beginning to feel tired not just from physical exertion – he was used to that – but from almost constant stress since leaving Fethiye. It would be a week on Friday, hardly an anniversary to be proud of with Julian and Fiona dead, and now Stellios and Costas as well as the Russians. And he was supposed to have resigned from it all. Sam dipped his head below the surface, as if in search of absolution from the sea. But when he opened his eyes there was still the prospect of a young girl with only half a mind. He had survived, but it was as if the gods preserved him only for the pleasure of their own amusement.

Sam lowered his face again. He had experienced this bone-deep weariness before but to surrender to it was to become careless and extravagant with life. Tomorrow was Thursday, the day before the ferry arrived at the island. In forty-eight hours it would all be over. He shook droplets of water from his face and stretched for the shore, sweeping back his arms to haul clear from lethargy and depression.

There was some improvement, a vague smile in response to his 'Hullo Sally', but she still wasn't ready to speak. Sam assiduously conducted a one-sided quasi-normal conversation. She allowed herself to be pulled up and walked to the beach, even co-operating by climbing into the dinghy. Sam tried to reassure himself. He had seen worse cases. Given peace and rest, she would recover. Onboard, he settled her on to the skipper's bunk and drew the curtain.

Kyriakos also stayed below, lying on a long bunk beside the saloon table. The rest of them worked on deck, unpacking and examining their windfall.

Part of the haul included three American-manufactured lightweight company mortars. Developed during the Viet Nam campaign, the sixty millimetre mortar was designed to be man portable, giving organic, high-volume fire support to long range infantry patrols. It took the Arabs only a few minutes to assemble the bipod, baseplate and tube. Sam passed them the sight mechanism and unpacked a high explosive bomb.

"Used one of these before?" he asked.

They looked at the nose with its bulbous cap and lined markings. The bearded Arab shook his head.

"It's a multi-option fuse. You turn it –" he twisted the nose section – "to one of four settings: high airburst, low airburst, point detonation or delay."

Aziz reached out, greedy for a new toy. Sam left it with them. Before he reached the wheelhouse a familiar, ringing 'plonk' assaulted his ears. He turned. Half a mile away a piece of hillside exploded.

The mortars would be invaluable, although some of the old, stone buildings on Kastellorizon could probably survive a direct hit. But in the Turkish armoury Sam had found one weapon system which, above all others, could prove decisive. They had removed probably the Battalion's entire reserve of anti-tank missiles: ten M47 Dragons, still in their packing cases, each one stamped with the markings of the McDonnell Douglas Corporation, St Louis, Missouri.

Sam had never used a Dragon, but one wire-guided, optically-tracked system had to be pretty much like another. He unpacked a tube and laid it on the wheelhouse floor. With the missile already inside, it was less than three feet long and weighed about twenty pounds. At the front of the tube was a single support rod. Sam lifted the missile, hinged down the stand and sat behind it, resting the centre of the launcher tube on his right shoulder. So far so good. Now he had to fit the combined firing and tracker attachment.

The optics slid on to a mount near the front of the launcher. Fully assembled, it looked like a length of drainpipe with a bulky pair of binoculars strapped on top.

It was a relatively simple weapon system to use. All the operator had to do was hold cross-hairs on the centre of his target. Commands passed through the wire guided the missile automatically, and although designed as a tank stopper the warhead would penetrate three feet of reinforced concrete. The only limitations were range – about a thousand metres before it ran out of wire – and the ability of the operator to lock on and hold, despite whatever might be exploding around him.

Sam carried the missile on to the foredeck and ran an instruction period, making each man go through the assembly process and test the optics. Finally he gave a demonstration firing, mainly to check that the weapons hadn't deteriorated in storage. As its gyro spun up to operating speed, the missile's gas generators hissed it from the tube. Inside the tracker an infra-red detector picked up a signal from the missile's transmitter, and measured the error between flight path and line of sight to the cross hairs. Using the optics' six times magnification, Sam had no difficulty in achieving dead centre on the Arabs' mortar scar.

Apart from any test factor, firing both mortar and Dragon would give the men confidence in their weapons – a useful morale booster.

At four o'clock the wind died. They heard the Riva at twenty to six. A few minutes later Andoula nosed the *Maria* cautiously through the entrance to bring her alongside the patrol boat. Whilst his men were helping with warps and fenders, Phivo joined Sam inside the wheelhouse.

"My friend," the huge hand settled on Sam's shoulder, "not without your help, we have our weapons. I think I should tell the others that we are now, as you British would say, formally under your command." He smiled, and tightened his grip. "But I should be happy to act as your First Lieutenant."

Although only confirmation of their agreement, it was a vote of confidence. Had there been any reservation, Sam knew that Phivo would not have hesitated to reverse his decision. But he was grateful for the gesture, particularly as in this part of the world any godfather would be reluctant to acknowledge publicly the authority of an outsider.

"Thanks." Sam placed his hand over Phivo's wrist. "I shall need an orders group, say in about twenty minutes. When we leave I'll drive the patrol boat, and presumably you will want to skipper the *Maria*. We'll split the men between us."

He grinned. "You have the better facilities, Second in Command, so do you mind if we meet on your yacht," Sam glanced at his watch, "at a quarter-past six?"

Phivo disappeared in search of Andreas. Sam wanted their armoury divided, half on each boat.

Alone in the wheelhouse, Sam opened out Admiralty Chart number 183 and leaned over the table, but apart from a time and distance appreciation there wasn't much he could plan. He tapped his dividers on the paper. A blind assault would be suicide. They had to know more about the Russians – where they were, what they were doing. The principles were the same whether taking on a small force or a field army. Without good intelligence you were lost.

He didn't hear her approach. Sam was still mulling over his problem when Andoula's hands closed round his upper arm.

"Phivo told me about the girl. I thought perhaps I could help. Another woman, and all that."

"She's below. Resting, I hope." Sam pointed to the companionway. "Down there and for'ard. Behind the curtained-off area to port." He reached out to hold her back.

"She was all right when I left the boat yesterday morning. After that, all I know is that one or both of those Russians came onboard, and that when she got loose from the engine room Sally went ashore and shot one of them to pieces with a Very pistol."

Andoula sensed his feelings of guilt and anxiety and turned to face him.

220

"I think she's been interrogated," Sam concluded. "No damage that's evident could have caused this reaction. Whatever it was, whatever they did to her, her mind's been hurt quite badly." He withdrew his hand. "Don't expect rapid results, and please, be careful how you go. Any attempt to force things might make her worse."

Andoula looked at him for rather a long time before stepping into the companionway.

With each man – apart from the Arabs – settled behind a large measure of his favourite alcohol, they listened to Phivo's opening words. His brief reference to the change of command received a general grunt of approval. Sam stood up.

"There are about forty men on that island," he began abruptly, "and they will be good. We got lucky today – don't count on it again. On the other hand, from now on we shall have the initiative."

He unfolded two charts on the carpet and weighted each corner.

"We're almost on the western tip of Cyprus, so it's only a hundred and fifty miles to Kastellorizon."

His finger traced the passage.

"We have a calm night, with little or no swell, so we can open up – say about thirty knots cruising. If we leave at seven, we can be there by midnight."

Sam wanted the men to be able to relax on passage, and at thirty knots they stood a good chance of avoiding the submarine. As he glossed over it, the door slid open and Andoula walked in.

"Before we mount an attack," he continued, "there has to be a reconnaissance. I can't risk going ashore in daylight, and the same goes for our final landing. The steamer is due on Friday. Tomorrow's Thursday. That points to a recce tonight, with the assault probably in the early hours of Friday morning. Between the two we lie up and rest."

"What about the girl on your boat?" The question came from Andoula. "She needs peace and quiet. Any more trauma could cost her what sanity she has left."

"Don't think it hasn't been worrying me," Sam replied evenly. "But I can't just put her ashore. She either needs the

221

support of people she knows, or specialist medical attention. I have to reach Kastellorizon tonight. There just isn't time to take her back to Akrotiri, which is the only British hospital, and then stand a reasonable prospect of being off the island before daybreak." He hesitated. "Besides, if she stays on the boat, she ought to be all right."

Even so, there was an element of chance. He could see that Andoula wasn't convinced. It looked as if she were about to round on him, but Phivo intervened.

"Enough." His thumb jutted towards Sam. "He's right. And don't get any ideas about taking her ashore yourself."

Andoula was catching his pent-up reaction to the events of the day. He stabbed his finger at her. "Costas and Stellios are dead. We shall need every man ashore, so you – " he pounced on the word – "will have to drive a boat."

This wasn't the safely legislated world of women's lib. From modern director and executive their relationship had regressed instantly. The veneer lifted, Sam suspected that any challenge from Andoula would have been met by the traditional back-hander. Her face on fire with rage and humiliation, she had the sense to keep quiet.

"Off Kastellorizon," Sam resumed softly, "we'll let the patrol boat pull ahead. When she throttles back the *Maria* will overtake, masking us from the shore. I shall go over the side. For reasons which will become clear, I suggest you lie up inside Kekova inlet. I may not be able to get back to you, but we shall be in touch by radio. If not before, I'll see you on the island."

He lifted his glass.

"Andoula, gentlemen, your health."

Gin and bitters burned his throat.

"Phivo will organise two crews according to experience. We leave in thirty minutes."

222

Chapter 14

Not as near dusk as he would have preferred, Captain Viktor Litov invited his officer of the watch to bring their Foxtrot Class submarine to periscope depth. There was a freighter going east-west about three miles away, probably outbound Cyprus, or maybe Lebanon, on course for the Rhodes Channel. He made a three-sixty degree search and waited patiently for her bridge deck to disappear over the horizon. Satisfied that there were no other ships – or aircraft – within sight, he flipped up the handles and ordered 'down 'scope'. As his periscope watchkeeper lowered the shaft into its well, Litov gave the order to surface.

The ship's intercom squawked a metallic warning. Next to the Captain, the Officer of the Watch began his incantation.

"Blow number one tank, blow number two, blow number three, blow number four . . . Shut number one valve, shut number two . . ."

A dull vibration settled through the ship as high pressure air blew into ballast tanks, forcing water through low level vents. The submarine lifted, stern first, then by the bow, and finally level.

Litov knew absolutely nothing about the man at his elbow who had boarded only twenty-four hours earlier. Until then it had been a routine patrol as part of what NATO referred to as SOVMEDRON, the Soviet Mediterranean Squadron. His two thousand-ton, three hundred foot submarine had been ordered to a rendezvous a few miles south of Crete where their passenger, who had arrived on the Island of Malta by Aeroflot, had transferred from a helicopter of the Soviet Merchant Marine.

The man carried what would have passed for a cassette radio, although not with the quality of sound usually associated with its discreet Japanese logo, because most of the set's interior was taken up with entirely different circuitry. Consular staff were on hand in case of difficulty, but in the event he had walked unchallenged through crew arrival. When the flight departed with a different steward he would be said to be recovering from some minor ailment, in the unlikely event that the Maltese noticed the difference.

Litov's orders were explicit. He was to afford the new arrival every possible assistance. When he had asked about the safety of his ship, the Admiral had been unusually evasive.

"Captain, if what your passenger wants is humanly possible, you are to do it. Should there be an accident – " his shoulders lifted – "you will be guilty. If you decline a request – " heavy stress on that last word – "then unless you can prove conclusively that it would have endangered your command," he shrugged again, "you will also be guilty."

The Admiral had seemed nervous but sympathetic almost to the point of condolence.

"You were chosen because of your experience. I can suggest only that you do your best, and wish you good luck."

Litov jerked back to the present.

"Open bottom hatch."

With the upper hatch open he preceded his passenger into the sail. The man extended an aerial. If Artamonov and Utkin were transmitting, he would hear them.

A hundred miles south-west of the submarine a Pchelka pilot eased back his throttles and circled just outside the Nicosia F.I.R., or Flight Identification Region. A shade more power, safely away from the backside of the drag curve, and into recommended range speed. If necessary they could stay up for hours as an airborne rebroadcasting station for the submarine. It could be a long, boring night but better than last time. They had run out of fuel on the bloody taxi-way. The pilot eased his straps and continued the interminable checks of instruments and horizon.

The submarine wallowed gently in the low swell. With her

224

captain on deck, the First Lieutenant had broken his rest to man the control room.

"Contact, bearing zero three zero." The sonar operator paused. "Not yet classified. Moving left. Difficult to tell blade speed. High revs and there's some shaft rub. Sir, might be two small vessels, fading fast."

The First Lieutenant nodded to the Officer of the Watch, acknowledging that he had heard the report. Probably a couple of pleasure yachts. In any case, nothing they could do about it. Certainly no reason to break silence. The Old Man had been a bit tense lately. No need to worry him till they came down from up top.

The shore party met neither their seven o'clock schedule nor the alternative an hour later. Litov entered Cypriot territorial waters to take station shortly before nine o'clock, one mile off Lara Bay. If the radio had failed there would be a light signal. At nine-thirty the submarine, with seventy-one men inside her, slipped below the surface. The Pchelka pilot turned thankfully for home.

In Moscow the controller of Operation Red Castle summoned his special forces adviser. For half an hour they sipped a Highland malt, discussing options and possibilities, but at the end of the day, failure to meet one schedule was too inconclusive – insufficient to justify an early withdrawal when the operation had yet to reach its climax. The two men were agreed. Despite an uncomfortable loose end in Cyprus, they would go ahead.

Two hundred feet below the surface and off watch in his bunk, First Officer Oleg Chekovsky realised with a sudden flush of guilt and panic that he had forgotten to mention a sonar contact to his Captain. Chekovsky was new to the ship, and still in awe of her skipper. He would leave it, rather than confess. Those two boats must be miles away by now.

Only two men on the submarine, Captain Litov and his passenger, knew the full background to their mission. The Admiral had been ordered expressly to forbid any detailed explanation to the crew. Thanks to rigid centralised control of the Soviet military machine, Oleg Chekovsky never understood the significance of what seemed to be only a tiny

225

omission. The midnight situation report – or sitrep – from Moscow to Kastellorizon mentioned only that a team inserted to take care of the patrol boat had yet to establish communications. When Samandag received the message and retired to his room he could not have known that Sam Verle was less than twenty miles away.

For the first hour Stavros had driven the patrol boat whilst Sam joined Phivo on the *Maria*. Thirty miles out, after a brief pause to bury Costas and Stellios and the Russians, he transferred back again.

Intermittent for a few minutes, but clear enough now and flashing, every five seconds: the lighthouse on Strongili Island, three miles south-east of Kastellorizon. Range of light, twenty miles. Fine on the starboard bow. Sam checked the radar scanner. Fourteen miles away.

For the past hour both yachts had been running without lights. Sam laid off a course for the Turkish coast and brought the patrol boat on to a more northerly heading. A glance over their port quarter confirmed that the *Maria* was following.

Sam and Phivo had refined their plan, such as it was, during the first hour of passage. Closing the coast before they reached the island offered the best chance of avoiding any lurking submarine. Once in-shore they would steam west, speed reduced to ten knots. Running side by side only the *Maria*, shielding the patrol boat from the island, would show a light – the single white of a local Turkish fishing boat. On an approach from any other direction they would be silhouetted, but hugging a backdrop of landmass their superstructure would be indistinguishable from seaward – and from the island less than a mile to the south on their port beam.

The harbourside village, normally well lighted, was in almost total darkness. Sam smiled. The darker the better. One by one, the kerosene lamps of the village disappeared behind an arm of land curving north from the westerly side of the harbour. It was less than seventy-two hours since he had swooped behind that peninsula to escape a machine gunner.

When Stavros and Aziz dropped his equipment over the side there was no time for farewells. Sam followed immediately. Even at ten knots, it was like hitting half-set concrete. A

226

quick wave to confirm that he was all right but already the boats were a quarter of a mile away. Water trickling over smeared black shaft grease brought a foul taste to his lips. Sam licked and spat. Lying in the sea, with cold water seeping under his wetsuit, he suddenly felt very alone.

Knowing how water temperature would affect his bladder, Sam had taken the precaution of drinking several cups of hot, sweet tea. Now, faced with an irresistible urge, he urinated freely, feeling the warm film spreading over his skin. With initial heat loss reduced significantly, Sam turned his attention to the board floating a few feet away.

He had intended to go ashore in the rubber dinghy, but the *Maria* had yielded a trove of equipment carried to amuse her passengers when the yacht was at anchor. Sam finned to the sailboard with its small, polythene-wrapped parcel lashed just for'ard of the mast slot. Sail and mast were stowed lengthways under bungee grips, available if he needed them, but for the approach Sam had brought a paddle from the inflatable. If the moon emerged through a high, shallow layer of fair-weather cumulus he could slip into the water and push the board. For now it was safe to sit astride it. Sam leaned forward, dipped his blade and J-stroked for the shore.

The Vathi Channel, a mile of open water separating Kastellorizon from mainland Turkey, was marked to the south by a small light set low on the seaward side of Kastellorizon's high peninsula. Down most of the island's west coast faults of rock slabbed sheer into the sea, but about three-quarters of a mile beyond the light was a small hook forming a tiny, uninhabited bay where except in a heavy swell he could beach the board. Sam had walked the island a couple of times during cruises from Cyprus. Fortunately the simplicity of its topography made it easy to remember. Climbing due east from the tiny bay he would reach a col. On his left, a seven-hundred foot hill on the peninsula; to the right, a ruined fort on the eight hundred and twenty foot peak of the island's spine. From the other end of the pass a steep track led down to the rear of the harbourside village.

Six hundred yards away the light changed from white to red. Approaching the coast at forty-five degrees, but beyond the loom of the beam, he would pass through a series of sectors – white again, obscured, another white – before the beacon disappeared astern, permanently obscured for the last half mile. The island rose, black, sheer and massive, from the water. He could hear waves lapping on invisible rocks less than a cable to port. Sam peered ahead, mentally shouting down his doubts. He couldn't have over-run. No. Ahead, three hundred yards, the outline of a little finger crooked into the sea.

When his flippers touched the bottom, Sam paused, holding the board just off-shore whilst he watched and waited. The first shot or stab of white light and he would be off, finning away underwater. But Samandag hadn't the men to picket the entire island. Nothing disturbed the timeless ripple of the waves until Sam hoisted his board ashore.

Rather than a Saco he had brought the more familiar Uzzi. Into Andoula's bag he stuffed his flippers, mask and snorkel, then sat on a rock to lace up his desert boots. He would leave nothing with the board in case it were discovered by some wandering patrol, despite a concealing layer of rocks and shingle. Twenty minutes later he settled the bag across his back, tightened its strap and set off up the hillside.

There was no natural path. Half the time it was a scramble, the Uzzi in one hand, the other forward on to rock or forever pushing back the bag. He stopped frequently. There was no point in arriving breathless at the crest, hearing destroyed by blood pounding past his ears. Despite the chill of the night he was sweating inside his wetsuit long before the slope levelled off into a ravine.

The feeling grew as he traversed the col. There was no evidence at all, just the promptings of some primaeval instinct all but bred out of homo sapiens by centuries of urban living. There was no noise but the wind on the back of his head as it funnelled through the high pass, nothing to see but grey slabs and shapes and black shadows, yet his pulse rate was being stirred by the same workings of imagination which turn familiar outlines in a child's bedroom into weird and menacing shapes.

No, it was someone, not some thing: from out there, either ahead or on one of the slopes, Sam sensed – a deep, gut feeling – that he was being watched.

228

He halted. Perhaps he should divert, pass round one of the peaks keeping just below the skyline. Instinctively he edged sideways towards the lee of a large boulder. But that shadow – too big, too solid . . .

The huge black shape leapt towards him. Sam bent his knees to twist and face, but the gap was too narrow. Before he could fire the Uzzi something rod-hard smashed down on his forearm. The weapon clattered on to bedrock as momentum carried them, locked together, across the floor of the ravine.

They broke apart on landing. Sam kicked out and scrambled clear, throwing the bag to one side. His right arm was numb. He needed time. But his opponent was up, too. A big man – maybe two hundred and thirty pounds – and in his hand what looked like a short chunk of wood. They were six feet apart, the Uzzi several feet away in the darkness.

Praying that his fingers would respond Sam crouched, extending his right arm towards the diving knife strapped to his calf. But before he could touch it, the attacker lunged.

No point in retreating. Sooner or later he would trip over backwards, or be caught by a blow. Go for surprise. Sam side-stepped but otherwise ignored the weapon and closed in. Fingers braced, he went for the eyeballs. Almost as if the move had been expected his opponent flinched away and recovered instantly, but Sam was able to land a solid knee to the groin before collecting a heavy blow on the temple.

He stepped back, blinking hard to clear his vision. Something warm trickled down the side of his face. The other man should have been doubled. He was crouched, and gasping, but by no means disabled. Sam would have to go in again. But this time he was able to extract the knife. Its six-inch blade glowed in the dull moonlight. The figure before him balanced, swaying from side to side on the balls of its feet. It spat in an act of defiance.

"Come on, ye Turkish bastard. I'm fuckin' waiting . . ."

Sam stood quite still, rigid with surprise. The man's size, that Scots' burr . . . There was no mistaking Angus Monro's voice.

Sam held his guard. There might still be an accident.

"Just who," he asked quietly, "do you think you're talking to?"

229

"Sam?" The voice was incredulous. "Is that really you?"

Sam slipped the blade into its sheath and moved closer. Angus peered at the familiar face under its black coating. But each man knew; this was just final confirmation. Seconds later they were hugging each other like ballerina footballers.

"Come on, mon, let's get off this track. Yon bastards patrol it once or twice a night. Normally I see them coming up from the village. They've been once already. When I saw you, I thought they must have spotted me and sent someone round the back."

Angus led off south, away from the harbour and up a steep slope to the island's summit. Out of sight from the ravine they squatted, sheltered from the wind by the ruins of an ancient fort. Sam gave a potted history. When he was told that the 'Turks' were definitely Russians, Angus raised his eyebrows and whistled softly but otherwise listened without interruption.

"Aye, well, you were right," he responded eventually. "There was a bit of a swell on Sunday morning and it was after breakfast when I finally left. The workboat's a seaworthy wee craft, but she's not built for speed. It was late afternoon before we reached Kekova. Not a yacht to be seen. I searched the whole lagoon, just in case there had been some misunderstanding. Nothing. No joy at the villages, either. By early evening I was knackered – tied up at one of the jetties, ate in a café and crashed out."

"We must have passed you on the way to the island," Sam observed quietly, "paddling those inflatables."

Angus nodded. "Next morning," he went on, "I started back. By then, I might tell you, you were being cursed up hill and down dale. I knew you wouldn't sail her against the prevailing westerly, not with a jury rig, so I had to assume that you'd got the engine running and for some reason, despite what we'd agreed, started to motor."

He looked across the water to Turkey. "There was nothing for it but to follow the coast by day, checking all the harbours."

"And inevitably," commented Sam, "you turned into Kastellorizon."

"To be honest, I thought that was where you would be." Angus stood, briefly, to look down the slope.

230

"Nothing," he muttered, making himself comfortable again. "Where was I? Oh, aye. After a while it did occur to me that the boat would be in a bit of a state, and Kekova's pretty primitive. So, the nearest hot shower and hotel room was this place." He tapped the length of wood into his palm. "I could imagine young Fiona telling you what she wanted." He paused uncomfortably. The girl was dead.

"It looked a bit quiet when I came in. Usually there's a few people outside the café, one or two fishermen mending their nets. At the time I didn't think much of it, but as soon as I get a line ashore some bastards armed with machine guns haul me off the boat."

Angus shrugged. "I got off pretty lightly. The Commander, this Ragip chap . . ."

"Samandag?" offered Sam.

"Aye, that's him. Well, after a few questions he told me to get back to the boat and stay there, then I'd be all right. He said they would be leaving after a few days. Till then, if they caught me off the boat, I could expect to be shot. Pretty blunt about it."

"So the tug's still OK?" asked Sam, an idea forming in his mind.

"Forget it," doused Angus. "There's a machine gun and mortar position on either side of the entrance. *Nessie* wouldn't get halfway up the harbour."

"Fair enough. But Samandag's warning hasn't stopped you from breaking curfew," Sam commented.

"Maybe it's because I live on the mainland and speak Turkish," responded Angus, his voice quieter and more serious, "but I've been left alone and certainly not ill treated. Those islanders are having a hell of a time."

His face turned towards Sam. "The first night was the worst. A few of the soldiers must have found some booze. They went from house to house after the women, and Samandag, or whatever his name is, let them get on with it. At the time I thought it was some sort of reward – now I see why." He paused and shook his head. "Screams, all night long. Men beaten senseless in the street. I kept thinking of Jenny, if it had been her . . ."

Sam waited for Angus to carry on.

231

"The next night – that was last night – I slipped over the stern and came out of the water on the other side of the harbour. Spent all night sitting on the summit with a torch. I thought if a boat came near enough to the south side of the island, I could try signalling or maybe swim out to it." He stopped. "Only some big stuff," he finished lamely, "way off in the shipping lanes."

They walked to the eastern end of the col and sat overlooking the village.

"Seems quieter tonight – perhaps Samandag thinks he's done enough," observed Angus cynically.

His arm extended towards the castle perched above the right-hand side of the harbour mouth.

"That's where the Russians have set up headquarters. Just below, in the museum overlooking the bay, is their living accommodation."

Sam had visited the museum. He had a vague memory of several rooms, airy and spacious; on the walls photographs from more prosperous times, the nineteen-thirties when the harbour had been packed with flying boats stopping overnight between Cairo and Paris. The museum's walls, like the castle, were carved from solid rock.

"Outside, on a sort of balcony, is the machine gun post and mortar battery. I saw both of them when I was dragged off to be questioned. The opposite post," Angus's arm traversed, "is on the hotel balcony. During the day about half the men seem to stay at the museum, a few man the mortar and machine gun posts, and the rest tend to congregate at the café."

"The one by the pier," confirmed Sam, "where the patrol boat used to be?"

Angus nodded.

"They patrol occasionally, no set pattern. I don't think there's an official curfew – the locals stay indoors anyway. Nights are the worst. I shouldn't think there's a woman under thirty who hasn't either been raped at home or dragged off to the museum. You have to hand it to Samandag. If he gets away with this, there'll be a media bonanza – those Greeks will go wild."

They sat for another ten minutes, talking over the options,

232

fashioning a plan for the morrow. When they finished Sam extracted the radio and extended its aerial. He didn't speak, but pressed the transmitter button five times, every other second.

Stavros, on listening watch in the wheelhouse, heard a series of distinct clicks. Even before Sam had finished, Stavros's glass of ouzo had been set down and he was reaching for his own switch. High on the hill, so loud that it seemed as if it could be heard down at the village, came his immediate response: three clicks, blown wide into the night.

Sam put the radio back inside its polythene bag and handed it to Angus whilst he fished for the spare magazines.

"Take the lot," he offered, passing them over with the Uzzi. "Plenty more on the boat."

Angus checked automatically that the weapon was cocked but on 'safe' and stowed the spare magazines with his radio.

"See you tomorrow," he said quietly, setting off down the slope.

Sam waited for three-quarters of an hour before a light came on in the *Nessie*'s forecabin. A few seconds later it went out. To a casual observer it would have indicated an early morning drink of water or trip to the heads. But Sam, starting back through the col, knew that Angus, with his precious equipment, was safely back on board his boat.

He wasn't expecting to meet anyone on the return journey – Angus had been watching the pass for hours. Even so he moved cautiously, keeping well clear of the skyline and pausing frequently to look and listen. Unarmed, it would be disastrous to run into some patrol which had worked its way round from behind the northern peak, out of sight from the ravine. But the only danger proved to be a tricky descent down the western face of the island – much harder than coming up.

Three miles away he could make out a deeper patch of shadow, as if the sea were heaped into a low mound. Behind the uninhabited island of Ayios Yeoryios, a barren lump of rock stretching a mile and a half east-west but only half a mile wide, waited the two boats. A nightly offshore wind dropping from Turkish mountains into the Vàthi channel veered a touch of northing into the prevailing westerly. Sam had spent many hours windsurfing in Cyprus but he regarded himself as no more than competent. He was certainly not expert – and he would be hard on the wind, not the easiest point of sail.

No need to paddle. Sam was confident that he was alone on the western shore. The sooner he was away, the better. He made a good start, but the wind was freshening with an approaching dawn. Soon, he found himself straining backwards for dear life. He lost count of the number of times he fell off, each time waiting a little longer for arms and back to recover before pulling up the sail, but all the time conscious of the need to be clear of Kastellorizon by daybreak. When he dropped the mast for the last time he hadn't the energy to pull the board on deck.

In the cabin, Andoula pushed a huge glass of Cyprus brandy into his hand. As Sam gathered strength in the wheel-house, Phivo was running the *Maria* due south. In an hour the sky would lighten from the east. No question of using a Turkish port, not with the gunboat, but Sam was confident that the Russians wouldn't return to Kekova. Deep inside the lagoon, past entrances too shallow for the twenty-odd feet of a submarine, they would lie at anchor. A quick calculation at the chart table. To be off the entrance by dawn they could stand out only for five miles before turning east. It was enough.

Alongside, he could make out Stavros at the wheel of the patrol boat. Up on the plane, they were running at over thirty knots but would be scarcely audible on Kastellorizon. If they were within sonar range, they would probably be taken for a couple of pleasure craft racing along the coast. Soon they would turn north east towards Kekova and disappear around the corner. Sam stripped off the top half of his wetsuit and headed below for a shower.

Chapter 15

It was still daylight, but not for much longer. Sam reached for his watch: ten-past seven. He had been asleep for over eight hours. He lay back and stared through the porthole. A deeper blue washed down over the sky, an indigo backdrop to fading lances of blood-orange and purple gold.

Overhead, someone strolled across the deck. With both boats anchored safely inside the lagoon, Andreas had drawn up a roster of two-hour watches. One man on the *Maria* with a sub-machine gun, the other alongside the pom-pom. Changes were to be staggered, one sentry to be halfway through when the other came on. Sam had no qualms about ducking the duty. They had been going for forty-eight hours. He had managed only two full nights' sleep and a few cat naps since last Friday.

Inevitably, after the recce, there had been residual tension. With Sally occupying the only private bunk on the patrol boat, Phivo had offered the *Maria*'s forecabin. But even if Sam had retired immediately there would have been no sleep. Instead, he and Phivo discussed the plan agreed with Angus. Phivo would brief the others during the day. Sam would give it a final run-over that evening. At half-past ten, adrenalin diluted by a third of a bottle of Phivo's Five Kings Brandy, Sam had walked over-cautiously to his bunk and crashed out.

Seven times the boats were approached during the day, mostly by fishermen selling their catch but twice by Kekova's café-restaurateurs, anxious to secure a windfall from the rich man's motor yacht and her unusual consort. The thin, grey ship flew no ensign and carried only a number painted on her side. Men balancing upright in a rubber dinghy were covering black numerals with grey paint. But she had to be one of theirs. To these local boatmen Kastellorizon was another planet. Not one of them connected the gunboat with an island only fifteen miles away. Gestures from her armed guards were unmistakable. In a country where the military traditionally held sway, the locals stayed away.

By dusk there was no novelty in the two strange craft with their unfriendly crews. And there was no telephone, even if someone felt moved to complain. But had the fishermen and restaurateurs returned, shortly before last light, even they would have wondered at the large red hammer and sickle being emblazoned on each side of the grey boat's super-structure.

They left at one o'clock and followed the previous night's pattern – close inshore, low revs, slow speed and only one light.

"One, this is zero over."

Despite having the volume set almost to nothing the mes-sage, soft-spoken but urgent, seemed to boom through his wheelhouse. Angus grabbed at the headphones. It was a long time since he had heard that voice over a radio. Memories stirred.

"One. Been watching since this afternoon. Confirm, no patrols out now. I say again, no patrols out now. Over."

"Zero. Roger out."

There had been a patrol. At five o'clock men walked up the path to the col. Angus had watched them with binoculars through a porthole. Shortly before last light they returned. Since then, no more Russians had ventured beyond the vil-lage. Sam's first party would have an unopposed drop.

Angus would have tailed any subsequent patrol and shot them in the back if they had seen the landing. There was a reasonable chance that a few cracks from the Uzzi wouldn't carry over the pass and down to the village. In any case, Angus could be back through the col before any follow-up group could set foot on the path. With care he had enough ammunition to hold the vital high ground till reinforcements arrived from the patrol boat.

But so far it was going their way. Angus was free to concentrate on his second objective. God bless black polythene bin liners. He tore off three, rolled the Uzzi and his radio inside clothing, and triple-wrapped the bundle. With most of the air squeezed out it would float awash. For five minutes he sat at the after end of his cockpit, developing full night vision and searching the harbour. On this side of the entrance the machine gun and mortar post was behind a curve of rock. Opposite and slightly right, the Russians were beyond his wheelhouse. Halfway round, outside the café at the foot of the jetty, a dozen or so men were drinking beer and talking, their vision confined to the pool of light from three overhead paraffin lamps.

It would be unwise to go straight across. Even from a hundred and fifty yards the shiny, wet plastic might throw a reflection. Angus stepped slowly down his boarding ladder. He would follow the harbour wall, within a bordering triangle of deeper shadow but a couple of feet out to avoid a murderous layer of thin, black, sea-urchin spines.

His approach to the jetty coincided with a surge of laughter. To the sound of palms slapping a table, Angus handed himself between piles and underneath the planking.

He was through to the other side and about to let go the wooden beams – a half second from the stroke which would launch him into open water – when a boot thumped on to the boards above. His bag was drifting into a pool of light. Frantically Angus reached out under the surface to hook his fingers into soft plastic.

The footsteps stopped. Angus froze. If necessary he could tear the bag, let it sink and swim deep, out to the middle and back to his boat. For ten seconds which seemed like thirty nothing happened, until behind him a falling stream thickened and reached out in a splashing arc.

On to the second half. Not all the way round. A few yards short of a point opposite the *Nessie*, Angus's foot found the prow of a fishing boat a couple of feet below the surface. As on two previous nights he climbed slowly, with scarcely a ripple, from the water. Houses were only a few feet away. Seconds later he scurried into an alley.

Sam took the patrol boat five miles beyond the harbour

entrance before turning south for the island of Ayios Yeoryios. Heading back east for the last three miles, engines restrained to a low burble, they were approaching Kastellorizon's west coast at a right angle and at less than ten knots. They had twenty minutes to run. But secure in the knowledge that there were no patrols on this side of the island, Sam could afford to trade speed for stealth. They would be inaudible from the harbour.

He studied the sheer rock profile and checked his echo sounder. Even a few yards from shore it was too deep to anchor. With the boat lying a-hull, he left Phivo and Stavros in the wheelhouse and went to help with the unloading.

Once, as a very inexperienced junior officer, Sam had been ordered to take part in a small-scale assault for which fire support failed to materialise. A handful of insurgents who should have been forced to keep their heads down were able to shoot almost at will. Until Sam's platoon reached grenade range, casualties were appalling. It was a lesson never to be forgotten. As he was the only one who knew the terrain he would guide the Arabs himself, to be certain they reached the right position.

Each Arab would take half a disassembled mortar, nearly thirty pounds a man, plus a few rounds of ammunition. Sam, John and Andreas would hump the rest.

It was slow progress ferrying five men, two bundles of mortar and box after box of bombs in one small dinghy. The weapon was rigged into back packs but ammo boxes had to be lugged, one by one, over each difficult patch. Sam would have sacrificed his pension for a couple of Bergens. They were soon sore-palmed and sweating. Arm and thigh muscles ached from pulling and pushing towards the crest, but half an hour later their tiny group entered the col.

At the far end Sam and the bearded Arab agreed their position on a map prepared from the chart. Using a hand compass they took bearings on three targets. Sam measured distances with the mortar's laser range finder and passed them to the Arab. With figures and fire plan agreed, Sam was confident that he could call for immediate support, with high probability of a first round hit.

Leaving the Arabs, the three men jogged back through the

238

pass and scrambled down to the tiny bay. A few yards away, held on station with an occasional touch of engines, the patrol boat bobbed quietly. Phivo nudged her in to meet the dinghy. Nearly four o'clock. With the mortar party in position, they were set to take Kastellorizon.

False dawn. A first, temporary shadow of light in the eastern sky. Andoula stepped out into the ambient pallor of a side deck. Behind her – gain turned up to a low hiss so that she knew it was working – sat a radio, its aerial poking out through the chart table window. For the third time in half an hour she looked at her watch.

Andoula had attended the final briefing. She sensed that her uncle might have preferred a different plan – he was sulking a bit – but Sam had been adamant. Some of them, he'd explained looking around pointedly, were too old to make a difficult approach march across the island carrying ammunition and anti-tank weapons. There was only one way to put all their heavy equipment in the right place, and that was by sea. If it went well, Andoula could bring the *Maria* into Kastellorizon harbour. If not, she was available to attempt a pick-up for the survivors, or at worst to intercept and warn the ferry.

She looked at the sky. It was definitely lighter now. Given the power of the gods, Andoula would not allow the dawn to come. She was fond of her uncle, who despite his archaic, Cypriot attitudes had been kind to her, but it was for the strange Englishman that she ached with anxiety.

She wondered about the girl now asleep in the forecabin. There had been the occasional, faint smile from her – perhaps the first hints of recovery. And how much did the girl mean to Sam? For those few seconds, when he had asked her to take care of Sally, an unfamiliar harrowed expression had etched on to his face.

Back in the deck saloon, Andoula put her weapon down next to the radio. Fortunately, she was no stranger to small arms. On their first business trip to the States her uncle had made her stay on and take a private course. At times, when they were working in Lebanon or Syria, she carried a handgun. Andoula disliked firearms but she was proficient. Any

239

young Turk pushing his luck with two women apparently alone on a motor yacht would be making a grievous mistake.

A few yards north of Ayios Yeoryios, Sam waited for daylight. When the solid outline of Kastellorizon began to assume a more intricate patchwork he started the engines. At a sedate ten or twelve knots they rounded the northern headland and turned for the harbour.

Sam had thought long and hard about the approach. They could have gone anti-clockwise around Kastellorizon but the last quarter circle would have been in full view of Samandag's headquarters. It was the most likely direction from which to see an unexpected Soviet vessel, but during the slow haul round that north-eastern quadrant the Russians would be trying frantically to make radio contact. He doubted if their disguise would last the distance.

But west-about, it might be different. Once round the northern tip of the island it was only eight cables – sixteen hundred yards – to the harbour mouth. And once there, they would be inside minimum mortar range. According to Angus the guard posts on either side of the entrance also contained a heavy machine gun. Three-oh calibre or similar. Rounds from that sort of weapon would make a mess of the wheelhouse and at some angles penetrate the hull. They had no Russian ensign to fly, but these men were soldiers, not sailors. A large hammer and sickle might just convince them for long enough . . .

As they headed south, hugging the peninsula, Sam realised that he was holding his breath. The port side post had seen them. Through binoculars he watched an NCO turn and shout towards the museum's open door. Another man ran out. Five cables to the entrance.

Above the harbour the Arab twisted the end of his beard and watched nervously. His mortar was laid on the hotel balcony. The first round would be triggered away. After that Aziz would plop them down the barrel as fast as he could.

From an upstairs hotel room Angus looked down over the Russians' position and waited for the patrol boat to close the entrance. The guests – a dozen or so Australians back to visit their birthplace – had not been molested, although one of Samandag's NCOs had examined their passports whilst his men looted the bar and kitchens. By day the visitors gathered for collective security in the hotel lounge. Each evening, after a carefully measured portion of their remaining rations, they retired before dark for another anxious and sleepless night.

It proved remarkably easy. Entry through one of several broken, downstairs windows, up a deserted stairway and along the corridor to an unoccupied room where since half-past three Angus had lain undisturbed. Below him, along the balcony, were four men – two for each weapon – surrounded by an improvised sangar of loose rock. Inside their emplacement a radio crackled to life.

On either side of the harbour, two machine guns tracked the patrol boat's bridge.

"Give them one more try," Samandag shouted inside to his wireless operator. The vessel was totally unexpected. Why had he not been warned? Suspicion touched every nerve, and yet she was wearing the Hammer and Sickle. Despite the mission's success, if he fired on one of their own vessels . . .

Outside the café, soldiers watched the boat's arrival with interest but no alarm. After all, she had been allowed to approach almost into the entrance.

Below him a group of people, intensely bored and there-fore curious, were emerging through patio doors on to the balcony. Angus swore. They had been prepared to accept a few injuries from flying glass, but if a mortar shell landed amongst that lot . . .

Sam noticed them too, and movement above at a window. Eighty yards from their port bow Samandag was shouting at the patrol boat. They were almost in the narrowest part of the entrance. It had to be soon. They couldn't afford to take the first strike.

"Fire!"

He bellowed down the companionway. Below, four of them engaged left through open portholes. Behind him, prone in the wheelhouse doorway, Stavros was shooting at the hotel balcony. First priority was the machine gun and mortar pits. Russians dropped from view – whether hit or not Sam had no idea. Slamming open the throttles, he caught sight of Samandag diving into the museum.

Angus watched men below duck instinctively as rounds

241

chipped and splintered the stonework. He screamed at the Australians: "Get back. Get off the balcony."

Four Russians turned to search for the strange voice. Angus put a long burst into the pit, hitting at least two of them. In three seconds of panic hotel guests surged inside. Angus ducked back inside his bedroom and waited for the blast.

Below, a Russian peered cautiously over his emplacement, seeking desperately to identify the threat from above and behind. The Arabs' first round landed twenty yards short, outside the dividing wall between dining-room and lounge. Blast flattened their makeshift shelter and shattered every ground floor window along the hotel front. A second followed immediately, screaming over the balcony on to the rocks below. The third, almost on their position, lifted a plume of debris – weapons, limbs and torsos spinning and twisting with bits of wood, strips of wriggly tin and chunks of white marble. There were no survivors. The patrol boat, her right flank secure, was curving to port behind buildings and rock which would shield her from Samandag's command area. Up on the hill, Aziz switched to his second target.

Sam watched as men on the square ran for cover. Those on the far side would be able to see the patrol boat.

Their deception had worked. Manning the pom-pom would have given the game away, but concentrating most of their lighter fire power on one position and leaving the other to Angus and the mortars had seen them safely inside. Now for the second critical stage. They still had to get ashore.

Throttles back, Sam hugged the curve of the harbour so that only a few of the Russians at the square would have line of sight. Phivo and the others were rushing up to crouch inside the wheelhouse. Sam flinched as a round from the corner café smashed through his centre screen, sending shards of glass in all directions. An anxious glance over his shoulder – this was as far forward as they could go and still be safe from the museum. She was making six knots. Sam put both engines hard astern and skidded her brutally on to the harbour wall. Water welled for'ard as twin screws attempted to claw her backwards. For half a second she was stationary. He banged the throttles shut and slapped her into neutral.

Stavros had moved on to the side deck to engage the café. Away to their right, a more distant chatter as Angus fired at extreme range. If they could suppress the Russians, just for a few seconds . . .

He thrust the radio at Kyriakos.

"Call the Arabs. Hit the square."

Kyriakos nodded, but Sam was already running through the portside doorway.

"Come on. Let's go . . . go . . . go . . ." He was screaming to encourage the Greeks. Everything depended on the next few seconds. Behind him, Andreas and John were taking lines ashore. A single round cracked past but the Russian fire was thinner. Sam sprinted for the pom-pom.

They couldn't hope to take out all the men around the square, but that wasn't the aim of the exercise. If the Russians held fast, firing from within those old, stone houses, Sam's tiny group was in trouble. They would have to clear the area building by building. Meanwhile, Samandag had all the time in the world to launch a counter attack. But Sam intended to force a different reaction.

From inside the café two soldiers watched a small group of men leap ashore. Lance Corporal Viktor Sobolev smashed another window and fired again in an attempt to stop what he recognised as a dangerous advance. The veteran of Afghanistan shouted to Mikhail Romanov, but at that crucial moment the young conscript who had passed every training test with flying colours held back. The veteran snarled – he would beat the shit out of Romanov later – and aimed at the running figures.

Sam's foot found the pedal. It was no time for finesse. Rounds crashed into the café wall; explosions boomed and ricocheted around the square, each blast echoing on into continuous thunder.

Sobolev's last round lifted at forty-five degrees as Sam's pom-pom shell smashed a window ledge inches below his chest. By the door Mikhail Romanov turned to see what remained of his comrade slide in a red, pulsing mass down the far wall. It wasn't supposed to be like this – outrageous noise, deafened in an obscene world of raw flesh and suffering . . . He gagged at the still moving corpus which had once laughed, and bought him a drink, and introduced him to their group. And like a wounded animal the private crouched, whimpering, crawling across the floor towards the kitchen and back door.

When the first mortar bomb reached the square Sam smelled success, at least for the landing phase of the operation. The Arabs were sustaining a slow, steady rate of fire.

Further back, in a house overlooking the jetty but round the corner from the patrol boat, Corporal Grigori Tikhonov crouched in a downstairs room. He had only twelve men. Maybe not that many by now. It looked as if those in the café might have bought it. He stopped thinking as another round crashed outside, threatening to shake the house from its foundations. Shells were exploding at ten-second intervals, making it impossible to disrupt the landing. Corporal Tikhonov forced himself to concentrate. That landing had fire support. It could be part of a much larger force. The section hadn't much ammunition. If the Major had to pull out, they could be cut off. It would be better to fight their way back to headquarters whilst there was still a chance.

He roared an order into the empty square, repeated it, and retreated to wait for the next round.

"Come on." He tapped the nearest man on the shoulder. They broke cover, running out of the front door and into a narrow side alley. High on the hillside, the bearded Arab watched ant-like figures scurry towards the bottom right-hand corner of the square. He reached for his radio.

There was still the pleasant cool of early morning. Andoula finished yet another walk round the deck and went in through the double after-doors, dropping her Uzzi on to the chart table. There was some fruit in the fridge.

She turned, the door half open, startled by a noise from the companionway, then relaxed as Sally's head appeared up the steps.

"Hello."

The greeting was nervous, hesitant, but for the first time the girl had spoken. Andoula closed the fridge door gently and stood up. She walked slowly towards Sally, her hands extended in greeting, but careful not to over react.

"I'm Andoula, hello. We were worried about you – welcome back."

She tried to say it lightly but the phrases sounded heavy, almost pedantic.

"I'm all right." Sally spoke in a quiet, calm voice. "I recognised the bay when I woke up and looked out from my cabin. It's Kekova, isn't it?"

Andoula nodded.

"It gradually came back," Sally went on, walking into the cabin and sitting in an armchair, "seeing the hills, and the lagoon. That's where it all started."

"And now you remember," said Andoula, half-question, half-statement.

A few minutes later Sally began to tell her. How Julian had died, and then Fiona, and about what had happened in Cyprus. It was a detached, almost impersonal account. Only when she described what they had done to her in Lara Bay were there any signs of emotion. She shuddered and faltered a few times but there was none of the outbreak of weeping which Andoula expected as part of a release from tension. This was outside her experience, but it was as if Sally's purpose in telling was no more than to fix the events in her mind, as she recalled them.

"I remember," she concluded, "killing that man. I have never hated anyone so much in my life. And nothing – nobody – was going to stop me from speaking to Sam. After that, I think something just snapped inside my head. I knew people were talking, but to let everything wash over me seemed the most natural thing in the world."

Sally hadn't eaten for over twenty-four hours. Andoula prepared a light breakfast of fruit and cereal with long-life milk. The end of their meal coincided with a burst of static from the radio. Andoula raced across the cabin but caught only two words, 'mortars' and 'square'.

"It's started."

Sally looked puzzled.

"Sam and Phivo, and the others. They think they can retake Kastellorizon. The patrol boat left before dawn. That's why we transferred you, last night."

The news worried Sally, but only for a moment. She had

known all the time, really, otherwise she would have asked where they were. It was one of the last sutures, drawing together a tiny gap in her memory.

Andoula was leaning over the chart table, her ear to one of the headphones.

"It's no good," she said eventually, tossing them down, "I can't make out what they're saying." She looked around. "It's these hills. I think we're being screened from Kastellorizon."

Her fingers drumming the table, she turned to face Sally.

"We're supposed to be listening, in case they need an emergency pick-up. It's no use sitting here. If they call us the chances are we won't hear."

Sally, immersed until now in her own thoughts, caught the anxiety and frustration in her voice.

Andoula hesitated. "I want to get closer, so we can be on hand in case they need us." She looked pointedly at Sally. "Are you sure you'll be all right?"

The English girl nodded in a slow, considered response.

"Yes. I shall need another holiday to get over this one, but I shan't run screaming into a corner if that's what you're worried about."

Andoula looked at her for a couple of seconds then made her decision. They would crawl gently up the coast and stop nearer the island. She started the engines and pressed a button for the electric windlass. Anchor chain clanked over the *Maria*'s bow roller.

It was as true now as ever before: war consisted of moments of intense activity and blind terror separated by long periods of boredom. Sam lay on the eastern ridge, lower than the one opposite, and studied a strip of land curving round to the fort.

He looked at his watch. It had taken half an hour to approach within sixty yards, doorway by doorway, their task complicated by a few brave souls emerging into the street behind them. But after giving vent to their relief, people were content to go back indoors.

They should be there soon. Sam had sent a Dragon crew comprising Angus and Kyriakos to face Samandag's head-quarters from across the water. Meanwhile, with Phivo, Stavros, Andreas and John behind him, he held the top ridge.

246

With only five men there was no chance of mounting a direct assault. But, conversely, they didn't have to. Samandag couldn't afford to sit cornered on the western end of the harbour for much longer.

Sam knew he was taking an almighty gamble. If they could keep the pressure on, force Samandag into trying to leave the island, then he believed he could win. But if the Russians chose the alternative, a break-out and counter attack, then with only a few magazines each and probably down to their last twenty rounds of mortar ammunition, Sam's tiny force was in trouble. By not occupying the village, he had deliberately left a path around the harbour. To leave it unguarded would have been too obvious but there were only two men covering from the other side. Meanwhile, they were dominating the high ground and the only other approach to Samandag's headquarters. Sam had no illusions. If his opponent made the right choice their final battle would be bloody but brief.

Samandag threw down the handset. No reports of additional forces heading for the island but the ferry wasn't due for over five hours.

He paced the stone floor. Why in hell hadn't they warned him? 'No contact, other than small craft and fishing boats.' Stupid, fucking submariner! 'No contact', and already a landing force, about which he knew practically nothing, had taken out half the harbour defences and bottled them up inside his headquarters.

The argument with that prick of a skipper had been short and bitter. It wasn't that the Foxtrot class carried no deck gun, only torpedoes, but her Captain had strict orders not to endanger his ship in the vicinity of Kastellorizon.

A light drizzle chilled the summer morning, but in Moscow the controller of Operation Red Castle was sweating. Flukes of mild panic weaved through his stomach. His plan, simple to the point of perfection, could not have anticipated such a landing. Any approach by forces from Greece should have been identified by the protective screen long before they could reach the island. Now, he had to assume that the ferry

247

would be warned off. It could be only a matter of time before follow-up forces arrived.

Studying a perfect model of Kastellorizon, he wondered what could be said at the daily briefing for a few, inner members of the Politburo. It all depended on what Samandag could achieve. The Major had to get his men off that island, but he was on his own. It was vital not to leave any wounded behind. The controller shuddered at the thought of a show trial. They would have to mount a damage limitation exercise – maybe denounce the action as unofficial – by Soviet citizens, true, but misguided Kurdish tribesmen. They could probably squeeze enough Third World support to survive in the United Nations, but politically it would be ten times more damaging than the Korean airliner fiasco.

It was unfortunate that he was forced to deny Samandag assistance from the sea, but it had been the right decision. A crippled, Foxtrot class submarine . . . Heat washed over his body. That would give the lie to any cover story they might develop. An odour of perspiration escaped from under his jacket. At the briefing he would tell them that the commander on the island was attempting to bring the operation to a successful, but early, conclusion.

Chapter 16

For the occupants' safety, Angus evacuated the hotel. Guests scurried behind harbourside houses to shelter at the rear of the village. The sight of ordinary people out of doors – the first for days – brought a few islanders cautiously on to the streets. Keeping clear of the waterfront they gathered in small groups to speculate on what was happening up by the Castle. Someone said they were Greeks; two of them had spoken in a sort of dialect. Their leader, said an old man who had worked the passenger liners, was English. Like mercury spilled on to marble the news burst into tiny, silver balls and rolled in every direction.

Two men dragged a body from the café. In the kitchen yard they found a young soldier, his face grey from pain and loss of blood, his right leg shattered above the knee by shrapnel from Sam's last round.

He was barely conscious. An old fisherman leant over him to cut away soaked, red cloth with a gutting knife. The young soldier asked for water. The old man ignored the strange language and worked to expose the boy's thigh, and then his stomach. He spoke over his shoulder, not caring whether they obeyed or not. Women drew back. Other men made no move to stop him. There wasn't a family left untouched.

The soldier on the ground realised that this was not medical attention. Romanov begged and tried to pull back in terror, dragging his crippled limb. Several of them dropped on to him, their knees on his arms, legs and chest. He roared at the pain his thigh, but even that all consuming agony disappeared when a hand seized his genitals and the blade sawed slowly into tissue. He screamed, an uncontrolled falsetto which echoed through every street and square in the village.

Last month, at his granddaughter's wedding, old eyes had flashed as he danced a Zorba. Four days ago, on that first morning, they had stripped and taken her in the street. His eyes were dull and expressionless as he threw two scraps of flesh on to the unconscious body. Soon it would bleed to death. Without emotion he wiped his knife on the Turkish tunic and walked to wash the filth from his hands at a tap in the yard.

There was movement again. A figure sprinted along the ruined parapet. Samandag was exploring, probing for strength and positions.

"Stavros, yours! Right-hand edge."

A few yards away the Saco opened up. Single shots. They had to conserve ammunition.

"Mortars, Castle. Two rounds, over."

Sam registered a faint double 'plop' high on the hillside. Seconds later another all-too-thin salvo exploded against stonework.

Below, in the museum, the remainder of Samandag's force waited, crouched and ready, eyes lifting nervously as shock waves passed through rock. Another strip of plaster slipped from the wall.

Samandag had lost ten men: two at the square, four from the hotel, a machine gunner outside his headquarters when the patrol boat opened fire and now three more from up top. Another three were wounded, but not seriously.

He was convinced that they faced only a small invasion force, probably less than his own thirty survivors, but more would follow if they sat there like rats in a trap.

Sam's radio clicked to life.

"Angus. We're ready. Over."

Faster than expected.

"Roger. Got everything?"

"Kyriakos persuaded a couple of locals to carry for us. Did it all in one trip. Ready when you are, over."

"Roger. Out to you. Mortars, how many rounds, over?"

"Okay." A pause – the Arab was counting. "Fifteen, one five, over."

Sam sucked his teeth. No point in putting off the evil moment.

"Roger. Out to you. Angus – it's all yours. Fire when ready."

"Roger out."

With cross hairs steady on the museum's outer wall, Angus thumbed down a safety catch and squeezed the trigger. Fins flipped out to induce a slow roll. Along the centre portion of its body sixty small rocket motors fired sequentially, their thrust vectored aft to throw the missile across the bay. It was an easy shot. The Dragon tracked faithfully on to its target.

The explosion boomed out across the harbour. Through the tracker's optics Angus watched a section of wall disappear into a cloud of dust which settled, slowly, to reveal a jagged five-foot hole. He dropped the launcher and ran behind the hotel. Another missile, from a different position. Through the hole this time, then wait to see what happened.

Samandag's men up top shouted that they were all right. So this was no prelude to an advance. But the enemy had them pinned down, almost blinded. Gradually, he would lose more men to mortar fire – or to what sounded like an anti-tank weapon being fired from across the harbour. His own mortars were useless. The men on the ridge were probably inside minimum range. In any case, the first salvo would serve merely to invite counter battery fire from a crew who already had the headquarters registered precisely. Deep inside the museum they were safe for a while, despite the pounding, but eventually the structure would crumble. Samandag shouted for those men up top to come down.

His briefing was short and crisp. Most of the enemy seemed to be on the ridge above so break-out would be along the waterfront. Their flank would be exposed but only for the first few yards, until they could turn into the village and work round behind the houses. Once in those narrow alleys they would be protected from mortar fire. But no one – he stressed the words – was to be left behind. It if were absolutely

251

impossible to move a casualty . . ." Samandag did not need to finish the sentence.

Men looked at each other. They understood. Besides, there would be no medical attention. Better a swift exit than waiting for death without morphine.

Each man checked his weapon. Samandag waited patiently till everyone was ready.

"First three," he ordered, "outside and cover us. He's somewhere by the hotel. Go."

Men sprinted out and dived behind rubble which had once been a balustrade. Eyes scanned the harbour. Alongside them a single file ran down the steps and along the quay.

"Sam, this is Angus. They're coming out. All of them."

"Roger." Those inflatables had to be somewhere, or had Samandag guessed their true weakness and decided to counter attack?

From the dining-room of the hotel Kyriakos opened fire, but it was extreme range for a lightweight Saco. Answering rounds from the Russians' heavier weapons whanged on to the building. He ducked behind a window ledge. Kyriakos was no coward but he knew when he was hopelessly out-gunned. Besides, he was supposed to provide only a token resistance.

Sam's small group took up a defensive position inside the old schoolhouse. Its walls were solid, and any attacker would have to cross open playgrounds. If necessary Sam would bring down final protective mortar fire right on to the building. Those in the open would come off worst. Anxiously, he looked out towards the village.

"I see them." It was Angus, back on the radio. "Looks like they're making for the square. A bunch of them have just crossed an alley and disappeared behind the fish market."

Relief, and a sudden intense burst of excitement. Early days, but just the faintest scent of victory.

"Roger. Sink the patrol boat."

A pity, but they couldn't risk Samandag making use of its pom-pom.

"Mortars, over."

"Mortars." It was the bearded Arab.

"Set all fuses for low airburst. All fuses low airburst. Over."

252

"Mortars. Confirm all fuses low airburst."

"Zero, roger out."

Up till now Sam had deliberately used only point detonation, even though airburst would have caused more casualties at the Castle. But unlike impact fuses, airbursts would be devastating over water. Samandag had been bounced into his most serious mistake of the operation.

Angus' Dragon penetrated the engine room and blew the decks off her. Inside a minute the patrol boat was blazing from end to end. An expanding, black cloud settled over a sector of the waterfront.

The islanders were surprised to see a running column of the invaders. They fled indoors, women and children screaming, but apart from an occasional shot into the air to clear their route Samandag ignored them. There had been enough brutality. If the politicians wanted more, let them come and do it themselves.

The last of his men reached the fish market without incident. Under cover of dense smoke from the patrol boat two of them opened its double-fronted doors. The rest ran inside.

The inflatables were ready, lined up on a concrete floor – watched over since Monday by Samandag's permanent guard at the square. Inside the market hall they primed carburettors and secured warps.

"Ready?"

Samandag registered his men's anxious drawn faces.

"Those that make it, run south-east. Don't drop a bleeper over the side till the island's off the horizon, and we're clear of all shipping. The sub will pick us up."

He looked around. Six boats. Eight men to most of them on the way out, now down to five or six.

"Good luck," he said quietly. "Let's go."

The first crew crossed ten feet to the water, lowered their inflatable stern first down a twelve-inch drop and lay prone on the harbour side. Covered by number one section the others followed. With smoke from the patrol boat screening their movements, three inflatables were on the water before Angus caught sight of running figures through a gap in the swirling black cloud.

253

"Sam, boats in the water! I hear an engine . . . two more. I think they're all starting up."

From Sam's position the boats, tucked under a line of buildings, were out of sight, but he heard the first scream of revs as a helmsman opened his throttle.

"Mortars, fire at will. Fire at will, over."

It was time to get down to the harbour.

The inflatable accelerated rapidly. In seconds it was planing through a thinning screen and weaving for the entrance. But because of the smoke it was halfway across the harbour before Aziz dropped a group of five rounds down the barrel.

From his balcony Angus watched the approaching flotilla. At least one boat would beat the mortars. He tapped Kyriakos. As the leading inflatable approached they opened fire.

The bobbing, speeding craft was a difficult target. Angus aimed again, following through. For two seconds they appeared to be missing completely. Metal raindrops spattered the water. The inflatable was drawing level. More short bursts of fire and the helmsman pitched sideways against his tiller, throwing the occupants across their craft as it slewed round towards the hotel. One man was in the water. Another reached aft in a desperate attempt to steer. His legs tangled in a mass of men and equipment. The helmsman made a valiant attempt to recover, but succeeded only in straightening their course. At thirty miles an hour the inflatable rammed the harbour wall.

Samandag peeled off, beckoning the others to follow. Frantic hand signals sent two boats side by side for the entrance. One of them ought to get through.

The bearded Arab had laid his weapon to perfection. As the second and third boats raced into a funnel a hundred yards from the entrance, five explosions threw down a hail of metal and blast. Water threshed and boiled. Caught in the open, both inflatables and the men inside them were shredded to pieces. One or two moved feebly in the water amidst a spreading pink pool.

They had ten more rounds. Adjusting after each shot the Arabs set out to blanket the harbour.

Circling desperately Samandag watched the advancing airbursts. His arms stretched sideways, fists shaking. It was the signal for line abreast. He made his guess. Formating on him they went clockwise round the harbour. The bearded Arab had traversed right.

Angus and Kyriakos watched a grey cloud explode harmlessly on the wrong side. With less than a full magazine between them they aimed for the nearest boat.

Alongside, Angus heard an empty 'thunk' from Kyriakos's breach. He aimed at the stern but the helmsman sat low, only his head and one arm visible. They must be down to half a dozen rounds. Angus resighted, swinging his last burst through the outboard motor.

His penultimate round shattered its electrics. The punctured inflatable lurched to a stop, collapsing into its own wash. The other two were streaming for the entrance. Angus watched, helpless as they parted around the debris of previous attempts, almost brushing the sides of the harbour as they swerved to avoid sinking boats and human flotsam.

They were through, and away. But Samandag's heart sank. It was senseless to go back. He had failed – nearly twenty of his men were still in that harbour, and at least six of them were alive.

Sam led the others in a frantic sprint around the quay to support Angus and Kyriakos. He needn't have worried. Angus, with an empty magazine but more swagger than a Sandhurst sergeant major, had accepted the surrender of six wet Russians and motioned them to sit, hands on head, on the foreshore.

As the *Maria* steamed slowly westward, Sally and Andoula tried to follow the course of the battle but the natural bowl of Kastellorizon harbour wasn't good for transmission. They stopped near the Turkish coast, two and a half miles from the entrance but shielded by offlying islands. Andoula let the *Maria* wallow. She heard a strange voice reporting boats in the water. That had to be Angus. They heard Sam call for mortars.

Two small, black blobs trailing a wedge of white foam streaked out from behind the islands. It could only be the surviving Russians. Sally tracked them through binoculars as they curved east and began to bear away south. Andoula reached out for the radio. Sally's hand gripped her wrist, fingernails carving half moons into her flesh.

"That's him, Samandag, in one of those boats."

Andoula pressed the starters. Sally had to snatch at the control panel as both throttles were pushed wide open.

It wasn't for Sally, despite what she had been through, or for Julian and Fiona whom Andoula had never met. It was not even for Sam. In part, it was for the Greek people on Kastellorizon, but most of all it was for Stellios, her kind, quiet-spoken 'uncle' with the ample wife and four children, and for the parents of Costas Araouzos, who lived in her village. An English education had failed to erase her Cypriot concept of justice.

The *Maria* was beginning to pound, her bow lifting high as twin turbochargers cut in to feed starving diesels. Andoula clung to the wheel. Thirty knots and still accelerating. Clear of the lee from Kastellorizon, the inflatables were forced to reduce speed in a moderate swell.

At a range of a thousand yards Andoula turned a few degrees to port until the *Maria* was roaring flat out for the two boats.

Above the noise of his outboard and the recurring thud of water Samandag detected a deeper, more vibrant sound. He twisted to look over their starboard quarter. Four hundred yards away, towering from his waterline perspective, a massive, white bow was tearing towards them.

Samandag screamed a warning and pointed. From both inflatables men attempted to open fire but accurate shooting was impossible. Those few rounds which did find their target disappeared into the looming knuckle of the *Maria*'s prow.

The inflatables divided but Andoula tracked inexorably on to Samandag's boat, anticipating his final jink precisely. Men threw themselves into the water seconds before the *Maria* slammed into the for'ard thwart. For five seconds the inflatable folded itself around the yacht's bow, only to slither aside a hundred and fifty yards from the red foam churned out by her screws.

Andoula hauled her round, leaning into the bank whilst she looked for the other inflatable. It was two hundred yards away, stopped in the water. Men perched on each side, hands raised in surrender, but she couldn't accept it, with only the two of them on board.

She swung off target, then back the other way. The *Maria*, rudders hard a-starboard, went into a full-bore, skidding turn, her hull pushing up a monster sidewall. The yacht passed within inches of the Russians. Tons of solid green water launched men and inflatables into an inevitable inversion.

Andoula throttled back and looked over her shoulder. Clinging weaponless to their upside-down craft, engine soaked and useless, the Russians were going nowhere. Sam could collect them at will. She turned for the harbour.

Chapter 17

They held the surviving Russians in the fish market, with Andreas and John inside to keep an eye on them. At first it took the rest of Sam's force to ward of an angry crowd of Kastellorizans. They dispersed, but only after warning shots were fired into the air. Sadly the incident soured relations with the islanders who waited morosely in small groups, well clear of the fish market, for the arrival of the ferry.

There were none of the usual local boats to bump alongside as soon as she dropped anchor. Angus took Phivo out in the *Nessie* to give an edited account of the invasion to her skipper. Captain Constantine Zavides spent half an hour inside his radio room before allowing only selected crew members ashore with food and medical supplies. The Russians were transferred aboard and placed under guard in a cargo hold.

Soon, Sam suspected, it would be a media jamboree. By that time he and Angus intended to be away; Angus because he had no wish to jeopardise his interests in Turkey, and Sam because as part of their agreement Phivo would remain as spokesman, and to negotiate on behalf of his men. Neither Sam nor Angus would be named, and there was nothing to connect *Soprano* with Kastellorizon.

Sam was not naive enough to expect that the full story wouldn't emerge eventually, but hopefully by that stage it would be yesterday's news. In the meantime Phivo would supervise the handover of prisoners to the Greek authorities. Sam shook hands with each of Phivo's men. They would meet again in Cyprus.

Phivo and Andoula stood on the waterfront near the harbour mouth as Angus, Sally and Sam boarded the *Nessie*, slipped her warps and steamed slowly for the entrance.

The charter party had been due to fly home tomorrow. Angus volunteered to drive to Ankara and brief the British Embassy. The Foreign and Commonwealth Office would set in train messages to the next-of-kin. Sam suspected that what they might be told would depend upon the course of a diplomatic hurricane which even now was only just beginning.

So for the next few days Sam intended to stay at sea. First, south for a hundred miles, well clear of Kastellorizon, and then east along the one hundred and seventy miles to Cyprus. The dog-leg would take at least two days, probably three. By then the worst of the Kastellorizon crisis ought to be blowing itself out. If not, he could always divert further south and push on for Tel Aviv.

From Angus's house Sally phoned her father. On her behalf, he would telephone her firm. She wasn't yet ready to face a barrage of questions, either from the authorities or from her friends' relatives. Neither did she feel able to return to the flat – at least not yet. But, Sally assured them, she would be all right on the flight. Her father would meet her at the airport and take her straight home to Yorkshire.

Seated next to Sam at the patio table she squeezed his arm and smiled.

"I'll be all right, really. Once I'm back where everything's normal, and everything's ordinary . . ." She tailed off, the sentence unfinished.

Her mind had returned but it was a delicate, fragile repair. The decision to fly home was the right one. She needed to be away from here, protected from all anxiety. Sam had thought of offering to take her with him on *Soprano*, but dismissed the idea almost immediately. It would need only a storm or some other incident during the first few days, and tender healing might tear beyond recovery. But she would be all right eventually. Scarred, perhaps, for a while, but the scars would fade, given time. Of that Sam was confident. He had seen it before – she had the strength, the courage of spirit, to rationalise and overcome what they had done to her. Andoula had told him everything on Kastellorizon after the ferry's departure.

259

Somehow it had made the carnage there, the taking of so many lives, easier to live with.

Later that evening, they walked together along the shore – arm in arm in quiet, almost unspoken companionship. Her foot turned a red stone left wet and glistening by a ripple of water. He would write to her, presently, and she would tell him truthfully how she was feeling.

Sam promised to call on the Monros again in a couple of months. Next morning, whilst Jean was taking Sally to the airport, he made the round of officials to clear himself and *Soprano* from Turkish waters.

For a while he was occupied with laying a course from Fethiye, and then, having lost no time in putting to sea, with the million and one aspects of checking over *Soprano*. Under a light breeze from the north-west, she nosed her way out into the Mediterranean.

There was nothing on the BBC World Service at lunchtime. Presumably the Greeks were considering carefully the text of their announcement. Somehow, it all seemed a long time ago. It was good to be standing on *Soprano* again, feeling her lift and dip to the sea.

Two hours ahead of London time, Sam almost missed the evening bulletin.

". . . following an attack on Monday morning, the island was occupied for four days. According to Australian tourists taken off Kastellorizon on Friday and interviewed briefly before being repatriated from Athens, the invaders wore Turkish military uniforms. Several of the island's inhabitants are believed to have been killed and a number, particularly women, are said to have been severely maltreated. Describing the invasion as an act of brigandry and barbarism, a Hellenic Government spokesman declined to speculate on who might be responsible. Significantly, it is understood that no allegations have yet been made against Turkish armed forces, although sources in Ankara report considerable high-level diplomatic activity. Further details are unlikely to emerge immediately, as Greece has declared Kastellorizon a Military Protected Zone, barring all landings until what it terms 'thorough investigations' have been completed.

"The tiny island, with only a handful of inhabitants, lies . . ."

Sam listened to a general description of Kastellorizon and its history, but surprisingly there were no so-called experts to offer opinion. The incident had not been ignored, but seemed to be attracting only the absolute minimum of media coverage. The following day it disappeared from the news completely. Sam had his suspicions, but they were not given substance until a few hours later when a Royal Air Force Nimrod circled low over *Soprano*.

He went below to switch on Channel Sixteen, the international call and distress frequency.

"Yacht *Soprano*," Sam responded, "send, over."

"You are asked to proceed directly to Akrotiri harbour, where you will be met. Over."

It was his choice; they had no jurisdiction. But, curiosity apart, Sam suspected that it might be very much to his advantage.

"Direct to Akrotiri harbour," he confirmed. "Wilco. Out."

The whistle of her engines whined to a roar as the maritime patrol aircraft climbed away from a setting sun.

They were there, waiting on the edge of the jetty in the small harbour just off the end of RAF Akrotiri's main runway.

"Welcome back." It was John White, the Sovereign Base Area's senior customs officer. It took only minutes to book Sam formally into Cyprus – but, more important, into British territory. No attempt was made to introduce a second man, who remained on the jetty until the customs officer returned ashore.

"Colonel Verle. May I come aboard?"

Sam stepped back from saying goodbye to his old acquaintance. The man produced a slightly battered but familiar identity card. He declined Sam's offer of a cold beer.

"May we talk below?"

"So that's it," he concluded, "the Greek Government were embarrassed, to say the least, considering how they've been sucking up to Moscow a bit, lately. It's my guess there never will be any accusations – not in public, at any rate. I wouldn't be surprised if they didn't wait for a while, to let the fuss die

261

down, and then quietly repatriate what's left of Samandag's team."

"But in private?" Sam asked.

His visitor smiled.

"Privately, we have a lot to thank you for. If nothing else, this business has at last made the Greeks realise who their true friends are – or should I say enemies?"

He shrugged. "Perhaps that's why they're so keen to hush things up, all that egg on their face. Either way, there'll be a bit more co-operation with NATO from now on, and right now the Soviet Ambassador isn't exactly persona grata in Athens. You'll not see too many of their Mediterranean Squadron being repaired or bunkered in Greek shipyards in future. I gather that Athens was even talking to Ankara this morning, and the Turks are co-operating in keeping things close to the chest."

"But eventually," queried Sam, "isn't it bound to come out? Inevitably some journalist or other is going to ferret about until he gets to the bottom of it."

A shake of the head. "You must have heard the World Service?"

Sam nodded.

"All governments involved have agreed to play down the story. Greece can keep the lid on Kastellorizon for as long as she likes. At the end of the day, if it becomes necessary, as a bottom line and a gesture of goodwill the Turks will accept a version blaming local brigands, but with no official government knowledge or involvement whatsoever."

He smiled. "It would make up for the fact that the Soviets used Turkey as a mounting base, which did cause Ankara some embarrassment."

"And it will not," speculated Sam, "be allowed to affect the new *entente cordiale* between Ankara and Athens."

They sat for a few seconds in silence.

"So I take it," went on his guest eventually, "that we can count on your co-operation in keeping this quiet – which is one of the reasons I had to speak to you?"

"And the other?" Sam queried.

"I think I'd like that beer now," asked his guest, "if it's still on offer?"

"Finally," he began again, setting down the can, "I've saved the best till last."

"How very 'foreign office'," Sam remarked.

The man grinned. "Along with requests for silence, at least for the time being, a very grateful Greek government has made available a substantial sum of money to defray expenses and recompense those involved. Where necessary, it will go to a deceased's relatives. Phivo assures me that he can vouch for his people on Cyprus. I expect that by now my colleagues in London will have been in touch with the Marchant and Cranleigh families."

"What'll you tell them?" asked Sam quietly.

"We shall blame local terrorists, pending the outcome of a Greek inquiry."

"Which will be a long time in coming."

"As you say." His visitor paused. "Miss Forbes' father has been most helpful, given the circumstances. When she has recovered a suitable version will be drafted which will satisfy her friends' relatives."

Sam told his visitor exactly what had happened to her.

"It will never make things right," he concluded, "but in my view a very significant sum should be set aside for Sally Forbes."

His visitor had lost his urbane, professional countenance. A rather white face dipped, twice, in acknowledgement.

Sam drove to Paramali that evening and watched the sunset. But despite the colours, despite a breathtaking view of the coastline, it was an empty, almost academic ending to the day. He knew why, wishing he hadn't come, almost as soon as he turned on to the track in John White's Land-Rover. Rocks and cliffs and the heady scent of wild herbs kindled powerful memories, but they couldn't replace people. Jenny and young Sam wouldn't be forgotten, but time had already offered the solution.

He walked back slowly towards the vehicle, his mind switching gently to the present. Time enough to drive to Akrotiri, return John's Rover, and still treat both of them to a steak at the little restaurant just off the base. The customs officer was a bachelor. Sam suspected that this evening

263

neither of them would be too concerned whether they drank one bottle or three.

He paid the price next morning, but considering the wine and the best part of a bottle of Five Kings brandy which they had demolished afterwards, on John's balcony, it could have been worse. Sam had only a hazy recollection of staggering back to the harbour, concentrating on a road which without warning kept slipping sideways from under his feet.

In – one step, two step; out – three, four. Not too much training lately. He would have to work to stay in condition, not run to fat after keeping it up for all these years. The morning was still fresh, but there was no breeze to stir the warm air. Sweat thickened on his forehead and chest, but in another mile he would be back at the beach.

He swam for twenty minutes until even the thinnest traces of pain disappeared from inside his head, taking with them the last cobwebs from his mind. Jean had given him some home-cured bacon which he had conveniently forgotten to mention to John White, and there were still one or two eggs on *Soprano*.

He was making coffee when the yacht swayed gently as someone came on board. He turned in the companionway to see Andoula stepping down into the cockpit.

She smiled. "So this is your boat. Aren't you going to offer me a cup of coffee?"

For a second he was lost for words. She was wearing bright yellow shorts, setting off long, golden-brown legs to perfection, and a matching blouse carelessly but carefully unbuttoned to display a double gold rope which disappeared between her breasts. She looked absolutely stunning – an effect to which Andoula had given a considerable degree of attention.

"Please, come on down." Sam reached for another mug. "Sorry about this – you make me feel as though I ought to have bone china."

It wasn't the greatest compliment she had ever received, but Andoula was content to have achieved her effect. As she slipped past him Sam caught a hint of expensive fragrance.

"Would you do something for me? There's a soft case, on the jetty."

264

It wasn't heavy, but Andoula had had no intention of making an unwieldy entrance.

Sam was still looking at her.

"Phivo sends his regards. All's well, and he'll see you when we get back."

"Get back?" he repeated lamely.

She nodded, very matter-of-fact. "He said I needed a holiday, after the past week, so he's given me time off. If it's not presuming too much, I hoped you might take me to Israel. If you'd rather not sail *Soprano*, Phivo said we could use the *Maria* . . ."

His arms went around her. She kissed him once, lightly, on the cheek. It was going to be all right. Andoula laughed to dispel her tension and stretched to whisper in his ear. "Shall I tell you," she asked wickedly, "about an option on a room at the Tel Aviv Hilton?"